Readers love
SUSAN LAINE

Femme Faux Fatale

"This book nails the film noir atmosphere, with both characters and settings conveying a sense of tarnished decadence."

—Love Bytes

"From the very beginning of this clever and suspenseful mystery, the author manages to paint a perfect picture of the environment, the characters, and the kind of "adventure" I entered when I opened the book."

—Rainbow Book Reviews

"I love a good cross-dressing book and add in all of the twists and turns of a murder mystery, and I was entertained from the start of the book to the end."

—OptimuMM

Summer Ride

"I love a good road trip romance, and with the added bonus of this being a reunion of friends, I was on board as soon as I read the blurb."

—Joyfully Jay

"…I liked the story. It was nicely written and held my interest."

—Open Skye Book Reviews

By Susan Laine

Falling for Rain
Flushed
Haunted Heart
How I Accidentally Slept with a
Prince
An Island in the Stars
Sage Advice
Sauna Lover
The Sensualist & the Untouched
Summer Ride
The Witching Hour

BEFORE… AND AFTER
After the Romance Novel
Kissing Lessons
Train to Somewhere
Dreams and Expectations

DREAMSPUN DESIRES
Femme Faux Fatale

HEROES AT HEART
Yellowbelly Hero
Yellow Streak
Code Yellow
Good as Gold

ISLESHIRE CHRONICLES
Lofty Dreams of Earthbound Men
Wishing Wings

LIFTING THE VEIL
The Wolfing Way
Genie's Wish
Hunter's Moon
Monsters Under the Bed
Love of the Wild
Stealing Dragon's Heart

SECOND CHANCES
Accidental Chemistry
Twice by Chance

SENSES AND SENSATIONS
Love in Plain Sight
A Luminous Touch
Sensible Commitments
Sounds of Love
The Sweetest Scent

THE WHEEL MYSTERIES
Sparks & Drops
Devil's Own
Fireworks & Wild Cards
The Disciple
The Wheel Mysteries: Books 1 & 2

Published by Dreamspinner Press
www.dreamspinnerpress.com

HOW I *Accidentally* SLEPT WITH A PRINCE

SUSAN LAINE

REAMSPINNER PRESS

Published by
DREAMSPINNER PRESS

5032 Capital Circle SW, Suite 2, PMB# 279, Tallahassee, FL 32305-7886 USA
www.dreamspinnerpress.com

How I Accidentally Slept with a Prince
© 2020 Susan Laine

Cover Art
© 2020 Tiferet Design
http://www.tiferetdesign.com/
Cover content is for illustrative purposes only and any person depicted on the cover is a model.
© 2020 Daniël Hasenbos
Daniel's Maps
https://www.danielsmaps.com
info@danielsmaps.com

Trade Paperback ISBN: 978-1-64405-817-6
Digital ISBN: 978-1-64405-816-9
Library of Congress Control Number: 2019953335
Trade Paperback published May 2020
v. 1.0

Printed in the United States of America

Acknowledgments

I WOULD like to wholeheartedly thank Daniël Hasenbos, the amazing artist from the Netherlands who drew the map of Riten Castle for me. Thank you kindly.

And also, from the bottom of my heart I would like to thank my mother for her continued support and love for my scribblings. I'll always be grateful for everything you've done for me. Love you, Mom.

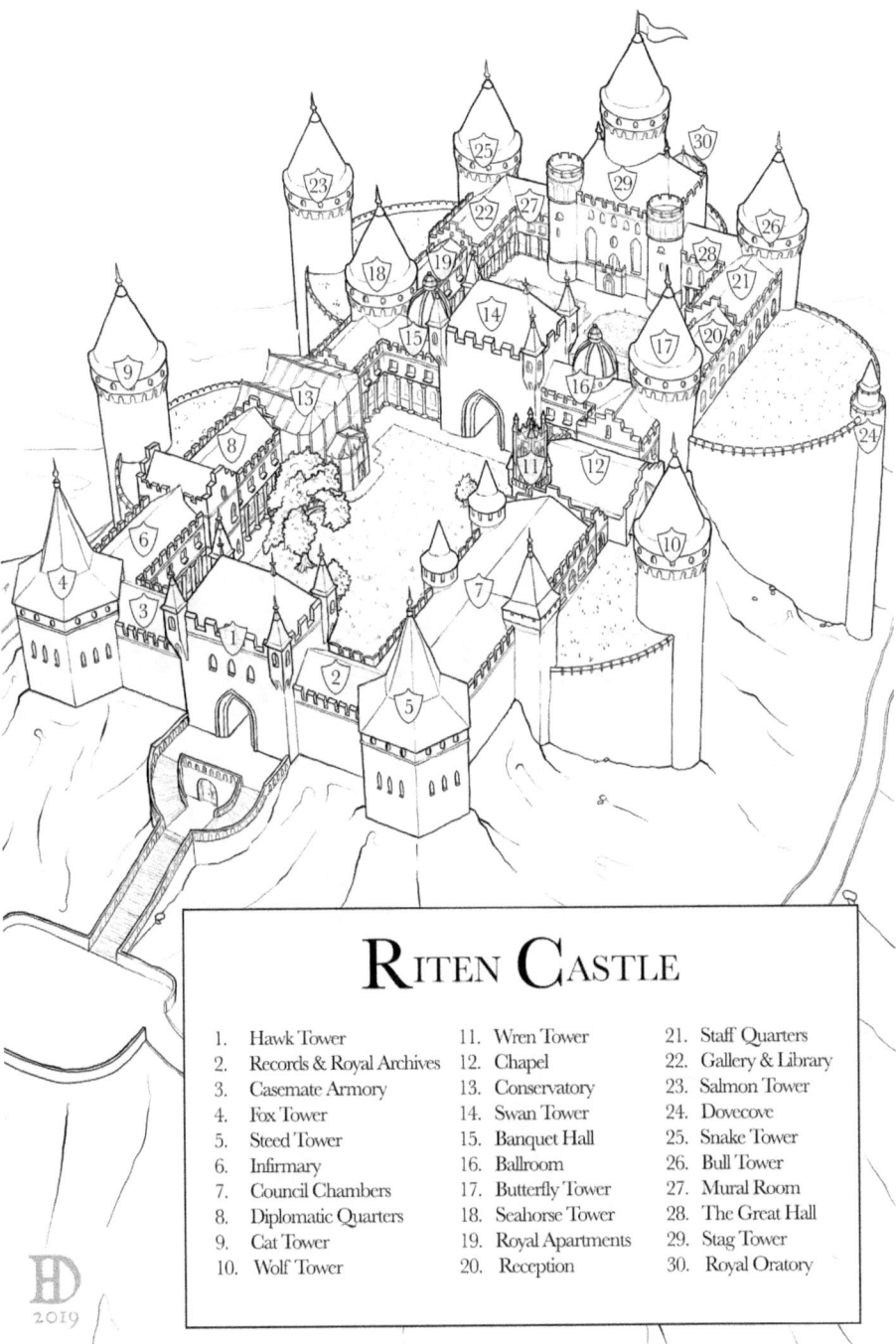

RITEN CASTLE

1. Hawk Tower
2. Records & Royal Archives
3. Casemate Armory
4. Fox Tower
5. Steed Tower
6. Infirmary
7. Council Chambers
8. Diplomatic Quarters
9. Cat Tower
10. Wolf Tower
11. Wren Tower
12. Chapel
13. Conservatory
14. Swan Tower
15. Banquet Hall
16. Ballroom
17. Butterfly Tower
18. Seahorse Tower
19. Royal Apartments
20. Reception
21. Staff Quarters
22. Gallery & Library
23. Salmon Tower
24. Dovecove
25. Snake Tower
26. Bull Tower
27. Mural Room
28. The Great Hall
29. Stag Tower
30. Royal Oratory

Chapter 1

I DIDN'T know if it was insomnia or jetlag, but I couldn't sleep a wink.

It was hot, as it always was in a tropical clime, even though the sun had set hours ago. The unfamiliar hotel bed, as preposterously lavish as it was, was lumpy. And cicadas were loud below my third-floor balcony, chirping away as if their lives depended on it.

My life, however, depended on adequate rest. Therefore, as my mother had advised me since I was a kid, I needed a glass of warm milk.

I called Domaine de la Lumière's room service, but it seemed they weren't open this late, because no one answered. Fuming and desperate, I decided to find the kitchen on my own and heat up some milk. How hard could it be? I was a college student, for fuck's sake. If I could microwave instant noodles, I could heat milk.

In the end, my midnight caper turned out to be a breeze. The kitchen was easy to locate, the appliances huge and modern but not overly complicated, and pots and pans were within reach. The drink stock in the walk-in fridge could have lasted for weeks, so I doubted anyone would notice me pilfering a little. I heated up some milk, poured myself a tall glass, cleaned up a tad, and left the kitchen.

I was tired; my eyes watered. I yawned and swore I heard my jaw crack. Ignoring all that, I slouched my way back to the empty elevator, banged on some buttons, leaned against the back wall, and closed my eyes. I practically fell asleep on my feet. But without warm milk, I knew something would startle me awake again, just like before.

The elevator pinged melodically, and the doors opened. I stumbled out toward my room in the dimly lit corridor, my hair falling over my eyes. My slippers shuffled on the wall-to-wall carpeting, creating sparks of static electricity.

Once at my door, I fumbled in the pocket of my bathrobe for the keycard, only to discover the door unlocked. I cursed my own forgetfulness and entered, blinking in the darkness. Hadn't I left the foyer light on? Oh, who cared?

I headed to the bedroom, rested the glass of milk on the dresser, pushed the covers aside, and snuck in. A musky yet delicate fragrance hung in the room, and I inhaled, liking the scent I hadn't noticed before. Sighing with contentment, I reached for my milk, drank it all down greedily, and then focused on relaxing my mind and body.

As usual with warm milk, I was soon fast asleep, more than likely snoring happily. The sweet scent probably helped too.

THE BED was so warm. It felt less lumpy than before. Perhaps I'd been too vexed at not being able to sleep to notice how comfortable it really was.

Sunlight peeked through a crack in the curtains. Morning had arrived. I yawned, stretched, and felt remarkably well rested.

I blinked up at the pompous velvet canopy on the four-poster bed, trying to wake up. What would I do today? I could go to the beach for a swim or the harbor market for some fresh fruit or maybe sunbathe by the pool. So many options, so little time. My vacation would only last a week, the duration of spring break, and I had wasted my first day feeling rotten and pouting like a petulant child.

"Good morning."

My boyfriend's husky voice beckoned me to naughtiness. I smiled languidly and closed my eyes again. I groped for my morning wood and gave it a little tug.

"Morning, babe," I purred back.

Then, in a flash of insight rare for my morning-muddled brain, I remembered I didn't have a boyfriend anymore. I'd dumped the two-timing SOB before I departed the country for my vacation to these near-tropical shores in the south of France.

I blinked and swiveled my head toward the speaker.

A man lay next to me on his side, leaning on one elbow, staring down at me with an amused expression.

And *whoa*, he was gorgeous. Not just handsome but possessing a mystifying charm I found oddly tempting.

He had short natural-blond curls that framed his face into a portrait of an angel come to earth. His sun-kissed skin had a healthy glow, and his blue eyes sparked with lightnings of joy. I think he found me quite a funny treat.

Strange. A faint recollection teased the back of my brain. He seemed familiar somehow. Had I seen him at the hotel yesterday? It was a big place, so… maybe.

I yanked the covers up to my chin and yelled a jumble of words, "Who the hell are you? What are you doing in my room? Get out right now!"

Unperturbed by my outburst, he studied me lazily. His slightly heavy eyelids gave him a dreamy, sensual look, like an exotic beast hunting its prey with ease. He had the fullest lips I'd ever seen on a grown man. His lower lip protruded outward ever so little, like an offering to the gods of kissing.

Since he was under the covers, same as me, I couldn't tell what his body looked like. But his exposed shoulders were broad and muscular, suggesting he was athletic and brawny all over. Or was that just wishful thinking on my part?

He chuckled at my outrage and waved about indistinctly. "Under any other circumstances, I would love to comply, you understand. But since this is not, in fact, your room...."

He left the sentence hanging in the charged air. The pregnant pause served to confuse me further. I refused to budge and stuck my chin out, glaring at him.

"You are mistaken, *sir*. See? My warm milk from last night." I waved madly at the empty glass on the nightstand. "See? My clothes on that chair and my suitcase right next to—"

As I rose halfway to sitting in bed, I gestured toward the opposite wall where two lounge chairs and a dresser formed a simple seating arrangement. And lo and behold, my belongings were *not* on the chair or on the floor or anywhere in sight.

What was on the chair, however, were clothes I had never seen before, all designer labels unless I missed my guess.

And above the dresser was a Gustav Klimt print.

I opened and closed my mouth like a fish on dry land. "Wait.... Wasn't that a... a Rembrandt print yesterday?"

Even as I spoke, my gaze swept the room in search of clues about the true occupant. I cringed and shrunk as I observed the large oak wardrobe in the wrong place, two big expensive suitcases with metal lining the sides, and two pairs of shoes in front of them, neither of them mine. Wrong paintings, wrong decorations, wrong wallpaper—wrong everything.

I slumped, my cheeks on fire. "Oh God, I... I'm mortified. I'm so, so, so sorry. I am in the wrong room." I hurried out of bed, only realizing I was in my underwear and nothing else as I stood there, searching for my bathrobe.

The beautiful man's eyes traced my slim, short figure, my messy brown hair with red streaks, unremarkable hazel eyes, and unflattering tighty-whities. I covered my crotch with my hands as I inched toward another simple chair by the nightstand, upon which rested my haphazardly thrown bathrobe. I was painfully aware that my erection hadn't disappeared, leaving me at half-mast. If my cheeks were burning before, now I was on fire all over.

I ducked my head to hide my reddened face, yanked the bathrobe over my bare body, tucked my feet into my slippers, and started for the hotel room door.

"Wait."

The man with the most amazing smooth sultry voice rose from the bed, slow and sure. I swallowed, trying to avoid his gaze and the sight of his body at the same time. But I had been right in my estimation. In all his athletic glory, this man was the epitome of perfect masculinity, with firm muscles, a broad chest, strong arms, tapered waist, long powerful legs, and a most delicious bulge behind his black boxer briefs.

Why couldn't I meet a guy like this at a time and place when I wasn't utterly humiliated?

After putting on a white silk robe that hugged his form like a second skin, he stepped closer on bare feet. Even his toes, with pedicured toenails, looked sexy. Sighing in defeat, I accepted the likelihood I wouldn't stop blushing anytime soon.

"May I ask, since this is not your room, how you got in here?" he asked.

A reasonable question. I thumbed over my shoulder. "The door was unlocked. I thought I'd forgotten to lock it when I went to fetch some warm milk from the kitchen."

He cocked his head, smiling at me again. "Why didn't you call for room service?"

I shrugged. "The phone number didn't work, so I assumed they don't deliver late at night."

The man smiled shortly. "This is a five-star luxury resort. Room service is open twenty-four seven."

Before I could say anything, he stepped around me and walked to the door. He tried the handle and the door opened. Clearly it was still unlocked. No keycard necessary.

"See?" I said, quite needlessly.

He faced me, one eyebrow quirked. He approached me without making a sound. His gaze met mine. "And you are…?"

"Oh." I coughed to clear my throat. "Oliver. Well, Ollie, as everyone calls me. Oliver Reed. Like the actor in the movie *Gladiator*." I extended a hand on automatic before considering if this was actually the right thing to do when trespassing.

Laughing, he took my hand in his. "Max."

As he didn't elaborate, I felt it would have been rude to ask for more. After all, I had barged into his room in the middle of the night.

As a sidenote, his hand was warm and strong, the skin smooth, no calluses or scars.

Awkwardly, I sidestepped him and backed toward the door. "Well, I, uh, don't want to keep you. Again, terribly sorry for the inconvenience." I knew he could call the police and have me arrested for trespassing or breaking and entering and god knew what else.

He did not, however, call the authorities. Instead, he bowed with a lopsided grin as a farewell. I nodded clumsily and took my leave in a hurry.

By the time I reached the elevator, I realized my faux pas: I was actually on the wrong floor. My room was one floor below his. Cursing my ineptitude, I made a mad dash into the lift and then back to my room. I didn't even dare breathe in relief until I had my back firmly set against the closed door, with me safe on the inside.

"Jesus Christ, what a fucking tool I am."

I could only hope my mystery host wouldn't hold my uninvited nightly visit against me.

"No, he won't," I told myself steadfastly, straightening up. "Because I am never going to see that man again." I nodded to cement my decision. "That's right, Fate. You have no power over me—because I'm never leaving this goddamn room again for the length of my stay."

My vow made, I hurried to the bathroom to take a cold shower. The enticing memory of the hottest man alive lingered. And my morning self-fun time had been so rudely interrupted.

Chapter 2

ALAS, I was not that lucky. Fortune didn't favor me, for I was not bold.

After I took a cold shower, I got the chills and had to take a hot bath with bubbles. I felt so silly. Even my reflection in the foggy mirror stared back at me with ridicule, my cheeks and neck as red as the bright-red stripes in my hair.

I got dressed in a T-shirt and shorts. I ordered breakfast from room service and confirmed that I had dialed the wrong number last night. No wonder no one had answered. I was also assured that any order placed at any hour would be met by the staff.

A continental breakfast later, I sat on my balcony, enjoying the cool breeze. It was early, but the sun was already blazing hot. I really needed to cool off if I was to be of any use to anyone today.

A knock on the door startled me. I figured it was a member of staff coming to retrieve my morning platter, so I opened the door.

My deep gulp had to be audible; it sure sounded really loud in my ears.

"Good morning, Oliver."

That reverberating baritone set my nether regions doing somersaults. It was the man from last night. Max.

I repeated his name in my head a couple of times before saying, "Morning, Max."

But my voice betrayed me and squeaked anyway, dammit.

I waited with bated breath to see what he wanted. He could still turn me in. Images of foreign jails passed before my overactive mind's eyes.

"May I?" Max gestured for me to stand aside and let him in. Embarrassed all over again, I did just that.

He sailed in gracefully, like a gazillion-dollar yacht. He was taller than me by maybe three inches, so I had to look up at him. But I sensed I would do so regardless of his stature, since from our attire alone it was apparent that he was way out of my class.

I stood in place in my raggedy T-shirt and shorts, shifting my weight from one foot to the other.

Max, however, wore an impeccable tailored suit. Not a wrinkle or a smear in sight. His blue silk tie matched the color of his eyes. A gentle, slightly musky fragrance wafted in his wake, and I recognized the scent from last night. His blond curls swayed as if touched by an unseen wind, giving him a look mixing high-powered businessman and world-class athlete.

As I closed the door, I noted two colossal bodyguards—at least I was pretty sure that was what they were—standing by the entrance: one male, the other female. They could have jumped out of the WWE circuit. Apparently this man with whom I had shared a bed last night was *Someone* with a capital *S*.

"H-how can I help you?" I asked in an effort to regain my equilibrium.

Without so much as a glance at my quarters, Max turned to face me. "During your midnight wanderings, did you by chance notice anything… unusual?"

I blinked in confusion. "You mean, like, in your room?"

He shrugged. "Wherever."

As he spoke, for the first time I caught the hint of an accent, soft and purring. Reminded me of French. Perhaps he was a French national. Foreign to be sure. Then I mentally slapped myself. *I* was foreign too; I was on holiday in France, not back home in Seattle.

"Um…." I scratched my head, trying to remember anything that might have stood out last night. Apart from the train wreck with Max, nothing jumped out at me. "Not that I recall. Why?"

His blue eyes flashed. "Would it surprise you to learn that I was robbed last night?"

I gasped in shock, my eyes widening. "Wh-what? How?"

Instead of explaining further, he studied me. "When you came back to your room after your adventure with me, was your door unlocked?"

My brow furrowed as I went over the insanity of last night. Had the door been locked? If I remembered opening the door with a keycard, as I did, was that an accurate memory?

Ashamed, I replied, "I-I can't remember. I wasn't paying attention. I'm sorry."

Max smiled kindly. "Don't worry, Oliver. You need not apologize." Then he got a cunning twinkle in his eyes. "I already knew the answer. Your door was indeed unlocked, same as mine—and everyone else's too. Last night, the entire hotel had quite the open-door policy in practice."

I stared in awe. "Holy shit."

He nodded toward my suitcase. "You might wish to check that your things are where they belong and that nothing is missing."

"Oh yeah, right."

I rushed to comply with his suggestion. I ransacked my suitcase and backpack for any signs of tampering. I found none. All my important items—passport, ID, wallet, money—were right where I had left them. I had few clothes and only two pairs of shoes, and they weren't lost either.

I met his gaze. "Everything's accounted for. You?"

Max looked down, hiding his eyes behind a veil of long golden lashes. Up close and in broad daylight, I noticed he had a couple of very faint freckles on the sides of his nose. Cute. A sudden urge to trace each and every one of those golden dots freaked me the hell out.

"Something irreplaceable was taken from the safe in my quarters."

I stood from my crouched pose. "Oh God, I'm sorry." He didn't look at me, but he inclined his head in acknowledgment of my sentiment. Then it occurred to me why he was there in my room. "I didn't take it, whatever it was. I swear. I'm not a thief."

Max chuckled. "I'm aware. The only thing you hid from me, rather poorly I might add, were your crown jewels." He winked at me. "Nothing like mine, to be sure."

I flushed with heat, a mix of arousal and embarrassment. Then his words hit home. "Wait. You had crown jewels in your quarters?"

Max harder, throwing his head back. The exposed column of his neck showed no trace of stubble. He had quite recently shaved. The golden skin was flawless and silky smooth. My mouth suddenly watered.

By the time Max stopped hooting, he was wiping tears of joy from his eyes. "No, I did not house the crown jewels of any nation in the small safe in my quarters. My father would kill me."

I cocked my head, baffled as usual in his company. "Huh?" My eloquence surprised even me—into embarrassed silence.

Mysterious as ever, Max didn't elaborate or explain. Instead he declared, "We should speak with the hotel manager. Perhaps that might shed light on the situation."

As I nodded my bewildered assent and followed him out of the room, I decided his twofold demeanor—how he spoke formally but behaved casually—was fascinating. I wanted to learn more about him.

I wondered how long he would be staying at the hotel and if there might be a chance for a little holiday fling.

BY THE time we'd reached the manager's office on the ground floor, I had discarded the idea of a foreign affair with the handsome stranger. He was way out of my league. And I considered myself as someone with healthy self-esteem.

At the manager's door by the lobby, a crowd had formed. Angry voices and rude gestures dominated the scene. I couldn't hear myself think.

I quickly gathered the facts, though Max had already alluded to them. A lot of people were missing a lot of priceless objects, ranging from men's and women's jewelry to bearer bonds, cashier's checks, and stacks of cash. A rare few rooms, all of them on the top floors, had safes that had also been burgled.

The manager raised his hands and tried to silence the mob but proved unsuccessful.

Then a sharp whistle pierced the air. Everyone whipped around.

Max smiled courteously, inclined his head like a true gentleman, and waved at the manager to speak his piece.

The manager, a tall, thin man with glasses, smiled in gratitude, adding a tiny bow.

Then he addressed everyone. "Ladies and gentlemen, I sincerely apologize for any and all inconvenience. Rest assured, the proper authorities have been contacted, and a full investigation will be conducted posthaste. We are hopeful that all your items will be returned to you in due course. Again, I apologize for the trouble."

The coterie of hotel guests drew an almost simultaneous breath. I knew what would follow, so I hurried to ask before anyone else could, "Excuse me, do these thefts have anything to do with all the room doors being open last night?"

People stared at me, some in astonishment, others in vexation. Pretty much everyone was surprised, though. Had they not noticed?

I raised my keycard above my head. "I could get into my room without my keycard. And to any other room too."

Max brought up his own as well. "I had a similar situation."

The manager blinked. A robust man in an ill-fitting suit that bulged at his side, revealing a weapon holster, whispered something in his ear. Since it was eerily quiet at the moment, the hissing was audible.

Though the manager kept up appearances, I saw beads of sweat pop up on his forehead.

He cleared his throat when the other man, probably hotel security, moved off, and he said with a grim tone that suggested all kinds of problems, "I regret to inform you that the computer system in the hotel which locks all the doors has been… hacked."

I exchanged glances with Max, who remained remarkably stoic. I envied his serenity. My own nerves were shot. Too much excitement for my second day on holiday. Geez.

Chapter 3

THE HACK sure explained why the doors were all unlocked.

Max spoke above the renewed din. "Are the door locks still malfunctioning? Or has the issue been fixed?"

Out of the corner of my eye, I observed a tiny twitch of Max's fingers, seemingly aimed at the poor manager. But it was over too quickly for me to make heads or tails of it.

The manager was barely able to conceal a sigh that spoke volumes. "I'm afraid the matter persists for the time being. As a precaution, I will be instructing security officers to patrol nonstop on all the floors. I assure you, no unauthorized person or persons will be allowed past the lobby. Any and all attempts will be thwarted."

That seemed to placate at least a couple of the patrons. A low murmur remained, though.

Perhaps to lift the sunken mood, the manager smiled a tad awkwardly and gestured toward stairs leading down. "The good news is that the hotel's own safes in the basement have proved hack and thief proof. Therefore, ladies and gentlemen, I would ask you to accompany my assistant here to check on your belongings secured there. One at a time, if you please."

As a line began to form, I faced Max. "I didn't store anything in the hotel safe. Did you?"

He shrugged. "A few things. Might as well check on them." He regarded me under his brow. "Would you mind accompanying me down to the vault?"

I hedged, rubbing the back of my heated, sweaty neck. My nerves were frayed. "Uh, I don't know. Isn't that, like, private? I doubt security would even let me go with you."

Max chuckled with a conspiratorial twinkle in his eyes. "Oh, I believe they will extend me every courtesy."

Though I had concerns about Max's overconfidence, I shrugged and nodded my assent. "Sure. I won't peek, I promise."

Max laughed as we followed an obsequious desk clerk down the stairs toward the vault.

MUCH LIKE an underground safe-deposit-box area in a bank, the hotel vault was hidden behind a large metal door. Next to it was a handprint identification screen, an iris scanner, and a numbered keypad. The hotel took security seriously, it seemed.

That fact made the full-hotel robbery even weirder. I concluded there had to have been an inside man. No other way to pull off such a large-scale heist in such a short amount of time.

A curious sidenote occurred to me: Where had Max's security detail been? They sure had not stood outside the door to his hotel room last night, or I wouldn't have gotten in so easily.

I shrugged the thoughts off in favor of following Max down the stairs.

As expected, the clerk tried to stop me from entering the vault with my host. Max, however, glared at the man for a brief second, and the next thing I knew, the clerk had scampered off, leaving me alone with Max.

"Voilà," he exclaimed, spreading his arms like a world-renowned actor.

I grinned. "You sure put the fear of god into him. Not bad."

A humble rosy hue colored his cheeks, but I could tell he was pleased by my compliment.

He found his box, which was one of the biggest in the vault, and used a key he had around his neck. I didn't think a neck was the most secure of places, but I was just along for the ride here. My commentary didn't matter in the end.

Max pulled out the box, brought it to the sturdy metal table in the middle of the vault, and opened it with his key. He studied the contents, which I could not see.

I grimaced again. Using keys as a security measure seemed so antiquated that I puzzled over why this place hadn't been robbed as well.

Then the thought occurred to me: maybe it had....

Max, however, quashed my idea by stating, "Everything's in its proper place."

I itched with curiosity, wanting to see what he had stashed away in his box. But I didn't dare ask or poke my nose where it didn't belong, so "Good" was all I said.

Max smirked at me. "Come on, then. I know you're dying for a look."

How did he know? My cheeks burned. "Nah. I'm good, thanks."

Max rolled his eyes, rounded the table, hooked arms with me, and walked me over to the other side. "I'm not a hoarder, but I do always travel with a few essentials. Though most are not of my own choosing."

Bewildered by this mysterious man who looked so familiar but whom I knew I had never met before, I peeked into the box. Not much there but a green folder stuffed with documents, stacks of cash—euros, and dollars—and a tiny black ring box. When Max opened the box, I saw a golden ring with a coat of arms I didn't recognize. It depicted a rampant unicorn with a crown over its mane.

"That's pretty cool. Is it a family heirloom?" I asked, pointing at the ring.

Max barked out a bitter laugh. "*Heir*loom, indeed."

Once again I stared at him, flummoxed. "Huh?"

The hotel manager appeared, hands clasped against his belly, an expectant look on his face. "I trust nothing is amiss, Your Highness."

I gasped, my eyes widening, my knees turning to jelly, and my heart damn near thudding its way out of my chest. "Wh-what?" I took an unsteady step back, staring at Max like a village idiot. "Wh-who are you?"

Before Max, who wore an annoyed expression, could speak, the manager had already continued in a haughty tone, "This is His Studious Highness, Hereditary Prince Maximilian IX Lukas of Noricia."

I stopped breathing for so long spots started to dance in my field of vision.

"Y-you're a… a p-prince?"

Max glared at the manager, who looked sheepish and cast his gaze down demurely. Then Max sighed and nodded. "Yes, I am. Is that a problem?"

I wondered how many people reacted the way I had, or if his regal station indeed posed a problem. My only concern was how much of an ass I had made of myself in front of him.

"No." I blushed, burning fire-hot, when I realized I had, in fact, shared a bed with an honest-to-god prince last night. "I-I would like to apologize for, uh…." I glanced at the manager, who clearly pretended not to listen. I couldn't say "last night," or misunderstandings would surely follow.

Max smiled, relaxed again. "No worries, Oliver. I had fun last night."

I was sure my eyes would bug out of their sockets as I stuttered to say something intelligible. "Oh, well, yes...." Then I remembered the ring, and I looked down at it. "So that's a... a royal signet ring?"

Max nodded. "Yes, a sign of my station, given to me by my father when I came of age. It dates back to the days of my great-grandfather, who is sadly no longer with us." He bowed his head minutely, and his gaze turned glassy. But the pose didn't last. He met my gaze. "Unlike the lion common in many European countries, the unicorn is the royal symbol of Noricia and the House of Lindau-Arbon."

I swallowed, nervous as all hell. "So, you're the, uh, heir to the throne?" I could have slapped myself silly. That was what he'd referred to when talking about family heirlooms.

"I am, yes. I do have two younger brothers," Max explained shortly. Then he took the ring out of its box and held it in his fingers. A slight frown marred his high, intelligent forehead. "I am confused, though. I was certain I had secured this signet ring in the safe in my room, not in here. That is why I came to see you this morning, Oliver."

A nagging thought rattled inside my brain. "If that's what you remember, then maybe that's what happened." I gestured at the undoubtedly priceless artifact. "Maybe that's not your ring. Just because it looks like it doesn't mean it is it, you know?"

I was babbling by then, wanting to show my smarts but not so sure about the accuracy of my assertions. I was guessing, not deducing with the brilliance of Sherlock Holmes.

Max frowned and raised the ring closer so he could inspect it more carefully, but he held it on the very tips of his fingers, as if it were a dangerous animal. His eyes narrowed as he went over the object millimeter by millimeter. Finally, his jaw clenched, and a cold, steely flash from his eyes told me I might have been onto something.

"You are correct, Oliver. This is not my ring. This is a fake."

The manager drew in a sharp breath and hurried closer. "That cannot be. A member of your security team brought this here last night for safekeeping."

"One of my own bodyguards?" Max demanded, anger lowering his tone to a growl like that of a beast. I shivered, glad I wasn't on the receiving end of the man's fury.

"Yes." The manager nodded, baffled if his scrunched eyebrows were any indication. "I don't understand...." The more confused he got, the stronger his accent became.

Who was this treasonous bodyguard? I wanted to know. Had he taken the ring to sell it for a fortune on the black market, perhaps to a collector, or had he taken it for more nefarious reasons?

The manager held the ring, turning it over in his hands, circling both the inside and outside, even slipping it on for a brief moment before flushing with embarrassment and quickly taking it off again. Then, frowning, he stared at his own fingertips. They stuck together as if his skin was sticky or gooey.

All of a sudden, the manager cried out. White foam gushed out of his mouth. He started to convulse. Then his eyes rolled around in their sockets, and he fell to the floor, limp as a wet noodle. His spectacles slid across the floor, one lens cracked.

Max knelt beside him, reaching for the manager's neck for a pulse.

I grabbed his shoulder. "Wait. Don't touch him. Just in case. You're the future king, for god's sake."

Max seemed irritated by my interruption, but he finally nodded grudgingly and stood again. Out of the corner of my eye, I observed him reach for his cell phone and call for an ambulance.

I crouched next to the unconscious man. As nervous as I was, I felt like I had to learn what had happened—for Max's benefit. The manager's chest didn't rise and fall at all. I brushed his neck, where the skin was cool and clammy. There was no pulse. I leaned over his mouth. I heard no sounds of breathing.

"He's dead." The fake signet ring had rolled away from his hand onto the floor. A tiny needle barely protruded on the underside the gold-and-gem-encrusted signet. "Shit. That was meant for you."

Max didn't touch the ring but checked his own hands. The manager's right-hand index finger had a blood smear on the tip. Max himself had no wounds.

"I'm fine," he murmured, staring at the ring and the manager, the corners of his mouth turned down. "Someone tried to poison me."

"The guy didn't give us the name of the bodyguard," I noted as I rose, pointing at the dead man on the floor.

Noises of hurrying feet came from the stairs, the stomping reminiscent of a stampede. Help was coming, but it was too late, at least for the manager.

Max had barely enough time to whisper to me, "Speak of this to no one" before the vault was filled with people, everyone from hotel staff to EMTs and the police.

I blew out a breath. Well, my vacation was off to a rocking start.

Chapter 4

Noricia, officially the Kingdom of Noricia, is a microstate in Central Europe. The land is a constitutional monarchy lead by the King of Noricia, currently King Gustav IV Caspar, the head of House Lindau-Arbon. As the first European country in history to do so, in 1979 Noricia established absolute primogeniture to determine the heir to the throne, currently Prince Maximilian IX Lukas. The King rules in conjunction with a sixty-three-membered Council of Ministers.

Noricia is bordered by Switzerland to the west, Liechtenstein to the south, Austria to the east, and Germany and Lake Constance to the north. An Alpine country, Noricia spans an area of 215 square kilometers (83 square miles) and is the fifth smallest country in Europe, with a population of 33,916.

The capital of Noricia is Vindeburg. The kingdom is divided into nine municipalities called cantons. Noricia is a member of the European Union, the United Nations, the European Free Trade Association, and the Council of Europe. Noricia has four official languages: French, German, Italian, and English. The country's state-sanctioned religion is Celtic Revival, and a large majority of the populace identify themselves as Neo-Celts....

My head spun. Reading Wikipedia entries didn't help. I sat on the bed in my hotel room, trying to eat a very late lunch and absorb the enormity of my recent encounter with a real-life prince.

I glossed over the history sections, noting references to the La Tène culture, the Roman province of Raetia, and the Noricum tribe in passing. I had a headache; my forehead and temples throbbed with heat.

I set the tablet aside and tried to arrange my thoughts from the jumble they were in. But no matter how hard I tried, I couldn't get past the realization that Max, the handsome man I had shared a bed with, was a prince. The notion was simply too enormous for me to focus on anything else.

I wondered if I would ever see him again, even if only to hear about the ongoing investigation into the death of the hotel manager. I had been escorted out of the area before I had learned anything more than what I had already gleaned, which was that the fake ring had been dosed with a lethal toxin set in an almost imperceptible needle on the inside of the ring. The manager had tried it on and taken the full brunt of the poison.

Max could have died. My breath hitched at the horrible thought. Max could have been killed before my eyes. Would I have been blamed? Would I have been the convenient scapegoat? Spending the rest of my life in a foreign jail paled in comparison to the worldwide spectacle of a public execution.

I quivered, covered in cold sweat.

Angry at myself, I shoved the vexing ideas out of my mind and headed for the bathroom, my intention to enjoy a nice hot bubble bath. I'm a dude but, hey, I like bubbles. Sue me.

I had started to take my T-shirt off when there was a knock at the door. Still fumbling with the shirt, I yanked the door open.

Max quirked an eyebrow as he surveyed my bare chest. "Am I interrupting you?"

I flushed with heat. That low reverberation, that soft hint of an accent—I was sold. I pulled down the hem of my shirt, hid my red face, and beckoned him in.

Max studied the room briefly. "I see why you might be confused about whose room you were in last night."

"An honest mistake," I quipped with a coy grin, since he didn't seem to loathe my trespassing. "How goes the case? Did you catch the killer or track down the guard dude?"

Max released a frustrated noise. "No to both. Firstly, there's a high probability that the parties who tampered with my ring, stole the original, and planted the fake one are not in this country. They are more likely to be back in my own country."

I nodded. The theory made sense. Those responsible wouldn't have needed more than a middleman for the exchange between the true culprit and a thief or a group of robbers. The additional items stolen must have been a bonus.

"Secondly," Max went on, "my missing bodyguard, Janos, is nowhere to be found. If he was the inside man, he might be dead. If he is still alive, though, I will turn the world upside down looking for him."

I liked this passionate side of Max, his steadfast determination, his just zeal, his strength of conviction. Where were all the guys like him when I was out on the dating circuit?

Max had reached the foot of my bed, where my food tray and tablet rested on a mussed-up blanket. He grabbed the tablet and smiled at me.

"Studying about my country, Oliver?" His teasing tone did funny things to my stomach, releasing a swarm of butterflies. "Why would you consult a piece of cold hardware when you have a warm, living and breathing encyclopedia of my country right in front of you?"

I gulped. I wanted him to leave; I wanted him to stay. Could I get past the fact that he was a prince and focus on the incredibly nice, cute guy behind the imposing title?

Max sat on the edge of the bed and crossed his legs, his back ramrod straight, an expectant look on his face. Nothing seemed to deter him. "Ask me what you will."

He had such a quaint, old-fashioned way of speaking. I sort of liked it. Those mannerisms seemed to fit him. Max was a gentleman of the highest order. Being a prince might have had something to do with it, or it could be his nature, his true character.

"Anything?" I inquired as I sat beside him at the foot of the bed, teasing him the way he had done with me.

Max chuckled. "Yes. However, I get a turn to ask a question after you. Fair play."

I nodded my agreement. "Why did the manager call you His Studious Highness?"

Max rolled his eyes. His cheeks pinked a little, as if he were embarrassed. "A lot of royalty, not just active rulers, have added nicknames. Some are given during the royal's lifetime, others after his or her death, to sum up their reign." He glanced at me, serious again. "I have always been a curious one. I excelled in my studies. Hence... studious."

"So if you weren't royalty, you'd be a scholar?" I asked.

Max sighed, a deep longing in his blue eyes. "No. What I really wanted to be was an athlete. I dreamed of the Olympics, of representing my country in the games and bringing back gold."

I whistled low. "Really? Wow. What sport?"

"Biathlon."

I blinked, not that familiar with sports outside of baseball and American football. "Is that the one where you ski and shoot?"

Max smiled. "Yes. I'm a pretty good shot, and in the Alps, everyone knows how to ski."

"I bet you'd be awesome. So why didn't you ever compete?"

A shadow passed over Max's face. "Dangerous sports are not allowed for members of royal families, especially the heir to the throne. I might jeopardize the continuity of the royal lineage."

I grimaced. "That's stupid. And it sucks. I'm sorry." Max inclined his head to acknowledge my sentiment. The mood had sunk, so I quickly changed the subject. "Does the rest of your family have nicknames too?"

Max nodded. "My father, King Gustav IV Caspar, is called the Just, for he has brought our country into the modern world and done so with compassion. He is known for progressive laws and initiatives." Then, with a salacious wink, he smirked at me. "I know *your* nickname, Ollie. Though I much prefer Oliver."

I coughed to clear my throat. My hands were sweaty. I'd never talked with a prince before in such an intimate setting. Last night didn't count.

"You have siblings?" I asked to steer the topic along safer paths.

"Two brothers. You?"

"One sister, younger."

Max straightened. "Ah. So, we're both of us the eldest child."

I shrugged. "Guess so. My sister, Elinor, is nothing like me. She's a whirlwind, rambunctious and carefree." I smiled at a memory from long ago that rose to the forefront of my mind out of the blue. "Elinor of Elsinore."

Max cocked his head. "Is that a reference to—"

"Shakespeare's *Hamlet*, yes. You see, back in high school Elinor starred in a production of *Hamlet*. She played Ophelia. And she took madness to whole new levels of crazy. When she jumped from the makeshift balcony—tethered, of course—the audience cried and screamed. One lady fainted. It was a total madhouse that night. I'm still surprised they didn't call the cops on her for almost causing a riot."

Max laughed till he had tears in his eyes. "Oh, I wish I had seen that."

I grinned. "Many wish they could *un*see it."

Max stared at nothing, longing in his eyes. "She seems like quite the character. Perhaps I will meet her one day. Then we can talk about crazy childhood adventures together."

I worried the inside of my cheek, pondering what kind of meeting was even possible for such an illustrious figure as a prince. Casual get-togethers with friends probably weren't the easiest thing to arrange.

"Elinor would love you," I murmured to say something, the mood too somber for my taste.

Max quirked a lopsided grin, hiding his gaze behind a thick veil of blond lashes. "I wonder if her brother would…?"

My breath caught. My heartbeat quickened. My mouth was suddenly dry as a desert. Had he really said what I thought he'd said? And what on earth could I say to that?

Like a coward, I deflected, "O-on Wikipedia, it-it says Noricia has four official languages. D-do you speak them all?"

If Max was upset by my timidity, he didn't show it. "Yes, I do. Italian not as fluently as I would like. I also speak passable Dutch, a fair bit of casual Spanish, and I'm trying to learn Mandarin Chinese."

I nearly choked. "Six languages? With a seventh in the works? Jesus. I can barely manage two languages adequately."

Max snickered. "English was the easiest to learn. We are bombarded by it on a daily basis. Hard to avoid picking it up. Besides, it is not a very, um, complex tongue. And the vocabulary is at times, ah, a bit narrow. The words I use, the long ones with aesthetic appeal or those with sophisticated significance, often go misunderstood."

I wasn't sure if I agreed with Max's interpretation. "English has a large vocabulary." Then I frowned, slumping. "It's dwindled in common use, though, so I guess you're right about that."

"Limited," Max said. I didn't think he was being facetious or insulting on purpose; he merely gave the subject his point of view. "There are English-speaking poets, writers, and artists who use the language exceedingly well. They are rare, however."

I cringed. I recalled my own half-ass tweets or commentaries where I didn't bother to check spelling or whatever. And abbreviations I got only as far as I needed them. All others might as well have been hieroglyphics as far as I was concerned.

"What is your other language besides English?" Max inquired.

"Spanish," I said proudly. "Like you said, passable, I suppose. I don't get to use it much in Seattle, despite my heritage and ethnicity. Much of our family still lives in Mexico."

"Is that where you're from, the great Northwest?"

"I was born in Vancouver, Canada, actually. But Elinor was born in the States, in Seattle." I wasn't quite ready to talk about my family to any great extent. Max was still largely a stranger to me. So, I moved on. "Your country is in the Alps?"

"It is an Alpine land, yes, although the northern border ends at Lake Constance. We get warm winds from the south, and the Rhine valley has a mild climate. The mountains aren't the tallest of the range, so...." He glanced at me with a whimsical expression. "Think of *The Sound of Music*, and you're in the ballpark."

I pursed my lips. "Never saw it."

Max gasped in feigned exaggerated shock, a hand on his chest. "Philistine. You must see it this instant. I insist." He removed his jacket, placed it over a chair, opened the top buttons of his white dress shirt, took off his fine shoes, creased his dress pants to ease movement, and inched backward until he leaned against a stack of pillows. "I can order the movie on pay-per-view at no cost to you."

I snorted as I backed up next to him, taking my tablet with me. "Dude, I've got Netflix." Then I realized what I'd said. "Um, sorry, Your Highness."

Max bumped my arm with his shoulder. "Please, Oliver, do not stand on ceremony with me. I get enough of that with everyone." Then before I could apologize again, he chuckled. "After all, it's time to... Netflix and chill."

I rolled my eyes, bumping him right back. "Behave."

Max merely settled more comfortably against the pillows. But he noticeably leaned into me. I found I didn't mind one damn bit.

Chapter 5

As THE day waned and night fell, Max admitted to himself he was starting to like this young American, Oliver Reed, quite a lot.

They watched the old movie, ordered room service, and chilled, as the service provider they had settled on suggested. This type of relaxation was atypical for Max, who had a daily itinerary set down by the minute. This trip was an exception, and he was thoroughly enjoying himself.

"What do you think of the movie so far, Oliver?" Max asked, watching a scene where Maria, with a dreamy expression, observed Captain von Trapp sing about a flower.

Oliver shrugged, popping a piece of popcorn into his mouth. "Lot of singing."

Max laughed. "It is a musical. You do know what that means, right?"

Oliver's cheeks and neck grew ruddy. He was a blusher; Max had noted this with glee earlier. He wondered if Oliver would be prone to the same reaction in bed.

Max knew Oliver was gay or at least bi. Oliver's response to hearing a man's voice in bed confirmed as much. Max recalled with satisfaction Oliver's sleepy, raspy purr, the way his hand had moved under the blanket, how his body arched up in the throes of dazed passion. Max wouldn't mind waking up next to this young man again.

"Do you get, like, free time or vacations for hobbies and such, or are you always on duty?" Oliver asked, his gaze aimed at the tablet screen rather than his companion.

"I am here, aren't I?" Max quipped back.

Though Max had traveled all over Europe during his lifetime, he had never before visited the Île de Porquerolles in the south of France, off the Riviera. The tropical climate and landscape had surprised him. It was the end of March, though, so it wasn't as hot as it got during the summer. Nonetheless, according to the staff at Domaine de la Lumière, the only five-star hotel on the island, temperatures had reached record highs thanks to climate change.

"True." Oliver stole a less-than-surreptitious glimpse of Max, who observed the look out of the corner of his eye. "But why'd you come here to Porquerolles? Are you, like, on a diplomatic mission or something?"

Max shook his head. "No. I do get vacation days, same as everyone else with a day job. But I rarely find the time to use them. This time my mother, Colette, was adamant. Apparently I've been too fidgety lately for her liking."

Oliver snorted. "You? Mr. Cool-as-a-cucumber twenty-four seven? I think not."

Max laughed. He realized offhandedly that with Oliver he had laughed more than he had in months, maybe years. Oliver had a way of relaxing him and bringing out the best in him. Quite an epiphany, Max mused, to want more time with someone he barely knew.

"Why are *you* here?" Max inquired with a casual tone.

Oliver sighed, sounding sad. "Spring break."

Max swallowed hard, his blood running cold. "You're in, uh… high school?"

Oliver barked out a loud laugh. "No, man. College. University of Washington. Senior year. At the end of the semester I'll earn a master's degree in culinary arts. I'm going to be a pastry chef."

As a reaction to hearing Oliver's interest, Max's mouth watered. He did the math in his head but sought confirmation. "So, that makes you… how old?"

Oliver smirked at him. "Twenty-one. You?"

"Twenty-nine," Max replied demurely. "Didn't you check that when you were perusing sites about my country?"

Max grinned when Oliver blushed again, red slashes rising to grace his high cheeks. Oliver murmured something unintelligible, and Max suppressed a laugh.

He didn't want to bring down the mood, but Oliver had awakened his curiosity. And if he wanted any kind of relationship, friendship or otherwise, with the young American, he had to learn more.

"Earlier, I sensed your reluctance to speak about your family. You've aroused my curiosity. But you don't have to tell me anything. I don't wish to pry."

Max let the suggestion hang in the charged air between them. He would wait for a moment, but if Oliver said nothing, Max would move on to lighter topics. He didn't wish to alienate his friend.

Oliver seemed to have a twitch in the corner of his eye, and he worried his lower lip. Clearly, he was anxious. Max was about to pull the plug before things got ugly, but then Oliver let out a long drawn-out breath.

"My dad drives a truck."

Max blinked. What was wrong with that? "You mean, an ice-road truck or—"

"No, a garbage truck." Oliver's chin jutted out, and he was frowning. Perhaps this subject had been met with laughs or derision before.

Well, Max wasn't like that. "That is impressive. Sanitation services are vital for a functional infrastructure and key to a sophisticated society. Without proper sanitation, civilization would grind to a halt. There would be riots in the streets."

Oliver's brow cleared, and the corner of his lips turned up. Lowering his eyes, he murmured, "Thanks. I don't think anyone's ever cared about how important garbage trucks and their drivers are."

Max smiled. "People might think garbage men are invisible, but believe me, if those services were unavailable, like during a strike, everyone would notice their absence."

Oliver met Max's gaze, a grateful sheen in his hazel eyes. "My dad would love you."

At the compliment, Max beamed. For an as of yet undetermined reason, Max cared about Oliver's opinion of him. "Would he like the Alps, do you think?"

Oliver snorted. "Just try to stop Paulito Ruíz from going down a slope, and you *will* have a riot on your hands." Before his laughter died down, however, Max observed a shadow pass over his face.

"Your father is Mexican American?" Max asked softly, realizing immediately that Oliver's reaction was about racism, not Max specifically.

"Legal," Oliver spat through gritted teeth. Then he slumped, his tightened features going soft and remorseful. "I'm sorry."

Max rested a hand on Oliver's bare arm. "Don't apologize. Hate seems to be the word du jour all over the world. Right-wing haters, fascists, and white supremacists do appear to dominate the world right now. But, Oliver, that won't last. Good wins out in the end. Keep your spirit strong."

The way Oliver blinked then, undoubtedly because of his eyes welling and with a gentle smile on his lips, convinced Max that Oliver had an inner light that shone through his whole being, like the soft glow of a lantern on a shadowy spring night.

Max gulped. Oliver was too beautiful for words, inside and out.

But was this the true man, or was it an illusion of the man Max hoped Oliver would be?

"What are your brothers like?" Oliver asked, his impassive expression belied by his eager tone.

Max hesitated. According to the unspoken rules of royalty, no member discussed private matters with outsiders. This included things that might at first glance seem innocuous or inconsequential. Every personal detail that got out was a potential threat. In the limelight it was hard to tell your friends from your foes. Many wore the same smiling mask.

Max doubted Oliver was the type to go blabbing to the tabloids for a quick payday. Still, he did have a shadow of a doubt hanging over him. Trust didn't come easily to him.

"My middle brother, Berengar I Clovis, or Ben for short, is a scientist. His plan is to drag the whole country into the light of modern science. His focus is on advanced technologies to combat climate change. He's the CEO of Lindau-Arbon Industries, a corporation developing futuristic solutions to today's problems."

Oliver nodded several times as he listened. "A visionary. Cool."

Max smiled. "You two would undoubtedly get along swimmingly." Then he grew serious. "My youngest brother, Johann VII Lothair, or John, is… something of a playboy."

Oliver chuckled, eyes still on the screen. "Typical. Younger children are more rambunctious, older ones more responsible. The younger child syndrome, trying and failing to catch up."

Max laughed off the comment, but he wasn't sure such a simple explanation excused his brother's antics. "Maybe. He hangs with, ah, a questionable crowd sometimes."

Oliver turned to him with an empathetic grin. "Don't worry, Max. They do grow out of their immaturity at some point. Elinor was a handful back when she was a kid, but now…." Oliver frowned, paused for obvious reflection. "Wait. Scratch that. Nothing's changed. She's still a damn hell-raiser." Oliver's bashful glance warmed Max's heart. "I'm sure your brother won't always be a dick, though."

Max sighed. "Some people never change their, um, dickness. Hmm, is that a word?"

Oliver cackled, his whole body shimmying. The movement sent his natural scent floating about as well, and Max inhaled, liking what he smelled. A hint of vanilla, perhaps from body soap, mixed with it.

"Young royalty have behaved badly before," Oliver reminded Max. "Like what that Prince Harry did at that party way back in the day, dressing up in a Nazi uniform. He probably didn't even really think about it. It was just goofing off. Your brother could be going through the same thing."

Max appreciated Oliver's comment. His baby brother could act like a total ass sometimes, so to have a perfect stranger defend him instead of berating him for his many misdeeds was a nice change. Condemnation was so easy these days, online and in the public eye.

"Thank you for saying that," Max responded in a husky, emotional tone. He sensed Oliver's sincerity, and that lifted his mood because it spoke volumes about the American's character.

Public discourse in America seemed awfully hate-filled these days and spread globally from there; that depressed Max. He was glad he wasn't king yet and didn't have to deal with leaders at that level. *Yet* being the operative word. His lull would end eventually.

"Things are changing," Oliver said somewhat absentmindedly, if his faraway expression was any indication. "Slowly but surely, all that hate speech and fear-mongering will end. Love prevails. I mean, think of Prince Harry again. Sure, he wore a Nazi uniform, but he also ended up marrying an African-American woman, Meghan Markle. That's progress, I guess."

Love prevails. The thought, spoken so casually, caused Max's heart to jump with hope. Not because he was desperate for love but because if Oliver was right, then things would level out in the end. Balance would be restored. Or, who knew? The scales could tip in favor of all the good things in the world.

"Would that be possible in your country?" Oliver asked, his voice lowering. Max observed his cheeks gaining a rosy hue.

"Marrying a nonnative or nonwhite?" Max asked with a purr, certain he knew what Oliver was asking in a roundabout way.

Oliver squirmed a little. "Either. Both. Anything."

"Any… one?" Max whispered, inching closer to Oliver, who appeared about ready to have a nervous breakdown. "As my scientist brother continues to remind me, anything is possible."

Chapter 6

OLIVER PANTED. "So you're gay? I've never heard of a gay royal before."

Max chuckled, relishing the warmth of Oliver's body next to his. "They do exist, you know. Throughout history *and* these days as well."

The tablet shook in Oliver's hands. Maria and the Captain were embracing in a moonlit gazebo, singing of love. Carefully, Max took the tablet from Oliver, turned off the movie, and placed the device on the bedside table. Then he took Oliver's hot, slightly sweaty hands in his.

"Am I being too forward?" he asked in a hushed tone, not wanting to upset his companion.

Oliver gulped; his Adam's apple bobbed. He shook his head, and his hair waved about gently. "N-no." He faced Max, a look mixing desire and concern lighting his eyes. "Can you...? Are you allowed to...? I mean, not just with a guy, but... like, a casual thing?"

"A one-night stand?" Max finished the thought for him, smiling. "Yes. Royals and aristocrats do have sex out of wedlock, you know. Not that I'm married."

Oliver blushed, rubbing the back of his neck self-consciously. "I-I wasn't sure. Still not, to be honest. This is, uh, kind of a lot."

A hollow pit opened inside Max's chest, and he deflated. "You're not having sex with a prince, Oliver. You're making love to a man. That's all. Underneath my titles and my clothes, I'm just a man like any other."

Oliver snorted. "Um, no. Have you looked in the mirror lately? 'Cause you're effing smoking hot, is what you are."

A stunning shade of maroon rose in Oliver's cheeks and spread from there. He was too cute for words. Max gently gripped Oliver's chin and tipped his head, bringing their mouths close. Oliver's eyelids fluttered closed, and a tiny sigh escaped his lips.

Max didn't wait. He kissed Oliver, softly at first, then more insistently, until Oliver opened up and let Max inside. Their tongues, hot and wet, glided against each other. The kiss was tentative and full of tender exploration. Max savored Oliver's taste, finding the salty flavor of popcorn mixed with his unique zest as delightful as his scent.

When they pulled apart, Oliver had his eyes shut and was licking his lips as if doing what Max had done and enjoying the sensory experience. Max smiled, pleased his kiss was far from unwanted.

"Shall we continue?" Max asked, needing confirmation.

Oliver blinked, a dazed look in his eyes. A goofy grin spread to his lips. "Yeah."

This time, they crashed into each other, all fiery breath, needy hands, and greedy tastings. Their lips fused, and their tongues dueled and made peace, over and over again.

With trembling hands, Oliver fumbled with the buttons of Max's shirt. Max saluted Oliver's actions with his cock, which rose to attention. He grabbed Oliver's dick through his shorts, found the hard length hot and throbbing, and rubbed back and forth. Oliver groaned, and his hips bucked.

"This too much?" Max breathed out. He wasn't a mind reader—he didn't know what Oliver liked from his sexual partners, so he had to ask.

Oliver murmured something unintelligible, his lips brushing over the corner of Max's mouth and gliding down to his neck to suck on a spot over his jugular. His whole body moved closer. Intentions clear. Consent given.

After a few moments of feverish groping and hot kisses, Oliver stilled and began to calm. Max pulled away. They needed a respite. Max didn't want to rush. They were both on vacation; they could enjoy themselves all night long; that is, if Oliver was amenable.

"Are you sure I'm not being too forward?" Max asked. Although he'd asked before, it seemed Oliver might have doubts.

Oliver blinked, a dreamy look in his eyes. His sensual haze seemed to dissipate slowly. Then he smiled. "No, I swear." He cupped Max's left cheek, his thumb tracing the cheekbone. "Your skin is so soft."

Max smiled back. "I moisturize. It won't do to look disheveled in publicity photos or in the newspapers."

Oliver bit his bottom lip. "Wow, I can picture you on trendy magazine covers."

Max leaned in and nuzzled Oliver's neck, loving the shivers his actions sent running through Oliver's body. "In that fantasy, am I wearing clothes or…?" He left the question hanging as he relieved his lover of his T-shirt and tossed it haphazardly over his shoulder and onto the floor.

Oliver sighed, and his eyelids fluttered closed. "Yeah."

Max chuckled. Oliver's answer was seriously lost in sexy dreams.

Oliver pushed Max's shirt off his shoulders, and Max inched closer to accommodate him. It was effortless and natural, as if they had done so many times before. While Max dragged off his sleeves, Oliver dipped his head and took Max's left nipple into his mouth.

"Oh." Max was taken aback by the sudden move but didn't question or stop it.

Oliver pulled back, his eyes wide in amazement as his fingers traveled across Max's chest. "Wow, you're so muscular. And your tan glows like honey and gold."

Max was pleased that Oliver appreciated his looks. Max worked hard at the gym to stay fit, which wasn't always easy while living in the lap of luxury with so much at his fingertips. It would be no problem to plop onto a couch and order ten meals a day from the castle kitchen. Exercise on a daily basis helped him stay healthy and athletic.

"You're not so bad yourself," Max teased, tracing Oliver's darker skin to his brown nipples, his sculpted pecs, and his flat stomach. There was so much to explore. He was especially intrigued by Oliver's tattoos. "What do these all mean?"

Max traced a colorful mural where images of plant life mixed with music notes.

"They're cultural," Oliver replied shortly, leaving Max filled with questions. "The plants are Mexican. Blue agave, ahuehuete, cempasúchil, poinsettia, jacarandas, stuff like that."

Max blinked. He'd not heard of many of those plants. He recognized the most familiar ones, like sunflowers and sycamores. "No cactuses?" he teased.

"Cacti," Oliver corrected him and then flushed red up to his hairline. "I mean, they're both right, I suppose. Forget I said anything."

Max studied the mural that covered the upper half of Oliver's right arm and his shoulder. He liked that Oliver had chosen flowers and trees instead of darker themes or power imagery. Given Max's Celtic background, nature-lovers were all right in his book.

"And the notes? Are you a musician too?"

Oliver shrugged. "I know my way around a guitar. Well, I know the basics." He sighed. "It's another cultural thing, I guess. Music, I mean."

Max took Oliver's hands in his and turned them around, surveying the yellow, orange, and red flames circling his wrists, burning a path up his forearms. "These are cool," he complimented in awe.

"No, they're hot." Oliver's blush deepened as he spoke.

Max snorted. "I adore your sense of humor, my dear Oliver. It's so unexpected." He grinned at his companion, who swallowed hard and blinked. "Do you have more tattoos? I can't see any."

When Oliver ducked his head and hid his face again, Max knew to expect delicious surprises the more skin he exposed. Max couldn't stand the wait, so he rose to his knees, shifted to a new position between Oliver's splayed legs, and started to remove his shorts. He wasn't sure what he would see, but Oliver's thighs, shins, and ankles had no ink.

"Aww," Max murmured, pouting a little.

Oliver chuckled. "I haven't gotten to my legs yet. I've been saving up."

Max turned his attention to Oliver's cock, which curved upward, hard and dark pink. He noted Oliver wasn't circumcised, same as Max. He gripped the throbbing shaft and slid the foreskin over the head a few times. Oliver groaned and his hips bucked.

"L-listen. When I broke up with my last boyfriend, I got tested for STDs, and I'm clean, but best be cautious, right?" Oliver waved toward the bedside dresser's top drawer. "I've got lube and condoms in there."

Max grinned. "Oh. This is that kind of vacation." When Oliver flushed once more, Max shook his head. "Don't be embarrassed. I'm overjoyed about that fact."

Oliver smiled. "Well, get to it, then." He wiggled theatrically to get comfortable, raised his arms behind his head, and lifted his hips, making his cock jump against his abdomen.

Max quirked an eyebrow. So Oliver had a dominant streak too. Promising.

Since this was their first time but hopefully not their last, Max decided they wouldn't cross some lines today. He yanked open the drawer, fished out the lube, popped open the lid, and squeezed the gel into his hands. Then he settled on top of Oliver, coated Oliver's cock with lube as well, and rested fully on top of him. Their cocks nuzzled each other, pressed together shaft to shaft.

Oliver spread his legs farther and cradled Max in his arms, kissing him softly. "Guess this is all we need right now," he breathed between kisses.

Max agreed. He was hungry for more, but the first time was like an appetizer—one didn't rush to the main course too fast but sampled the savory hors d'oeuvres first. He hoped they would have time for more in future days.

For now he relished the feeling of a hard, hot body beneath him, panting and rocking, a lover entwined around him. Oliver's kisses tasted so sweet, his body burned, his breath fanning warmly into Max's mouth. Their hands wandered and touched expanses of skin, firm muscles, strong limbs.

"Oh, I've missed this so much," Max whispered against Oliver's neck and licked a spot there to suck.

Oliver shuddered. "God, me too." His nails raked across Max's back, undoubtedly leaving crisscrossing red scratches as proof of ardor.

All of a sudden, Oliver turned the tables and flipped them around to straddle Max's hips, showing his strength. Max shivered. He loved a man who could—and would—be a man in bed.

Oliver grinned down at Max, his palms resting on Max's chest. "Can't let you have all the fun."

Max chuckled, grabbing Oliver's buttcheeks and squeezing them. "I don't know. I have no problem with this position. So much access."

"Too bad your fingertips can't see," Oliver said with a mysterious wink.

Max gasped. "More tattoos?" He almost asked if his companion had a tramp stamp, but he'd never liked that term. The buzz of sex received an added spark from curiosity.

Max started to wiggle in an effort to roll them over again, but Oliver gripped his wrists, brought them up over his head, and held Max in place. Oliver's balls pressed against Max's in the best way possible, and the resulting fever boiled inside Max's stomach.

"Nu-uh. My turn now. Missed your chance." Oliver's teasing tone did funny things to Max.

"I'll get another," Max said, his voice rising a bit at the end in the hope Oliver would grant him that possibility.

Oliver's smile widened. "I sure as shit hope so."

Max laughed. He couldn't remember if he'd ever done that with his past lovers. They hadn't really been chuckling types. "Well, you've got me. What are you going to do?"

Rocking back and forth, Oliver put weight on Max's cock and balls.

Max sighed. "You're evil." He sweat bullets, wanting so badly to come but also wanting the sex to continue longer, to prolong the moment.

Oliver seemed in tune with Max's needs since he lowered himself on top of Max and rubbed his erection against Max's. Oliver then cupped Max's head and kissed him, tickling his sensitive lips with the tip of his tongue. He kept backing off and giggling every time Max tried to capture his mouth.

"I swear, I could kiss you for hours," Oliver murmured against Max's lips, which tingled as if sparks danced on them.

Max stared up at Oliver's hazel eyes burning with dark flames. He swore he'd never seen anyone more beautiful. His past affairs had left him physically satisfied but emotionally hollow and cold. Oliver brought warmth, humor, caring, and sensuality to their lovemaking.

"M-me too," Max confessed, feeling more exposed now than five seconds ago, even though he'd been just as naked then.

Oliver glided his hands down Max's arms to cradle his head between his arms again and kiss him thoroughly. But as Max got into it and tried to suck on Oliver's tongue, Oliver retreated yet again and laughed mischievously.

Max could play this game too. He snaked a hand between their writhing bodies, fisted both their cocks, mashing them together, and started to jerk off leisurely. When he tightened his grip, Oliver moaned. When he swiped a thumb over their leaking slits, Oliver shuddered. And when Max urged Oliver to press harder with a hand on his lover's buttocks, Oliver pumped his hips in a way that signaled he was close.

"Oh, ohh, *ohhh….*" Oliver kept panting, his kisses turning sloppy and eager.

Max saw his window of opportunity. He wrapped both arms around Oliver's back, rolled them around, and covered his lover, pinning him to the mattress with his bulk. Using his toes for traction, Max rubbed his cock against Oliver's dick, both trapped between their swaying bodies. Oliver groped and gripped frantically, his kisses sweet in their silent intensity.

Max's climax tore through him with the force of a hundred wild horses, his cock erupting in one giant surge of pure ecstasy, hot splashes spraying his skin. He felt like melting away into the bed.

Then an answering groan heralded a new heated burst of come when Oliver bucked his hips and spilled his seed between them.

Max gathered Oliver into his arms and kissed him softly, stroking his arms, neck, and back, his touch gentle. They rested side by side, savoring the afterglow and sharing little kisses and pettings.

Neither spoke of what had happened or what lay ahead. Yet, it was silently understood this would not be their last stop.

Chapter 7

I KISSED a prince, and I liked it....

Funny how that beat worked for any occasion and any lover. Katy Perry must have been a genius. Or whoever wrote the song.

After that night, my second night on the island, Max and I fell into a rhythm. We spent our days traversing the isle and taking in the sights. We sunbathed on beaches of pearl-white sand or lounged under the shade of pines and eucalypti, inhaling scents of rosemary, evergreen, and sea salt. We trekked across meadows filled with colorful flowers and swarms of butterflies as the sun cast its rays down upon us. Each picnic treat tasted like ambrosia, every drop of water as sweet as nectar.

We talked about everything, from light topics like favorite songs and movies—we both loved comedies—to more serious ones, like the rise of fascism and racism. Every word we shared seemed golden and meaningful but was, in the end, as fleeting as the sunny days.

Max and I spent our nights making love. His weight settled above me, his breath hot at my neck, his lips pressed against mine, our hearts beating as one, our bodies moving in perfect sync. I treasured every finger-shaped bruise on my hips, every bite mark on my shoulder, every hickey on my chest. They were signs of his passion and ardor.

I had never felt so blessed by life's bounty.

Everywhere Max and I went, however, we had company: His security detail, led by a petite but formidable Thai woman named Lawana, who was a former kickboxing world champion, shadowed our every step. I could always see at least one of them out of the corner of my eye, and I knew more were hidden around, watching us and our surroundings like hawks.

There was no sign of Max's signet ring. No demands for money had been made to the royal family, no ransom exchanges, no blackmail notes. It was as if the ring had fallen off the face of the earth, and the matter dropped with it. I was surprised how unconcerned Max seemed. But as we spent more time together, I learned he kept things close to his chest, revealing nothing, like a consummate diplomat—or actor. I wondered how much of what he showed was smoke and mirrors, how many expressions were mere masks he changed with each new person. How much of the true man did I ever see?

When I rested in his arms at night, his embrace at once tight and tender, his face lax and his body warm, I figured this would be as close as I got to his real being. He let his guard down with me at those times, even if only for a few days. That meant something, though I wasn't quite sure what.

After we had spent another day lying on the beach and swimming in turquoise waters, our skin hot and browner, wet and sandy, he swept me into his arms in his suite and danced me around the room. His laugh echoed about, and I chimed in. His strong thigh moved between my legs, pushing against my privates. Heat sparked within me. A hunger for him.

As we tumbled down onto the comforter, I muttered, "Have you had many lovers?"

Max shrugged, seemingly unoffended. "A few. You?"

I grimaced. "Came here to nurse a broken heart, actually." When Max quirked a questioning eyebrow at me, I continued, "My ex was a cheating dickhead. That about sums it up."

Max nodded slowly, a rueful gleam in his eyes. "So, I'm the rebound guy?"

I cupped his cheeks and met his gaze. "You're no one's rebound. You're amazing. I…."

Swallowing my words, I had to stop there. What could I say? That I was starting to feel something for him? Ours was a foreign affair. I had no future with him, no chance at all for more than this short assignation. He was a prince; I was… not.

I didn't want him to be sad, though, or have to guess my words, so I stated quietly, "I'll miss you."

Max smiled at me, the same longing shining in his eyes as undoubtedly shone in mine. I certainly had to blink back a few unbidden tears.

"I shall miss you as well, Oliver. You're a wonderful man. Your ex was a fool."

Max was good for my self-esteem. With him whispering compliments in my ear, I felt like the king of the world. Ha! Fat chance of that. He was more likely to fill that position than I—literally.

Max dipped his hands beneath my T-shirt to the hollow of my back. His palm was warm and dry and insistent. He pulled me close, pressing our bodies together. Even through the thin layers of clothing, I could tell he was as aroused as I was.

Max had a single-mindedness when it came to sex that I quite liked. He made it impossible to feel nervous or jittery over his station, for when I was with him, I only saw the man. The incredibly hot, desirable, smart, funny, utterly gorgeous man I wanted in my bed, between my legs, on top of me, inside me.

"Oh, really?" Max purred, a wily grin on his face. "Get on the bed, then."

Had I spoken out loud? With him, anything was possible.

I hurried to comply, yanking my shirt off and tossing it carelessly over the edge of the bed. He gripped the waistband of my shorts and inched them down, so slowly that I urged him to move faster by raising my hips from the mattress. His wicked smirk told me he was doing the slow routine on purpose.

I groaned, my dick already hot, hard, and leaking. I palmed the length, but Max slapped my hand aside and wagged a finger at me.

I growled. "Get on with it, dammit."

Max chuckled evilly, removed my shorts all the way, spread my legs with first his hands and then his shoulders, and dragged his tongue from the root of my shaft to the tip, following the thick vein beneath. I jolted and moaned, delighted beyond belief.

Quickly, I recalled my senses and placed a hand over his silky blond hair, stopping him.

"W-wait. Sh-shouldn't you use, um, a condom? Just in case."

Max pursed his lips and sighed. He must have hated the taste of latex as much as I. But we needed to play safe. I couldn't jeopardize a lover. I refused to, especially one who would one day rule a whole nation.

"Fine," Max grumbled, fished a condom packet from his shorts pocket, tore it open, and slipped it on my penis. I closed my eyes and fisted the sheets, praying for patience and endurance. The cool latex smothered my shaft, but his mouth was hot and tight and, *oh shit*, I seriously doubted I could last for more than a minute or two.

"Hey, uh… why don't you get undressed and let me have a taste too?" I suggested, a little awkwardly for I was fast losing my self-control. Perhaps with his cock in my mouth I could hold back the inevitable or even turn the tables on him.

Max chuckled and shook his head, a wicked gleam in his eyes. "No. This is my treat. Double entendre intended."

Reluctantly I had to stop him, squeezing the base of my dick hard to stave off the inevitable. "I-I won't last if you go on." Max looked ready to argue, but I shook my head. "Please fuck me."

To make my point, I squirmed, rolled over onto my stomach, and shoved my ass up.

Max pressed a hand over the small of my back and pushed me back down. He straddled my thighs and kneaded my buttocks and back. I stifled a groan; as if I needed a massage.

Then Max purred in awe, silencing my protests. "I love these."

His fingers, like feathers, traced *my* feathers. "It's Quetzalcoatl, the Feathered Serpent, the Aztec god of wind and learning." Then I remembered I had already told him that. "Sorry."

"Don't be." I couldn't see Max's face, but I heard his sigh. "It's so beautiful, full of life and color, so vibrant."

I turned my head on the pillow. "What tattoo would you get?"

"I can't get one. It isn't appropriate for royals. My mother would kill me." Max sounded sad about that; perhaps he felt he was missing out. "Maybe a unicorn…?" he mused.

I didn't want him to be melancholy when we were supposed to be enjoying each other and the many pleasures of sex. "A unicorn, eh?" I snorted. "Well, that'd be fitting. All things considered."

Max released a curious breath. "Whatever do you mean?"

"It's your family emblem, of course." Then I chuckled. "And… the unicorn is a rare treat, like a mythical ideal man, someone unobtainable but highly coveted, uncatchable but always pursued. The absolute yummiest, dishiest, sweetest, sexiest man alive."

Max was silent for a moment. Then he burst out laughing. "I'll be sure to remember that if I'm ever given permission to get a tattoo."

I smiled and moved on, not wanting to bog things down. "I'm thinking of getting ink done on the small of my back. The Pyramid of the Sun in Teotihuacán. What do you think?"

Max touched my back all over until finally settling to the top of my buttocks. "Couldn't ask for a more inspiring canvas." Then he buried his fingers in the soft cushions of my buttcheeks. "I do like this shadow image of a bull." He slapped my right butt where I indeed had a dark gray tattoo of a bull's head in profile. "I love seeing it wiggle."

I laughed. We'd done a little bit of the old slap-and-tickle. Max seemed unfamiliar with a lot of things. He wasn't a virgin, obviously, but clearly his past lovers hadn't been as thorough, creative, or romantic as they should have been.

I felt Max was starved for affection. I wanted to give him what we both needed.

"Are you going to fuck me or just play with my ass?" I asked, smirking over my shoulder at him.

Max winked. "Can't we do both?" He kneaded and massaged the soft but firm mounds with vigor and delight.

I giggled, unable to help myself. His touches both tickled and turned me on. "Just remember, buddy. You play with fire, you get burned."

Max chuckled, and the sound was hot and wicked. I shivered at the dominant tone, heat building in my groin. I rested my head on the pillow again, sighed, and relaxed. I had no doubt that whatever he had in mind, I would enjoy it.

Inching backward down my legs, Max leaned in, parted my asscheeks, and licked a line up my crack and over my twitching hole. Then the tip of his tongue pressed into me, soft and wet and warm and, *damn*, I was dying. The lewd noises out of his mouth were hot as hell. Whether or not Max had done this before, he sure knew what he was doing. I melted under his ministrations, left a pool of jelly.

Then, with an enviable show of strength, guile, and dominance, Max shifted down the bed, grabbed both my legs, and flipped me onto my back. Out of breath, I could only ogle him in wonder.

"Have I set you on fire yet, my dear?" Max asked, his voice teasing and amused.

Before I could answer, he'd flicked open a tube of lube, coated his fingers, and probed my entrance with purpose. These weren't the actions of an inexperienced man. Maybe his previous lovers had been thrilled by the idea of being fucked by a future king. Personally, I was way more thrilled about the prospect of being fucked by the kindest, smartest, most gorgeous man I'd ever met, with a cock that would have made professional porn stars weep with envy.

"Fuck me and find out," I dared him, flicking my tongue at him.

Max merely chuckled—and added another finger to pry me open. Even alone, I liked playing with my ass, so I knew what to expect. I loosened up and pushed out, meeting his tender intrusion. With a breathless laugh, Max shoved his digits in deeper and made tiny little circles that widened me and at the same time drove me mad with desire.

"There's that light of lust I was waiting for," Max purred, his baritone vibrating through my rib cage, along my nerve endings, and down the length of my prick. "Now for the hot spot."

And Max poked and prodded my prostate till I cried out and arched up, primed and ready to go. I flushed with heat inside and out, sweaty and hungry and weary and charged.

After lifting my legs onto his shoulders and raising my butt off the mattress, Max aligned his condom-covered cock with my hole and pushed in. Pressure increased, as if all the air was pushed out of my lungs, but I met that with my own push back until his cockhead breached the tight rings of muscle and entered me.

We both gasped. Max studied me, his lips parted, his eyes as dark blue as an erupting thunderstorm. He asked me without words if I was all right. I smiled and nodded, happy he was being so attentive and gentle. Not all my exes had been so considerate.

No more words were needed. We spoke the language of lovemaking now. Glances, gestures, touches, kisses. Max leaned in, captured my lips for a brief kiss, and finally hovered above me, arms straightened at my sides as he pushed in deeper. Max was big; he was bigger than any of my previous lovers. My ass tingled, hungry for him, waiting to swallow him whole.

At long last, fully seated, Max sighed. "A-are you all right?"

I couldn't speak. I'd never felt stuffed so full to the brim, near the breaking point. God, but I wanted this so badly. I nodded, swallowing and trying to breathe normally.

First Max moved slowly, rocking back and forth, giving me time to adjust. Gradually, he picked up the pace. His abs rubbed my shaft, caught between us, whenever he pressed tight against me, never stopping his movements within me. When he started gliding over and jabbing my sweet spot on purpose, I knew I'd blow before him.

Max lowered himself fully on top of me. I wrapped my legs around his waist. He gathered me into his arms and thrust harder and faster. Little by little, he drove into me deeper, until I was losing it. His lips sought mine, and we kissed, our tongues entangled, our lips fused.

Then Max pounded into me. The movements of his tongue matched the lunges of his cock. I was in heaven. I'd enjoyed anal sex before, but somehow Max seemed attuned to me, pushing all the right buttons. Then he gripped my dick and started to pump me, again in time with the punches of his cock and tongue.

"I… I…. C-coming…," I managed to murmur into his kisses.

Max growled. Frissons of pleasure cascaded over me at the sound, his caresses, and his motions. I was lost. I tore my mouth away from his, screaming when I came, his hand continuing to wrench every last drop of my hot, creamy essence spilling between us.

Max conquered my lips again. His hips jerked, in rhythm at first, then erratically as he neared the edge. Finally, perhaps because I sucked on his tongue or raked his neck with my nails or tightened my legs around him, Max came. He grunted into my mouth as his cock spurted its seed into the condom. Even through the latex, it felt like molten lava, burning me from within, just like he'd promised.

I giggled and broke the kiss. He smiled down at me, and I knew contentment.

As we lay there side by side, panting like beached whales, our limbs entwined, I murmured in between gasps, "Whoa, I don't know about you, but I fucking hate that this has to end." I shuddered, feeling the blood drain from my face. "Sorry. Didn't meant to curse."

Max barked out a laugh as he discarded the used rubber into a trash can. "I don't mind harsh language, Oliver." He faced me, a sad smile dangling on his luscious, swollen-from-kisses lips. "And I hate that we must cut our dalliance short too."

I giggled. "Dalliance? Wow. Never had one of those before."

"First time for everything." Max winked at me. Then he regarded me with a more serious gaze. "What will you do once you graduate?"

I shrugged. "I'll likely apply for a job in a restaurant. That's how it usually goes, I suppose. Or I could try to find funding and start my own culinary business. But that's not something I'm ready for. I'd love to be, like, a pastry chef. Who knows? I might ask my professors for advice based on my skill set."

"Can't you estimate your skills yourself?" Max asked, turning to his side and cuddling next to me. The way he nuzzled my neck, giving me goose bumps, suggested he was getting ready for round two.

"They judge things more dispassionately, I guess," I managed to murmur before desire swept me away in its roaring tide and sent me headlong into another lovemaking session with Max.

I wished we could have gone on like that forever.

Chapter 8

MY LAST day arrived far sooner than I would have liked. That morning was bittersweet in the extreme. Max and I didn't speak. We made love once in the bed and again in the shower, stopping several times in between bouts of packing to kiss and hug and be close to each other.

We even took the time to eat a proper continental breakfast and watch the movie *Royal Flash*, with actor Oliver Reed in it. It was one of my favorite old-timey films, so I was glad that Max enjoyed it too. Perhaps because it portrayed royals in a country near to his.

I'd promised myself that if I had a brief affair while on my vacation, I wouldn't get attached. I had failed. I'd also vowed not to cry. When Max held me, my suitcase finally shut and knowing I had to go, I let a couple of tears fall hotly onto his shoulder, wetting his shirt.

"You're the best time I've ever had," I whispered in his ear, his blond hair tickling my nose, the scent of saltwater and lavender on his skin from our moonlight dip last night. The line seemed vaguely familiar to me, perhaps from a movie; I didn't care because the words rang true.

Max embraced me tighter and whispered in my ear, "As you have been to me, Oliver."

I released a watery laugh. "Not fucking likely."

Grumbling, Max tugged on my hair to chastise me, the sting there and gone. "Do not call me a liar, Oliver."

He kept repeating my name, I noted. Was that a tell?

"I'm sorry. I just… I really don't want to go."

Max bussed my temple. "But you must. Your future, your whole life, awaits."

I almost let it burst out that I didn't want a future without him, but common sense stopped me in time. I was being foolish. You couldn't fall in love with someone in a week. Love at first sight was a myth; it had no basis in fact.

I would get over Max. But this wasn't the way it had been with my ex. I had self-respect, so cutting ties with a cheating dirtbag had been easy. This separation from Max would cut deeper.

I had to be the one to stand strong on my own two feet. So taking a stout breath, I pulled back from Max's arms and gave him an unsteady smile.

"You're right. I do have to go." I made a final check around the room to see if I'd missed anything. There was nothing. I strapped on my backpack and grabbed my suitcase. I stopped in front of him. "Unless you, like, want a male concubine or something."

Max laughed, his head thrown back to show his neck. This gesture reminded me of the day we'd met. It was hard to believe it had only been seven days ago.

"Please, Oliver. Do *not* tempt me."

Though there was humor in the tone, I thought I saw a glimpse of something darker in his eyes when he spoke. Perhaps he wasn't as unaffected as he seemed. Maybe he liked spending time with me as much as I enjoyed his company.

Duty called, however.

I nodded, slouched to the door, crossed the threshold with Max in tow, and closed it, putting a definitive end to one of the best chapters in my life, if not the very best. Without a word between us, Max escorted me to the elevator. He took my hand and held it throughout the ride. Once in the lobby, though, he released me. Did I sense reluctance, or was that just wishful thinking on my part?

I handed in my keycard, and the concierge called a taxi service, courtesy of Max. I started to argue the point—the airport shuttle bus would work just as well—but then I thought about sitting in the bus, waiting for it to leave, and all the while watching Max through the window, unable to touch him or speak to him. That would suck ass. So I relented and let him pay for the service.

A cab soon drove up to the curb in front of the hotel. The sun was climbing the sky fast, and the heat was already sneaking underneath my clothes, smothering me. Waves of evergreen and rosemary wafted through the air, full of sweet memories. But a cold fist clawed at my chest from the inside, the knowledge I would likely never see Max again.

As the cab driver grabbed my suitcase and placed it in the trunk, I faced Max. I extended my hand to shake his. He didn't try to hug me goodbye. I appreciated that. I feared I would fall to my knees sobbing if he did.

The crinkle of paper seemed loud in the melancholy silence. Max frowned in puzzlement and studied the rumpled piece of paper on his palm, left there from our handshake.

I waved a hand, about to stop him from unwrapping it. "My contact info, you know, if you want to drop me a line or call me or whatever. You know, just in case."

I could barely hear my own voice. It sounded thin and hoarse and awkward in my ears. Was I being pathetic and needy? My face heated with embarrassment.

But then Max smiled, leaned in, and kissed both my cheeks. The continental arrivederci, so to speak. But instead of an air kiss, he touched me. His lips were warm and soft against my skin.

"Thank you, Oliver. I might just take you up on that."

His conspiratorial wink made me smile. Despite this parting of ways, I was grateful to life and fate for giving me this moment with him. Max was one of a kind. I was truly a lucky man.

"Goodbye, Max," I said, proud that my voice sounded steadier. I even managed a polite half smile.

Max gave me an admonishing look. "Au revoir, Oliver Reed."

He stepped back, and I stepped into the cab. I waved, and he waved back. As the cab drove away, the green, sunny scene turned blurry. I watched it speed by through a veil of fresh tears.

My heart ached. I hadn't felt this bad when I'd broken up with my ex, even though I'd known him longer. Eleven months compared to a week. Yet the connection with Max had from the start felt more profound. Had the cause been the haste of it all, how he and I had both plunged headlong into an affair because there was an end date attached?

Time flies, as the old adage went. Soon I would fly too, on steel wings across the ocean—back home where I would tell myself I didn't miss Max at all.

"STOP MOPING already."

I fake-slapped Elinor's hands away from my graduation cap, which she had straightened for the umpteenth time in preparation for the post-ceremony family photo session. "I'm not moping. I'm not some lovesick puppy."

Yet even as I said the words, my tone told me I was lying—to myself and everyone else.

And judging from the sarcastic chuckle Elinor let out, she was on to me.

"Shut up," I mumbled. I shoved the cap back, thus ensuring it was definitely crooked, and fiddled with the collar of my graduation robes, which felt too constricting.

I wasn't sure exactly what was bothering me, but I had a pretty good idea. It was May; it had been two months since my liaison with the handsome European prince.

It wasn't like I'd googled him every couple of days; more like every damn day. In the publicity photo on the royal family's website—yes, they had their own website—he stood tall and dignified. He wore a uniform with blue shoulders, arms, and neck, a white middle, and a green hem, decorated with white sashes, white-gold buttons, and about a million medals.

I peered into those blue jewels Max had for eyes and tried to see something familiar there. But I wasn't that lucky. It was just a picture.

He had written emails to me, and I back to him. We never spoke of those sensual nights or the many pleasures we'd shared. I told him about my boring classes, the papers I wrote, career plans I was wavering between. He spoke of casual things: how the scent of the forest made him think of me, what book he had read in his rare spare time, the type of pillows he liked. It was all so random. I understood he couldn't talk about important things in emails anyone could intercept, so I acquiesced to the reality that this would be as close to him as I would ever get again.

"Great. Now your cap's got dents," Elinor harrumphed at me, jolting me out of musings all too dark and gloomy for my graduation day.

I glared at my little sister. "Not my fault. The cap throwing is a dumb tradition anyway."

"Stop being mean to your sister," my mom, Valerie Reed, called out, putting an end to the sibling disagreement.

I sputtered, "You always take her side."

Elinor flicked her tongue at me, wisely keeping her back to our mother and her almost-all-seeing gaze. She took risks; that was for sure.

Valerie fumbled with her digital camera. "I saw that, young lady."

Elinor smirked at me but bowed her head when she turned to Valerie. "Sorry, Mom."

I rolled my eyes. "She's not sorry, Mama."

"I know, dear," Valerie said, smiling congenially as she raised the camera to take my picture. "Now, big smiles."

I posed attentively, the way a dutiful son did, as my mother captured my image for posterity, for family and friends, for later reminiscing. My face felt like a wax mask after the first five minutes, my smile frozen on my lips.

"Are we done any time soon?" I spoke through gritted teeth and a smile that had stopped being genuine four and a half minutes ago. "I can't feel my cheeks anymore."

Elinor chuckled next to me, pretty in her summer dress—and combat boots, rainbow-colored streaks in her hair down to her ears, and nose ring. She would never fit into a mold or an easy-to-define type. I loved that about her. She wanted to be an engineer, and she could fix any machine at the house and outside it. Our car ran like a dream because of her alone. I dared any man to challenge her and escape unscathed.

"Just a few more," Valerie said, shifting from side to side to get better angles, as though she had suddenly transformed into a professional photographer.

"Where's Dad?" I asked, not daring to scan my surroundings for my father. Mom would be upset if I messed up her perfect shots.

Before either Valerie or Elinor could respond, I heard my father's deep bass voice, soft and husky, coming closer from behind me. He was speaking with someone, probably one of my teachers. Dad was pretty active when it came to his children's school experience, and he knew all my teachers and professors by name and specialty.

"Yes, I'm very proud of my son's accomplishments. He's a good boy."

I smiled at my father's high praise. My education meant so much to him, for he hadn't been able to follow that route himself, though he'd wanted to. Higher education was too expensive in this country, and our family was too poor to afford it. Both Elinor and I were fortunate that we'd earned college scholarships. I never forgot that stroke of good luck.

"Indeed, Mr. Reed. I very much agree with you."

Gasping, I recognized the voice and whirled around to face the owner of said voice in a rush.

"Holy. Motherfucking. Shit. *Max?*"

And that was how I ruined one of my mother's perfect shots.

Chapter 9

FLUMMOXED AND on the edge of passing out, I stared at Max, who strolled along the path through the university green with my father. I was faintly aware of my mouth hanging open like that of a fish on dry land. My eyes felt like they might pop out of their sockets at any second.

Elinor sidled next to me and shoved her elbow into my side, rather painfully I might add. "So that's the infamous Max whose name you've been moaning every night in your sle—"

I slapped a hand over her mouth as I watched Max quirk an amused eyebrow, having heard the interrupted comment.

I laughed like a bona fide lunatic. "Ha-ha-ha! She doesn't know what she's talking about. She, uh, hallucinates at night. Yeah, she smokes way too much pot."

"She… what?" Valerie called out with a sharp look at Elinor, who just giggled.

"Hello, Oliver," Max said, his baritone doing funny things to my stomach and making my toes curl. "You didn't think I'd miss your big day, did you?"

"Well, I…." I rubbed the back of my neck, self-conscious and staggered. Could this be real? My skin was hot to the touch. Was madness contagious? My family were all staring at Max, so he couldn't be a product of my feverish imagination.

My mother cleared her throat loudly, scowling at me. I blushed and realized my faux pas at not introducing everybody. But when I opened my mouth, not a peep came out. I had, in effect, landed in a heap of dog doo without anyone's help.

I smiled at Max, again like a crazy person, and raised my hands before me in a time-out sign. "Would you, uh, excuse us all for a second, please, Max? Don't go anywhere," I added in a rush. If he vanished, I might literally die right then and there.

As Valerie collected righteous indignation at being ignored, I frantically waved at my family to gather around me. As my baffled parents and sibling came closer, we huddled, hands on each other's shoulders, like a football team.

"Okay," I stage-whispered, enunciating slowly because if I knew my mom, and I did, these could be my last words on the face of the earth. "Don't anybody freak out, okay? No one can know about this, but... Max, um, is kind of a big deal."

"Duh." Elinor rolled her eyes. "We kind of already know you like him a lot."

"No, that's not what I mean," I countered.

"Come on," Elinor whined. "Not like we didn't figure out you two had amazeballs sex during your trip. So spit it out already, bro," she demanded, her face an eager question mark. Man, my sister could always break a logjam—with Thor's hammer, no less.

I sighed and slumped. "I'm serious. Absolutely no one can know he's here with us, okay?"

I glanced around quickly, expecting foreign spies hiding in the bushes or armies of paparazzi swarming around us, invisible and invincible. There was, however, nothing and no one. I was losing it.

Lowering my voice again, I said, "Max is the heir to the throne of the Kingdom of Noricia."

The only one who remained passive and unreadable was my father. My sister looked about ready to burst out of her skin and start screaming aloud that her brother had slept with a prince. My mother was fuming.

"He's a—" Elinor started, her voice rapidly climbing toward ear-shattering levels.

I shushed her quiet with mad theatrical handwaves. "Yeah, he's an honest-to-god prince, okay? Now shut up."

"And you kept your family in the dark why, exactly?" Valerie's clipped tone made me cringe, the way I always had as a kid when she admonished me, usually with good reason.

I stole a glimpse of Max standing there, handsome in his charcoal-gray business suit, blue silk tie, and black shoes. His appearance impeccable and beautiful, he smiled, his blond curls shining in the sun and competing with the light of mirth in his eyes. He was a vision.

Man, I'd missed him so much.

I faced my mother again. "I couldn't say anything. I was sworn to secrecy. And I promised myself I would never reveal anything about what went on between us. I mean, what if the tabloids got wind of it? Or freaking spies or something?"

"Good boy. *Buen chico.*" My father patted my shoulder, seemingly pleased. "Your character is true. You are trustworthy. Keeping a secret in this day and age is certainly not easy, what with everyone carrying a camera and exuding greed and selfishness. No, you did the right thing."

I smiled. Paulito had an awfully posh way of speaking when he was being wise. I wanted to be like him when I grew up.

Valerie narrowed her eyes as her gaze shifted from her husband to me. Finally, she pursed her lips as if dismayed still, but her features relaxed, and she nodded. "Well, he's here now. So are you going to introduce us or not?"

I flushed, abashed. My mother could scold with the best of them. I loved her.

I plastered a nutty, lopsided grin on my lips, purely on instinct, and made frenzied gestures in Max's direction. "Max, these are my parents, Paulito Ruíz and Valerie Reed, and this is my sister, Elinor." Then I added softly, "Guys, this is Prince Maximilian IX Lukas of Noricia."

Max raised his arms subtly. "Please, I beg of you, no bows or curtsies. I am supposed to be here incognito."

He winked at us to show he was making a request but wouldn't be terribly upset if we missed a protocol cue. He was nice like that. My heart jumped to my throat.

Max shook hands with everyone, behaving like a perfect gentleman. His winning smile did more for my case than a million of my apologies. There was only one word to describe him: dashing. I was mildly embarrassed by how much I wanted him right then. Bad timing.

"We should perhaps adjourn to your abode," Max suggested. His polite tone and obvious sophistication clearly made a good impression on my family. I nodded several times, and before I could comment, everyone else also agreed. My parents were private people, so regardless of his title, they understood Max's concerns. And I think they felt the situation was slightly surreal, as I had, and our home turf would aid the acclimation process.

"WHEN YOU said you lived in Seattle, I imagined an apartment in the city." Max roamed around our living room as though he belonged there. "We're not that close, are we?"

Max had followed us home in his rented SUV with Lawana at the wheel. I wasn't sure where he and the guard were going to stay—our house is small—but we could worry about that later.

I shook my head. "No. As I'm sure you noticed, we're over an hour's drive away from campus. I guess I still think of this as the greater Seattle area. My folks think I'm crazy." I glanced about, taking in the familiar sight of my childhood home. "This is Whidbey Island. Come on. I'll show you around."

The back deck overlooked the strait, with a rocky shore below, and pines surrounded the house in thick copses. There I escorted Max. We were alone; my parents and kid sister had made themselves scarce. This reunion was weird enough as it was.

"Is that the Pacific Ocean?" Max asked, gesturing toward the waters.

"No, that's the Strait of Juan de Fuca." I pointed over the restless bay. "At night, when the weather's clear, lights from Port Townsend can be seen from here. And those peaks on the horizon, that's the Olympic National Park." I stared at the distant mountains, just white puffy hills overlooking the green shoreline and blue sea. I'd missed the view. I hadn't always come home from campus, even if my weekends had been free.

"Do you go hiking there?" Max asked, leaning against the creaking wooden railing, his gaze aimed at the faraway mountains beyond the bay.

"Yeah, sometimes. There are some awesome biking trails there too. If you've never tried mountain biking, you should. It's a great workout." I took up position next to him, studying his profile instead of the familiar vista. "Max, why are you here?"

He didn't face me, but he did quirk a smile. "What a warm welcome, Oliver."

Heat filled my cheeks. "I didn't mean it like that." His chuckle told me he'd been joking, so I bumped shoulders with him. Max laughed a little more, so I felt better and reassured. "I just didn't expect to see you, is all. Like, ever."

Max nodded, hiding his eyes behind a veil of golden lashes. "Nor I you." Only then did he turn to me with his whole body, his elbow still resting on the railing. "I have been keeping an eye on you, though."

I blinked in surprise. "Me, why?"

"I suppose I waited to see if stories or pictures of me would surface on the covers of tabloids."

I clenched my fists and my face hardened. "I didn't tell anyone about us or what happened. Not a soul."

Max smiled softly. "I know. And judging from the rather amusing and dramatic huddle scene back at the university, I gather you didn't even tell your family."

I raised my chin, suddenly angry, as if I had been accused of a heinous crime while being as innocent as the driven snow. "It wasn't my secret to tell. And even if it had been, I'm allowed to have a private, classified, personal, intimate…." I struggled for the right word.

Max stepped closer. My anger evaporated, leaving behind only the warmth of rising desire. He placed his palm over my arm and squeezed gently. "I meant no disrespect, Oliver. I… I have misplaced my trust before. Perhaps that has made me a bit skittish."

The last remnants of my vexation abandoned me. "I get that. I'm sorry."

Max's smile widened from rueful to grateful. "Thank you, Oliver. You truly are a prince among men."

This time when I blushed, I felt the fire licking at me all over, inside and out. I chuckled awkwardly. "Uh, thanks."

Max closed the gap between us. The heat of his body seemed to transfer to mine. His breath smelled of apples and cinnamon. Cookies, or maybe scented coffee?

Max brushed the tip of my nose with his. "Aww, you are so cute when you blush. Like an adorable little tomato. I am so happy to see you again."

I fidgeted, avoiding his gaze. "Surely you didn't come all this way just to see my red face, did you?"

Max moved back, observing me like a cat staring at a mouse. "To be honest, Oliver, I traveled halfway across the world because I was rather hoping you and I could continue our…." He swished his wrist about in a telling gesture.

I grinned. "Our dalliance?"

Max laughed so hard he had tears in his eyes. "Touché. And as a matter of fact, yes, indeed."

My mind was blown by the notion that Max had enjoyed our time together so much that he traveled to the other side of the globe to see me. My ex hadn't even bothered to trek from the living room to the kitchen to fetch me a drink—though he went there to get *his*, of course. But he'd been a selfish bastard; Max was his polar opposite.

I wasn't 100 percent sold on Max's idea, though. Not because I had a special someone or specific plans for the summer, but because I couldn't see where this thing between us could go. Long-term schedules weren't my thing, but this seemed so… indeterminate.

"Uh, for how long?" I asked, hoping I didn't sound like I wanted to get rid of him, which was the furthest thing from my mind. "Aren't you worried someone will find out? I mean, we're not in Europe, sure, but folks here do recognize famous people. Sometimes."

Max inclined his head to show he understood my concerns. "I cannot say with any certainty for how long, Oliver. A few days, a couple of weeks, or the entire length of the summer? Depends on my schedule and yours."

When he spoke, I finally caught on. "Wait. You're suggesting we make this… thing between us into a permanent arrangement?"

The languid, seductive look on Max's face spoke volumes. "You're a smart man, Oliver."

Chapter 10

I COULD barely contain my enthusiasm. Although I had reservations, despite my heart threatening to beat its way out of my chest. "I can keep a secret, no problem. But Whidbey Island is a pretty small place. I can't promise—"

"Your family seem nice," Max interjected. "If you are worried about them—"

"They won't post anything about you, either, I swear," I cut in. I knew my parents both believed in honor and honesty, and I knew my sister who, despite being rebellious, would never betray a confidence.

Max nodded. "I had a feeling they would do no such thing. I like your parents. I especially like your sister."

Somewhere from inside we could hear a giant "*Aww.*"

"Ellie, stop eavesdropping!" I yelled as loud as I could over my shoulder.

Max burst out in hapless giggles. After a few seconds, I chimed in, seeing the humor in the situation. And the melodramatic "*Aww*" from inside was even bigger this time.

"She's wonderful," Max mumbled between chortles, holding on to his stomach.

"No comment," I remarked dryly, but my lips spread into a wide grin. "So, am I reading the reason for your visit right? You want to continue our affair?"

Max calmed, but the light of hilarity in his eyes remained. "Yes. Would you be amenable to that sort of arrangement?"

I hesitated. Not because I didn't want him—goodness no—but because our lives were an ocean and two continents apart. It would be hard to schedule a single regular rendezvous. Long-distance love affairs burdened the heart and everything else to boot; would a long-distance booty-call be any different?

I could see the advantages to his having a semiregular sexual partner, available whenever the need arose, all kept under a cloud of secrecy. He wouldn't need to search for any other man and risk exposure. I'd proven I could be trusted.

But what was in this arrangement for me? Yes, fabulous sex with a handsome man. In the long run, though, I had a lot to lose. My career, my credibility, my anonymity—all gone if….

"I'm supposed to spend the summer looking for work," I murmured slowly, not wanting Elinor to hear, but needing Max to listen and understand that I wasn't rejecting him, but that I simply had reservations about his proposal. "If I do get a job, it would likely be here, in the States. Your life is back at Noricia."

Max demurred, his smile unwavering. "It is true that I have innumerable duties back in my home country. I am supposed to rule it one day. But…."

I held my breath, my heart on overdrive. So much depended on his next words. A great deal of my future, I dare say. Would I continue with or without him? I had accepted the likelihood that it would be without him, so this opportunity was rare and special, not one I wanted to miss.

Max touched my arm as if he could read the trepidation haunting me. Perhaps he read my face instead of my mind.

"However, I firmly believe that if and when two people decide to be together, no power in this world can stop them. Not even distance. I'm certain that two reasonably intelligent adults can figure out a solution to any problem."

His confidence gave me a boost as well. "Okay."

I blushed yet again. A plain response seemed wholly inadequate to convey the multitude of feelings inside me. I might have looked calm, but within me raged a whirlwind of hope, joy, expectation, and an endless anticipation of sexual satisfaction.

"I never imagined we could pick up where we left off," I confessed. "I thought I'd never see you again. I'd resigned myself to that fact and mourned it every day since we parted."

Max embraced me. His consolation was laced with sensual promises. "Oh, Oliver, I missed you too."

I hugged him back. His strong muscles rippled under his clothes. I buried my face in the crook of his neck, inhaling the scent of his clean hair and expensive cologne. He smelled good; he felt good. I wished we were alone together somewhere and that we didn't have any clothes on.

But I remembered practicalities, so I pulled back a bit. "There's a lot we still need to discuss. I mean, are you going to come to me every time, or—"

"I do have a private jet and flexible hours," Max reminded me with a grin as he bussed my cheek. He had no stubble. His face was so soft against my grittier one, as my stubble was starting to show after a long day.

"Well, yeah, I guess that's one point to you," I whispered while my brain rattled like a gourd by rising passions. I didn't want to talk anymore. I wanted him on top of me.

"So, how about a ride?" Max murmured into my ear, his voice beckoning me to naughtiness.

I stared back, wild-eyed and crazy aroused.

Max merely laughed. "You've a dirty mind, Oliver. Oh, I like that. But I meant a bike ride. Noricia and its peaks are known for hiking, rock-climbing, and bike trails as well, so I'm proficient in all national sports. Perhaps you could show me that famous national park of yours."

My fatigue over the graduation ceremony was abruptly gone, and I nodded eagerly. "I'd love to. But the Olympic National Park is a couple of hours drive away, so… what about one of the bike trails here on Whidbey Island? Lots of nice places to see here too."

Max inclined his head as a sign of acquiescence.

"You can borrow my bike, Max" came Elinor's shout from the shadows inside the house.

I rolled my eyes, but Max merely laughed.

MAX WAS a fit athlete, I noted fast. He had both endurance and speed, and he left me in the dust as he cycled past me on one of the more challenging stretches of the Kettles Trails close to home.

I grinned. Max was competitive. Then again, so was I. The race was on. Sometimes I was in the lead, other times he was. We sped up, passing each other time and again, the scent of pines mixing with fresh sweat, and the scenery whisking by. Our dirt bikes sent pebbles and dust flying, so it was best to stay beside my rival rather than behind or in front of him.

We flew, time flew.

After about an hour, at the trail head of the mid-difficulty path we'd taken, we fell off our bikes onto the dirt, panting roughly, our chests heaving. My voice was gone, my heart thudded hard enough to deafen me, and I was sweating in places I didn't even care to think about.

I glanced beside me where Max lay, gasping for air. His skintight riding outfit left nothing to the imagination. I would have drooled if my mouth hadn't been so dry. I was dying of thirst. For water or Max's juices, I couldn't say.

Lawana, who had ridden behind us the entire way, had reached the end the same time as us. Only she seemed unaffected by the grueling ordeal. She stood by her bike, rolling her eyes at us, her chest barely rising and falling.

Who was she, Wonder Woman?

Her serene gaze swept the forest around us, scanning for possible threats. I'd never seen anyone as efficient as her. Where did she hide her weapons? She had to have at least one on her.

She seemed to be an excellent bodyguard, and she'd been promoted to the position of head of security for Max after Jonas Of-No-Apparent-Surname had gone missing back at Porquerolles. Of him, there was no news. Whatever had happened to him, it remained a mystery.

Max and I staggered, and Lawana walked, back to their black SUV with tinted windows and drove back to our house. Once there, I let him hit the shower first. Sure, I could have used Elinor's bathroom, but she was too particular and protective about her space, so I didn't dare.

And the thought of getting naked, hot, and wet at the same exact place where Max did the same made my heart miss a beat and my dick stiffen a little. The familiar buzz of anticipation filled me. Max and I would undoubtedly have sex before long. I could barely contain my enthusiasm.

I waited patiently, standing in the middle of my bedroom, watching the bathroom door like a hawk. I didn't realize I was worrying my bottom lip until I tasted blood. Gnawing something just seemed fitting at that moment. It dawned on me that I was nervous. For reasons I couldn't rationally explain, Max meant a lot to me. Being close to him again, just the two of us, excited and unnerved me.

The gush of water ceased. I held my breath. Rustling of fabric, probably towels, followed. Then the door opened, and a cloud of steam billowed outward.

Max stepped across the threshold. A white towel hung low on his narrow hips; I could see the mouthwatering V-shape of his hipbones. A few errant droplets glided down his sun-kissed skin, some getting stuck on his visible abs, the rack of perfect muscles revealing how much he exercised.

Max dried his hair on a smaller white towel. A hissing sound emerged as a result. He smiled and winked at me. I blushed. Was I salivating like a dog after a bone? More than likely.

Embarrassed at being so obvious, I slunk past him into the bathroom and shut the door.

From behind it, I heard Max say, "If you need help washing your back, or any other body part, do not hesitate to ask. I'm here to serve."

I damn near swallowed my tongue. The temptation was killing me; my libido was killing me. But I couldn't succumb—or *my mother* would kill me.

I cursed because the only thing ahead of me in the near future was an ice-cold shower.

"WE DON'T have a guest room," I said as an apology at dinner later that evening. Mom had made my favorite, chicken enchiladas, in honor of my graduation day. I addressed Max, though. "We have an unlived-in room but it's not empty. We use it for storage, mostly. It has a pull-out couch, but… that probably wouldn't work for you. So, I'll take the couch, and you can have my bed."

Max cocked his head like a baffled dog. "Your bed is a queen. We could share it."

"No, you couldn't," Valerie cut in, her steadfast tone putting an end to the debate.

I sighed. There was no use countermanding my mother. Once she set her mind, it was written in stone. Not even dynamite would make a dent in her decision.

Instead of the conversation dwindling, though, to my surprise Max spoke. And I was taken aback by his whole proclamation.

"Are you Roman Catholic, Mrs. Reed?" he asked.

My mother frowned as if both offended and confused. "Yes. As is my husband and our kids. Are you?"

Max shook his head. "No. With a Bohemian army, my people fought against Catholicism in the early seventeenth century at the Battle of White Mountain[1]. Though we were caught between the forces of the German Catholics from the north and the Holy Roman Empire from the south, we won. It was a war of attrition; we had to resort to guerilla tactics in the Alps. My mountaineers knew the area well, and despite the fact we were

---

1 The Battle of White Mountain was fought on 8 November 1620, and it was a decisive victory for Roman Catholicism. Protestantism was eradicated, and the Holy Roman Empire was able to advance to Germany and outlying countries.

outnumbered by the enemy, we came out victorious. Had we not won the battle, it is highly likely Catholicism and the Holy Roman Empire would have encroached onto a much larger domain farther to the north."

"Your people aren't Protestants, though, either?" I noted, vaguely remembering something along those lines.

Max smiled at me. "No. We fought against Protestantism as well in the late seventeenth century at the Battle of Black Valley[2]. Similar strategies were employed, and no form of Christianity advanced in our little nation. We were apparently too small a people and too isolated a kingdom to merit further actions against us."

"So, you're not religious at all?" my mother asked, and her clipped tone and rigid posture told me this conversation was going downhill fast.

Max met her gaze with his own steadfast one. "On the contrary. In the late nineteenth century, there was a revival of our traditional tribal faith, Celtic paganism, a movement which has extended to this day."

Elinor sighed with obvious admiration and longing. "That's so cool."

"Is there a point to this history lesson?" Valerie asked briskly.

I grimaced inwardly. As much as I wanted her to be quiet and not insult our guest, I couldn't talk back to my mother, not at our own table, in our own house.

Max nodded. "Yes. The Catholic Church teaches that, while homosexual desires are not sins, homosexual acts are a violation against nature and divine law."

I closed my eyes and slumped. Yup, a Titanic-level disaster and icebergs of religion ahead. All hands to escape rafts.

Then Max surprised me by saying, "I cannot speak for your level of spiritual devotion, Mrs. Reed, but considering Oliver is here with us and not out on the streets, alone and homeless, you chose your son over your faith."

I looked up at my mother in shock. I'd never really thought about her religious beliefs and how much it had cost her to pick me instead of her relationship with God. I knew she loved me; that was all that mattered to me.

Did she hate or despise me for her having to make such a personal sacrifice?

---

2 The Battle of Black Valley is an invention by the author, and not a real historical event.

Valerie raised her chin in defiance. "I believe in a loving God. He and I are on close enough terms that no human priest or holy scripture can compel me to hate my own son. He would embrace Oliver, not bash his skull in. Only humans are so cruel."

Max nodded in obvious agreement. "That being the case, and to bring the conversation back on track, Mrs. Reed, while I appreciate your desire to protect your son, I should also note that neither he nor I are children anymore. I journeyed across the globe to be with Oliver, to lie next to him at night and hold him with the certain knowledge that I am with someone who both cares for me and makes no demands of me. A rarity, to be sure. If you find something shameful about an act of love, then he and I shall find another establishment to ease your concerns."

Shocked, I couldn't even blink. No one had ever spoken like that to my mother. Max's words were at once respectful and rebellious, reverent and derogatory. I couldn't make up my mind if his manner was grown-up and wise or childish and insulting.

Cringing inwardly, I stole a glimpse at my mother. I expected her to tell Max off and order him to leave the house immediately. She had a firm concept of guest courtesies, and this was not it. I decided then and there that if push came shove, I would leave with Max. Maybe my mother would forgive me later on.

Valerie had narrowed her eyes, and her mouth was set in a firm line, as if she disapproved of everything. Finally, she said, "There is absolutely nothing wrong with love between two consenting adults. So, Your Highness, you may share a room with my son for the extent of your stay, provided you show a modicum of discretion."

Max bowed his head. "We will be as quiet as church mice."

I gulped. My head was spinning. The world had turned upside down. My mother had changed her mind—and Max had used the word *love* when describing our burgeoning relationship. I couldn't catch my breath. Was the floor tilting?

Or perhaps I wasn't slipping out of my chair but falling… in love.

Absurd. Impossible. Insane.

Then I glanced at Max's blue eyes and dove into their depths, not caring if I'd ever surface.

Chapter 11

"Psst. Oliver, are you asleep?" Max whispered in the dark of the night and nibbled on my earlobe, giving me goose bumps.

I fisted the sheets. How could I sleep with him so close? I felt the nearness of his warm body, and I longed to touch him with my hands, my lips, my heart. His feverish palm rested over my belly, the heat of him spreading outward like ripples in a puddle.

"What do you think?" I grumbled.

Max's chuckle filled the private, shadowy cocoon of my bedroom. Then his lips sought mine, and we kissed. He stole my breath away, leaving behind a pool of surrender and relaxation.

Passion overtook me, and I wrapped my arms around him and flipped us so that I lay on top of him. Max spread his legs to accommodate me. He wound around my body like a vine, crushing me to him, his mouth hungry, devouring mine.

I grabbed him everywhere I could reach, as greedy as he was. I fumbled a hand between us and aligned our cocks so that we rubbed against each other with each push and glide. He gripped my buttcheeks and massaged gently, then with more vigor. I shivered, desire burning my skin.

"Harder, Oliver," Max urged me with a hoarse whisper.

I rocked against him faster and stroked our cocks vigorously. The sensation of his hot shaft pressed against mine, pulsing and throbbing, our tips nudging and exchanging precome-wet kisses, sent me hurtling toward the edge of delight.

His tongue in my mouth swirled and licked, and I sucked in his taste. His legs tightened around me, his arms shaking, his nails digging in. I wanted more; I craved every inch of him.

Hunger like this was unknown to me. I'd known the desperation for climax before, but this felt different—the yearning to be close, to share pleasure, to kiss without end. Lovemaking couldn't last forever; could the feelings awakened by it last?

"Oliver, my sweet Oliver, please…," Max begged, his head thrown back, his body arching into me.

I was lost. His voice, his body, his flavor, his scent. All those sensations washed over me, a tidal wave of passion, and we surfed the crest to a blinding orgasm, mutual and perfect. His and my come mixed, white globs of hot, sticky substance that drenched my hand. I let go, slumped over him, and together we lazily swayed to the rhythm of our heartbeats.

"Aren't you glad you hadn't fallen asleep?" Max asked, out of breath, laughter in his voice.

I giggled into his neck. "You're really something. Smartass."

Max merely wrapped his arms around me, sighed with contentment, and promptly fell asleep like a baby. I rested my head against his chest and drifted off to dreamland to the sound of his heart.

MY FIRST summer vacation week was a repeat of the perfection of my spring break.

Max and I spent all of our time together. We only saw my family at breakfast or dinnertime. They didn't seem to mind, but I could tell Valerie wanted me to search for employment. I knew she would bring up the subject one day soon, probably at supper, and put me on the spot. I couldn't escape her queries without looking like an ungrateful brat.

One morning, though, things took a turn. Max had been with us for just over a week, and my folks liked him fine. But Valerie had long-term goals for me, which were a stable job and a steady paycheck. Over our meal, I caught her glancing at me surreptitiously, each time about to speak, and I knew my vacation was at an end. I had to be a responsible adult.

Before Valerie could speak, however, it was Max who silenced everyone.

"Mr. and Mrs. Reed, and Ms. Reed, of course, I would like to extend my gratitude for giving me this rare reprieve from my royal duties and for allowing me to spend time with your son. I adore Oliver. He is unique, the rarest of jewels."

My mother took my hand over the table and squeezed, a teary veil over her green eyes. I had to swallow or turn into a waterfall as well.

Max studied us all with a smile on his lips. "With that in mind, I would like to make you all a once-in-a-lifetime offer. I would like to invite you to Noricia for the summer. You would be guests of my family at Riten Castle, or Schloss Rishen as it is pronounced."

I stared, my jaw practically on the ground. My family stared as well, their mouths gaping too. The shock of the surprising invitation reverberated through the air like an electrical charge foretelling the first crack of a storm.

Max grinned, his gaze flicking among everyone at the table. "Well, ladies and gentlemen, what do you say?"

"A-are you serious?" I managed to breathe out, stuttering due to nerves.

"Please tells us you're serious," my sister called out, her voice rising to a high pitch as her excitement grew.

"As the grave," Max declared solemnly, as if he were reciting a ceremonial address in front of thousands.

I rose from my seat, my knees unsteady. "B-but if we all go with you, there's no chance of keeping things under wraps. Everyone will find out, you know, about us. I thought you wanted to avoid that."

Max rolled his eyes. "I am not sleeping with all of you. And I am allowed to invite and house friends as guests. And—" He smiled softly and a bit shyly at me. "—I would love to show you my homeland, Oliver."

Whenever Max murmured my name, my heart leaped up to my throat. Tears burned my eyes. I blinked them away and forced myself to swallow down my emotions. "I… I would love to."

The small smile on Max's face spread to his eyes, his whole demeanor. "Thank you, Oliver. You make me so very happy."

"I'm in!" Elinor exclaimed before the echo of Max's words had dissipated.

"Ellie, behave," our mother berated her, with little effect on my sister, who bounced on her seat, about ready to burst out of her skin.

I turned to my parents. Concern colored Valerie's expression as she worried her bottom lip, while Paulito remained stoic as ever. They exchanged glances.

I was wary, barely daring to keep my hopes up. I owed so much to my family. If they said *no* now and demanded I spend the summer trying to find a job and a place to live, I felt I'd have to comply. It was my duty, not just as their child, but as an adult. Perhaps that was me being overly responsible.

I also knew they had their own jobs and responsibilities. It'd be hard to leave those behind for a trip without a specific end date, if they decided to come with me at all. I didn't want them to lose their jobs. I consoled myself with the fact that if push came to shove, there was always a need for both nurses and sanitation engineers.

It was my father who nodded his assent. "I don't want to deny my son the chance to see the world before he settles down. And I've been reading up on Noricia as well. I'd like to see it."

Elinor whooped loudly and clapped my shoulder hard enough to almost knock me off the chair. She had strength in her petite form.

Valerie tutted. "Ellie, stop this instant." To Max, she said, "I agree with my husband. This is a rare opportunity. My son can go."

I took her hand. "You're coming with us, right?" I felt like a kid again, wanting my folks to be near if and when I did something amazing, or if I needed something.

Paulito nodded. "We will, if that is okay with our employers, your mother, and His, um… Max."

Valerie remained hesitant. Her brow was furrowed, and lowered eyelashes covered her eyes. I couldn't tell what the problem was. Was she afraid of losing her job? In this economy, it was a risk to stay off work for any reason.

Finally, she sighed. "Fine. We'll go as a family. We simply need to plan this out step by step and not rush into things."

Before Ellie could deafen us, Max's chief of security, Lawana, hurried into the dining room with a determined stride and a hardened expression. She leaned in and whispered something in Max's ear. I watched as Max's smile slipped away.

"What's wrong?" I asked, so agitated all of a sudden that I could scarcely draw breath.

Max met my gaze. "It seems our secret has been uncovered. There are pictures of me at your house in the papers."

I gasped. I froze, unable to function. How? We'd been so careful.

Elinor, who had fumbled with her iPhone, growled and jumped to her feet. "I don't fucking believe it. I'll kill that fucking jerkwad."

My heart skipped a beat. "What? Who?"

Elinor shoved her phone across the table to me. On the screen, I could see a slightly smudgy photo of our house, with Max and me standing in front of the living room window. I was gesturing something, and Max was laughing. His hand was at my waist, and it could not be interpreted as casual.

It was intimate.

I remembered that day. I'd been showing off our front lawn, kept meticulously short by my dad, and told Max a joke. We'd been spending time close together in my room right before and after the picture had been taken, and it showed.

"Kill who?" I asked, searching the photo for clues but unable to find any.

Elinor cursed like a seasoned sailor. "Check out the right-hand lower corner. See anything familiar?"

I studied the photo with greater attention to detail. What I'd thought was a smudge was in fact the hood of a maroon-colored car, dirty and rusted through.

I drew in a sharp breath and snarled. "That miserable asshole. *I* will kill him."

"Forgive me, but who are we talking about?" Max asked politely. I couldn't gauge his mood.

I flushed with heat—a bit with shame but mostly with boiling-hot anger. "My ex. That's his piece-of-shit car. He must have come by for whatever reason, seen us, recognized you, and taken pictures. He's a greedy dickhead, so I'm guessing he sold them to the tabloids." I looked up at Max, chewing on the inside of my cheek so I wouldn't cry. "I'm so sorry."

Max waved his hand dismissively, as if it had transformed into a magic wand with which he could make our problems disappear. "I cannot fault your taste in men, my dear Oliver, seeing as I am also in that category."

He stood, smoothed out the wrinkles in his clothes, and glanced at all of us in turn. I knew I'd never see him again and, depressed to the core, I slid down my chair, wanting the ground to open up and swallow me whole.

Then Max proved me wrong. "So, family Reed, how fast can you all pack?"

Chapter 12

"THAT'S THE money shot right there," Oliver whispered, staring wide-eyed at the glorious vista of the summer Alps.

Max chuckled and watched with delight as his companion suddenly blushed beet-red. He wasn't so innocent that he didn't know what the term *money shot* meant. He liked the sexually charged atmosphere between him and Oliver. It seemed to expand around them and form whenever they were together, in company or alone.

"You know, this view makes me feel like I should start singing "The Sound of Music," Oliver commented, gesturing about indistinctly.

"Go ahead," Max suggested with a wicked grin. "You wouldn't be the first, I assure you."

Oliver winked at him. "Only if you yodel with me."

Max rolled his eyes. "Pass. Hard pass."

As Oliver laughed and returned to his sightseeing, Max studied him at length.

The hasty packing and rushed journey from the States to Noricia on a private jet had given Max the opportunity to learn more about the relationships of the Reed family—and about Oliver's ex-boyfriend, Rick, who had broken Oliver's heart. Apparently, the odious man had caught sight of Max at Oliver's graduation, gotten jealous, decided to investigate—basically spy on them—and then betrayed them to the press. One last "screw you" to Oliver from the finest of men... not.

Oliver had seemed so crushed by Rick's actions that it had taken most of the trip overseas for Max to reassure him that Max understood and would not hold someone else's wrongdoings against Oliver. After a hundred and one kisses at the back of the private plane, Oliver had finally calmed. Max counted that as one of his major wins.

Now, here they were, in Max's homeland.

They had departed from the States midmorning and, after a twelve-hour flight, arrived at Zurich airport the morning of next day. From there, they'd flown on a private helicopter to St. Gallen Airport, which was right next to the border of Noricia. There they had entered two black, unmarked, and reinforced SUVs with tiny Norician flags—tricolor with three vertical stripes (green, white, and blue), and a crown depicted in the white middle stripe—attached to the sides of the hood. No sounds entered the spacious, luxurious cabin, and the tinted windows camouflaged the outside world. After an hour-long drive, it was midmorning again, but on the next day.

And they could finally stop for a bit of fresh air by the side of the mountain road, one of the very few up in the hills covered in asphalt.

Paulito and Valerie were talking in hushed tones, holding hands. Elinor was taking pictures and selfies with her phone. She was practically bouncing on the balls of her feet with excitement. Her rebellious hand gestures and flicked-out tongue amused Max.

The snow had mostly melted, and the rugged but slightly glistening peaks were showcased in various shades of green in their lush, undulating meadows and vibrant, dense forests. Colorful wildflowers dotted the grassy lowlands with splashes of white, yellow, orange, and pink, and sent their delicate fragrances floating along the crisp winds. The temperature had climbed a tad above twenty degrees centigrade, and the sun blazed hotly from the clear blue sky. Bees buzzed and butterflies flew by.

High pastures saw a few hikers with backpacks here and there on the footpaths, while herds of cows appeared, idling and eating grass, their cowbells chiming as they roamed about. The coppery dings reached a long way in the natural silence and echoed over the range, accompanied by bird songs and interspersed with an occasional moo.

The rustic serenity of his homeland never failed to draw on Max's heartstrings.

As did the young man beside him who seemed utterly captivated by what he saw. Max heard Oliver sigh with deep contentment. Max could relate. Sometimes, despite his occasional wanderlust, he felt he never breathed so easily or so well as he did at home. This was where he came from, his home soil. He was part of this earth.

"I think I'll fall in love with this country before you," Oliver remarked, a dreamy look in his eyes.

Max grinned. "Yes. But you will fall for me, too, in the end."

Judging from the endearing blush and the shy smile on Oliver's face, Max had him there.

"THAT'S THE capital, Vindeburg, down in the valley below." Max waved indistinctly at the panoramic view of the old town far beneath their lookout spot by the gray ramparts. "There are many things to see. The Norician National Museum holds a permanent exhibit on our cultural history and Celtic traditions, the Grand Gardens contain both sacred groves and the burial mounds of past chieftains, the Council Hall is one of Vindeburg's oldest, best-kept buildings, the Temple of Rosmerta showcases ancient votive offerings, and the Royal Concert Hall…."

Max realized he quite liked being the tour guide for people he enjoyed spending time with. With visiting dignitaries, a special aide was usually selected from the palace staff for that purpose. Max didn't get to show his expertise on those occasions.

"Will there be paparazzi at the castle too, like at the airport?" Oliver asked, sounding timid.

Max held back a grimace. As the private jet had landed, a band of reporters had flocked the place, taking pictures of Max, Oliver, and the Reed-Ruíz family. Airport security and royal guards had disbanded them after a moment, but it was clear that the cat was out of the bag.

"No," Max reassured Oliver, taking his hand and squeezing gently. "Reporters are allowed on castle grounds only for scheduled press conferences. No one will harass you there. Also, the Royal Press Officer will handle any PR issues that might arise."

"Cool." Elinor whistled. "How does one get that job?"

Max chuckled. "By being an amazing problem solver with a flair for drama and a face that can keep a secret, not to mention knowing how to hide bodies." Elinor's eyes twinkled. Was she contemplating a career change? Max smiled at the idea.

"That the place you live in?" Oliver pointed upward toward where, amid the forested mountainside, rose an impressive structure of conjoined buildings and towers that dominated the hilltop.

"Yes, that's Riten Castle." Max suppressed a chuckle because Oliver sounded surprised, his eyes wide, while he sported a tiny frown between his brows at the same time. "Let me guess. You were expecting Neuschwanstein?" Oliver's cheeks turned red as rubies. Max nudged him with his shoulder. "Don't worry about it. Again, you wouldn't be the first."

Oliver nodded slowly, seemingly hesitant. "It sort of looks similar…."

"The original castle consisted of a medieval keep and an inner wall," Max explained, talking as they drove the last leg of their journey toward the palace, windows open. "There have been sieges, earthquakes, wars, and bombings, but the palace stands. The current castle is the visionary work of a Prussian architect from the early nineteenth century whose work was heavily influenced by English Gothic Revival, German

Romanticism, and the French Châteaux of the Loire Valley—very much like Neuschwanstein. The stone used for Riten Castle, however, is closer to earth tones than white. Hence the different look."

Max didn't say out loud that he felt the palace looked too much like Hohenzollern Castle in Germany to stand out on its own merit. That jealousy and envy still occasionally burned like acid. He wished Riten Castle had been built with a little more originality, but after two centuries it was tough to complain about it now. Still, Riten was bigger than either of the other two, so they had that going for them.

A paved serpentine road climbed from the valley up to the castle, winding like a string around the entire mountaintop. Between elevations, six terraces featured lush, verdant gardens where people were milling, most of them taking photos.

"Lots of people about," Elinor noted, taking snapshots of the terraces as well.

"The public gardens are open year-round for tourists," Max replied.

"Not a lot of cars around, though," Elinor noted. And she was correct. No vehicles appeared on the winding road, on the move or stationary at roadside.

"There's a gondola lift up from the valley, from Vindeburg, that's operational year-round. It reaches the highest level of the Royal Gardens, so most people come up via the lift and then hike back down the mountainside. There are many easy, scenic paths."

Max pointed at the gardens on various elevations where trees, hedges, and flowerbeds mixed with marble statues and fountains. "The six terraces have individual themes, each one dedicated to two of the thirteen Celtic astrological trees. Growing them in these harsh climes proved challenging at first, but we've managed."

"That's so cool," Elinor murmured, her tone full of awe. She gasped, pressing her nose to the glass. "They're so big and majestic." Each species of tree flourished, green and tall, on their own spots of land, surrounded by shrubberies and flowerbeds. Plump leaves rustled and waved in the wind. Summer made everything beautiful.

Max smiled. Elinor's enthusiasm was infectious. "Alders and hawthorns grow on the highest terrace and, as symbols for royalty, oak and holly grow in the Outer Bailey, or outer courtyard to put it in simpler terms. Oh, I believe you can see the castle front already."

Both Oliver and Elinor stuck their heads out of the car. Max knew his security detail, Lawana especially, frowned upon opening vehicle windows before they were inside the castle walls. But these were his friends and guests, and he doubted anyone was out to get him—despite all that had happened in the spring in Porquerolles when his signet ring was stolen and replaced with a lethal weapon. No new incidents had occurred since then.

Crown Plaza, a round open area in front of the castle, was graced with a wide set of stairs, a perron, leading up to the main entrance. A protruding portico preceded a raised portcullis that served as an outer door. Beyond the arched passage under the curtain wall was a set of double doors, but these, the main gates, were almost never closed.

At inception, there had been a reinforced tower and a booby-trapped barbican in case of an attack. However, that gatehouse had been destroyed in World War II by an unlucky bomb strike and never rebuilt.

Max was fine with that engineering and design choice since he preferred the new entrance over the old, imposing one that had cast a looming shadow.

Oliver whistled low, his gaze already on something new. "Wow. Tall towers."

Max studied his excited companions. He didn't need to see the castle, for he had grown up there and was familiar with every vista, every corridor, every room. "To mirror the six wood-themed terraces, there are thirteen towers on the grounds, each named after one of the thirteen Celtic zodiac animals. Noricians call this place the Thirteen Towers."

"Which one is yours?" Oliver asked, glancing wide-eyed at Max over his shoulder. He was buzzing with curiosity, a look that suited him well and gave Max a heated lurch low in his stomach too.

"The Snake Tower is mine," Max replied and watched with amusement as an adorable little redness crept over Oliver's cheeks and neck. Clearly his thoughts had veered toward the naughtiness Max had anticipated by using a hushed, seductive tone. Thankfully, the Reed parents were in the other car.

"Which one belongs to your parents?" Elinor asked, breaking the charged silence.

"The Stag Tower, which was the original keep and the first and largest of the thirteen towers, belongs to the King and Queen. It's called the Royal Chambers by the staff. The Throne Room is on the ground floor."

"So…." Elinor winked shamelessly at Max. "Since you're well-behaved royalty, I guess you never call your toilets thrones, do you?"

"Ellie!" Oliver scolded with a shout, his cheeks flaming.

Max laughed so hard tears streamed down his face. "Actually," he retorted wickedly, "I call my bathroom the *little* throne room."

Elinor giggled, joining in Max's mirth. He liked her direct, naughty sense of humor.

They quieted as the cars veered around their last curve toward their destination.

"This place is… amazing." Oliver spoke in a quiet, reverent tone that made Max happy. He had wanted to impress Oliver, for reasons he wasn't quite ready to delve deeper into.

The cars stopped at the round plaza in front of the steps. No tourists were allowed there when the royal family was in residence. In the summer, most of them were, if they weren't out of the country on diplomatic or representative missions.

On each of the three landings stood guards. All wore the blue-white-green national uniform, like the one Max had on in his publicity photo. The guards carried swords and spears, but they were for show. These guards were the ceremonial wing of the Fox Tails, as shown by the unicorn emblem on their chests.

The actual guard contingent of the Fox Tails dressed in full body armor and carried high-powered weapons and the fox insignia. They were hidden from sight, like the vast array of futuristic, high-tech security and surveillance machinery protecting the entire area.

Oliver, Elinor, and Max exited the vehicle at the foot of the stairs and waited for Paulito and Valerie to join them. Lawana set up a perimeter of guards around them without saying a word.

"The old gatehouse is gone," Max explained as they ascended the stairs slowly, taking in the sights. "The new entrance is less threatening. The Hawk Tower above it, though, was rebuilt after WWII as a symbol of perseverance, endurance, and farsightedness. It was the only part of the original gatehouse that was reconstructed. We felt it should be preserved since, apart from the Stag Tower, it was the oldest of the thirteen towers. Legend has it, as the settlement was built, a hawk nested there, bringing good fortune to the royal residence from the Great Goddess…."

Behind and above the portico rose a large, rectangular, light-brownish gate tower with a bulwark at the top. A stone plaque embedded into it, directly above the colonnade, depicted a rampant falcon. Vines crept up the walls, with pink and purple flowers blossoming here and there amid the greenery.

"Does anyone live in there?" Oliver asked, pointing up at the Hawk Tower, which rose high enough to encompass four levels and had two corbelled side turrets about midway up its length. A hawk nested over one to this day.

Max shook his head. "No, no one ever has. It's a guardhouse and a control room, manned twenty-four seven. Everything that happens in Riten Castle is monitored from there. But it's not a barracks."

As Elinor kept taking pictures, Max matched steps with Oliver who shyly, just for a moment, touched Max's hand. Max replied to the gesture by taking Oliver's hand in his. Side by side, they entered the wide but shadowy passageway under the curtain wall and into the castle proper.

"Here we go," Max murmured to himself, suddenly unsure if bringing his lover home was a good idea after all.

Chapter 13

"THIS IS the Eastern Drawing Room."

Oliver and his family ogled the open space with a vaulted ceiling depicting the night sky as a dark blue background with golden stars, large french doors open to a balcony, and a decor that was straight out of the Arabian Nights. All that was missing was a hookah.

The stucco walls were painted yellow and decorated with glass mosaics of arabesques and ivory inlays. Ottomans with fluffy pillows and wooden carvings lined the walls, a low coffee table was placed before each, and rich, ornamental carpets covered every inch of the stone floors.

"This is beautiful," Oliver declared, his gaze sweeping the room.

Max was gratified that his companion appreciated his home. "I'm glad you like it. There was an eastern exotica craze when this castle was constructed, and this room is a result."

Lawana approached him and handed him a small black locked case. "Everything is ready, Your Highness."

"Ah, excellent." Max waved at the others to gather round. He opened the case and revealed a number of keycards attached to lanyards. "There is a keycard for each of you. Though this castle is old, we no longer use traditional keys to lock doors. The mechanisms are state-of-the-art. All guests, residents, and staff are required to carry keycards that also serve as IDs."

"So, these are like all-access backstage passes at concerts?" Elinor asked after snatching the one with her name on it. She glanced at Valerie, whose eyebrows had risen. Elinor blushed and very awkwardly chuckled, "Not that I would know anything about that sort of thing."

Valerie rolled her eyes. "Nice save, young lady."

Max suppressed a laugh and went on, "The keycards serve a multitude of purposes and have several functions. They open the doors to your quarters and show the guards and staff the areas you're allowed to enter. In addition, they have built-in proximity sensors regarding areas that are off-limits to you, as well as radiation detectors, among other things, so heed the auditory warning signals."

"Radiation?" Oliver asked, his head cocked to the side in bafflement.

"Yes. We live in an age of hateful fanatics and dirty bombs. Riten Castle is prepared for any and all emergencies." Max waved behind him with a vague gesture. "As we came in, you probably noticed that all hallways and corridors have not only watercoolers and coffeemakers but green and red call buttons on the walls. Red alerts guards, green summons staff."

"How efficient—in an elitist sort of way," Elinor muttered, attaching the keycard to her belt.

Max liked her straightforwardness. It was refreshing to be condemned so publicly. He wasn't used to it, but he wasn't about to chide her for it. She seemed to rebel against existing conditions, not Max's family or lifestyle specifically.

A middle-aged, brown-haired, round-faced woman entered, dressed in a befitting trouser suit and sensible pumps. She clutched to her chest a brown tablet with the royal crown on the back, tapping the screen even while her gaze was aimed at Max.

She curtsied according to custom. "Your Highness." Her accident was decidedly German.

"Freddie." Max smiled and gestured to the others. "Reed family, meet Frederica Hoffman, the Royal Press Officer. She takes care of all statements to the media. She'll contact you if there's a problem." Max stared at her with narrowed eyes. "Of which there shouldn't be any."

Frederica laughed, loud and infectious. "Of course not, sir." She opened a thick brown leather notebook and handed everyone a leaflet. "This covers the main issues related to proper court conduct. Naturally, none of you should speak with any reporters or outsiders in the castle. There are other guests staying on the grounds, but your quarters in the Swan Tower are separate from theirs. Also, the schedule of upcoming events should be studied with care—"

"Yes, thank you, Freddie," Max cut her off and told her with a look to leave, which she did with a kind smile and a curtsey. To the others, he explained, "There are formal dinners and the like, but the only event you need to be aware of is the Summer Solstice Festival and Feast. That we will all attend at the Banquet Hall and Ballroom."

"Awesome," Elinor said, her mouth gaping, her eyes wide with excitement.

"Sounds cool," Oliver agreed with a bashful smile and a cute blush. Max wanted him so badly, but he suppressed his desire in favor of keeping up a princely facade.

When a fair-haired, spectacled young man dressed in the gleaming black pants and vest of a servant brought in fruity cocktails for the guests, Max inquired, "Pieter, have you seen my parents?"

The servant bowed. "Yes, Your Highness. The King and Queen are presently in the Grand Gallery entertaining another guest, Lady Kira von Montfort-Bregenz."

The blood drained from Max's face, and an icy shock shot through him. "Wh-what is she... I mean, who invited her?"

Pieter, the servant, appeared unfazed, his gaze aimed at a point below Max's jaw. "I believe His Highness Prince Johann invited Lady Kira to stay for the summer."

Max clenched his fists as anger rolled over him. He barely controlled himself, even though he was aware that his guests were looking at him funny. "And where is my dear brother, Johann?"

Pieter bowed. "Last I saw of him, Your Highness, Prince Johann was at the Royal Stables with his companions, Karl Jünger and Otto von Thürer."

Max suppressed a grimace. Johann's latest friends, Karl Jr. and Otto, were the worst kind of entitled aristocrats, spoiled little ingrates who behaved like they owned the country, the world, and then some. "Thank you, Pieter. That will be all."

The young servant bowed again and left, closing the door behind him.

"Is something wrong?" Oliver asked quietly as he approached, a look of concern adding a slight furrow between his eyebrows.

Max forced a light smile to his face. "No, everything is fine." He resisted the urge to repeat his words, knowing that would cause further confusion and weirdness. "Would you like to see your rooms in the Swan Tower and freshen up before the meet and greet?"

"Yes!" Elinor exclaimed sharply, though she seemed perfectly etiquette savvy from Max's point of view.

Max avoided the silent question in Oliver's eyes and prayed nothing else would go wrong.

THEY DIDN'T make it as far as the guest quarters, though. Inside the eastern ground floor's maze of stone corridors covered by thick rugs and featuring tapestries and paintings on the walls, they bumped into three men whose immaculate attire smelled of horses and hay, sunshine and dirt.

Max seethed, but he tried to be the better man and show his proper nature by smiling politely at his younger brother. "Johann, there you are."

Prince Johann had that age-old boyish charm. Then again, he was only twenty-two. Not quite as fair as Max, Johann had spiky, dirty-blond hair, green eyes, and two adorable dimples. Too bad, Max knew, that Johann's character didn't live up to his looks.

The Thürer twins, arranged beside Johann, had similar features, teeth bleached too white and with an overbite, slightly overthick eyebrows, and a couple of dueling scars on their faces. Max didn't hate them, per se, but he hated the petty, mean-spirited influence they had on his little brother. In their company, Johann behaved like an overindulged brat.

Johann's contemptuous gaze swept over the Reed family.

"Who ordered Tex-Mex?" he asked, his tone oozing disdain. His friends snickered behind their hands.

Max was mortified. He got so angry that he shook from the force of his rage. No matter how petulant and childish Johann could be, this was a new low even for him. Max couldn't bring himself to look at Oliver for fear of what he would see. Would this end their relationship before it began?

Before Max could berate his brother, however, which he was loath to do in public, Johann said, "My apologies. Poor joke." His fake sincerity echoed in the halls.

Silence thundered around them, loaded and awkward.

Then the quiet was broken by Elinor's swift response, "A poor joke for poor people, eh? How thoughtful of you." After that, Elinor started singing "Brown Girl in the Ring" by Boney M. Max smirked.

Johann and his friends stopped laughing in an instant. Their expressions hardened. Elinor's snarky remark and song snippet cut through their spiteful mirth like a scythe through wheat. Max would have bounced up and down with glee had that been appropriate.

With a menacing snarl, Johann whirled around like a tornado, obviously planning on making a flashy exit with his comrades. His departure, however, was cut short by a woman's smooth voice.

"Thank you, Your Highness, for inviting me to Riten Castle for the summer."

Max cringed inwardly. He would recognize that harmonious cadence anywhere. He prayed for the ground to open and swallow him whole. Unfortunately, that did not happen, so he turned and calmly faced the train wreck that lay ahead.

The midheight woman was thin as a reed. Her designer dress, burnt orange, hugged her body like a second skin. Whether this was a good look for her was up for debate. Her hair, the color of tarnished gold, was raised above her head in a complex coiffure. Her delicate features gave her a pixie-like appearance; the only thing missing was pointed ears. Hazel eyes greeted people with an inner light.

Johann gave a smug chuckle and bowed with theatrical flourish. "Believe me, Lady Kira, it was my pleasure. And I know Max here is as eager to see you as I am."

Max gritted his teeth but refrained from making a scene. He inclined his head as well and said politely, "It is an honor to see you again, Lady Kira."

Despite the tightness of her dress, Kira curtsied. "Good to see you as well, Your Highness."

Before Max could defuse the situation threatening to erupt, Johann declared loudly, "Oh, don't be so wooden with your bride-to-be, brother, or she might think your stiff back's the only hard thing about you."

Max could have killed Johann then and there had they been alone. Of course if it had been the two of them, then news of Max and Kira's engagement wouldn't have decimated Max's small chance at happiness.

He more felt than saw Oliver flinch and then go rigid next to him. Would he grow cold too?

Max quickly, if too late, took charge of the situation. "I look forward to speaking with you, Lady Kira. At the moment, though, I will show my guests to their quarters. Good day."

He ushered the Reeds away from Johann and Kira as fast as he could. Max noted that when he placed his hand on the small of Oliver's back, Oliver quickened his steps to move away from him.

Max suppressed a sigh. Things were going downhill so fast he estimated the next couple of minutes would undoubtedly find him at rock bottom.

"It's a lovely—" Oliver started to say in a tiny, squeaky voice once they had reached the lavish, spacious guest quarters in the Swan Tower—where wood-paneled walls, rich decor, a well-lit fireplace, a four-poster bed, and dark wooden furniture added welcoming touches of warmth.

That was good, for there was none in Elinor's voice when she interjected, "So, Max, you're engaged to be married? Did you bring Ollie here to be your secret lover? Or did you just want to rub your fiancée's nose in your sordid sexcapades?"

"Ellie!" Oliver called out, his voice shaking from frustration. "Knock it off. I'm sure Max will explain." He faced Max and looked at him pointedly, much calmer than Max felt, lowering his voice. "You will explain, won't you?"

"Why don't we give the two some privacy?" Paulito offered. Though his husky voice exuded composure, his adamant command was heard by all. Grumbling under her breath, Elinor followed her parents out of the room.

Oliver cleared his throat, fidgeting in place, seemingly nervous. "A-are you really engaged to... her?"

Max sighed. "Not as far as the public at large is concerned, but... sort of. It's complicated."

Oliver frowned but appeared to control his rampaging emotions. Max was grateful for that. "Complicated how? I know royal marriages used to be arranged, but surely not anymore, right?"

Max hedged. "My mother, Colette, arranged the match for us when Kira and I were infants. Quite a long courtship, wouldn't you say?" Max chuckled to alleviate the tension in the room. When Oliver's frown deepened, Max hurried to continue. "Kira and I aren't close like two beloveds would be. We certainly have never been lovers. She's more like an estranged sister to me. My mother still wishes for Kira and me to wed. But my father, Gustav, hasn't allowed news of the engagement to become public because of my... well, my sexual orientation."

Oliver crossed his arms and shifted his weight from one foot to the other, a deep, contemplative expression on his face. "So, you're gay, not bi?"

Max nodded emphatically. "Yes. I want a man, not a woman, to be my life partner."

Oliver worried his lower lip, continuing to hug himself. Max wanted to embrace him but knew that would be unwelcome at that moment.

"John brought her here to remind me of my, uh, previous engagement."

Oliver grimaced. "Sh-should... should me and my folks just leave?"

"No!" Max reined in his alarmed tone and wished he could be somewhere more private with Oliver, alone on a desert island, the two of them, bathing in the sun on golden sand, skinny-dipping in the turquoise waters, kissing. "I will sort this out, Oliver. Please give me another chance. Don't leave."

With a visible gulp, Oliver finally nodded, even if the gesture was hesitant. "Why didn't you tell me about her, and your situation in general, before?"

Max gestured for them to sit on a fancy couch tucked in the corner. Though covered in velvet cushions, the seating was less than comfortable. Max had known this conversation lay ahead, but he had hoped to whisk Oliver away in a whirlwind romance and cloud his judgment so that when the ugly truth came out, it wouldn't be enough to drive a wedge between them.

"I-I was afraid you would decide to up and leave right then and there," Max confessed. "And I wasn't ready to leave you in the past, like a dream from a night before. I'm still not ready."

Oliver shook his head, though the exact emotion behind it remained murky. "That wasn't your call to make. My ex, the jackass, you remember him? He cheated on me and lied about it for months. I'm lucky I didn't catch anything from that miserable jerk. But you? I thought you were different. Honest."

"I am," Max assured him as best he could after being caught in a lie by omission. "Despite my brother's antics and my mother's blind insistence, nothing will ever come of Kira and me. She and I are not in love, and we will never marry, not each other anyway."

Oliver seemed a bit relieved upon hearing that, but Max found it difficult to gauge his mood. "I don't want to cause friction between you and... her and your mother and your family. Maybe I should go. Maybe this was a bad idea."

Max shook his head. "No, Oliver. You don't really believe that, and neither do I. We are good together, you and I—"

"In bed," Oliver interjected and cut a bloody gash across Max's heart, hopes, and dreams. "Perhaps we should leave things at that, at great times in the sack, but not try to be anything more."

At first Max couldn't tell if Oliver really meant that. Then he heard a hint of underlying sadness and saw a shadow of resignation pass over Oliver's animated face. That merely served to strengthen Max's resolve not to surrender.

"Now I'm certain you don't mean that." He took Oliver's trembling hands in his. "Do not give up on me yet, Oliver Reed. Give me one last chance."

Oliver wavered. "I don't want to be the other woman. Does this Kira believe she is going to be your wife? Does she want to? Does she… love you?"

Max appreciated Oliver's reluctance to step on another's toes, especially in affairs of the heart. That simply made Oliver shine more brightly in Max's eyes. Like following elusive, mysterious fairy lights, Max hoped Oliver's moral compass wouldn't lead him astray. Why did this matter so much to him? Max had tried to figure that out most of the past spring but found no answers as of yet. What made Oliver so special and worthy of this dedication and level of pursuit? Max couldn't give a rational reply. Maybe one day.

"Kira does care for me, I think," Max offered in the spirit of honesty. "I've known her all our lives. We played together as children. But love? I doubt it. She has never shown any signs of that kind of devotion."

Oliver chuckled suddenly, surprising Max. "You're gay, like me, but you sure don't know a lot about women if that's your take on things. Women can appear one way on the outside but inside be another. What you see is what you get is true for men but not for women."

Max smiled wickedly. "And, um, what makes you such an expert?"

Oliver blushed. Max had his answer. Oliver hadn't always known he was gay, or he was bi. He'd slept with girls. It wasn't a deal breaker for Max. In any case, that experience and/or knowledge put Oliver ahead of Max in many ways.

"Aren't you a dark horse," Max murmured, leaning into his companion.

Oliver smiled bashfully. "You might have better luck betting on Ellie. She sure showed your brother. What's up with him? Is he, like, a homophobe or something?"

Max's mood sank. "Johann grew up knowing he would likely never have to take the throne. Born to high station, no responsibilities—"

"Only the wealth and prestige of being a member of the royal family?" Oliver finished for him. "I get why that would make him a first-class douchebag, but a racist one too?"

Max didn't have to be a mind reader to anticipate where this was going. World War II had happened nearly a century ago, but old sins cast long shadows. The evil legacy of the Nazis endured. And Noricia was awfully close to Germany. Back then they had been overrun, like so many other European countries. They had not collaborated with the Nazis, and as a result their towns and castles had been bombed, their people killed or enslaved, and their treasures stolen or burned. Even after all this time, they were still recovering.

"Johann believes in entitlement by birthright," Max replied with caution. He didn't want to sell his brother short. "Not specifically white people. Just royalty and aristocracy."

Oliver harrumphed. "His comment was racist. But if he believes blue bloods deserve to stay at the top and rule over everyone else stuck in the muck, then he's a fascist too."

Max nodded slowly. Fascist leaders were on the rise all over the world; finding one in one's own family didn't seem that big of a stretch. Yet he hoped Oliver's interpretation was wrong and that Johann was simply too young to know any better. He hung out with the wrong crowd, that was for sure. He was easily influenced, and those von Thürer twins, for example, did him no favors. But to leap to the conclusion Johann was inherently bad? No, the big brother in Max refused to believe that.

"I'm sorry," Oliver whispered. "I didn't mean to suggest your brother's, like, a lost cause or something. Maybe I'm reading too much into—"

"No, you don't have to apologize, not after that racist joke." Renewed anger reared its ugly head inside Max. "I'm sorry he said those things, and I'm even sorrier if he really thinks those things. That's not the John I know and love."

Oliver squeezed Max's hand. "Or maybe he just thought his words would be a funny jest. Having a bad sense of humor doesn't automatically mean he's a bad person."

Hearing Oliver defend Johann even after their disastrous introduction lifted Max's mood, and his heart skipped a beat. His determination to keep Oliver close grew.

"Listen. We'll figure all this out, I promise. My brother, my parents, my... non-fiancée. All that. But you can't bear witness to any of it if you're not here."

At Max's final plea, Oliver smiled. "Okay."

And so, with one word, Oliver brought Max out of the shadows and into the light.

Chapter 14

MAX AND I found Lady Kira von Montfort-Bregenz in the Conservatory. No point in wasting time to assess the competition for Max's affections, if she was that.

Arched glass ceilings and walls revealed a stunning vista of rolling green hills and distant snowy peaks, vast meadows dotted by wildflowers and tall dark green trees in expansive forests. Inside, a tropical jungle surrounded us, with the scent of orchids and the smell of wet, warm dirt floating about. I felt surrounded by life and nature in all its glory.

The scene was almost enough to reduce me to tears—had I not noticed the young lady seated at a white wicker table on a white wicker chair.

While I was still mad at Max for keeping this liaison a secret from me, I sort of understood too. If Max was telling the truth and there was nothing between him and this woman, then maybe it could be seen as unimportant. Maybe. Could I be that mature and civilized? That remained to be seen.

"Your Highness." Lady Kira spotted us approaching and stood with a swift, graceful move that would have put swans to shame. She curtsied, her head bowed. She made the gesture seem natural and effortless. I was glad I wasn't a girl, because I'd never learn that.

"Lady Kira." Max bowed to her, if a tad stiffly. After straightening up, he gestured at me. "This is my dear friend, Oliver Reed."

The way Max emphasized the word *dear* made me grimace inwardly. Way to rub someone's nose in it.

I offered my hand in greeting, and Kira accepted. She held my hand as lightly as bird, and I was afraid to really shake in case I ended up breaking those delicate bones.

"Nice to meet you," I said, hoping to sound polite and kind.

Her smile, though courteous, stayed aloof. "The pleasure is all mine, Mr. Reed." She had a Swiss accent, but she nonetheless spoke fluent English.

I longed to ask her then and there if she had designs on Max. But surely that would have been rude beyond belief. I curbed my curiosity and prayed for patience.

For a moment an awkward silence reigned. I could hear birds chirping, leaves rustling, and the drip-drop of sprinklers and tiny fountains. Low to the ground, the glass of the greenhouse was colored. but higher up it was clear. The air was hot and humid. I detested both. But Kira seemed perfectly suited, not a tear of sweat on her skin and not a crease in her dress. I guess that was her talent. She portrayed a consummate aristocrat.

Could I go for chitchat? "This place is lovely," I said, waving about at the Conservatory.

It was Max, however, who responded, foiling me. "Thank you, Oliver. Though a separate structure, this Conservatory is themewise connected to a botanical garden and an orangerie on a tier lower down the mountainside."

I blinked in confusion. "What's an orangerie?"

Max winked at me. "Just a fancy word for a greenhouse with fruit trees."

Out of the corner of my eye, I observed Kira hide a smile behind her hand. I blushed with shame. Was that a word everyone should know? I felt like an idiot.

Then Kira said, "Don't worry, Mr. Reed. Apart from the tour map of Riten Castle, no one here uses that word." Kira looked at Max, chiding him with a theatrical glare, but her smile gave her away.

Max chuckled. "What she said." His warm gaze landed on her— and I felt a surprising sting of jealousy. "You always know the right thing to do, Kira."

The young lady quirked an eyebrow. "Yes, Your Highness. I do."

Their relationship seemed amiable and close despite Max's assertions to the contrary. What was the old adage? How best friends made for the best lovers and life partners? *Shit*.

"Excuse us, Your Highness," Kira said then, her tone betraying nothing of her mood. "May I have a private word with Mr. Reed?"

An icy chill shot through me, freezing me in place for a long instant. Max seemed concerned. Finally, with a visible gulp, he nodded. "I'll be outside in the waiting room."

"Which one, exactly?" Kira remarked with a roll of her eyes and a lopsided grin. "There are hundreds in this damn place." Wow, she cursed in front of a prince too. The two of them had to be close, no matter what Max swore.

"Bite your tongue. You're a freaking lady," Max scolded her before giving me a sympathetic look and walking away, her laugh escorting his departure.

And so I was alone in a literal hot seat with *my* prince's bride-to-be.

I SAT on a chair opposite the lady who could be the future queen of the land. It was so warm and damp in the greenhouse that my clothes stuck to my skin. Or was the sweating the result of my poor nerves?

"Please, if it's too hot for you, take your shirt off," Kira advised.

I blushed before I realized I was wearing both a T-shirt and a dress shirt, the latter given to me by Max on the plane. New formal clothing had been waiting on the jet for us, each the perfect size and cut. Remarkable what you could do with money.

So I yanked off my white dress shirt that sported wet spots under my armpits and around my collar. That sure didn't help the redness evaporate from my face. I left my T-shirt on and tried to ease my uncomfortable jeans from my thighs. I wasn't particularly successful.

I scrambled to find something to say to fill the awkward silence. But what did you say to your lover's bride-to-be without mentioning the rainbow-colored elephant in the room?

"I like your name," I murmured sheepishly.

Kira smiled in gratitude. "Thank you, Mr. Reed. Half of my lineage hails from the Prussian Empire. My grandmother was the cousin, twice removed, of Grand Duchess Kira of Russia. I was named in honor of her."

"Cool." In hindsight, I probably could have been more eloquent, but that was the first word that came to mind. "So, uh, you're, like, a lady of leisure?" I asked, both out of curiosity and to keep the conversation going.

Kira shook her head a little. "No, I'm the President of the Norician Palace Department. I'm in charge of a large organization dedicated to the preservation and maintenance of Norician cultural heritage—everything from castles, mansions, and chapels to gardens, lakes, and ruins."

My eyebrows rose to my hairline; I felt it. "Wow, that's even cooler."

Kira cocked her head, her smile staying firmly in place. "You know what… Oliver? I believe you actually mean that. Yes, I think I see why Maximilian likes you so much."

The blood drained from my face. Yet I was perspiring all over. Maybe it was just the humidity. "Oh." That had to be to stupidest comeback ever.

Kira shook her head with an empathetic look. "Don't worry, Oliver. I know you and Max are together. I'm not an idiot. I've been aware of Max's proclivities since early adolescence."

I wasn't sure how to react, so I asked, "But… you are engaged to him?"

Kira sighed. "It's complicated."

I snorted. "That's what Max said."

Kira chuckled. "He was right. Max and I, we played together at the royal hunting lodge near St. Gallen. We spent many a happy summer there. Our parents, perhaps seeing how well Max and I got along, decided we were the perfect match. By blood, I suppose I'm closer to royalty than…."

She didn't need to finish her sentence. To Max's parents, royals or aristocrats were better or more desirable than commoners. That didn't bode well for my chances. I slumped in defeat.

"So do you think Max's parents are more amenable to their son ending up together with a man than a… a commoner?"

I felt ridiculous and ashamed to even use that word. It should have become obsolete from civilized nations ages ago. But the truth was, the rift between the rich and the poor grew wider every year.

Kira hesitated. I couldn't read her expression. She could have had an excellent career as a diplomat—or a professional poker player.

"You should speak with them yourself," Kira said. "I imagine Max will want to introduce you to them as soon as possible, so as not to cast a shadow over the whole summer."

"What are they like?" I ventured to ask, though I wasn't sure she was willing to part with that kind of privileged information.

"King Gustav is an avid hunter and fisherman," Kira offered.

I cringed. I was an animal lover. I didn't eat red meat. I did eat fish, but not ones I'd caught or gutted myself. The mere thought roiled my poor stomach.

"He's also an historian by education," Kira continued while studying my features, obviously having realized I seemed to have little in common with the King. "And a devoted reader and fan of the classics."

I sighed. While I liked to read, I hadn't perused the classics since high school. And history was composed of books covered in dust and people turned to ashes long ago.

"Queen Colette, on the other hand, is more active," Kira moved on. "She breeds show horses, collects art, and is something of a fashionista.

Also, she grows flowers, especially orchids. The terrace gardens are her pet project."

My defeat had been written before I'd even arrived, it seemed. I was gay, but I knew nothing about fashion or art or upper crust animal hobbies or flowers. Yup, I was as good as gone already.

"What is it you do, Oliver?" Kira asked then, surprising me with her curiosity. I'd surmised she wanted nothing to do with me.

"I graduated from college this past spring. Degree in culinary arts. I'm looking for a job."

Her expression betrayed nothing of her thoughts or feelings.

Basically, I was informing her I was unemployed, poor, gay, and nonwhite. Sure, over the past couple of decades royalty had married commoners and mixed ethnicities all over the monarchies of the world. But I suspected none of them shared all of my so-called undesirable traits.

For the first time, for real, I wished I hadn't met or fallen for Max. Well, half wished.

I met her gaze as levelly as I could. "Look. I don't want to waste your time, nor am I an expert in diplomatic lingo, so… do you have feelings for Max or—"

"No."

"—or do you harbor aspirations of becoming Queen of—"

"No."

"—of Noricia…. Wait, what?" I admit I was flummoxed.

Kira giggled, not like a little girl but like a full-fledged lady, with class. "While I have no doubt that I would make a great queen, I don't believe I would make a good wife for a man I did not love." She locked gazes with me in earnest. "Do you understand?"

I nodded. "There may not be any arranged marriages in the western world anymore, but that doesn't mean marrying for love should be taken for granted."

Kira raised her chin. I could swear her outlook regarding me had changed.

"Well said, Oliver. Quite eloquent and diplomatic."

I blushed. In some ways, Kira reminded me of Elinor. Both had spunk and sass. It came out in different ways, but the underlying spirit was the same. I had to agree with her assessment: Kira probably would have made an excellent queen.

"What about a marriage of convenience?" I asked, blurting out things on my mind without further thought.

Kira laughed. "I'm willing to bet you didn't plan on saying that." As I was busy bursting into flames, she smiled. "To be honest, I'd considered that. When I was younger. But now... you see, if I marry Max, I might become queen and be able to do many wonderful things for this country. But I also wouldn't be able to marry anyone else. And I refuse to entertain the possibility of keeping an in-house lover. Many rulers have had them—some still do. I would not."

Her tiny chin jutted out defiantly; I was in awe of her. I figured that even if Max and I had no future, Max could do a hell of a lot worse than Kira. They would make a lovely power couple.

I had to shake my head then. What was I doing? Trying to matchmake my lover with a woman? I was losing my mind.

"Since we are speaking so candidly," Kira said, and a steely note brought a hard edge to her tone. "What exactly are your intentions toward Max?"

"Other than the horizontal mambo?" I quipped, immediately regretting my outburst and turning red as fire. I coughed to clear my throat as Kira quirked an eyebrow and pursed her lips to contain a laugh. "I mean, I like him. A lot. I didn't know he was a prince when we met. I just thought he was a hot guy."

Kira didn't ask for particulars. That raised her a few rungs in my estimation of her character. "And now?"

I shrugged, feeling lost and confused. "I don't know. Maybe he and I are only compatible in bed."

Kira snorted. "I highly doubt that."

I reared. "I'll have you know, Max and I rock the bed in more ways than—aaand you didn't mean it like that. Got it. Whoops. Anyway, he wasn't forthcoming about being royalty or about *you*. Both things I learned by accident." I frowned when I realized what that meant. "He claims to be an honest man but... there's some evidence to the contrary."

Kira narrowed her eyes. "'Every man has three characters: that which he exhibits, that which he has, and that which he thinks he has.' I believe it was Alphonse Karr who said that."

I frowned in bewilderment. "So?"

Suddenly Kira leaned closer and took my hand across the table. "Don't be so hard on him, Oliver. Max is forced to hide much of his true nature. But trust someone who knows him: he is a good man, honorable and honest. He simply needs the right time and place to show it."

Lately, I'd heard it said many times that things were complicated. I had to accept the likelihood that this was, in fact, an understatement. Max and Kira's relationship, for one, was vastly different from the one I'd imagined upon first hearing about their engagement.

But would there ever be a time when Max was honest of his own volition? Or was I trying to build something with another liar?

What kind of situation could I create to induce Max to display his true colors?

Chapter 15

"So, Max... have you had sex in every room in the castle?"

Max sputtered, not having expected Oliver to behave in so forward a fashion, especially after finding out about Max's engagement and lies by omission. "No, I have not. I don't think anyone in the history of this place has. Do you know how many rooms there are in here? Hundreds."

"And?" Oliver smirked. "Practice makes perfect."

Max's cheeks caught fire at the thought of making love to a beloved in the heart of his home. "You are aware that my parents live here too? And that there are security and servants and cameras, not to mention tourists, everywhere?"

Oliver shrugged. "Excuses. A house, or in your case, a castle, is not a home until you've had sex in every room. You know, to christen it."

Max chuckled. "And does that mean you've done the nasty in every room in your house back in Seattle?" Oliver stopped his aimless wanderings and smiled. His smile spread wider and wider until Max couldn't misinterpret the gesture any longer. "Well, you do get around, my dear Oliver."

Oliver's face turned ruddy, but his grin remained. Then he waved about. "This is quite a hall."

Max glanced around, but he knew the Throne Room well. As a child, he'd not been allowed to play there, but all the ceremonies involving his station as the crown prince and heir to the throne had taken place there. He wondered sometimes if perhaps he'd been able to familiarize himself with the stately hall as a kid, he wouldn't be so intimidated by it and what it entailed still.

The notion of becoming a king and sitting on that chair freaked him out. Not all the time but on occasion.

An arched ceiling created an impression of a subterranean vault, even though the cupola was painted with pictures of the sun, moon, stars, clouds, and winds. But since the hall covered two floors, there was no shortage of space. The marble floor bore a mosaic of nature imagery, with all the animals and trees of the Celtic zodiac present. The walls were either paneled in light wood or covered in rich tapestries, all picturing vines and flowers.

The Ivy Throne itself, uncomfortable in spite of the soft deep-green cushion, was made of oak. The backrest had a carving of a unicorn on it. Behind the seat, like an altar to nature, stood a statue of the triple goddess carved out of an oak tree. The maiden and the crone held on to the throne while the mother held a crown above it with both hands, as if to anoint a ruler.

"I'm willing to bet you're overjoyed that thing's not made from the melted swords of your enemies," Oliver jested, pointing at the throne.

Max laughed at the *Game of Thrones* reference. "We are a nation of peace and nature. In times of war, we've remained neutral, or secretly sided with the good guys, such as the Allied Forces against the Nazis. As for our foes, we turned them into friends."

Oliver smiled at him. "You're a romantic, sentimental sap. I like it."

Max appreciated the praise. "If I were that sentimental about the past, I'd request the three thrones of old back. You see, the land used to belong to three tribes that ruled together. Each had their own seat of power: the Juniper, the Snowbell, and the Ivy Throne…"

Max let his voice drift off when he noticed Oliver wasn't listening but was instead glancing around the hall with curiosity.

"Are those the crown jewels?" Buzzing with visible excitement, Oliver pointed at the display cases that stood on the left side of the hall from the direction of the throne. He rushed over and leaned in to inspect them.

"No, they're replicas," Max explained, joining his companion. "The real items are kept safe in the vault beneath the castle." He shrugged nonchalantly. "They are exact replicas, though."

Oliver cocked his head and studied the glittering artifacts. Max smiled, well aware that his lover was searching for flaws or oddities. Nonetheless, no one would have known they weren't the real thing at first or even second glance.

Oliver straightened, a frown between his eyebrows. "The crown looks… weird."

Max nodded and stared at the unusual piece resting on a pillow of royal purple velvet behind bulletproof glass.

Three separate crowns seemed to meld together, embedded in concentric circlets surmounted by ornaments. The rigid band was composed of bronze below, silver in the middle, and gold at the top.

Horns that spiked upward and nearly blocked each other out were shaped like the stylized leaves of plants, with bronze strawberries below, silver poplars in the middle, and gold three-leaf clovers at the top. A cap of green silk velvet, soft and billowy, covered the middle. The design choices might have seemed perplexing to the untrained eye, but their Celtic heritage accounted for them.

As for the plentiful embedded gemstones, the crown sported one hundred thirty-five diamonds, ninety-three emeralds, fifty-four sapphires, three rubies, and a single amethyst. The purple gem was a nod to the royal color, the rubies to royal blood, and the rest symbolized the sea, land, and sky.

"Why does it look like it's got three crowns superimposed?" Oliver asked, a baffled look on his face.

Max smiled. "It's called the Triskelion Crown. See the engraved symbol around some of the gems?"

Oliver leaned in again, his eyes narrowing. Slowly he nodded. "That triple spiral?"

"Yes." Max was pleased with Oliver's interest. "The triskelion image was sacred to the Celts, and it's sacred to the Reconstructionist Neo-Celts in our country as well."

"Why?" Oliver didn't seem to understand the importance of imagery, especially in matters of royalty. Max could relate. It was hard to be interested in things that had nothing to do with you. Basic human condition.

"Certain numbers, like three and nine, were important to the Celts." Max waved at the statue behind the throne. "The triple goddess—maiden, mother, and crone. She watches over us, the royal family and the throne, and judges the true value of the person sitting on it. According to lore, if anyone unworthy were to sit upon this throne, the goddess would be displeased and bring the whole mountain range of the Alps down upon us."

Oliver whistled low in awe. "Wow. Savage." Max laughed. Then Oliver pursed his lips. "Although, the castle sits on top of the mountain."

Max had to wipe tears of joy from his eyes. "It does at that."

Oliver gestured at the display again. "So, I get that the number three is a big deal for you guys, but I still don't get why three crowns had to be superimposed like that."

"For that, my dear Oliver, I would have to school you in the history, culture, and traditions of my country. Do you think you might be up for that?" Max used a teasing tone to show they didn't have to do this if Oliver found it boring.

"Oh." Oliver worried his bottom lip, appearing pensive. "Maybe later." He stepped back and forth slowly, as if doing an absentminded dance.

Max followed Oliver's gaze to the Triskelion Crown, the Clover Scepter of King Matthias I of Noricia, the coronation vestments of past kings and queens, the three rings of the country's three historical tribal leaders, the Wolfsbane Sword of Warrior Queen Beatrix V, and the Royal Trinary Star Ring of Noricia. He knew them well, especially the originals.

"They're nice crown jewels, all in all." Oliver shrugged, as if he hadn't a care in the world. "I've seen yours."

Max closed the gap between them, hugged Oliver at the waist, and bussed Oliver's exposed neck. "That you have."

Oliver wrapped his arms around Max's neck. "Say… have you ever done it on the throne? Sex, I mean? It looks sturdy enough."

Max laughed against Oliver's hair, which smelled of apple shampoo. "No, Oliver, I confess I have not." He nodded over his shoulder without looking. "You do realize there are at least a dozen security cameras, with microphones, pointed at us even as we speak? Not to mention guards standing at every entry and exit point?"

"Yeees, but…." Oliver stared at him wickedly. "They do work for you. You're their boss, so they wouldn't tell anyone, would they?"

Max kissed the tip of Oliver's nose. "Maybe not. But they would watch the whole thing from start to finish. That's their job."

"Oh." From Oliver's tone, it was hard for Max to tell if he was disappointed or still determined.

Max grinned. "I had no idea you had such kink in you, Oliver. Exhibitionism?"

Oliver's bashful blush pushed all of Max's buttons. They hadn't covered the kink subject. Sometimes it was easy for Max to forget that, overall, he'd known Oliver for a mere fortnight; there was simply a long interval between those two weeks.

Then a curious thought occurred to Max. He considered Oliver's motives for exhibitionism. Was this a subtle attempt at bringing out Max's hidden side? He was well aware he had lied to Oliver, who must have felt betrayed, especially after already being deceived by his former lover.

Perhaps this was Oliver's way of trying to see Max honest, not hiding anything, showing his true self?

"What's yours?" Oliver whispered into Max's ear, ending the suggestive, seductive murmur with a lick along Max's earlobe and a soft suck of the tender flesh there.

Max swallowed hard. He was starting to get aroused and having a tough time following his train of thought. Images of doing erotic things to Oliver clouded his mind and his judgment.

"Mine?" Max gripped handfuls of Oliver's hair and forced him to face Max. "Fucking you on that throne."

Oliver giggled, glancing at the throne over his shoulder with an assessing gaze. "And here I thought your delicate untouched flower hadn't blossomed in every room."

Max laughed at Oliver's ridiculous choice of words. "My delicate flower? Careful. I'll spank your butt till it's redder than your face."

Oliver bit his bottom lip, as if to stifle a moan. His eyes darkened, and his smile faltered. It seemed the idea of entering the domain of kink excited the young American. Max purred inwardly at the multitude of possibilities that bloomed inside his imaginative mind.

Gripping Oliver's hips tight, Max started to steer Oliver backward toward the Ivy Throne.

Oliver gasped, and his eyes widened in shock. "Max? Y-you weren't serious... w-were you?"

Max offered his companion a mischievous grin, fully intent on delivering on his promise.

Oliver shook his head vehemently. "N-no, Max, you can't. We can't. I was effing kidding."

"I wasn't," Max replied and continued to push Oliver back till he hit the lowest step and had to fumble up toward the royal seat.

Just when Max had Oliver where he wanted him, tumbling buttfirst onto the throne with an astonished look on his face, a loud knock came from the double doors. Without waiting to be bidden entry, Lawana walked in. She neither bowed nor curtsied. And whatever she thought of the situation, with Max pinning Oliver to the Ivy Throne, forever remained a mystery.

"Your Highness, your parents are ready to meet you and your guests."

Max sighed and nodded. Oliver blew out a breath of relief, sagging on the royal seat. Max chuckled and watched with delight as Oliver flushed as red as the cutest tomato on the planet.

Max cussed low. "Damn. Cockblocked by my own chief of security. Should I fire her?"

Oliver leaned in and kissed the tip of Max's nose and then his lips, the touch soft and fleeting. "Considering she just saved you from making an ass of yourself in front of your entire security force behind the cameras, I think she deserves praise and a raise."

"I agree," Lawana deadpanned.

Max cupped Oliver's cheeks and kissed him again. "I beg to differ, my dear Oliver. I dare say it was you who was about to make an ass of himself."

Oliver's cheeks turned even ruddier. Laughter bubbled inside Max like champagne. He had never felt this happy with a boyfriend before. Because that was what Oliver was to him.

Could Max make his parents see that too?

Chapter 16

I'D THOUGHT the Throne Room was impressive. But the Grand Gallery was truly awe-inspiring.

Max and I were guided to the entrance by Lawana and a stiff but polite butler-type woman—a Lady Usher called Wilhelmina van Apeldoorn, apparently—in an impeccable uniform that hugged her form like armor. As if I wasn't already overwhelmed.

My family already stood at the closed doors, waiting for us. I winced thinking how late Max and I could have been, and the mussed-up state we would have been in. I doubted I would have been allowed to even meet the King and Queen stinking of sex.

Elinor smirked knowingly at me, and my cheeks flamed.

"Shut up," I told her, even though she hadn't uttered so much as a syllable.

Before the doors opened, the Lady Usher instructed us how to bow and curtsey, how to address the King and Queen, and how to shake hands. The rules of etiquette were quite complicated, I mulled glumly. I would have thought that living in the twenty-first century had done away with such pointless rituals by now.

Finally, the Lady Usher left. The wide, tall wooden double doors opened with a deep boom. I shivered with trepidation.

A towering woman approached us, her stern expression promising swift revenge for any and all offenses. Her black hair was cut short in a bob, and her dark eyes inspected us from above a regal nose that resembled the beak of an eagle. She had on a dark blue uniform with a white sash across it and medals pinned to her chest. Clearly, she was someone important.

"Family Reed-Ruíz?" she inquired, her deep, husky voice surprising me with its bass tones. It was a powerful, commanding voice, like that of a military general. When we silently nodded, she declared, "I am Gudrun Kühl, the Marshal of Ceremonies. I will present you to Their Majesties. I trust the Lady Usher has instructed you on proper etiquette?" After we had once again nodded our affirmatives, she waved. "Follow me."

So my family and I, plus Max, entered the lion's den.

On the left side of the Grand Gallery, floor-to-ceiling windows, interspersed with large french doors, provided illumination. One the right, tall crystal mirrors added a sense of space and reflected the light. Gilded chandeliers and numerous wall sconces turned the room into a prism of rainbow-colored sparks. I felt I might go blind.

The air was cool in spite of the sunshine. Most of the french doors were open, letting in the crisp mountain winds. I was relieved. Though the halls, rooms, and corridors of Riten Castle were all large, it was still summer, and it was hot inside. Plus, the Grand Gallery was facing southwest.

There were no pieces of furniture anywhere in sight. The vaulted ceiling with its graceful wooden arches was comprised of numerous murals and relief carvings depicting Celtic myths and divinities, nature motifs and symbols, and scenes from the history of the kingdom. I wasn't aware I was staring like a village yokel until my sister jabbed me in the side with her elbow.

Only then did I notice the other people in the room.

Even without crowns or capes, jewels or medallions, it was easy to tell who was who.

King Gustav stood as tall as his son, but he was thinner, and his shoulders slumped slightly, as if he spent a great deal of time hunched behind a desk. Paperwork was endless, it seemed, even for royalty. His silver hair was cut short, and he had no beard, but he had a pencil mustache, thin and white. Somehow he made it work. His face and body appeared bony, with sharp edges, and his eyes were a colder shade of blue than Max's. If there existed a stereotypical mid-European look for men, he embodied it.

The King stood with his hands behind his back in a military pose. He wore a suit and tie, the former charcoal gray, the latter the same shade of icy blue as his eyes. A silver tie pin with diamonds added a touch of quality, as did the signet ring on his left pinky.

Queen Colette was a stark contrast to her husband. She was short and curvaceous, and her features had a graceful softness to them. Her golden hair, trapped in a simple coiffure, had a few silver strands here and there, giving her an aura of otherworldly beauty. I suspected she'd been coveted by all the men back in the day. Her eyes were light green with hints of blue, like a delicate work of art portraying an ethereal spring.

She wore a pale green Chanel tunic, cinched with a light-brown belt with a gilded buckle that fit her round figure and accentuated it in all the right places, the way only an elegant designer dress could without drawing attention to her weight. Or at least that was how I envisioned women's dresses were meant to work, not being an expert or anything. Like her husband, she wore no distinct jewelry.

The King and Queen were the main attraction, to be sure. The couple we had arrived to meet. Max's parents.

But they weren't the only ones in the room waiting for us. Two other men stood there, slightly to the back, perhaps due to their lower status.

While King Gustav carried his age well, one of the other men did not. Lanky and pasty, he had a gray mustache and beard, gray hair, and gray eyes. His whole look and demeanor, even his suit and tie, were dull and void of color. I wondered if he really was as boring as his appearance suggested.

But his eyes held a steely glint as he stared at me—with open hostility. He didn't even bother to hide it. So either a career politician whose facade had cracked, or a novice who hadn't yet learned to disguise his feelings. Either way, it was obvious I'd made an enemy in absentia.

The other man was short and portly and exuberant, his hazel eyes twinkling, his pudgy lips smiling, his bald head—adorned with Celtic tribal tattoos—gleaming, and his green robes making him seem like either an actor in a fantasy or an escaped mental patient who thought he was a wizard. His smile was earnest, and he bowed eagerly at me.

I smiled rather awkwardly and nodded back.

The Marshal of Ceremonies cleared her throat and, with a surprisingly far-reaching voice, declared, "The Reed-Ruíz family from the United States of America: Paulito, Valerie, Oliver, and Elinor." Then, after a short pause, perhaps for drama, she boomed, "His Royal Highness, King Gustav IV Caspar of Noricia. Her Royal Highness, Queen Colette II Sophia of Noricia."

I gulped. I'd met the parents of boyfriends before, but this was on a whole other level of awkward and surreal. Their gazes were level, their expressions inscrutable, their statuesque presence inexplicable. I couldn't read them at all. What did they want from us?

The back of Max's hand touched mine. Like a ship caught in a tempest, I reached for his offered anchor, seeking a grounding force. His instinctive awareness of my unspoken needs made my heart skip a beat.

I also didn't know whom to address first.

Thankfully, my father came to the rescue. As the head of our family—or so my mother let him think—Paulito Ruíz approached the royal couple, stopped in front of King Gustav, bowed his head so expertly I wondered if he'd done it secretly his whole life, and then extended his hand for a greeting.

"Thank you for inviting us, Your Majesty. On the flight here, I studied the castle brochure. This Grand Gallery is stunning. The history shown here is rich and fascinating."

Flummoxed, I stared at my father's unassuming conduct, so natural and humble, yet in no way obsequious or fake. He was my idol. As a Mexican American, Paulito had a traditional masculine role engrained in him since childhood, but his true nature was kind and quiet, hardworking and honest. He didn't need to show off to anyone.

The King shook my father's hand. "Welcome to Noricia, Mr. Ruíz. If you are interested in the history of the land, I hope you and I will be able to converse on the topic."

Paulito nodded. "History was always my favorite subject in school, Your Majesty."

A small smile tugged at the corners of Gustav's lips. "Mine too."

I noted he had a distinct German intonation, different from his son's soft French accent. The King had a composed voice, a bit thinner that I would have expected. Nonetheless, he was used to public speaking.

Paulito faced Queen Colette, bowed, and shook her hand. "Your castle is truly a wondrous place, Your Majesty."

Queen Colette inclined her head minutely. "Yes, we are privileged to call Riten Castle home. You are most welcome."

Her voice had a melodic cadence, as though she was more used to singing than speaking. I wondered what she would sound like belting out a song at the top of her lungs. Probably amazing.

Valerie joined Paulito, curtsied, and shook both the King's and Queen's hands.

Where Paulito had behaved in a calm manner, Valerie smiled radiantly. Her joy had always been infectious. It had brought poor shy Paulito out of his shell when they had met as teenagers.

Now I watched her magic work on Queen Colette. They shared a few words about fashion, gardening, and the castle itself. A smile now graced Colette's full lips as well. I could finally see where Max had inherited his luscious lips. At the thought of Max's mouth, I blushed like a damn teen.

My parents waved me and Elinor closer. I had hoped to make a better impression than that of a red-faced yokel. Too late now.

"N-nice to meet you, Your M-Majesty," I squeaked, my voice breaking as I shook hands with King Gustav. Mine were hot and sweaty, his strong, smooth, and cool. I was so embarrassed.

When the King quirked an eyebrow, I could have kicked myself stupid. Apparently stating the obvious—what an honor, pleasure, or privilege it was to meet a royal—was bad form. The Lady Usher had told us this, but my muddled brain had forgotten the rules of etiquette. I could only pray the royal family wouldn't hold my faux pas against me.

Elinor took charge of the situation, addressing the Queen. "The terraced gardens outside are simply divine, Your Majesty. You must employ hundreds of groundskeepers. I love trees. Seeing so many and so well maintained… I'm in love."

I cringed inwardly. Informal was Elinor's natural state, although I couldn't quite decide if her flow of words qualified in this instance.

Queen Colette, at least, seemed pleased, her cautious smile widening. "You are kind, child. Unlike the King and your father, biology was my favorite subject in school. I do believe I fell for the gardens at Riten Castle before my husband."

Her warm glance at King Gustav subtly demonstrated their close relationship. I envied their bond. I wanted to love and be loved for the rest of my life too. Girls were taught to want that, but guys should be allowed to get in on that action, in my humble opinion.

"Aww." Elinor's whisper made the Queen giggle. She had magically broken the ice between us. I considered that a win—for my sister anyway. Too bad Max wasn't courting *her*.

How could it be that of all four of us, I had given the worst impression when I'd had the most time to prepare?

THE MARSHAL continued. "The Right Honorable Karl von Thürer, prime minister of Noricia. His Holiness, Grand Druid Theo Weiss."

During the first declaration, the tall, thin man nodded stiffly, the gesture so small I would have missed it if I'd blinked. At the second introduction, the short, plump man bowed deeply from the waist, the edges of his robes sweeping the floor.

I knew instantly which man I liked and which I disliked.

All of a sudden, Valerie chuckled. "Grand… what?"

I was mortified. "Mom!"

Valerie had the good grace to look ashamed and blush. I'd inherited that trait from her—times a dozen.

"You're Catholic?" King Gustav asked my mother, who nodded along with my father.

I shook my head to steer attention away from my parents, whose beliefs contradicted the faith of the land—and my own. "I was baptized, but I'm not particularly religious, Your Majesty."

Max squeezed my hand and smiled. "Neither am I."

The prime minister growled. "It's a disgrace that the future king of our country refuses to adhere to the spiritual traditions of our people." As anticipated by his appearance, his voice was dull and monotonous, as if sentences were nothing more than a string of gray pearls that never ended, not even for something as mundane as breathing.

"Tsk," the Grand Druid scolded, wagging a fat finger about. "Ours is a religion of nature, peace, and harmony. For the prince to deny his true nature and pretend to have faith would be a worse transgression. Not everyone receives the gift of faith. Doubt serves a purpose, too, in the grand scheme of things."

Karl von Thürer crossed his arms over his chest. "You're too accommodating for your office, Theo. The prince seems to have forgotten that Celtic beliefs are our state religion. What kind of example is he setting by—"

"He is following his nature," the Grand Druid interjected. "That is all we can ask of a man."

"That, and that he betters himself," von Thürer cut in, grimacing.

"You don't need religious belief to be better," Elinor said out of the blue, startling the two arguing men. "Simply claiming to be religious seems to excuse folks at churches or temples or mosques of all sorts of ugliness, which it shouldn't."

"Ah. We have a true skeptic among us." Theo Weiss laughed and bowed to my outspoken sister. "In my humble opinion, faith and ethos are not mutually exclusive."

Elinor rolled her eyes. "If your faith tells you you're exonerated from everything bad you've ever done simply by being a member of the church, your faith is all wrong, because that is not how morality or culpability work—"

"Ellie, please stop," I murmured. This had gone on long enough. My sister could turn any discussion into an argument if she had an opposing viewpoint. A meet and greet with my boyfriend's parents didn't seem like it should be one of them.

Elinor bit her lower lip and nodded. "Sorry, Ollie. Didn't meant to get on a soapbox."

"You have firm opinions, a strong backbone, and a sharp tongue, young woman," Queen Collette said with a quirk of her lips. "I like that in a young person. It gives me hope for the future."

"And the fact she insulted me, the Grand Druid, and Your Majesties at the same time is of no consequence, ma'am?" Karl von Thürer said with a prickly expression.

Queen Collette narrowed her eyes. "If a man cannot stand a jab at his politics or his faith without becoming angered, then he is not much of a man."

King Gustav sighed and cut in, "Careers in politics should have taught all of us tolerance and patience. Words cannot hurt us. Therefore, we shouldn't overreact to them."

The prime minister looked like he'd swallowed a lemon. I wondered how such an angry man had become a part of the government of a land that seemed so peaceful. For the record, I despised Karl von Thürer already. Him and his kids.

Frederica, the Royal Press Officer, entered and hurried over to the King and Queen. "Your Majesties, your meeting with the Austrian delegates is scheduled to take place in twelve minutes in the Clover Drawing Room."

I stared. She must have had one hell of an internal clock. That, or she had a cheat sheet on her tablet or notebook. Under those clothes, Frederica must have had strong arms for carrying all that around.

"Very well," King Gustav said with a curt nod.

"Thank you, Freddie," Queen Colette added with a warm smile. She turned her attention to me and my family. Well, mostly me. "I hope my husband and I get to enjoy your company again in a less formal gathering."

Then she and the King sailed out of the room with Frederica in tow.

Almost to the second, once the door had closed, Karl von Thürer seemed to have concluded there was no need for polite pretense. He bowed to Max so minutely that, in my eyes at least, it bordered on disrespect. Then he left the room as well, head held high.

Theo Weiss approached Max and me with an apologetic smile. "He just can't help himself." Then he shook my hand forcefully but kindly with both hands. "Welcome to Noricia, Mr. Reed, and to Riten Castle.

I'm sure we'll be seeing each other again, if not before then at the Solstice Festival. Good day."

He bowed with a flourish, grinned at Max, and waddled out of the room with surprising speed.

"What an unusual dude," I commented.

Max chuckled. "Theo is a character all right." He touched my arm, a tender gesture I saw as almost too intimate for public view. "So? How was it? Did this compare with meeting your other boyfriends' parents?"

I smiled. "They're a bit reserved. Not like my folks at all. But I liked them. And they didn't seem to hate me."

Max harrumphed, pursing his lips. "Why would they? You're adorable."

Given my mistakes at court etiquette, Max's statement was a bold-faced lie. But I appreciated the sentiment. In any case, I'd finally met the King and Queen, and I'd survived, if not entirely unscathed, at least mostly so. Did this gathering bode well? I dared to hope.

Now that social responsibility had been taken care of, though, I could look forward to my summer-long dalliance with Max. And I had so many delicious plans.

Chapter 17

DESPITE THE awkwardness of the first meeting with King Gustav and Queen Colette, the following two weeks proved beyond fine.

My family scattered to the four winds. Paulito and King Gustav spent a great deal of time together, discussing history, infrastructure, or fishing. Valerie and Queen Collette found a common interest in gardening, and the two could walk and talk for hours on end in the terraced gardens. As for Elinor… well, she found her own amusement by becoming Karl von Thürer's shadow. Wherever he went, she was there too, arguing over every conservative thing imaginable, never once letting herself be put off by the maelstroms of fury the prime minister was capable of.

And me? I ignored everything in favor of spending time with Max. From what his mother had implied, my relationship with Max had an expiration date.

Which was becoming a problem because my feelings for Max grew every day. Not because I was lost in the luxury and glamour, privilege and excitement. Max was a dream come true. All my life I'd wanted to be with a man who would be honest with me, a true gentleman, a prince among men. I'd dated enough cheats and liars and jerks. Max was different.

Or… was I simply lying to myself? Because I had not really forgotten the fact that Max had been less than forthcoming with me about Lady Kira. Was my whole affair with Max just wishful thinking, a fantasy brought to life briefly but never forever?

Yet it was hard to remember those things when I lay in Max's arms in silk sheets in a king-size canopy bed in the Snake Tower or when trekking along green hills while holding his hands or exploring every nook and cranny at Riten Castle.

It was amazing how many out-of-sight places there were outdoors in the hills and how many blind spots there were in the castle. Cozy chalets, cool woodland copses, shadowy rocky crags, and lush Alpine meadows gave shelter for Max and me to spend our love, whether under a golden sun or a silver moon. Inside, the castle had named rooms, like the Throne Room or the Grand Gallery, that all had unseen surveillance systems. But the unnamed rooms, like anterooms and private quarters, didn't, so those were the spaces Max and I employed for our sexual escapades.

I was not seduced by my surroundings as much as I was drunk off him. Max was like a drug that coursed through my veins, granting me endless waves of pleasure.

That being said, I did like the ease with which everything flowed. I'd never had this sort of relaxation where I didn't need to think about whether I had enough money for food or my phone's payment plan or books for school or clothes to wear. Here, everything was free. Sort of. I knew the taxpayers of the kingdom paid for the food I ate, the power I used to charge my phone and laptop, the roof over my head, the bed I slept in. It was heady to feel like nothing had a cost when in truth I knew better.

One night, as Max I sat together in a large lounge chair on the balcony of his tower, a grand view of the entire valley and the peaks beyond below us, I had to ask. "Do you ever feel entitled by not having to worry about stuff like money? Your people pay for your upkeep and—"

"Sort of," Max cut in, bussing the top of my head, since it rested over his chest as I was half lying on top of him. "The king receives an allowance from the Treasury. It's called a sovereign grant. It's basically his cut of the profits from crown-owned estates, while the rest is given to the Council of Ministers to dispatch for the welfare of our country. Other members of our royal family receive income from our own estates. None of them are salaries, if that is what you're after. Our work is royal work, but it's not the same as regular work. Ours is a rich family even without the royal titles. We own land, property, and businesses. This castle is kept under the watchful eye of a government supervisory board, but we own it, along with many others. These crown estates are national monuments, but they're also, strictly speaking, the property of my family."

I raised my head to peer into his eyes. "So, if you weren't a prince anymore, you'd still have money?"

Max grinned. "I am a man of means." As he said that, his hands slipped lower onto the small of my back and then dipped to cup my buttcheeks.

I giggled. "You mean an octopus, don't you, with your wandering hands?"

"You disapprove?" Max teased, lifting his hands theatrically over his head.

"Dumbass," I reproached him in a playful tone. I pushed up with my hands and kissed him. His sweet taste flooded my mouth and my senses.

He swept me away with his embrace. An hour or so later, we could check off sex on the tower balcony in our sex-in-the-castle bucket list.

Why was I asking him about his fortunes? Was I secretly hoping that he'd stop being an heir to the throne so I could have him all to myself? I had to admit that was pretty selfish of me.

Then I realized, apart from a few reservations Max had expressed, I didn't really know what he wanted out of life. Maybe he wanted to become King of Noricia after all? For his family, his people, and his country?

Later that night, I returned to the balcony, leaving Max asleep in the fabulous bed. I stared out into the dark summer night. Unfamiliar stars blanketed the sky above me, and tiny flickering lights dotted the river valley below, proof of the settlements there. The scent of pines and other evergreen tree sap wafted into my nose, an odor I knew well from my home. Yet here, in a foreign land, they seemed strange and magical.

I didn't know my place here. Was that the reason I was wondering if Max could give up being a prince? Because I knew I couldn't stay here, doing nothing but looking hot on the prince's arm at banquets and formal functions? I could not be a trophy husband. I wanted my life to mean something, for my actions to matter, for me to leave a legacy of my own, hopefully to better the world by improving myself.

Where did a love affair fit into my plans for the future? Did it at all, in spite of my growing feelings for Max?

All I had were questions. And underneath these strange stars, I had no answers.

A SMALL brook bubbled beside me as I walked on a dirt road winding through green meadows dotted with colorful flowers. The scent of fresh earth, delicate flowers, and clean air made me heady. A well-maintained wooden fence separated the path from the rising conifers that sloped up the mountainside. The path led downward toward the valley far below. Behind me and far ahead of me, the snowy peaks of a rugged gray range made me feel small. It was hard to gauge distances, but here it wasn't the destination that mattered but the journey.

"Is that a good spot?" I asked, pointing at a field covered in bright yellow dandelions. The meadow spanned far and wide, and we had an unobstructed view in all directions. The scents of fresh grass and evergreen resin floated in the air, and birds sang unseen in the foliage.

Max nodded with a smile. "Go ahead. Spread the cloth; I'll bring the basket."

I hopped over the fence to wade through the ankle-high grass. I didn't know if it had been mowed or if this was as high as it got around here. Nonetheless, I made my way to a sunny spot, laid down the checkered woolly blanket we'd brought with us, and plopped down. The sun was hot on my face, and I adjusted my sunglasses so I wouldn't go sunblind.

Max ambled slower, his gaze sweeping the hills and woods and streams. I watched him come closer. Unlike me in my tourist-casual T-shirt, jeans, and sneakers, Max had opted for slacks, a dress shirt with the sleeves rolled up and top buttons open, and a vest to hold it all in place. He looked good enough to eat.

"What are you looking at?" he asked as he sat down opposite me with the basket between us. I didn't know if it was the sun twinkling in his eyes or joy. Either way, it was a great look for him.

"You," I confessed. "I can't decide if I'm hungrier for picnic snacks... or you."

Max ducked his head, but I saw the cute bashful smile he sported. "Thank you, my sweet Oliver."

He moved aside the little red-and-white checkered cloth from on top of the basket and placed several plastic containers onto the blanket. Roasted, salted chicken wings with sweet-and-spicy sauce, caramelized apple slices, chorizo crostinis with apricot jam, prosciutto-apricot focaccia, asparagus, pea, and radish salad, creamy potato salad, old-fashioned lemonade, blackberry-almond cake, spongy brownies, mojito-dipped watermelons... I was salivating just staring at the dishes as delicious aromas wafted into my nose.

"Dig in," Max said, waving at the picnic offerings.

I didn't need to be told twice. I gobbled huge chunks of everything. Once sweet, sour, and savory balanced on my tongue and my stomach rumbled its thanks, I glanced over Max's shoulder.

"Would she like to join us? We have plenty here."

Max shook his head. "No. Lawana would never allow herself to get distracted while on duty. Not even by a rumbling stomach. Then again, she eats like a bird. I thought having access to luxury cuisine would get to her, but nothing does. She can't be persuaded."

"Even with foods like this?" I blew out a breath. "She's crazy."

Max chuckled. "Crazy good at her job."

We munched on the meal for a while, enjoying the crisp mountain air, the bright sunshine, the soft meadow beneath us, the babbling brook close by. Everything was so idyllic, the vista picture perfect. I sighed with contentment.

Things began to feel awfully surreal, as if all this was happening to someone else.

"Max?" He faced me in quiet anticipation. I hesitated, wondering how to phrase my thoughts. "I know you grew up here, at Riten Castle, but… don't you ever feel like you're missing out?"

Max cocked his head like a baffled dog. "What do you mean?"

"Everyday stuff, you know?" When Max shook his head, I clarified, "You have a whole staff dedicated to your, um, whims."

Max chuckled. "My whims?"

I waved about in general, harrumphing in frustration. "Come on. Like, isn't it weird to know some stranger is, for example, washing your dirty underwear?"

Max laughed. "Oh, you're talking about chores." I nodded, so Max went on, "Doing the laundry or the dishes, vacuuming or dusting, making dinner or going grocery shopping, is that it? I'm missing out on the minutiae of everyday life in a relationship?"

"Yes." I studied him, curious about his attitudes. "Doesn't it ever bother you that those are mundane things everyone who lives outside of a castle has to do on a daily basis—except you?"

Max winked at me. "How do you know I've never done my own laundry?"

I snorted. "Maybe it's me, but I can't see you bending over a washing machine or sauntering about with a dust buster."

Max grinned. "In this image of yours, am I wearing a maid's little black outfit of frilly lace?"

My jaw dropped in surprise. Max had a way of lofting bombs on me. There was so much I didn't know about him. "Stop. I don't want to get a damn hard-on outside in front of your bodyguard, okay?"

Max chuckled, amused by my embarrassed blushing. Finally, he said, "It is different, I grant you that. My lifestyle compared to yours. It's true that I don't have to do any household chores every day. A staff of over a hundred strong does that for me, my brothers, and my parents, not to mention friends and guests staying at the castle."

I nodded. "Was it odd for you back at my family home on Whidbey Island? You saw how I live. My small room that I had to clean twice a week, my dishes I had to wash after using them, my own laundry I had to do. I'm not a, what's it called, a gentleman of leisure, like you."

Max shrugged. "Wealth and privilege have their advantages."

I frowned. "I don't know if I could live like that. For a time? Sure, it's awesome not having to worry about that stuff and just being able to enjoy myself. But in the long run? It's weird to say, I know, but I think I'd miss doing my own laundry and shit."

"If that's the case," Max drawled, grinning at me. "I'm sure we can make that happen. You can stay here and always do your own laundry. I'll be sure to inform the staff."

"You're missing my point," I growled but couldn't help smiling. The lengths he was willing to go for me warmed my heart.

"Oh shush," Max scolded me softly.

He inched closer, lay down on the blanket, pulled me beside him, and sighed. Max didn't speak, and neither did I, listening to the fluty sound of the breeze, birds singing in the trees, crickets playing their own tunes, and the beat of Max's heart. The sun's glare made me close my eyes, and I soon dozed off.

I WOKE up to a dog barking. Startled, I rose to find Max patting and hugging a big sheepdog with a wildly wagging tail and a tongue that lolled out to lick at Max's hands and face. A sudden pang of jealousy and envy surprised me. I shoved the feelings aside as stupid. How could anyone be jealous of a dog?

"What's this?" I asked.

The excitable dog heard me and bounded over to me, a furry weight landing on me.

"*Oomph!*"

Max laughed and didn't lift a finger to help me as my face was covered in dog spit.

"Pumpkin! Get off him!"

A short, stout old man carrying a rucksack and holding a bendy staff approached us. Lawana walked alongside him but kept her distance. I noticed her hand stray to her belt holster.

The golden-hued sheepdog jumped off me and hurried to its master.

"I'm sorry. Pumpkin's big on people," the man said. He had a craggy face that had likely seen a lot, but his eyes were youthful and lively. His broad smile revealed a few missing teeth.

"Pumpkin?" I asked as I got up with Max, my voice hoarse after the impromptu exercise.

The old man smiled at the canine who sat beside him, patient but its tail wagging like a serpent. "Yes. Sir Pumpkin von Jumps-A-Lot. Bravest and barkiest of all knights in the realm."

I laughed, and Max chimed in.

"Forgive me. Archibald Chantry, at your service. Call me Archie." He extended a hand for me and Max to shake. His British accent became more noticeable now he wasn't gruffly rebuking his pet.

For a second I didn't know what to say. Should Max and I tell this stranger who we were?

But I should have known better than to worry.

"I hope my dog didn't scare you, Your Highness," Archie said, addressing Max.

I blew out a breath of relief, not having to pretend. Max had to be well known in these parts; it was his country after all, and not a very big one.

"Not at all." Max dismissed Archie's concerns with a kind smile and a bow. "Pumpkin didn't attack me, only my friend here."

"Hi. I'm Oliver," I introduced myself.

Archie nodded. Then his gaze traversed the peaks. "Lovely day for hiking."

"And picnics," Max added, gesturing toward our blanket and basket.

Archie smiled. "That it is, Your Highness."

I knelt on the blanket. "Would Pumpkin like a snack?"

Archibald nodded, so I waved a piece of turkey sandwich in front of the dog. With a glance at Archie, the animal came to me, gobbled the tiny morsel in one bite, and returned to its master.

"Good boy," I complemented the young canine, who studied me with eyes as hazel as mine. "He's a pretty one, isn't he?" I realized I'd switched to baby talk only when both Max and Archie gave me amused looks. I blushed.

"Well, I best be going," Archie declared. "Day's a-wasting. Good day to you, gentlemen."

As he went, he whistled, and Pumpkin followed him fast and ran past him toward the path.

"Did you know him?" I asked.

Max shook his head. "No. But he's a citizen, and he's served in the Norician militia." I stared at Max with a silent question. Max smiled. "He wore the unicorn emblem with a star around it. Sign of the Norician Army."

I shrugged. "He was nice, anyway. As was his dog—from which you failed to rescue me."

Max giggled. "You had the situation in hand."

"No, the situation sat on top of me like a warm, hairy blob." Max laughed more, and I was pleased knowing I'd made him happy. "How come you don't have a dog? A cute little pup. You seem like a dog person. Come to think of it, most royals have pets."

"We do have hounds, if that's what you mean." Max lay down on the blanket again, and I snuggled beside him. "The castle zoo is small—"

"The castle... what now?"

Max chuckled. "It's not a very big zoo. A few animals under our protection or given to us as diplomatic gifts. There's a place for them close to the orangerie down the hillside."

"Ah." I mused on the news. "They're not pets, though."

Max sighed. "Johann's not an animal lover, and Mother is a cat person. We had a litter of puppies when my brothers and I were kids. When the dogs eventually died, it felt wrong to take new ones."

"Oh. I'm sorry. What was your little one's name?"

"Not Sir Pumpkin von Jumps-A-Lot." We both laughed. Then Max's cheeks reddened. Finally, he admitted, "Her name was... Princess Hilda of Forestfire."

I couldn't hide my amusement. "What kind of name is that?"

"When I was six, there was a huge forest fire near the castle," Max explained. "It cut down a whole swath of forest. We could see the blaze light up the sky, even at night. It was scary. My little Hilda was born two nights later."

Despite the frightening tale, I giggled. "I bet that was fun, running up the hills, calling for Hilda. How many shepherdesses and milkmaids did you—"

Max moved so fast I couldn't stop him. His fingers found all my most ticklish spots, and soon I was wiggling like an eel and had tears streaming down my cheeks as Max tormented me. When he ceased at long last, he glared at me.

"No. Mocking. My. Hilda. Understood?"

I conceded immediately. "Yes. Yes. I give. No mocking your princess.... Man, no wonder Kira never stood a chance—"

Max tickled me mercilessly at my continued jibes, and I was howling with mirth and agony at the same time. I squirmed, but he was relentless.

"Okay, I swear I'll be good. Please."

Max pulled back, his eyes ablaze like a lightning storm. "Oliver, I shan't warn you again. I will have you thrown out of the country. This I promise."

I rose onto my elbows, every part of me hurting in a good way. "I won't do it again, I swear." After Max observed me with narrowed eyes of suspicion, I relented all the way. "Max, I promise. I'm done."

"Fine."

Max remained grumpy after that and refused to let me near him. He shot daggers at me with every gaze. I suppressed every chuckle at his cuteness overload.

The wind began to pick up as the afternoon waned. We gathered our belongings and headed for the nearby chalet with Lawana in tow. The mountain lodge was property of House Lindau-Arbon, so Max was familiar with it.

"Here's our little cabin," Max said as we stepped inside.

"Little cabin, huh?" I remarked dryly, closing and locking the door behind him and me.

At that moment, thunder boomed above us, darkness descended, and the pitter-patter of droplets showered the roof, walls, and windows.

"Looks like we made it just in time," Max commented, staring out the windows, the vista obscured by summer rain. The bright afternoon suddenly seemed like late evening.

Lighting flashed across the sky. The sudden burst of light reminded us that the lodge was pitch-black now. Max hurried to the light switches, since I didn't know where they were. This was not the cozy chalet we'd been to earlier, which had been more like a round hut with a firepit in the middle and wooden benches around it.

This one was luxurious in every respect.

The lodge's exterior was constructed of light wood and gray stone, and the interior was decorated in beige and light gray hues. A freestanding fireplace dominated the living area, surrounded by a plethora of soft gray tweed couches piled with plump, faux-fur pillows. The fire was lit, which surprised me a bit. Were we not alone?

I checked the fridge, intent on raiding it for every last bit of supplies to stave off starvation. It was, however, fully stocked. I popped a small strawberry amuse-bouche into my mouth and snatched a plate bearing slices of sticky apple-and-ginger cake, based on the scent, and placed it on the marble counter.

"You really owe your staff a raise," I said, holding up a fresh jar of peanut butter, which I put back without tasting.

Warm, strong arms wrapped around me from behind. Max peppered my neck with hot kisses. My jeans got a little tighter in the front, and I wiggled to find some room for my swelling member.

"Did you know we'd be coming here tonight?" I asked.

Max chuckled, the sound reverberating through my body. "I might have hinted something along those lines to the staff and Lawana. Which is why she's not in here with us but outside in the guest cabin."

"Mmm...," I moaned when Max sucked on the juncture of my neck and shoulder. In passing, I thought how weird it was for a mountain chalet to have an adjacent guest cabin. "With everything so well taken care of, even the fridge filled with food, I'll become fat in less than a year."

"I'd love you the same even if you had way more meat on your bones," Max quipped—and rubbed my aching cock through my jeans. "Ah yes, hot flesh, hard boners."

I burst out laughing. Max joined in, kissing my neck every few seconds.

Thunder clapped outside, making the ground quake and rumble. Or was that my overactive imagination?

"We're not going to get buried under an avalanche, are we?" I asked, concerned.

"No. Wrong season." Max whirled me around to face him, hugged me again, and kissed me repeatedly and insistently. I opened up for him, and our lips fused and our tongues entangled. I loved kissing him. I really liked when he got all alpha aggressive on me.

When Max pulled back, he rubbed his nose against mine. "I could easily get used to this."

Please do, I said in the safe confines of my mind.

Then Max frowned. "What you said about well-stocked fridges..."

"Huh?" I was confused. Hadn't we been about to retire upstairs for the night?

Max locked a serious gaze with mine. "When you spoke of everyday chores, I know that you really meant responsibilities. How to maintain a household and keep a relationship going when the mundane intrudes. How it's not always sunshine and roses or champagne and caviar."

I blinked. That had sort of been the underlying reason, I had to admit. "Okay, yes, sure."

Max pressed his forehead against mine. "I want you to know that I understand. Just because anyone in a relationship with me would have less ordinary, menial things to worry about, there would still be normality."

"Normality," I repeated on automatic. So that was his issue about my issue. He was worried I saw him as an entitled aristocrat, not a regular Joe to live a quiet life with. Not a normal man.

Max embraced me tighter. "I am more than my title, Oliver."

"I know that, Max," I reassured him, shushing him silent. "You've told me a million times already. And I get it."

"No, you don't." Max pushed away from me and ran a hand through his hair. He radiated frustration, and he started to pace. "I have slept with men before you. Not many, but enough to know myself."

He paused for thought, and I didn't dare interrupt him. He clearly had something on his chest, so I waited for him to get it off.

"Those I've been with," Max said slowly, as if weighing every word carefully. "They knew from the start that discretion and secrecy were the name of the game. But I also knew their characters. They weren't like you."

"Like me?" I parroted, unsure where he was going. My hard-on faded away.

Max gestured for us to move to the large couch, one of several around a low wooden coffee table. He landed with a heavy thud, as if his troubles gave him more substance. I sat next to him but gave him his space. He still wouldn't look at me, but even though it seemed he was about to open the lid on the ex-files, I sensed I was held in higher regard than my predecessors.

Then Max's words confirmed as much.

"With you, Oliver, it's easy for me forget that I used to have low standards when it came to the men I was attracted to."

Max took my hand and squeezed. I think it anchored him on a turbulent emotional sea.

"Two were from Noricia, one a nobleman, the other a commoner. Three were foreigners, two dignitaries and an envoy." Max made an angry motion with his hand, as if to dismiss his own words. "I used to believe I was a relatively good judge of character. The truth is, I wasn't, but I've become better as a result of my... assignations."

I suppressed a snort. Assignations? At least I'd gotten a dalliance. Wait, what the hell was the difference again?

"They were good for me because they enabled me to learn what kind of man I am and how to hide that part of me from the world. They were bad for me because they didn't love me. Not that I wanted them to. Thrill seekers, royalizers, boy toys, gold diggers. I was out of luck for love but in luck for plenty of sex. Quantity over quality."

I blinked. Five men? Didn't seem too excessive. I'd been with more guys than that. Then again, my taste in guys sucked ass. Max and me, two unlucky peas in a sexual pod.

"With them, I could be a gay man with ease. But with you, Oliver…." Max faced me, tucked a leg under his knee, inched nearer, tugged on my hand to bring me closer, and leaned into me. "With you, Oliver, I can be myself. Not a prince, not a gay man. Just a man. Do you understand?"

I nodded. "The way you are when you're not wearing a crown or having sex. The normal, basic you. Ordinary, plain, boring, dull as dirt—"

"All right, all right, funny guy. I'm glad you get the gist." Max giggled, and with that, the mood lifted again. "But yes, something to that effect."

I think Max was still worried he was inadequate for a normal relationship with me, so I quickly said, "Don't worry, big guy. You're plenty enough for me exactly as you are."

It was Max's turn to blink. He seemed bewildered. Then his face melted into a broad smile, and his eyes welled up.

I embraced him, and he wiggled into my arms.

"I knew you'd get me," Max murmured into my ear. "I hoped you would."

I kissed his cheek. "Of course I did. I'm a fucking genius."

"If so, why haven't you suggested we go upstairs to bed?" Max seduced me with his words and a hushed tone that made me shiver inside and out.

I couldn't get up fast enough. Double entendre intended.

Chapter 18

WE STUMBLED into bed, kissing ferociously, our limbs entwined, our bodies half-dressed. He ground his erection against my hip and made needy little groans at the back of his throat.

Then Max surprised me yet again.

"Oliver, w-will you fuck me?"

Flummoxed, I drew in a sharp breath. "A-are you sure?" When Max nodded, eyes wide like a rabbit in panic mode, I knew he was nervous for a reason. "You've not done this before, have you?"

Max swallowed hard. Finally, he nodded. "I've always wanted to but... there was never the right time, the right circumstances. The right guy I could trust. I trust *you*, Oliver."

I was worried about his first time. What if I got it wrong? I'd bottomed more than topped. Most of my cheating exes had preferred it that way, and I'd been too naive to say no. They'd not been bad or violent. My experiences were good enough, I suppose. I liked bottoming.

But good enough was not enough for me and Max. He should have a stellar experience. I had doubts about being able to deliver.

Still, I vowed to try and give him pleasure.

"D-do you know, are there any condoms in here?" I asked, buying time to get a handle on my frayed nerves.

Max nodded toward the bedside table. "The chalet concierge service is excellent. There will be condoms, lube, cock rings, nipple clamps—"

"Okay, latex is sufficient. No need for bells and whistles." Then his words hit me. "Wait. This place has a fucking concierge?"

"Yes. A concierge, a chef, and three valets. Standard staff contingent for a royal chalet of this modest size with only three bedrooms and a single guest cabin."

I started to laugh and couldn't stop. When Max was warm and willing in my arms, it was hard to remember this pliant man was a prince who had hundreds of servants at his beck and call.

Max appeared baffled. "What's so funny?"

I wiped a tear from the corner of my eye. "Really? First you give me a speech, and a damn fine speech at that, about how you're a pretty regular guy—and then casually mention that five servants are standard for a royal chalet. Yup, normal."

Max pinked. He seemed embarrassed. I pushed up and kissed him.

"Don't go into a funk. I'm fascinated by this contradiction in you. The regal gentleman and the horny hunk, the good friend and the posh prince. It's all you. I don't like one side more than the other. It's you."

I felt the thought bore repeating. Max gulped. He studied me for so long I was certain the mood was wrecked again. Then a smile pierced the funk. He dipped down, captured my lips in a searing kiss, and brought his body back into full contact with mine.

We managed to undress without tearing anything, fabric or limb. One sleeve here, a pants leg there. Soon our naked bodies crashed together, our passion rising fast.

Then Max shifted, yanked open a drawer, fumbled out a packet of lube and another of latex, and handed them to me. Quite an achievement as he never broke his kiss with me.

I tried not to get swept away by his first-time jitters. I kept my own memories fresh in my mind and eased him with every kiss, touch, and word. Max calmed and even managed to smile in a relaxed manner.

I flipped us around, rose onto my haunches, and urged him to roll over onto his stomach. He obliged but he'd stiffened again. I massaged his back to get him to let go of his anxieties. His broad shoulders, strong lean back, and firm round buttocks beckoned me to grope and fondle, but I restricted myself to soft, gentle strokes and only an occasional harder kneading to loosen his tightly bunched muscles.

I leaned over him, molding my front to his back, and simply held him and let him get used to my weight on top of him.

He turned his face on the pillow and showed me his profile. "Th-thank you, Oliver."

I smiled wide. I'd succeeded. He'd hidden his face in the pillow at first but now he let me see him. Max exposed himself in a way one could only do with a trusted lover.

Tonight, that someone was me.

I kissed my way down his strong, sinewy back, planting one over each vertebra, and licked and nipped here and there too. Max whimpered and clutched the plush gray comforter.

We hadn't turned on the lights, and the stormy skies were dark. Curtains were drawn in front of the french doors to the balcony and windows. But light wood timbers above on the slanted ceiling and around us in the walls reflected what little light there was. With the dim lighting, the mood was intimate, as if the world faded to obscurity.

Only we mattered. Only Max mattered.

I bit into the fleshy parts of his butt, and Max groaned, his hips bucking a little. With steady hands, I pushed him back down, spread his asscheeks, and licked a line over his puckered pink hole.

"Oh my Goddess…," Max breathed out. I thought I heard a sob in there but wasn't sure.

I flicked my tongue over his hole, licked around it, and probed inside as best I could, though it wasn't deep. By then Max had melted into a wobbly mess. I kept rubbing his butt everywhere to get him to relax, so that when I added a lubed finger to the mix, Max's body succumbed to me.

"Tell me if you want me to stop," I urged Max to speak his mind. "Tell me if it's okay?"

Max shook all over. He seemed at once trying to pull away and push back, like he couldn't decide which. So I proceeded gently, letting him get used to it. When I felt the ring of muscles cave, I added another finger. Inside I made the tiniest circles, expanding his channel.

"O-Oliver, p-please, n-now." Max's plea sounded as if it emanated from the deepest core of his being, the baritone gravelly and grave.

My hands trembled as I put on the condom and lathered it amply with lube. I realized I was either breathing really fast or holding my breath, so I made a conscious effort to calm down. I didn't want my nervousness to add to his.

"I'll be gentle," I promised, aiming my cockhead at his hole.

Max nodded, a private little smile on his lips. "I know. I trust you."

Pride and love bloomed in my chest, filling my heart with warmth. I eased into him slow and steady. I popped in, the tight pressure around my cock just this side of pleasure. He was so tight, even after my ministrations. I rubbed the small of his back, his buttocks, and his hips until his body relented and I could enter deeper.

Max's channel swallowed me whole. When I was finally in all the way, we both let out long sighs of relief. I rested on top of him, pushing his legs farther apart with my knees and holding most of my weight off with my straightened arms.

"You okay?" I asked, careful not to move until he gave me a sign.

Max grasped at my arms and brought me down on top of him fully. I felt his torso move up and down as he breathed. I kissed his upper back and neck and whispered sweet nothings into his ear to soothe him.

"G-go," he finally murmured, and I knew he didn't want me to leave.

With incremental motions, I made love to him. At first he felt like a rigid plank beneath me. Then he began to undulate to my pace, and I got in and out deeper. Max moaned and shivered. I kept my arms around him, and he seemed to appreciate that.

"Max, talk to me."

"I-I'm good," he muttered. While his voice was tense and strained, his body stayed relaxed, and the tension in his face unwound. His long eyelashes fluttered over his cheeks, and he began to pant.

I smelled his fresh sweat and the spicy scent of his expensive cologne as I buried my nose in his hair and picked up the pace, going in deeper, a bit harder, faster. Max responded beautifully, his body moving with me, his moans reaching higher pitch. Together, we undulated back and forth, my cock inside him, his channel silky and hot and wet with lube around me.

I could have stayed like that forever. I was in no rush. I glided in and out at a slow tempo, getting both of us riled up gradually. Max's muscles flexed, and his channel constricted for a moment. I almost came then and there.

"O-Oliver, a-are you close?" Max asked, and this time I could read the strain in his voice as that of man skating on the edge.

"Yes. You?"

"Uh-huh." Max had never sounded less eloquent. It made me smile to know I'd reduced him to an animal in heat, unable to communicate in anything more than one-syllable grunts.

I kept one arm wrapped around Max's upper chest and wound the other lower to take a hard grab at his prick. Max moaned and bucked his hips. That made his cock slip easily against my palm, which was slick with lube and sweat. Max started thrusting into my hand, so I thrust harder into him. He let out hisses and whimpers, and I panted roughly against his neck. The scent of Max's warm musk grew in the air, thick and arousing.

After a moment, our rhythm became brutal, the lovemaking turning into a rough pounding. We were both chasing our orgasms now, lost in a sea of sensations. Any pain or discomfort would be lost under the flood of pleasure and satisfaction.

"Oliver, I—"

Max didn't get further. His whole body jerked, his cock jumped and swelled, and he shot out hot, creamy come. New spurts kept coming, coating my hand, his lower abdomen, and the comforter. His ass gripped the entire length of my throbbing shaft in a velvety vise.

It was too much. Pleasure and the need to climax churned in my stomach. Groaning raggedly, I felt my balls pull up and my seed explode through my cock into the latex. I kept pumping, my hips moving as if they had a mind of their own. Max touched my leg with his hand, as if to remind me I was with a man, not just fucking some nameless guy.

"Max, God, you're so fucking hot," I murmured amid hoarse breaths.

Max giggled, wiggling under me. "I'm a prince to everyone, a future king to most, and a god to you. Hmm, I can live with that."

I laughed, and he laughed with me. I held on to him as my spent penis slipped out of him. I rolled us over to our sides so my dead weight wouldn't pin him too hard. Max needed his breath too.

After a few heartbeats, Max turned to face me. I was afraid of what I'd see. A wide toothy grin greeted me, even though his cheeks were wet. I wiped away the moisture with the pad of my thumb. He kissed my digit, and then he kissed my mouth.

Though I'd just come and couldn't again for a while, a frisson of electricity shot through me when our lips met. Static electricity—or true love? Perhaps one day I'd find out.

APART FROM my accidental stay in Max's bed in the spring, there had been another thing that had brought us together. Max's missing signet ring. Since the theft in France, there had been no leads or updates. At least none had been shared with me.

During the third week of my stay at Riten Castle, the first piece of news emerged. And it wasn't good.

Karl von Thürer stormed into Max's private solar early one morning, waving an offending document. He thrust it to Max's face. "Care to explain, Your Highness? This is a blatant transgression of your judiciary powers. I will never countersign this travesty. I will report this to the Council of Ministers and the King and Queen. This kind of challenge will not go unanswered."

Remarkably calm in the face of such accusations, Max rose from his seat at the breakfast table, wiped his mouth with a napkin, and addressed the raging prime minister, "Explain yourself, sir. I know for a fact you were taught basic manners, same as I. This intrusion will not stand."

For a second it looked like the reddened blowhard that was Karl von Thürer was in serious danger of exploding. But after a couple of breaths, he calmed. He shoved the document toward Max.

"This is your doing. But I will make sure it will be the last decree you will ever make."

That said, he rushed out of the room, slamming the door behind him with a heavy boom that echoed in the stone halls of the castle.

I grimaced. "What's that guy's damage? Was he dropped on his head as a kid? Or did he have a heart transplant, and they forgot to put in the new one?"

Max chuckled but without much mirth. "The von Thürer family has been a stout supporter of the royal family and monarchy in general for generations. But as you've observed, he can be quite, um...."

As Max searched for words, I jumped in. "A dickhead? Moron? Jerk? Dumbass?"

Max laughed so hard he had tears in his eyes. "Recalcitrant. But deep down he has only the best interest of the country and its citizens at heart."

"Ha. If he has a heart." I nodded toward the papers in Max's hands. "So what's that?"

Max shrugged. "No idea. If it's a royal decree, as he implied, it does require the signatures of both myself and the prime minister." He read the paper from top to bottom, and I could tell from his darkening expression that whatever was on there, it wasn't good at all. By the end, Max sported a frown and cheeks reddened in anger. "Karl was right. This is completely wrong."

"What?" I asked in alarm, rising and closing the gap between us. I reached for the paper but then thought better of it. If this was a sensitive administrative document, I really shouldn't read it.

Max, however, passed the paper to me. "I have to get dressed." He already had on proper pants and a clean white half-open dress shirt, so he looked fine to me, but apparently that wasn't enough for meetings on the highest level.

As Max readied himself, I studied the document with care. It was a royal decree that imposed significant monetary sanctions on citizens who refused to hire immigrants for their places of business. If those sanctions failed, a chance for loss of citizenship and even deportation were possible second-tier penalties.

I stared at the paper, puzzled. When a fully dressed Max returned from his big walk-in closet, I asked, "What's the problem here? Isn't it good to have a more diverse staff?"

Max shook his head. "It isn't about that. We already have strict antidiscrimination laws in place. They extend to the workplace. Threatening citizens like this is unconscionable. Financial sanctions and even a prison sentence are possible for breaking the antidiscrimination laws, but loss of citizenship? Banishment? That is horrendous."

I blinked. "Then why'd you sign this?" Max's signature, written in beautiful calligraphy, was confirmed by a wax seal from his signet ring. Then it hit me. His ring…. "Oh shit. Someone else wrote and signed this. But von Thürer doesn't know that, and that's why he yelled at you."

Max sighed, slumping. "My parents and I decided to keep the theft of the signet ring a secret. I've been using a replica from the vault. But it won't stand up to scrutiny. The age and intricacy are all wrong."

I chewed on the inside of my cheek, worried now. "Why do you still sign things like this? Any copy of the ring could—"

"It's tradition, I'm afraid," Max said, putting on his jacket and looking rather dishy in his suit and tie. "All royal decrees and documents are archived for posterity and research. They must look the part. Signatures with flourish, wax seals, royal emblems—necessities, each and every one."

A gentle knock came from the door. Max bid them entry. Elinor peeked in, her eyes firmly shut. "You guys decent?" When I laughed, she opened her eyes and smirked. "Nice." She studied Max's refined outfit from head to toe and gave a thumbs-up. "Even nicer." Then she grew serious. "Was von Thürer in here? I thought I saw him head this way."

I groaned. "Man, you've got to stop following him around. You are aware that people in here practice dueling and shit?"

Elinor rolled her eyes. "I'll challenge him to a fist fight, street style. He'll go down like a dead tree, dull and gray. Timber!"

Max chuckled. "I adore you, Ms. Reed." Elinor gave him the stink eye, and Max blushed. "I mean, Elinor."

She blew him an air kiss. "What did the big meanie want?" Elinor asked, her suspicious gaze flicking between Max and me. "Did he give you a hard time? And no, I'm not talking about dicks, just dickheads."

Max chortled for a moment. "Listen. Karl can be a little intense sometimes. He's passionate about the affairs of this country."

"Maybe so. But *your* affairs are none of his business," I interjected like a smartass.

Max leaned in and kissed my temple. "No, they certainly are not. Now, if you'll excuse me, I must find my parents posthaste."

He left before I could say anything. Then I told Elinor what the stolen signet ring had been used for. Both Elinor and I were children of immigrants, so perhaps our views were colored by that fact. Immigrants often could not get jobs in a new land despite having the training or the expertise. This was not the case everywhere, but the rise of hate crimes against immigrants had put both of us, and everyone we knew, on guard.

In spite of that, Elinor surprised me by saying, "Being exiled from your home seems a bit drastic for not hiring someone, don't you think? One should always be allowed to hire the best person for the job, not to fill quotas. I can see why Max is worried his name and reputation are being used in this way."

I don't think I'd ever been prouder of my sister than right then. Not even when she did that sick backflip with a skateboard, right over a cop's head. He'd not been amused. But I was glad that there was no hate in Elinor's heart.

"We'll figure this out," I vowed, though I wasn't sure we should be meddling in affairs of state. "No one's going to bring Max down." In my head, I finished the sentence, *unless it's me doing it, inadvertently, that is.*

In the meantime, while secret things were slowly simmering beneath the surface, Max and I should try to enjoy ourselves. No telling when everything would end.

Chapter 19

"Wow. Holy shit."

Max laughed at Oliver's shock. "Think you could whip up something sweet and delectable in here?"

The double entendre was lost on Oliver, who surveyed the vast kitchen on the ground floor of the Bull Tower wide-eyed. Max understood that Oliver, an aspiring chef, was naturally curious about a facility where traditional mixed with modern and luxurious.

Countertops gleamed clean and pure, made of stainless steel. A massive fireplace dominated the back wall, the farthest away from the doors leading to the anteroom of the Great Hall. A spit with a skewer had been there once. Now it was no longer in active use, as the floor was heated in winter months. Shelves with copper pots, pans, kettles, and mugs lined the walls, as memoirs of times past. The whitewashed stone walls shone spotless, and the arched ceiling had new light fixtures that left no corner in shadow.

"Where is everyone?" Oliver asked, peering inside every cabinet and drawer, even opening the two doors on each side of the fireplace, one leading to the pantry and larder and buttery, the other outside to the kitchen gardens and to the confectionary kitchens.

"It's late," Max explained, glancing at the clock high on the wall, where it kept perfect time. According to the device, it was after ten at night. "We're between shifts."

"I thought Riten Castle had twenty-four seven room service," Oliver said absentmindedly, leaning into whatever was in front of him.

"It does, yes, but the staff need not hang around here twiddling their thumbs if no one makes a request." Max waved at the door on the right. "That leads to the servants' quarters. I assume the night staff is there, probably in the lounge area. If you desire something, I can summon—"

"No." Oliver smiled. "If I want something, I can make it myself. Do you think anyone would mind?"

Max chuckled. "The Royal Chef, Ariana Delacroix, might have your hide in the morning, but only if you don't tidy up after yourself."

Oliver giggled. Then he sighed in awe. "I can't believe how modern this place is. This is all high-end stuff. Walk-in refrigerators, blast chillers, gas-electric ovens with french doors, and, and…. Man, there's so much room to experiment with recipes."

Max loved how excited Oliver got about what interested him. Like a happy little puppy. Max wanted to stroke his companion. "Well, then, make me something. Your signature dish, how about that?"

Oliver gasped. "I-I don't have one. I'm not a chef yet."

Max shrugged. "All right. Your favorite food, then. What you make better than anyone else."

Oliver's cheeks pinked, and he worried his bottom lip. Max would gladly have done that for him. Oliver rubbed the back of his neck self-consciously and glanced around, longing shining in his eyes.

"Come on, my dear," Max coaxed gently. "Who knows when you'll have a chance to cook or bake in a palace-level industrial kitchen? Go on. Be daring." He winked at his lover. "If you do, later I'll show you the confectionary."

Oliver's eyes rounded to saucers, and his jaw dropped. "C-confectionary? You really have one here?" He ran to Max and hugged him tight. "Please, show it to me."

Max pretended he hadn't heard anything. "I'm feeling kind of peckish…."

Oliver pulled back, scowled, and even growled. "Fine."

He stomped toward the fridge like a mortally wounded man. Max suppressed a laugh so as to not aggravate his newest chef too much. His mouth watered at the thought of eating something delicious that Oliver made—and then eating Oliver. Yes, that sounded like a good solid plan.

Max sat down on a steel barstool, crossed his legs, and watched Oliver in action. The young man was a whirlwind of motion. Without ever having been inside the Great Kitchen at Riten Castle, Oliver seemed to know where everything he needed was. He laid out ladles, bowls, and ingredients perfectly as he set to work.

Max had never spent time in the kitchen. He wasn't sure if he wanted to know how his food was made. It was served to him on fine china and crystal with the royal emblem engraved on their delicate surfaces. But observing Oliver pushed all the right buttons in Max. His desire to be sated took on extra meanings.

Oliver buttered two teacups while self-rising flour, caster sugar, butter, and eggs mixed in a food processor. He chopped what smelled like ginger, grated what looked like an orange, and added them to the mixing batter. He poured golden syrup into the teacups, and then chopped a peeled pear and added the chunks into the teacups. He then added the batter and put a circular piece of parchment paper on them. Instead of the oven, though, Oliver blasted the cups in the microwave for a few minutes.

While he was doing that, he also diced some more pears, placed them in an ice cream maker, and poured sugar syrup on top. The machine swirled lazily, and Oliver added a whiff of pear brandy and then cream, let the maker stir, and then placed the bowl into one of the blast chillers.

The third thing Oliver did was boil water to a simmer, add cocoa powder and milk, and then keep on whisking. Max didn't need to understand cooking to know what that would be. He was salivating already.

All in all, the whole process couldn't have taken more than a quarter of an hour at best. Max was impressed at Oliver's ability to multitask.

Oliver set the dish down. Max could see it was some sort of pudding. Oliver smiled. "Voilà. Pear and ginger pudding, hot cocoa, and finally pear ice cream. Enjoy."

"Thank you, my sweet Oliver," Max said and dug in with gusto.

The hot chocolate was smooth and creamy, the pudding springy and moist, and the ice cream crisp and sweet. Flavors burst on his tongue— pear, ginger, sugar—and the mix of hot, lukewarm, and icy were baffling but absolutely delectable.

When he was done with his half, he sighed with contentment. "Oh Oliver, please promise me you will stay here and cook for me every day."

Oliver blushed and smiled bashfully. "Okay."

Now that Max had satisfied his stomach, it was time to turn his attention to his other needs. Oliver licked his lips to get all the sticky syrup there, and Max could have screamed, he was so horny.

"I'm glad you liked it," Oliver said, sounding proud of himself, if still sort of shy.

Max wasn't listening. He spotted a glop of ice cream on the corner of Oliver's lips and didn't resist the urge. Max dove forward and licked the delectable morsel away. Then he proceeded to kiss Oliver again and again until they were both breathless.

"Mmm, you taste so sweet," Max purred. He rose from his seat and pulled Oliver into his arms.

Oliver wound his arms around Max's waist and pushed closer. Max rubbed his groin against Oliver's, and Oliver sighed and moaned a little, the sound more like a whine. Max let his hands roam. He slipped them underneath Oliver's shirt and felt glorious skin.

Oliver's knees buckled. Max cupped Oliver's buttcheeks and lifted him into his lap. Oliver wrapped his legs around Max's behind.

"A-are we really going to do this here?" Oliver murmured wantonly into the kiss. "I mean, anyone could come."

Max chuckled. "Oh, someone will come, I assure you."

He plopped Oliver down onto the countertop and started to lift his shirt. Oliver complied, raising his hands accommodatingly, but his gaze flitted across the room to the doors.

"No one will disturb us," Max reassured, though he wasn't certain. "And even if they did, I am the crown prince, you know."

That seemed to calm Oliver, who smiled and then kissed Max. His scrumptious flavor flooded Max's mouth and body like a drug he couldn't get enough of. He was fast growing addicted to everything Oliver.

Why bother breaking such a delicious habit? Max sure didn't see any reason to.

Divesting Oliver of his clothes was hard work since the guy was sitting and squirming at the same time. His hands were never still. Max kissed him over and over as he undressed him. Finally, Oliver was naked, while Max still had everything on.

"Ah." Oliver pulled back to breathe and unbutton Max's dress shirt. His fingers fumbled, and he grumbled under his breath, but Max said and did nothing. When Max's torso was fully exposed for Oliver's delight, Oliver sighed with happiness. He traced the curves of Max's firm muscles and the lines of his sleek, athletic build. Oliver's eyes were huge and dark, glistening brilliantly. His total focus on Max's body made Max beam; he loved that his hard work at the gym paid off with such appreciation and naked hunger.

Oliver leaned in and captured one of Max's nipples between his lips, sucking and nipping and licking. A frisson of pure pleasure shot from the point of contact straight to Max's cock. He loved when a man played with his nips.

Oliver tried to lick his way down farther, but he was foiled because he was sitting. He growled, but Max silenced him with a thorough kiss.

"May I fuck you?" he whispered the crude words into Oliver's ear.

Oliver giggled, face flushed, pupils dilated. "God, you don't need to ask."

Without missing a beat, Oliver pushed Max back, showcasing his very erect prick dripping precome, wiggled off the countertop, and turned around till he was lying on the surface with his backside in full view. Max's mouth dried at the sight.

"Oh Oliver, the sweet things you do to me," Max murmured as he fished a fresh packet of lube from his pants pocket, coated his fingers amply, and probed Oliver's entrance. Oliver groaned and pushed back so fast that Max's fingers popped in and slid in even farther. From there on out, the prepping process was easy. Oliver's channel undulated around Max's fingers.

"For fuck's sake, get on with it already," Oliver snarled, clearly in need of more than what Max's fingers provided.

"You're so impatient," Max chided softly. "One day I'll use restraints on you and force you take your time to fully enjoy—"

"Max, please, I can't hold on." Oliver's voice cracked, and a sob wracked his body.

That was Max's cue to get on with it if there ever was one. Without delay, he replaced his hand with his cock and pushed in steadily. Oliver rocked back and forth, moaning and trembling. He was so beautiful, he took Max's breath away.

"Shh, relax, love," Max encouraged, placing his warm palm over the small of Oliver's back. The muscles there jumped at the touch. Max moved in slowly but surely until he was fully seated inside. "All right there?"

Oliver groaned and dropped his forehead to his arms on the countertop. "Y-yeah." Then he glanced over his shoulder, a feverish, dark light in his eyes. "Hard, Max."

Nodding, Max knew Oliver was not commenting on the state of either of their dicks. No, this was a plea by a lover to be taken hard and fast and rough. Max wasn't really into that, or at least he hadn't thought so—until he'd met Oliver, who didn't mind a bit of rough and tumble.

Max wrapped his arms around Oliver's waist and yanked him onto his cock. Oliver started and moaned, going pliant. Max grabbed Oliver's hips, pulled back slowly till he was almost out, and then shoved in hard.

"Goddamn, yes," Oliver murmured.

Max set a brutal pace, as Oliver obviously wanted. Judging from the way Oliver's hushed voice turned high-pitched and shrill, egging him on with a litany of lewd words, Max was doing everything right.

After a while, he changed pace and did what he wanted, using long, deep strokes to draw out Oliver's hushed pleas. Max kissed his way up Oliver's back to his sweaty, heated neck. He wound his arms around Oliver's torso for leverage and relished how Oliver placed a hand over Max's arms, reaching for him like an anchor in a sensual storm.

Oliver tasted like pears and sugar, and Max lapped at the flavor.

"I could taste you forever," Max whispered. "First you bake for me, and I'll eat the dessert off your body. Then I'll have my salty surprise, drinking straight from your fountain."

Oliver laughed amid pants. "Jesus Christ, Max. How you can speak so fine when fucking a guy is beyond me. You turn sophisticated words into dirty ones."

Max grinned. The praise made his cock swell even further. He rammed his dick into Oliver, who clung to him with both hands now, eyelids fluttering closed as he showed his profile to Max. Max kissed Oliver's cheek, a sloppy sideways smooch. He held Oliver tighter and pounded into him. His pants fell to his ankles, and the back of his dress shirt was glued to his sweaty back, but he didn't care. He had to have Oliver, had to give him pleasure, had to make them both come like shooting stars.

"I… I can't…. Please, Max," Oliver muttered, his voice shaky and husky.

Max snaked a hand lower and gripped Oliver's shaft in a firm hold. His sweaty hand glided like a charm over an already precome-slick cock. He stroked hard and fast, in time with his thrusts. He was close too; he could taste it.

"Ah, ahh, ahhh… I'm coming!" Oliver cried out.

Oliver jerked, and hot, creamy jets of fluid coated Max's hand. Max continued to stroke and thrust, the pressure building and building till it hit boiling point. With a hoarse shout, he came and shot his seed—directly into Oliver.

"Oh no, what have I done?" Max murmured, dropping from ecstatic heights so fast it was a wonder he didn't leave a man-shaped indentation on the ground.

"What?" Oliver asked, his voice sluggish, his face a portrait of rapture, his lips curved in a sleepy smile.

Max stared. He'd never seen anyone so stunning. The confession hurt. Trust was already an issue between them. "I-I forgot the condom. I'm so sorry."

Oliver frowned. He wiggled his butt a bit. "Oh. So you did." Then he chuckled. "So what? We've had this talk before. You're clean, and so am I. We've done the checkups with a doctor. What's the problem?"

Max sighed. "I guess I should have asked—"

"While we were doing it?" Oliver snorted. "Not fucking likely. Way to break the mood when we both already know where we stand. So, knock it off, okay? You're ruining my buzz."

Max smiled, pulled Oliver into a hug, and kissed the tip of his nose. "Sorry. Won't happen again. Thank you for getting tested for me."

Oliver rolled his eyes. "Didn't do it for you specifically. Not exactly a chore for me to have that monstrous cock inside me, filling me up, nothing between it and me. Love it."

Max blushed. He'd rarely talked this directly with his lovers. No, not lovers. Sexual partners. Max hadn't loved them; he'd cared, but only a little. They hadn't been enough to draw him out of his shell and induce him to trust them.

With Oliver, trust came easily. Perhaps because Oliver was too trusting for his own good. Oliver didn't lie. What you saw was what you got. Quite unlike Max. Opposites attract, he pondered.

Oliver scrunched his nose. "Man, now I'm all dirty. Syrup and spunk. Great."

Max laughed. "No worries, my dear. I know the perfect place to fix that."

"Wow." Oliver shook his head with a grin. "I keep saying that, don't I?"

"A little," Max admitted. "But I don't mind." He looked around as if seeing the familiar room for the first time. "It's so easy to take this for granted. Thank you for reminding me not to. And to see the world anew."

Oliver blushed cutely and ducked his head. He started to remove his clothes again, and Max followed suit, watching Oliver's exposed nudity with renewed voracity.

"This is what your country's known for?" Oliver asked once he was naked and stepped into the hot tub. Wooden steps helped smooth the descent into the rippling warm waters.

"Yes." Max entered the bath after his companion. "There are a multitude of hot springs and health spas in the land. We're in that part of the Alps where we're lucky to enjoy geothermal energy. The heat is used for our homes and spas, among other things."

"Like Iceland," Oliver said as he slid under the surface, sighing happily as he rested against the smooth stone edge. "This is amazing."

Max let the water wash over him till it reached his neck. Then he lay back and relaxed. His troubles melted away in the hot water.

"What else is here in the Seahorse Tower?" Oliver asked, his eyes closed, curious still even though he sounded and looked sleepy.

"Hot tubs here on the ground floor, showers and regular baths above, saunas above that, and a recreational area with a bar and a lounge at the top, complete with a wraparound balcony. Plus, there's an indoor swimming pool in the adjacent building. Also, this Seahorse Tower connects with the conservatory that's on the western side of the Outer Bailey, as you know."

Max knew all this by heart. He could shut off his brain and give a lecture about the castle if need be. He'd spent his childhood exploring every room and hall and then rummaging in every nook and cranny. A bit older, he'd been schooled on the history and importance of the place and taken pride in learning it all. This was his home, but it was also the center of the kingdom. Royal obligations to the past were significant, not to be taken lightly.

Oliver slipped deeper till he was submerged up to his jaw. "With all these wondrous things here, why do you ever leave?"

Max sidled over, caught Oliver in his arms, and cradled him in his lap with ease. "If I'd never left, I'd never have met you, my dear."

Oliver pursed his lips, pensive. "Yeah, I guess that's true."

Max nodded. "So no regrets. More than a fair trade."

Oliver shifted to sit astride Max's thighs. Max pulled on Oliver's hips to induce the man to scoot closer, which he did. They embraced in the natural bath and held each other close. Their hands traced lazy, idle patterns on each other's skin, and occasionally they shared a kiss.

"Did you like the movie we watched after dinner and before, uh, dessert?" Oliver asked, his bashful smile endearing.

"What, *Beetlejuice*? Yes, it was fun." Max hummed a few bars of the coconut song from the movie, and they both laughed.

"I love that scene," Oliver confessed. "One of the best in any comedy film."

"The leading lady, Catherine O'Hara, is a great actress," Max agreed, inching his hands up and down over Oliver's back. "In that scene in particular, she shines. She sells the idea that her body's been possessed by a reggae-loving ghost."

Oliver giggled and threaded his fingers through Max's wet hair. "Tell me a ghost story about this castle. Surely you must have ghosts here?"

Max grinned mischievously and teased, "Oh, you mean specters like the Crimson Queen and the Gray Monk and—"

"Yes, yes!" Oliver exclaimed, excited enough to bounce on top of Max.

"—and the Blue Knight and the Green King and the White Rabbit and—" Max continued.

"Wait. Hang on a minute." Oliver's eyes narrowed in suspicion. "Those aren't real, are they? You're totally messing with me, aren't you?"

Max laughed so hard he had tears streaming down his cheeks. "Of course I am. Ghosts aren't real!"

Oliver pouted, arms crossed. "Says who?" He shot daggers at Max with his gaze. "You don't know. No one does. Science hasn't proved they exist, sure, but it hasn't disproved their existence either."

Max's eyebrows crept to his hairline. He never would have pictured Oliver as a spook chaser. "Is that your secret vice? Ghost stories?" He didn't make fun of his lover because everyone had some concealed little fancy that was completely preposterous, but people indulged in them anyway.

Oliver's lower lip protruded to show how hurt he was. "Yeah. What's yours?"

"Bad karaoke," Max confessed, which earned him a wide-eyed stare and a suppressed giggle. "Yes, I know. I can hold a simple tune, but beyond that I'm totally tone-deaf. Got into karaoke on a diplomatic mission to Japan, and the habit stuck."

Oliver smiled. "Don't tell me you have a studio hidden somewhere on the grounds so you can sing to your heart's content when no one can see or hear you?"

Max shrugged. "Maybe. Maybe not. Not telling."

Oliver chuckled and closed the gap between them again, moving to sit skin-to-skin. "So, if you're not telling me that, are you going to tell me that ghost story or not? I mean, what kind of castle do you guys have here if you can't afford even a single supernatural resident, or even a guest?"

Max couldn't stop chortling. Since meeting Oliver, he'd laughed more than he ever had before in his whole life. And he'd been a relatively happy child.

"Fine," he finally said. "I'll tell you a story about the Pink Pony who—"

"No, tell me a *real* story," Oliver complained, shaking Max by the shoulders.

Max kept a straight face. "I am. How do you think we got a unicorn as our family emblem?" At first Oliver paused for thought. Then he apparently read Max's face right and splashed water over him. "Stop. No. Please, show mercy."

Oliver answered by sloshing even more till they were both soaked, their hair dripping, their eyes filled with water. But they both laughed, unable and unwilling to stop.

Then their lips met, and the bathroom turned steamy in more ways than one. Moaning with uncontrollable passion, they touched each other with wild abandon. Then Oliver climbed over Max's cock and lowered onto it. Water wasn't the best lubricant, but Max had no intention of stopping Oliver, who seemed to know what he was doing.

Once Oliver had settled, it only took a moment for him to start moving. Up and down he went, like riding on horseback.

"Did you really have sex in every room back at your house?" Max asked, incredulous, as he embraced Oliver and planted a swarm of kisses over his neck, clavicles, shoulder, and cheek.

Oliver giggled, breathless from the motion and taking a cock up his butt. "Have you had sex in every room here at the castle?"

Max growled. "No. You know I haven't."

Oliver smirked. "Yes. You know *I* did." Then he closed his eyes and let out a long, satisfied sigh. "But you and I will get there. One day. Every damn room in this place. I swear it."

As Oliver's quickening movements brought Max to an intense, earth-shattering crescendo, with Oliver teetering off the orgasmic edge mere heartbeats later, Max knew he'd never been happier about the present or the future.

Chapter 20

THE SUMMER Solstice Festival and Feast came around faster than I'd expected. And I sure as shit wasn't ready for that hustle and bustle. Corridors that had once been empty now filled with staff and guests finding their way about, decorations appeared where there had been none, and certain areas became off-limits until the big day.

Max explained to me that I simply hadn't observed servants about because they used hidden underground corridors to get between buildings. The royal family had similar passages to move about unseen. Apparently, there was a whole warren underneath our feet that I had no access to. Shivering, I realized I didn't want to go there. Claustrophobia reared its ugly head.

On the morning of the Festival, I awoke in Max's bed—alone.

The First Prince was busy getting dressed in front of a tall mirror in the corner.

The Snake Tower was luxurious and spacious. The bedroom had one centerpiece: the king-size canopy bed in the middle of the room. The fireplace, a walk-in closet, the bathroom, and three lounge chairs were all arrayed around it. It seemed rooms like these were called solars; I hadn't known that before.

"You snore," I said out of the blue.

Max sputtered. "I do not."

"Yes, you do. You make this cute little *tuf-tuf-tuf* sound."

"Again, I do not."

"I caught you on video," I said in a singsong tone. Max turned, his smile faded, and his eyes dimmed. I'd gone too far. "I'm kidding. I swear."

Max turned back to the mirror. His happy expression hadn't returned. "I wasn't worried. The court erases any unsanctioned videos or photos about the royal family on social media. That is one of the reasons why we have a press officer as well as a press and an IT corps."

I gasped. "Really?"

"Yes."

The easygoing grin returned to Max's lips, and I sighed in relief.

"There's a whole complex mechanism of secrecy behind Freddie's innocent, warm smile," Max explained. "Do not be fooled. She might look like a lost little lamb but she's a—"

"A wolf?" I clarified.

Max chuckled. "You better believe it."

I wasn't wise to the relationship between the press and the court, so I decided to change the subject. "Our whole house could fit in this room," I murmured, leaning onto my elbow as I watched him get dressed.

Max glanced over his shoulder, a warm twinkle in his eyes. "You need to put something on too. In the olden days, nudity during the solstice celebrations wasn't unheard of, but now…. Do you want your naked butt showcased on every tabloid around the globe?"

I blushed. The image of naked butts did funny things to me. But I got out of bed in a hurry and rushed to the bathroom to get ready. When I returned, I found Max had placed the clothes I was to wear on the bed. And for the first time I also took note of *his* outfit.

"Wh-what are you wearing?" I asked, staring dumbfounded. I pointed at the garments on the bed. "And what the heck is that?"

Max laughed. "It's Summer Solstice, love. This year's theme is the Court of the Sun King, Belenos. He's a Celtic sun god of the Noricum tribe that used to live in these parts before our people came here. Naturally, at the celebration all hosts, guests, and staff assume solar court guises."

I gulped. "You mean, it's a masquerade ball?" I'd never in my entire life been to a real-life masquerade. I wasn't sure how I felt about it. The upside was that my face might be covered, so if I blundered, no one would know it was me.

I studied Max who, of course, looked divine. He wore an old-fashioned jacket with a vest and cravat, tight pants, and boots—all white and gold, complete with jeweled adornments. In short, he sparkled.

"If you're, uh, the Sun Prince or whatever, what exactly am I?" I asked, scrunching my nose as I studied my skintight clothes. They were dark gold, almost golden brown, and instead of white they had splashes of red and orange—and they also seemed a lot more revealing than his attire.

Max giggled wickedly. "You're my cupbearer, of course." He winked at me, which told me that was a title with additional benefits—for him anyway. "So hurry up and get dressed."

"What's the rush?" I grumbled, starting to put the infernally tight clothes on. "Don't these shindigs last well into the night?"

"Yes, they do," Max admitted. "But this is a solar festival. So, the whole thing will be in full swing by noon, afternoon at the latest. And it's already well past ten. We must hurry. The face painting starts soon."

My mouth gaped. Face painting? Were we five years old now? I didn't even want to know.

"What's on the agenda?" I asked, suspecting I'd not see much of Max during the celebration. If this was a national holiday, a religious feast, and a rowdy carnival all rolled into one, the heir to the throne would undoubtedly be in high demand.

Max was making the finishing touches to his costume. The short, waist-length cape of white-gold he wore over his right shoulder made him look like a knight of old. I wanted him bad, but the timing was worse than impossible.

"The Banquet Hall and the Ballroom both open half an hour before noon," Max explained absentmindedly. "This gives people time to gather for the King's commencement speech at around ten to twelve. Don't worry. My father knows when to keep things short. Then, at precisely noon, we have a laser light show. We used to have fireworks but we're trying to avoid air and noise pollution. Hence, the light show at the Outer Bailey. After that, there's entertainment of all kinds to enjoy, or you can mingle or dance or… or whatever your heart desires."

"Anything?" I asked salaciously.

Max chuckled, giving me a leisurely look from under his long eyelashes. "Within reason."

"How available will you be?" I inquired, as if I hadn't a care in the world.

Max came to me, wrapped his arms around me, and kissed me hard on the lips. "For you? Always." Then he slapped me on the butt. "Now put a sock in it and get moving. I do not want to be late."

Scowling, I did as he asked. I admit, in spite of the costume, I was curious to see how modern Celts partied. Not that I'd observed Max to be particularly religious. Perhaps he preferred to keep that to himself. The prime minister had hinted that Max was a deficient prince because he wasn't a lackey of the church. To me, Max's lack of religious fervor meant he was a decent man. Religion seemed to drive people crazy.

"This is ridiculous. I'm not going out there like this. I freaking refuse."

My pants only reached midcalf, my shirt had no sleeves and was tight enough to constrict breathing, and I had little slippers for shoes. I was seriously underdressed compared to Max.

I crossed my arms over my chest and growled. "I'm not going."

Max grinned. "Aww, you look so adorable. Cutest cupbearer ever." He was trying to sweet-talk me into doing this; I could tell. I avoided his attempt at a hug. He laughed at me. "Are you going to make me chase you, my dear?"

My blood ran hot as magma. I shivered at the thought of him hunting me along the castle corridors. What would he do to me once he caught me? My dick hardened at the mere thought.

And because I was distracted, Max easily grabbed me into a bear hug.

"Now I have you," he purred. Then he looked at me with those puppy-dog eyes and fluttered his eyelashes. "You will come with me, won't you?"

I blushed. "Come on, Max. If I wear this, everyone will know you and I are… you know."

"So?" Max shrugged. "This is a summer festival, a day of love and laughter and music and wildness and sex. No one will care."

I doubted his self-confidence. Surely it would be unwise to frolic like a nymph(o) on the castle lawn? Not exactly discreet, that. What would his subjects say if they knew of his proclivities?

He bussed me on the cheek and lowered his voice. "Please, Oliver."

I couldn't resist that hushed plea. Silent, I nodded and let him win this round. I hoped he wouldn't lose everything as a result.

A knock on the door startled us.

Max opened the door. Johann stood there, looking equally dashing in white and gold.

"Ready?" he asked. For the first time, Johann sounded normal to me. He wasn't belligerent or mean-spirited or adversarial. He seemed excited about the party. I considered that a good thing.

"Have you seen Ben?" Max asked his brother once they stood outside the room.

Johann grimaced, straightening his jacket. "No. Him and his experiments. We'd be lucky to catch a glimpse of him all day." Then he regarded me down his nose, doing a once-over. "He cleans up well."

I whistled low. "Wow. A compliment and an insult in one. Nice." I looked at Max. "Have I been too dirty? Outside of bed, I mean."

Max rolled his eyes and smirked at me. "Behave."

"Yes, sir." I clacked my heels together. "I promise to misbehave."

"Shut up, you," Max scolded me, yanked me out of the room into the hall, and closed the door so I couldn't retreat.

And off we went to the Summer Solstice Festival and Feast.

WE LEFT the Snake Tower behind, crossed through the Great Gallery, the Royal Library, the private apartments, and a covered colonnade with a view of the wide sunlit lawns of the Inner Ward. Then we entered the Banquet Hall.

The dozen chandeliers weren't lit, but the floor-to-ceiling windows allowed the bright sunshine in. French doors were open on the southern wall to the Outer Bailey, and a warm summer breeze rustled the lilac-colored curtains and the pink wax flowers. Sweet fragrances floated about from clean linens, fresh flowers, and filled food platters on two long tables on both sides of the room, covered in white cloth with gold trimmings. Little Norician flags fluttered a foot apart on the tables amid china and crystal flutes engraved with the royal unicorn emblem and the words Lindau-Arbon. Countless staff members stood in perfect unbroken lines against the wall, their uniforms pristine, their faces schooled.

I stared at everything in awe as I trailed after Max and Johann through the empty hall.

"Is this where the dancing happens?" I asked since the floor had been cleared of any clutter of furniture. I'd passed through here before with Max on our tour of the castle, and I recalled couches and armchairs, coffee tables and credenzas.

"No, stupid," Johann snorted, causing my blood pressure to rise. "That's what the Ballroom is for. This is the Banquet Hall, where guests—namely foreign dignitaries and ambassadors—can mingle with the elite of our country while savoring a nine-course buffet."

I suppressed a growl. "Not all of us know about this sort of thing, you know."

Johann stared down at me. "No, commoners usually don't." Then he wheeled around on his heels and walked off, head held high, as if the ground near me was made of dirt and smelled funny.

I took a deep breath and counted to ten in Spanish. "I know he's your brother, but dammit, dude, he's such a jerk."

Max took my hand and squeezed. "I know. He hasn't always been this bad, though."

I met his sad gaze. "So it's me, then? The Tex-Mex gay guy he can't stand?"

Max leaned in and touched his forehead to mine. "Don't let him get to you. He's my problem, and I will deal with him. All right?"

I hated the idea of being the wedge that separated the brothers. I didn't want to be a point of continued contention. But what could I do? Johann had his preconceptions and elitist views, and I doubted I could change them overnight, if ever.

It was best left to Max. He and Johann were brothers, after all. This was their issue to resolve.

"Ollie, look at me!"

I nearly jumped out of my skin. Elinor's holler rang throughout the three-story-high Banquet Hall. I was surprised the dead didn't rise and scream at her to shut up.

"Jesus fucking Christ, woman!" I called out in frustration.

"What was that?" Valerie asked, her voice sharp and demanding obedience.

"Sorry, Mama," I murmured and heard a similar sentiment from Elinor.

Only then did I really look at her. She wore a white-and-gold cocktail dress, high heels—and had wings on her back.

"What the...?" I gawked in surprise.

Elinor snickered. "I'm a solar sprite."

"A what?"

"A solar sprite." Elinor shrugged. "It's from this book I read: *Gremlins Are Malfunctioning*. Quite a hoot."

I blinked. I'd not read that tale. "So you're like a sun fairy?"

"Something like that." Elinor twirled on her toes like a ballerina, even though she wore high heels. She waved her hand about as if she were dancing the lead in *Swan Lake*. Behind her, the wings made of silk and jewels—*please don't let them be real*—fluttered and undulated. She was stunning.

"You're beautiful," I said like a dutiful big brother, though I meant it too.

Elinor smiled at me. And did I see a misty veil in her eyes? She quickly looked away, hiding her emotions from me. I really did love her. I wanted to say it out loud, too, but the place was too public, and she was already teary-eyed.

My parents had been given costumes for the ball as well.

Clad in dark gold, Valerie resembled a rococo queen straight out of Versailles. Her dress had a low-cut neckline, tight bodice, and a skirt with a wide pannier that was lavishly decorated with bows and ribbons, lacy waves, and flower patterns. Her brown hair was raised high on her head in a stiff coiffure adorned with huge feathers and yellow flowers.

"Mom? Holy shit," I exclaimed in pure and utter shock. I'd never seen her like this.

Valerie beamed. "Quite a difference to my usual look."

I had no words. Thankfully, Elinor did.

"Mom, you look amazing. Like a proper queen."

"Agreed," said Paulito at her side.

Like Max and Johann, Paulito wore form-fitting pants, a dress shirt with a vest, and a short cloak draped over one shoulder. Was that the fashion back in… whenever that was? I wasn't an expert on Celtic sun gods or courts of any kind. In any case, my father looked perfectly presentable in his attire, the hue dark red this time.

Compared to everyone else, I felt naked and exposed. At least no one seemed to notice, or if they did, they didn't call attention to my cupbearer's uniform.

Only Max leered at me on occasion, his gaze traveling up and down on my skin. I swear I felt it everywhere, like a real-life touch.

"Good morning, everyone. Your Highnesses."

Frederica sailed across the room—dressed in a white-gold shepherdess outfit.

I damn near swallowed my tongue trying not to burst out chortling, remembering how Max had described her as the wolf among the sheep. How apropos.

"How is everyone doing on this most glorious day?" Frederica chirped. Before anyone could comment, she moved on, which seemed to be a habit of hers. "Now, I trust you're all aware of the importance that this celebration goes without a hitch, hmm?"

Max and Johann nodded pliantly, which seemed to expedite things, so my family and I followed their lead.

"Excellent," Frederica declared, bouncing on the balls of her feet. "Onward. There will be a select few reporters about this evening among the other guests, so no excessive drinking."

Max glanced at Johann knowingly, a gesture which Johann ignored. I wondered if the party prince, as he was known, would embarrass the royal family tonight.

"Which reporters?" Johann asked, though he appeared disinterested. Perhaps he just wanted to divert attention away from himself.

"De Lange from the *Vindeburg Tribune*." The pointed look Frederica gave Johann didn't go unnoticed by me or Max.

Johann snarled. "That damn presstitute? Why the hell was she invited?"

Frederica's cheery disposition didn't falter for a second. "Your father invited her."

"To keep you in check, no doubt," Max commented dryly.

Johann glared at his brother. "That last article was hardly my fault. She ambushed me." He scoffed and crossed his arms over his chest. "If de Lange had an ounce of journalistic integrity, she wouldn't have published those pictures."

"Oh, she had plenty more that never made it to print or the internet," Max said dryly, evidently piquing Johann's interest, since his scowl changed into a confused frown. "She had photos of you literally with your breeches down. Instead, the only one out there is you kissing Ambassador Fowler's daughter."

Johann blinked, his cheeks turning rosy red. "I, uh, well... Madeleine Fowler is a rare breed. A beautiful aristocrat. Most of them tend to look like horses."

"How fitting, since you seem to treat women like animals," Elinor cut in, her gaze trained elsewhere as if she'd not said anything or said only innocent things.

Johann looked like a lightning rod gathering a charge.

Max broke the tension. "Who else besides de Lange is coming?"

"Patrice Chevalier from the *Norician Times*, of course—" Frederica offered.

"Good. At least he's both polite and discreet," Johann cut in, seemingly pleased.

"That's because he's both a Royalist and a lover of wine," Max remarked with a sigh. "Last Summer Solstice security found you two passed out in the wine cellar, if I recall."

"Yes, but he never wrote about that," Johann admitted with a smirk. "Who else?"

"Alois Zest from NPR. He's conducting interviews with a couple of the guests," Frederica replied. "NNBC is broadcasting the entire event live, with an assortment of host and guest interviews, so be prepared."

I noticed how Max flinched when the radio host's name was mentioned. The pink rising to his cheeks told me this reporter was either an old fling or the one that got away. Max had never spoken of his exes in detail, and I'd never pried. Now I regretted my discretion and politeness.

Johann chuckled. "This should be interesting." His knowing gaze landed on me, which confirmed what I already suspected. That was why I was able to keep a straight face. Johann's smile faltered at my blank expression.

"All right." Frederica closed her leather notebook with a soft thump and gave each of us a meaningful look. "This is an important event. One of the highlights of the social calendar. I expect all of you to be on your best behavior."

Then she walked off, tapping her tablet without looking at it. She really was a consummate professional. I would have hated to have her job.

Johann shrugged and sauntered off in search of snacks.

I went to Max and gave him a chin-lift to indicate we should move away from the others. With a sad look, he followed me to the open french doors that gave out to the park—the hollies and the oak trees and the beautiful lawn—of the Outer Bailey.

Before I got a word in edgewise, Max said, "Alois Zest, one of the most popular hosts of Norician Public Radio, is a former bedmate of mine. We met when he interviewed me on his show. He and I were not in love. It was merely a, uh, an inconvenient affair."

I kept the raging emotions, mainly jealousy, out of my face. "How long did it last?"

"We met a second time at a party much like this one, got to chatting, and… one thing led to another. He would come to my tower after midnight via one of the secret entrances. He'd stay for a few hours and leave."

"No, I meant—"

"I know what you meant. It was over well before Winter Solstice Gala last year. But he was my most recent lover before you in the spring."

I hesitated. "Is he the jealous, obsessive type? Should I steer clear of you the whole festival?"

Max smiled. "No. You see, Alois's parents are conservative. He hasn't come out to them. That is only one of many reasons why he stands to lose as much as I if word got out about him and me. He will say nothing."

"You're not getting me," I said, slightly frustrated. "Does he want to get back together with you? Especially if he sees you with someone else?"

Max gripped my hips and pulled me close till we were almost touching. "No, he does not." Hedging, I wanted to ask him how come he sounded so sure of himself, but then Max kissed me, and I relented.

Secretly, I hoped I didn't live to regret my trust in him or his confidence in an ex-lover.

AT TEN minutes to noon, King Gustav stood behind a makeshift podium on the highest steps of the stairs leading up from the Outer Bailey to the terrace of the Swan Tower. Dressed in amber-hued, gold-and-jewel-adorned clothes and a long cape, with an honest-to-god crown on his head—*was that real?*—he stared out at the crowd gathered there. Every guest had something yellow or gold on their costumes. Most wore those colors exclusively. All the clothes were extravagant and luxurious, as befitting the Court of the Sun King.

The last theme party I attended was a stupid toga party at a college frat (not mine), and the one before that was a Cowboys and Indians birthday party when I was eight (not my birthday). I felt wholly out of place.

King Gustav gave a speech. It was in German, so I didn't understand. Then he switched to French, then Italian, and finally English. "The sun is shining, and both Great Sun God Belenos and I, along with everyone here at Riten Castle, wish to cordially welcome you to the Annual Summer Solstice Festival and Feast. Eat, drink, and make merry. Salut!"

He toasted with a flute of champagne. Everyone in the audience raised their glasses and called out *salut*. I followed suit. My glass overflowed with a pink fizzy drink, and my tongue tickled as the bubbles popped. I tasted strawberries and alcohol and sugary sweetness.

"I love this," I murmured to Elinor beside me.

Elinor snickered. "Everyone loves champagne cocktails."

The light show alluded to by Max started. Colorful lasers danced in the sky, turning the place into a sunshine club experience. Projections reflected on the upper parts of tower walls in each direction: The Bull Tower showed a stampede of golden bulls, the Stag Tower had a mountain with a sparkling, rampant buck on top, and the Seahorse Tower was enveloped by a blue ocean scene floating on its surface. Everywhere I dared to look, flashes of blinding color radiated images or beams.

Elinor glanced around. "Where's your special guy?"

I suppressed a longing sigh. "He's around. Hobnobbing with guests, I suppose."

Elinor bumped my arm with her shoulder. "You should mingle too. Get to know people. I mean, who knows? You might spend a lot of time here in the future."

I took a sip. Okay, more of a gulp. I was buying time. I couldn't think beyond the summer. I simply couldn't think that far ahead. And I didn't want to confess that to Elinor. She would have intervened. Somehow, she would have tried to fix things, and I had to do that myself. I just didn't know how to fix something that wasn't broken—not yet, at least.

Maybe the simple truth was that royal affairs weren't meant to last.

"You mingle," I told her. "I want to watch."

"People-watch or stalk like a saber-tooth tiger?" Elinor clarified, her lips pursed. But she didn't wait for a reply, simply danced into the Banquet Hall where, after the King's speech, a lot of people had already gathered.

I could relate. They all wore elaborate, old-fashioned costumes—the women in ball dresses that had to weigh tons—while the air was getting hotter by the minute. Any shelter or shade had to sound appealing until nightfall.

I wasn't wearing enough to break a sweat. I might get sunburned, though, so I traipsed inside too. I hadn't eaten much of a breakfast, and it was past noon, and the tables had spreads I had only ever dreamed of. Nine courses? Geesh. And the options? My mouth watered at the sight, the smells, the anticipation. A grand buffet in a real-life castle?

I wasn't about to turn away.

Saddles of wild boar roasted with juniper berries, quail with truffles, bite-size walnut and orange flavored ice cream, stuffed salmon trout baked in red wine, turbot in tarragon sauce, rosettes of partridge breasts, grouse pies, lobster medallions, chicken breasts poached in white wine, fried capon served with potato salad, fritters stuffed with cherries in a kirsch syrup, chestnut soup….

My head spun. I was grateful the dishes had labels, placards engraved with gold lettering because some I wouldn't even have recognized. Even the scents threw me. Everything seemed like something else. I was weirded out. And I was plenty envious. This was the level I aspired to reach as a chef. But upon seeing the complexity and detail on these edible works of art, I doubted I could ever accomplish such majesty even if I had weeks to complete them.

Nonetheless, I sampled a little of everything. Almost every dish in the main course had either meat or fish in it. The meats simply melted on my tongue. The taste was out of this world—buttery and creamy, smooth and savory. My eyes hungered almost as much as my belly.

I was so focused on tasting the numerous options that I failed to notice the lady beside me.

Chapter 21

"YOU MUST try the roasted duck with crispy potatoes and mulled wine cherry sauce. It's absolutely divine."

She wore a simple white silk dress with a wide yellow silk sash under her bosom, the attire revealing her svelte figure so well, she might as well have been naked. Her dark orange hair was raised in a loose hairdo over her head, with escaped curls framing her delicate face. A golden sun had been painted around her right eye. She reminded me of Lady Kira but had an approachable warmth to her, complete with dimples and an open smile.

She extended a hand for me. "I'm Tulip."

"Like the flower?"

"*Oui, exactement*." She touched her hair. On the jeweled headdress, a red tulip had been attached. I couldn't smell it at all; maybe it was fake?

I shook her hand. In hindsight, I probably should have kissed it. "I'm Oliver."

She popped a purple grape in her mouth. "You're new. I'd remember seeing you before." She did a once-over on my body. That coupled with the purring French accent, and I shivered in spite of being wholeheartedly gay. Maybe she reminded me too much of Max, whom I was already missing badly.

"I, uh, I'm a guest of the royal family," I explained vaguely. "And you?" I added to steer the idle chitchat to her. Safer topic to be sure.

She waved her hand about and giggled, her voice like silver bells. "Oh, I come to all of these shindigs. They do get ever so boring sometimes. Nothing new to see." Tulip batted her eyelashes at me. "Except someone new. You sound American?"

"I am." I was stumped for something to say that didn't outright reveal every damn thing about me and Max. "First time at the Solstice Festival, though. Is it always so, uh... shiny?"

Tulip laughed. "Well, it is a celebration of the sun, isn't it?"

She made me think of birds-of-paradise, colorful and bright, and also of pretty little dolls dressed in silk and lace, with porcelain skin and big childlike eyes. Was this the result of wealth and good breeding, so to speak?

"Are you, uh, a Norician noblewoman?" I asked, hoping I used the right term.

Tulip quirked an eyebrow. "Aren't you cute? Too adorable. I'd like to crush you to my breast like a puppy and kiss you all over."

I blushed, my skin so hot inside and out that it was a wonder I avoided spontaneous human combustion. "I, um...."

Tulip cocked her head, suddenly assessing me. "You do look familiar after all." She perked up. "Have we slept together?"

"No!" I sputtered. When people glanced in my direction, I forced a strained smile on my lips and lowered my voice. "I mean, no, we haven't... milady."

She shrugged, shifting about as if dancing to a tune only she heard. "Ah well. I dare say I'd remember that. You're just too cute for words. Cuddly."

Grimacing inwardly, I stepped away from her, making it seem like I was just inspecting the endless buffet platters. But she followed me, tiptoeing to stand by my side again.

"I can't recall where I know you from," Tulip said, sounding pensive. I cringed. Did ladies of leisure read foreign newspapers, especially the gossip section? I wished she were more civilized. Then, out of the blue, she asked, "Have you tried Chicago pizza?"

I stared and blinked. "Um, yes?"

Her eyes grew impossibly large, like those of a Japanese anime character. "Ooh, tell me everything." Before I could so much as make a noncommittal noise, she said, "I've seen you in the papers, haven't I?"

I stared down at my plate, praying for guidance from a beer sausage. "Have I seen *you* in the papers?" I asked back. A bit childish, I thought, but company is as company does.

Tulip laughed. "Aren't you funny?" All of a sudden, she gasped and snapped her fingers. "Oh my goodness. You're the First Prince's—"

"Is this sorbet or ice cream?" I interjected in desperation, pointing at the tiny strawberry-shaped objects in an ice-chilled silver bowl.

Tulip blinked, her full lips rounding in a soundless O. "Ice cream," she replied.

"Oh. I could've sworn it was sorbet." I chuckled in such an awful fake style it was a miracle no one paid more attention. "Oh well. I guess we all make mistakes. One thing can look so much like another, you know what I mean?"

For a while Tulip stared at me. I couldn't read her at all. Then she smiled—in a way that contradicted her prior genuineness. "You're a smart one, aren't you? No wonder Max likes you."

I frowned. "You mean, His Studious Highness, Prince Maximilian?"

Tulip chuckled. "You tow the party line well for an American. Speaking of which, what political viewpoint do you represent, Mr. Reed? Are you a right-wing conservative fascist or a left-wing socialist tree-hugger?" My hackles rose as my suspicions grew. She smiled like a predator. "You're cautious; I'll give you that. Is it really so hard to be true to yourself?"

She accentuated the last question by rounding her eyes into a display of picture-perfect innocence. Had I not heard her before, I might have been fooled.

"Who are you?" I asked.

She curtsied. "Tulip de Lange, at your service, Mr. Reed."

Her name rang a bell. "You serve the people with your writings, don't you? Or rather you serve their insatiable curiosity with the dirt you dig up."

"Such contempt for a representative of the free media," Tulip said. "Then again, perhaps you cater to both sides of the aisle, as any dutiful chef would. Not like that sister of yours. There's no mistaking where her loyalties lie. Such a strong feminist in the making. A would-be engineer, I hear, breaking the barriers between the sexes."

I held back a gasp. She knew an awful lot about me and my family. "What do you want, Ms. de Lange?"

"An interview with the First Prince's lover, of course," Tulip replied matter-of-factly. "How did you two meet?"

I paused to see if she had more. When she waited for me to speak, I did. "I heard yours is one of the two major newspapers in the country, highly regarded and very respectable. From your line of questioning, seems more like a tabloid."

Tulip's eyes flashed. "We all serve a purpose and carry out a necessary function to protect our country."

At first I was surprised by her patriotic fervor. Then I heard what she didn't say. "You fling the dirt first so no one can beat you to the punch."

Tulip quirked an eyebrow. "I was right. Definitely a smart one."

I leaned in a little. "Doesn't it bother you that people think so ill of you when it's—"

"What, undeserved?" Tulip shook her head. "But it isn't, now, is it? I play in the mud with the pigs. One gets… dirty. No avoiding it."

Her style of ending statements with questions should have been a clue about her identity. Alas, I'd been taken for a ride by the dimples. "Does anyone know the truth?"

Tulip laughed merrily. "The truth? The whole truth and nothing but? Aren't you a quaint little American? Such an innocent."

"Were you going to say naïve?" I asked, teasing.

Tulip's smile widened, revealing pearly-white teeth. "Changing words to fit your meaning, eh? You'd make a fine journalist." Then she cast a seemingly casual glance about, but I wasn't fooled. "People form opinions based on their own prejudice. Why bother telling them off when they won't listen? That sounds illogical, doesn't it?"

I sighed. "Well, even if no one else knows, I do."

Tulip winked at me. "I bet there's a lot you know. Max must have been very impressed by you from the start at, oh, where was it again?"

I rolled my eyes. "You're a persistent one… aren't you?"

Tulip giggled, leaned closer, and kissed me on the cheek. "You're sweet."

"You do get around. Both of you." Johann's sneer broke the bubble of friendship that was starting to form between Tulip and me. He stared down his nose at us.

"Ms. de Lange, scrounging the bottom of the barrel for slime, I see. And Mr. Reed, kissing strange wenches in public already? I never would have guessed. Sharing stories of your two-faced adventures, eh? I didn't mean to interrupt your bonding of like minds."

I shook with rage.

Tulip, however, laughed. "I have tomorrow's headline for you, Your Highness. *Party Prince caught in a compromising position.* What do you think? So many possibilities."

Johann gritted his teeth. "I've done nothing tonight."

Tulip smiled. "But you have on so many other nights. Who could tell the difference?"

Johann took a step forward. "That's slander. I will have your head on a platter, de Lange."

Tulip stepped closer as well. "Are you threatening the free media, sir? Would you care to make a statement on record to that effect? I'm sure our people would love to see how their tax crowns are used to support your many indiscretions and hate speech. Who knows? The Republicans might gain an upper hand in the Council over the Royalists."

Johann's face paled but his eyes flashed like steel. "You're crossing the line. Unpatriotic to the last." He glanced at me; I felt a chill despite the sunshine. "Are you plotting with her to end monarchy in the kingdom?"

I opened my mouth to deny his accusations, but, as usual, Tulip got there first.

"Oh, I was plotting. He tried to stop me." She stared me down, condescension burning me like flames. "A foreign agent for royalty, is he, Your Highness? You plant him before me to try to distract me. It won't work. I'll write what I want."

She sent a shriveling scowl at Johann, then me, and walked off, her high heels clicking on the white marble floor set with tiny black diamonds. I stared after her, utterly confused.

Johann inched closer to me while watching Tulip's retreating back. "Be careful with her. She's a vile Republican who disguises her agenda in her writings." He looked at me as if seeing me for the first time. "I'm curious. Were you defending the royal family because of Max and what you can gain from him or because our house has ruled here for centuries and we deserve to keep the Ivy Throne?"

Everything hit me at once. Realizations and epiphanies. Tulip had made herself appear like a political adversary for Johann and then accused me of conspiring with the Third Prince. That in turn made Johann a tentative ally to me—even though he continued to doubt my motives.

Man, Tulip had a handle on manipulation and intrigue. I was duly impressed.

I met Johann's gaze. "I don't care about your wealth or power. I only want Max for sex."

Then I stomped off as well. It felt good to have a little revenge and sting the elitist pig with something that would undoubtedly leave him seething. Not that what I'd said was true; I wanted Max for much more than his body. But the slap against Johann's arrogant face was called for.

"I'm slightly offended. You only want me for sex? Or do you just like canopy beds?"

I smiled at Max's words and faced him. "Eavesdropping? How amoral of you."

Max grinned at me. "It's my castle."

He stole a glimpse over his shoulder, where Johann was speaking with the prime minister's twin sons. Johann looked pissed, but then again, he seemed to have a resting bitch face. The von Thürer twins were snickering and pointing at people. Boorish jerks.

"I was trying to annoy him, you know," I told Max, who nodded with a smile. "You think his head would explode if he tried to imagine a world without royalty and where commoners or gays rule countries?"

Max laughed. "Maybe." Frederica drew closer and waved at Max, who sighed. "Duty calls. How are you enjoying yourself so far?"

I hesitated. "Food's amazing."

Max nodded. "Taste everything. Who knows? Perhaps you can concoct your own future signature dish from the inspiration you receive today." I could tell he wanted to kiss me but didn't. He bowed and walked off with the Royal Press Officer.

I felt abandoned and cherished at the same time.

Throwing caution to the wind, even at the risk of a stomachache later, I dug into the dishes. Every mouthful was a novel experience. I ate and I googled on the free Wi-Fi in the castle grounds. I learned that most of the dishes had hundreds of years of tradition behind them. Culture dictated certain foods and drinks, but modern aspects were added as well. I didn't think they had champagne cocktails in the seventeenth century, or whenever this kingdom was founded. I vaguely recalled it had been a duchy first…?

"You must try the spit-roasted swan with redcurrant jelly. It's to die for."

I smiled and faced Tulip. "You have a knack for fitting into every situation."

She winked at me. "And butting in where I don't belong and getting into trouble."

I grew serious. I liked her and didn't want her to get hurt. "You didn't need to do that with John. He still doesn't trust me."

Tulip shrugged. "Maybe not. But at least he believes you're not here to abolish the monarchy. You, an American and a Democrat? He thinks you're everything that's wrong with modernity."

I harrumphed. "America's not so modern right now. Old white men are trying to drag us back to the dark ages, kicking and screaming."

Tulip touched my arm in sympathy. "Even despots meet their end eventually. Whether by not being elected or by the hanging rope."

"Now when hate crimes against people of color by white-supremacist douchebags are on the rise, anything could happen." I shook my head, sad for so many reasons. But defeat wasn't an option; that much I knew. We had to fight for our freedom, our rights, for progress, and for democracy. Even if a corrupt government threatened to take them all away.

Tulip bussed me on the other cheek, perhaps for symmetry. "Aww, don't look so glum. It's a party. Light burns away darkness." She gripped my arms and pulled me toward the doors leading to the Swan Tower and the Ballroom beyond that. "Come, my young American. Dance with me."

I could have resisted, but I suspected resistance was futile with this woman.

I SHOULD have brought my sunglasses with me. For the Ballroom was enough to blind anyone with its brilliance.

An arched glass ceiling created prismatic rainbows everywhere. A white marble floor matched the white walls decorated with golden ornaments. A grand piano stood in the southeastern corner, with a low stage for an orchestra. Live music played, a tune reminding me of a Viennese waltz. A few tables dotted the walls between tall french doors and floor-to-ceiling windows, all lined with beverages of all kinds. In the doorways stood unicorn statues that shot colorful confetti out of their horns every few minutes. Gold streamers hung here and there across the grand hall.

I was stunned into silence. Then Tulip swept me away into a twirling dance amid a hundred other couples in a large circle around the room. I did my best to follow her lead and managed not to step on her toes more than thrice.

"So, what's with the Royalists and Republicans?" I asked, leaning into her ear. Tulip seemed to be a political expert, among other things.

"The Council of Ministers, like the country as a whole, is comprised of three groups," Tulip explained, her warm voice fanning my neck. "The Royalists, the Republicans, and the Moderates. It's not your typical right-wing, left-wing division."

I knew a bit, so I said, "The prime minister is a Royalist, isn't he?"

"Yes," Tulip confirmed. "Basically, Royalists want Noricia to continue as a kingdom while Republicans would prefer a democratic state with an elected president—with them doing the electing, not the people as a whole. Moderates stand in between and maintain the status quo, which means both royalty and democracy. That's the current constitutional monarchy. They hold a majority in the Council, so they've been able to implement modern reforms."

"King Gustav can veto?" I ventured a guess.

"Yes, but it's rare for the King and Queen to interfere in the legislative process. You see, King Gustav is the head of state, and an elected Council enacts the law. But Noricia is also a direct democracy where registered voters, basically everyone born in this country as well as every registered citizen, can propose constitutional amendments independent of the legislature."

I had always sucked in civics class. "Okay, so… three parties can make laws?"

Tulip smiled at my undoubtedly bewildered expression. My head sure hurt.

"Yes: the King, the Council, and the people. As a matter of fact, it was a citizen's initiative that led to the Equal Marriage Act which is now law of the land."

"Wow. Cool." I couldn't imagine a situation like that, where a citizen might be enlightened enough to make a proposal to bring forth progress. Not in America; not in a million years. If anything, the country would likely be set back in time. A single educated, civilized person might be able to propose something that benefited everyone—but that proposal would most likely be shot down by special interest groups and corrupt politicians. Ring around the rosie.

Tulip chuckled, unaware of my ruminations. "Yes, the law is in your favor. You and Max."

To avoid answering, I gestured toward an older gentleman with white hair cut in a trendy fashion. He wore a business suit, only it was completely white, with gold cufflinks and a yellow-gold tie. He was speaking with Max.

"Who's that?"

Tulip followed my gaze. "Ambassador Robert Fowler from the States."

I shivered, remembering the rumor going around about Johann's relationship with the ambassador's daughter, Madeleine. "I didn't know that," I stated rather stupidly.

"Keeping up with the names and faces of the ever-changing diplomatic corps is a task best left for government officials and state bureaucrats," Tulip commented, scrunching her pretty little nose. Her gaze traveled the room. "I wonder where Madeleine is, though. With the Third Prince?"

To divert the subject further away from restless waters, I asked, "How often do these citizen amendment proposals get through?"

"Quite often, if they have merit. The potential new legislation has to benefit more than one person, you understand. And it should be about progress, not stagnation or worse, regression."

If I'd been a citizen of Noricia, would I propose a future law where gay royals were allowed to rule and marry whom they pleased? The law wouldn't benefit more than the person wanting to wed a royal, though. At the moment, that was me.

Wait. What was I saying? I didn't want to marry Max. That would be hell on earth.

Wouldn't it?

Who was I asking, besides myself?

I shook my head, angry at my heart for wanting impossible things and my mind for trying to rationalize insanity and solve impossible equations. The world had progressed a lot, but not enough for a gay king and his... what?

No, I was being ridiculous. My thing with Max was an affair, nothing more. A summer fling with an expiration date. I really ought not to forget that fact.

Chapter 22

MY HEART, though, refused to listen. It told the rest of me it was in love and expected the rest of me to fall in line.

"How well do you know Max?" I asked Tulip de Lange. Shrewd journalist that she was, she might know him quite well.

"Isn't that my question?" Tulip chuckled. Then she sighed. "Forever, I suppose. My whole life. He is the First Prince, isn't he?" She twirled me around so fast I almost tripped over my own feet *and* hers. "See that gentleman with him now?"

It took me a moment to spot Max. He'd traveled from his earlier post. Now he was speaking with a young man who was, for the lack of a better word, pretty as a picture. Long dark hair with green highlights flowed like a cascade over his shoulders and down his lean back. Short and slender, he was like a pretty girl, only he was a boy—dressed in a cupbearer's outfit similar to mine.

A twinge of jealousy bit my heart.

"Who is that?"

Tulip snorted. "Your predecessor. Alois Zest."

The little spark roared into open flames. Holding it back was a hard thing to do. I recalled Freddie mentioning him by name. "The radio guy?"

Tulip giggled. "Oh, that casual comment must have taken an effort. As opposed to running across the room and tearing Alois's long hair off his head."

I smiled in spite of my raging emotions. "Pulling hair? That's more of a chick thing. I'd just knock his perfect teeth in." I cleared my throat. "Not that I would. First, I'm a gentleman. Second, I have no personal relationship with the First Prince."

Tulip threw her head back and laughed, just like Alois did across the room. He didn't touch Max, but he leaned closer. They appeared to be whispering like a pair of lovebirds. I bit my cheek not to cry or shout or... something.

"You were invited here by the First Prince, weren't you?" Tulip said with a knowing smirk. "The buzz says you and he are close personal friends."

"Says who?" I asked, daring to flirt a little, though I knew that wouldn't throw her off the scent. "Heard it through the royal grapevine? You're a journalist. You should know better than to believe in gossip and innuendo."

Tulip studied me with a twinkle of mirth in her eyes. "Oh, if I put any stock in rumors, I'd not ask you about your affair with Max, but about what happened in France." I kept a smile on my face; inside I crumbled. She whispered to me, "You wouldn't want me asking about that, would you, Mr. Reed?"

I swallowed down so many emotions that it was a wonder they all fit. "P-please, call me Oliver."

I remembered I hadn't told her my last name. She'd known who I was from the start. I really needed to stop allowing myself to be ambushed like this.

"What do you know about Alois?" I asked, peering past her to Max and the young man with the long, luscious locks.

"I know Max cared more about him than he cared about Max. I also know Max cares more about you than he ever did about Alois." Tulip locked gazes with me. "But I also know that Alois had and may still have designs on the First Prince. Ambition was always his strong suit. Or did you forget, Oliver, that whoever wins the First Prince's heart may become the next Royal Consort of Noricia?"

I gulped. To be honest, I had let that slip my mind in favor of long mornings in bed with a man I loved. He'd been so adamant about insisting he was just a man, not a title, that I'd forgotten said title and all that came with it.

Tulip shook her head, bemused. "What a precious little darling you are, Oliver."

I blushed. So, she'd figured me out without my uttering a single syllable.

Then I remembered that Max had told me Alois was still in the closet. My first thought was how on earth could Tulip even know about their affair when, according to Max, he and Alois had been secretive and careful to the point of clandestine. Who or what were Tulip's sources, and what was her end game? Her vast font of information scared me.

But then my second thought returned me to Alois and his ambitions. How could he have any designs on Max if he wasn't out with his family or society at large? I snorted inwardly. Perhaps Alois marrying the future king would go a long way in appeasing his family's animosities toward having a gay or bisexual son. Greed could be a blinding *and* an eye-opening experience at the same time.

Regardless of Alois's motives, I had faith in Max—and my number one concern right now was Tulip and her unceasing probing. It was clear that the longer I spent time with her, the more likely it was I'd falter and spill the beans by accident.

"I-I don't feel like dancing anymore," I said weakly, pulling away from her.

At first she looked surprised, her eyebrows raised. Then a tiny smile showed her sympathy. "I apologize, Oliver. Please, try to enjoy the festival. I may not know Max as well as you do, but I know he would like it if you did."

Then she curtsied and ambled off, sharing a few words and giggles with passing guests. Everyone must have been aware who she was. Yet no one treated her the way Johann had, like an enemy.

I mingled, sharing nods and the odd pleasantry here and there. No one recognized me, so they left me alone. Perhaps they were wary of strangers, or maybe they had nothing to gain from a nobody like me.

Out of the corner of my eye, I spotted Tulip huddled in an alcove in the Banquet Hall. She was conversing with a tall, burly, fair-haired man with a short, trendy beard. Their expressions seemed casual, but to me something seemed off. With a curtsey and a bow, they went their separate ways.

I pushed the encounter out of my mind. Too much rattling inside my skull already.

There was a mix of languages at the party. I missed all the snippets in German, French, and Italian, but I caught a few in English and even a couple in Spanish. One conversation in particular caught my ear, and I couldn't resist eavesdropping. I couldn't tell who was talking to whom, but I could distinguish four, maybe five different speakers.

"Ambassador Fowler will likely be recalled to the States after all that unpleasantness."

"Fowler must be so embarrassed about his daughter's indiscretion."

"Guess someone should have taught her that a foreign country is not a college sorority where anything goes."

"Ms. Madeleine's absent from the festivities today, I see."

"Can you blame her? She should be mortified. After all, her choice of bedmates is ending her father's illustrious diplomatic career."

"We don't know that. King Gustav respects Fowler's experienced counsel. He may choose to keep him on, if not as an ambassador, perhaps a consul or envoy?"

"I agree. Why should the King send Fowler packing? I mean, it's not like the girl bedded one of the princes."

"Who did she bed, then?"

"Some reporter. That radio personality who's on almost every day."

"Alois Zest? The young man from *Afternoons with Alois*? Well, I never knew he had such lofty aspirations."

"I heard he's not too particular about who he screws. Men, women, highborn, commoner, foreign, domestic—it's all the same to him. As long as he can benefit."

"In that case, he must be an aristocrat."

Everyone laughed at the jest. I grimaced and snuck farther away, mostly to hold back nausea. Had I stepped back in time? These people seemed to believe that being born into a rich and powerful family was an advantage that came with certain undeniable privileges, like a foregone conclusion. I didn't get that kind of thinking.

I was mystified by the exchange too. Hadn't Tulip moments ago inferred that Prince Johann and Madeleine Fowler had indeed slept together? Yet these guests, who should be in the know, seemed to think Madeleine had slept with Alois. Maybe she had, maybe she hadn't. I didn't know.

But I did decide I didn't like Alois Zest one damn bit.

Of course, trusting silly rumors might make me misjudge a man....

The air smelled of foods and perfumes and fresh mountain air. I left the Ballroom in the direction of the Outer Bailey and found myself in the sunshine under a mighty oak. Even beneath the foliage, I was still hot, caught in the dappling sunlight. I inhaled and tried to rediscover my center. In this place, I didn't know who I was. What was my role to play in the grand scheme of things?

"Hello."

I started. I'd closed my eyes and leaned against the tree trunk, trying to calm down. Now I faced a pretty young man who screamed twink and bottom with every ounce of his being. Alois.

"I'm Alois Zest." He thrust his hand at me and smiled. If I hadn't made a vow to dislike him, I might have found him tempting. But he had nothing on my Max. "And you are...?" he asked.

I pushed off the tree and shook his hand, a bit more forcefully than usual. "I'm Oliver. And you wouldn't be much of a reporter if you didn't already know that."

Alois flashed a winning smile. "I see there's no point in pulling the hair over your eyes."

"The wool," I corrected. "Pulling the wool over your eyes." Alois had a French accent as well. The gay part of me found him eminently fuckable, but the rest of me hissed in fury.

He inclined his head. "Yes, wool, of course."

I saw from his reaction that he'd faked his ignorance, perhaps to ingratiate himself to me. My dislike of him grew.

He studied me. "Are you and Max together?"

"Are you and Madeleine Fowler together?"

His smile faltered, and he glanced around as if to see who might be listening. "I don't know what you mean."

"Ditto."

His eyes flashed. "I see there's no point in pretense either."

"To be civil?" I clarified. "Nope."

I turned to leave. He put his hand on my arm to pull me back, and that was it for me. He'd gotten on my last nerve. The straw that broke the camel's back. I swiveled around fast and discreetly punched him in the groin. He grunted quietly and doubled over. I kept him upright, though, escorted him toward the nearest bench, and plopped him down.

I leaned over him and whispered, "I'm not some pampered nobleman. Reporter or not, touch me again and I'll wipe the floor with your remains. Got that?"

Alois blinked up owlishly and nodded.

"What's going on here?"

I cringed as I straightened up. Alois looked pleased, like the proverbial cat that ate the canary. Max stared at me and Alois, his face unreadable.

"Your boyfriend assaulted me, is what," Alois muttered.

"Did you, Oliver?" Max asked.

I faced him. "Yes."

For a while no one spoke. An awkward, tense silence that could have been cut with a knife ensued.

Finally, Max said, "What did you say to him, Alois?"

The young reporter stood, wincing in pain. "Why are you taking his side? He hit me."

Max sighed. "I know you, so you more than likely deserved it." Before anyone could speak further, Max added, "Ambassador Fowler is looking for you. So is his daughter. One is furious, the other amorous. I'll leave it to you to figure out which one is which."

A panicked look animated Alois's pretty face, and he glanced around like a frantic animal. He worried his lower lip, and beads of sweat popped on his forehead.

Max stared at Alois, and I could see there was no love lost there. The cold blue flames in Max's eyes could have frozen anyone. Yet his next words implied he empathized. "I'll catch everyone's attention with a speech. Then you can get away unnoticed. Just like old times."

Alois swallowed; I saw his throat work. He forced a smile, nothing like the carefree one I'd seen on his face earlier. Alois was trapped by his own actions. And Max's words left much up for interpretation. If Alois was bisexual and a social climber, maybe he had slept with both father and daughter? *Eww* was the only word I could think of. It was a miracle his parents could be so oblivious to their son's publicly well-known audacious and raunchy behavior.

"Thanks, Max," Alois breathed out.

"His Highness," I corrected.

Alois shot daggers at me with his eyes. Then he noticed Max's icy ire, and he bobbed his head like a jack-in-the-box, murmured something along polite lines, and hurried off, keeping his head down.

Max faced me. I couldn't tell if he was disappointed in me. I was disappointed in myself. But I didn't want to apologize. Not about this.

"I'm glad your taste has improved," I said dryly.

Max narrowed his eyes. Then a flicker of a smile graced a corner of his lips. "Not my taste. My judgment." He wanted to touch me; I could tell. "Don't go punching any more guests, please? Even if I might have slept with them."

Then he was off, vanishing into the Ballroom crowd.

As for me, I was so done with this lameass party.

BAD LUCK refused to leave me alone, though.

On my way through the Banquet Hall, I was accosted by Ambassador Robert Fowler, a glass of whisky in hand, the amber liquid sloshing about as he moved. "Are you Oliver Reed, the student from Seattle?"

I shivered. His cool tone told me in no uncertain terms that he disliked me. *Dang, why me?* I didn't even know him. "Uh, yes?"

"I'm Rob Fowler, the current American Ambassador to Noricia." He sipped his drink, and his breath stank of alcohol. I grimaced inwardly. He examined me from on high, like I was a bug under a microscope. "According to the newspapers, you're the First Prince's companion."

It wasn't phrased as a question. "I'm His Highness's friend, if that is what you mean."

My careful response warned me that if Max and I continued our liaison, I would be telling these sorts of lies forever. Being with a gay prince necessitated discretion. The thought saddened me. I'd been raised and taught to be honest, with myself and others. Now, simply by having an intimate relationship with a prince, I had to become a skilled, believable liar.

A realization hit me hard, like a bolt of lightning.

I did *not* want to spend the rest of my life walking on eggshells and lying till I knew no other way to be. What did that mean for me and Max?

"Ahem." Fowler's cough brought me back to the moment. "Mr. Reed, what kind of student are you? A political major, perhaps?"

"No, I have a master's in culinary science."

Fowler's bushy white eyebrows shot up. "I beg your pardon?" As his eyebrows lowered, I could tell his suspicions grew. "How did you and the First Prince meet?"

I was going to answer *on holiday*, but I refrained. "Excuse me, sir, but how is that any of your business?" I wasn't usually confrontational, but when did the details of my life become public property? At heart, though, I knew the answer—when I'd met a handsome prince from a faraway land.

"Don't be impertinent with me, boy," Fowler growled with a deep bass for a voice. I bet he made excellent speeches.

"With all due respect," I countered. "I don't know you, and I don't owe you a single answer about my friendship with His Studious Highness."

All of a sudden, Fowler grinned. "I see you're not susceptible to intimidation, and you use deliberately vague phrases. Good. That should help us avoid a scandal."

A chill ran up and down my spine. "Why would there be a scandal?"

Fowler shrugged, sipping his whisky. "We've always suspected there's more to Prince Maximilian than meets the eye. There are rumors about his proclivities. Can you confirm that for me? Is the First Prince bisexual?"

So the ambassador was on a fishing expedition, trying to wrangle information from me based on our shared nationality. Would he call me a traitor if I refused to respond? I decided to find out.

"If you have questions about the First Prince, I suggest you direct them to him or the Royal Press Officer, not me. I will answer none."

Then I turned around and walked away. I shook with pent-up rage. The nerve of that man to interrogate me about Max.

I calmed when I anticipated that this encounter would likely be the first of many. Whether I had to dodge reporters or dignitaries, I would have to learn the subtleties of diplomacy at the highest rungs of society. This was an unfamiliar field for me. I think I'd handled the ambassador fine, but I sure as shit hadn't made a friend. If anything, I might have burned a bridge back there.

"Here. Have a drink."

Frederica handed me another fizzy pink champagne cocktail. She seemed to loom around. Had she observed me and Fowler talking?

I accepted the flute with a nod, but I didn't drink. "I didn't tell him anything, if that's what you're worried about."

Frederica smiled, her dimples showing. "I figured Rob would test the waters with you. It's rare for someone like him to discover a new source of information close to the royal family. It's only natural for him to try and take advantage of the situation."

"What is the official position of the court when it comes to Max?" I inquired.

"Matters pertaining to the princes' personal lives are subject to speculation but not up for discussion in the media, be it local or global. Thus far, public discourse has given royal families everywhere some latitude. And certain questions are never asked. It would be impolitic."

I blinked in confusion. "I'm sorry but… what did you just say?"

Frederica chuckled, then leaned in and lowered her voice. "All right. Neither Max nor his parents have made any official statements regarding Max's orientation. It is generally accepted fact that the First Prince will carry out his duty when he becomes king."

This time I didn't need to ask. Freddie meant marriage and children. Max was supposed to do those things due to the very nature of his position, so no one had cause to think differently. The people expected Max to live up to his role as their future king.

"But if Max has had, um, other affairs before, how come no one's noticed?" I asked in a hushed tone, glancing around to see who might be listening.

"Any liaisons royals have before their eventual marriage are usually kept out of the press," Frederica replied. "Tabloids spread rumors; that's the nature of the beast. Reputable publications might write articles about court-approved boyfriends or girlfriends, but even those are kept discreet and general in terms. It is understood by the media that any outrageous exploitation of the monarchy has poor results. Gossip is one thing, slander another. The people don't usually like to read negative stories about their rulers. Unless, of course, there's plenty of evidence to back up any allegations."

I whistled low. "Wow. You have a way of talking about things and at the same time not answering me. So Max's previous stuff was never discovered, or if it was, no one talked about it?"

Frederica nodded. "Something to that effect." She clinked her glass with mine. "Don't worry, Mr. Reed. So far you've done well."

I snorted. "More like barely held my head above water. I'm waiting to drown."

Frederica laughed. "I wouldn't worry. Tonight is a special occasion. Normally, Riten Castle is off-limits and not open to the public. These guests today, including reporters and ambassadors, will be gone by tomorrow morning."

As Frederica sailed away like a majestic barge, the crowd acknowledging her presence with waves, nods, or hellos and moving out of her way, I had to admit I was glad Fowler wouldn't be here tomorrow. I'd had enough of him to last me a lifetime.

In the end, though, if I stayed with Max, in whatever capacity, this would be my life. I'd have to grow used to people like Fowler and de Lange. The trouble was, I didn't know if I could, or if I even wanted to.

The real question was, was Max worth it? My head and my heart gave two different answers.

In any case, I snuck out of the Banquet Hall, across the Inner Ward, and ran to the safety of the Snake Tower. The guards knew me and let me pass.

Max wouldn't be there for ages, but I took a seat in the anteroom on a narrow, uncomfortable settee-like couch made of dark wood and covered with dark-purple velvet cushions. I settled in for a long wait, already grimacing at the discomfort of the chair.

In here, at least, no one would disturb me. That was good because I had a lot of thinking to do.

Chapter 23

THOUGH APART from Oliver, Max was determined to enjoy himself during the Solstice Feast. And he did until he observed from afar the trials and tribulations Oliver faced.

Oliver had handled Tulip rather well, appearing first guarded, then amused. The two even danced together in the Ballroom. A lovely couple, Max mused, and felt a twinge of jealousy. He knew he was being ridiculous.

When Oliver encountered first Alois and then Fowler, Max knew without a doubt that the party was a bust for Oliver. Glum and angry on Oliver's behalf, Max watched as Oliver snuck out of the festival, looking sullen and worn. And it was early still; the celebration wasn't even in full swing yet.

Max was about to chase after him and console him, possibly in bed for several hours, but an approaching man caught his attention. With a lifetime of experience, Max plastered a polite smile on his face and readied for the encounter.

"Orell. Happy Solstice Day. I trust you are enjoying yourself."

"Happy Solstice Day to you, Your Highness. Oh yes, what wonderful festivities. The King and Queen have surely outdone themselves this year."

Max bowed a little. "I'll be sure to mention your compliments to my parents."

Orell Schaffhausen was both the leader of the Royalist party in the Council and the interior minister. Karl von Thürer had been the previous leader of the Royalists. Due to his position as prime minister presiding over the entire Council, Karl could no longer assume the role of party leader; that would have been highly inappropriate and unorthodox.

Orell was a staunch believer in tradition. His aristocratic roots traced back to the origin of the kingdom. As such, his loyalty to the monarchy stemmed from noble privilege within the class system rather than any particular devotion to the royal family itself.

And that explained why Orell could be trusted only so far.

For a portly man, Orell carried himself nimbly and with distinction. He was an avid hunter who often trekked the woodland hills in search of defenseless animals to slaughter—which was why Max despised him. Hunting was no longer an accepted practice among the royal household, and Max preferred it that way.

Orell fancied himself a jolly, jovial man, but he showed that side only during good times. When offended or in the shadows, Orell could be cold and ruthless. Any opposition to royalty and the aristocracy was met with a hard, unforgiving heart.

Orell had a habit of twirling his fingers through his thick golden mustache and equally thick golden hair, which stood in spikes. He prided himself on those things because other men in his family had heads as bald and round as pebbles on a beach.

"So, I hear Lady Kira von Montfort-Bregenz is staying here at Riten Castle."

Max gritted his teeth. It was an egregious breach in protocol to address a royal without them initiating the discussion and choosing the topic. But Orell had never adhered to rules that made him subordinate to someone else. And as usual, he was as subtle as a brick through a window.

Regardless, Max had noted Kira's absence on this festive day. He couldn't help but wonder where she was. Perhaps she was avoiding Max or Oliver, or both? Max hated the idea of losing Kira, who was like a sister to him.

To Orell, Max said, "I assume so. My brother, Johann, invited her. As you know, she is close to our family."

Orell nodded, grabbing the lapels of his white-and-gold outfit, with its lacy ruffles and layers of expensive fabrics, as if he were preparing to make a speech. He behaved like a pompous blowhard at times, Max knew, but in his opinion, all politicians were full of hot air and zero substance.

Only then did Max notice the other man standing beside but a little behind Orell, reverent and quiet, hands clasped behind his back, his craggy face emotionless. Max's heart skipped a beat, and he fought hard not to show his apprehension on his face.

Archibald Chantry, the trekker from the hills. What is he doing here?

Orell cleared his throat. "Her ladyship is a fine woman. Fine breed indeed. She would make an excellent queen, wife, and mother."

Max wanted to scream. Inside the safety of his head, he did. Still smiling outwardly, though, he shrugged. "Lady Kira has but to say the word, and I will gladly pass my future throne and royal duties to her slender but more than capable shoulders."

At first Orell blinked. He didn't get the jest. Although Max was only half joking.

Out of the corner of his eye, Max noticed Archibald's lips twitching as if he was holding back a smile.

Then Orell harrumphed, clearly annoyed by Max's dismissal. As a Royalist, the continuation of the primary royal lineage mattered to him.

"Max, you are young, yes. But you near thirty. It is time to settle down."

Max's hands clenched. He was too vexed about Oliver to bother with this arrogant fool a second longer. "You forget yourself, Orell. For a man with your background, you of all people should remember your place."

Orell paled and gulped. He stole a glimpse around to see if anyone else had noticed him being chastised by the First Prince. When he found no one, he ducked his head as if studying his toes.

"I-I apologize for my abhorrent conduct, Your Highness."

Max relented. He'd have to deal with Orell for years to come in some capacity. No point in burning bridges. "I realize that as First Prince, my future plans interest numerous parties, including you. But until I am ready to announce them, there will be no further speculation in my presence. Do I make myself clear, Orell?"

"Y-yes, Your Highness. Clear as crystal."

Being allowed to use a first name with someone who couldn't use it with him gave Max control in most situations. It was one shield against intrusive queries about his private life. At the moment, the power grab gave him a thrill. Orell needed to be brought down a peg. He'd gotten too complacent of late, too forward, too overfamiliar.

In the end, though, Max understood that he couldn't dodge these questions forever. Sooner or later, he would have to marry and carry on the family name and the royal line.

If he didn't, there would be public uproar, and the Royalists, with Orell in the lead, would rise up in arms, possibly leading to a coup. Noricia was among the very few nations in the world where there had never been a coup or even an attempt during its centuries-long history. Max would be damned if he became the cause—or the scapegoat for narrow-minded dimwits.

"Your son serves in the militia, does he not? Do you think he would amenable to a city or a castle posting? Or does he prefer the thrill of adventure in the great outdoors?"

The diplomatic attempt to mend the sudden rift between them was successful because Orell was ambitious and vain. He loved talking about his accomplishments, one of which was his eldest son. Orell's wife, Irina, was a second-rate ballerina from Russia but a first-rate Mayor of Vindeburg. She was the only thing in Orell's life he took no credit for; she wouldn't let him.

"Ah, yes. Timur makes my wife and I very proud."

Orell stood taller and pushed his chest out, rolling on the balls of his feet. He seemed quite pleased with himself. Max let him have his moment in the sun.

"Timur is on duty at the southern border, up in the hills. He seems to like the post, but a castle posting.... I might be able to persuade him to consider it."

Max smiled and nodded. He knew this was a safe topic because he would not have to offer Timur anything. Timur was as stubborn and willful as his mother, and he had no patience for the intricacies of court or the hubbub of a city, not even for the ladies. Orell would never succeed, so in the end the offer was moot.

"Is there perchance a lady in his life?" Max asked.

Orell asked about Max, so Max asked about Orell's son. Seemed fitting since Orell wanted to discuss family planning. But it also seemed ill-fitting because now there was a danger the conversation would slip back toward Max.

Orell chuckled, at ease again. "No, not for Timur. He's too busy sowing his wild oats. When he's not on duty, of course. Ah... he's young. Let him have fun and enjoy the many pleasures of women before enjoying the company of only one."

Orell had a double standard, like all politicians. Max and Timur were separated by just a few years. Yet freedom seemed to be only allowable for one, according to Orell. His hypocrisy turned Max's stomach, but he kept up appearances.

"Speaking of the ladies...." Orell actually winked at Max, who had trouble reining in his temper. "Three of the nine noble families have brought their daughters here, and I know for a fact they would all love a dance with you, Your Highness."

This was not new for Max. No matter where he went, someone was always there offering their daughters, cousins, or friends as potential mates. Max had a plan in place for such contingencies.

"Oh. Have you noticed, Orell? Looks like a storm is brewing."

Bewildered, Orell shielded his eyes from the sun's glare with his hand and peered through the nearest window. "Clear blue skies, Your Highness. Not a cloud in sight."

Max smiled.

Then a young lady, dressed in a provocative ensemble of white and gold, approached them. An opening in the front of her dress showcased her golden stockings, and her low neckline exposed her ample bosom. Add to that show youthful exuberance, full lips painted cherry red, and fluttering eyelashes, and Orell forgot all about Max, his wife, and everything else, and whisked the lady toward the dance floor.

Max sighed in relief. *Stormy weather* was a code he used with his security detail so they would arrange a quick extraction or distraction to extricate him from any situation. At a party, that meant lovely young women or men to dance with the guests.

"Thank you, Lawana," Max murmured discreetly. He didn't need to hold his earpiece to hear her acknowledging snort. Max let out a soft chuckle at her irreverent sarcasm.

Orell had vanished into the throng.

But Archibald Chantry still stood in place. Max steeled himself for a confrontation.

"Good to see you again, Mr. Chantry."

Archibald bowed deep. "And you, Your Highness."

Max studied the man with mild trepidation. "You're Orell's secretary?"

"Personal assistant, yes, sir." Archibald glanced at the councilman in question, swept away to dance with a beautiful girl. "I'm personally not political, but I do want to stay in the know about our government and how it works."

"You served in the militia?" Max asked, indecisive about the secretary's ulterior motives.

Archibald nodded and straightened proudly. "Yes, sir. Twelve years. Achieved the rank of major. Best time of my life."

"I should call you Major Chantry, then," Max commented, impressed at the military man's devotion to his chosen craft.

Archibald shook his head. "Thank you, sir, but I'm retired. The rank is no longer relevant." He frowned, his gaze still on his employer. "Permission to speak freely?"

Max suppressed a smile at Archibald's quaint phrasing, as if Max was his commanding officer. "Granted."

Archibald faced Max, his expression solemn. "I did not tell anyone, even Mr. Schaffhausen, about our encounter up in the hills, sir. It's no one else's business."

Max narrowed his eyes. "Are you a Royalist?"

Archibald ducked his head briefly. "Like I said, Your Highness, I'm not political. But even if I were, I'm of the firm belief that matters of the heart with royals cannot be and should never be legislated or decided by others, be it the Council or the people."

Max waited to see if Archibald had more to add, but the secretary grew quiet, his look serious and expectant. "I appreciate your words, Mr. Chantry. And… your discretion." It wasn't an admission of anything but an acknowledgment of Archibald's sense of tact.

Archibald smiled shortly, there and gone. "Mr. Schaffhausen is a fine politician and a good man, in spite of his at times rash temper and habit of speaking out of turn. But not even he is entitled to know every little detail about another's private life. Same goes for me, sir."

A part of Max still wavered on Archibald's intentions but no longer about his sincerity. If Archibald managed to keep the secret of Max and Oliver, that didn't matter in the long run. Max was the First Prince of Noricia. He'd not be able to hide forever. Someone would talk, sooner or later. But he had a feeling that person wouldn't be Major Archibald Chantry.

"How is Pumpkin?" Max asked, changing the subject.

Archibald's features softened. "Still jumping on people like a bulky furball made of dog spit and hot tongue, sir."

Max laughed. "Good to hear."

Wilhelmina, the Lady Usher, approached, curtseyed to Max, and indicated with a mere look that Max's attention was required elsewhere; a signal that he'd spent too much time with one guest.

Max shook Archibald's hand. Since touching wasn't encouraged between royal and commoner, a handshake wasn't customary, but he felt it appropriate in this instance. "Be well, Major Chantry. And hug Pumpkin for me."

"I will, Your Highness. Thank you." Archibald's hand was firm, solid, and full of scars and calluses. A professional military man's hand.

When he left, Max wondered if this was what it felt like to make a friend. A warm glow in his chest told him Archibald was a good man. Maybe they could meet again out on the trail and be bounced once more by a huggable dog.

So the Royalists didn't know anything more about Max than before. Orell had picked a topic he wanted answers to, not realizing that his own secretary harbored a secret about that very thing. Coincidences happened. Max knew he couldn't keep the Council or the people in the dark forever. But maybe for a few more weeks? Would luck be on his side?

Max sipped his drink now that Orell and Archibald were both gone. Two down, endless more to go.

"I've never seen the Ballroom this shiny, Your Highness."

Max smiled in spite of his foul mood, even though this was another breach in strict protocol. "You say that every year, Silvan." Turning to face the man speaking, he added whimsically, "You know, my blue jacket still has those stains from those infernal berry bombs. I seem to recall a promise by you to dry clean my—"

"I'd never presume to find the kind of luxurious laundry services Riten Castle provides, Your Highness, so I didn't even try." The man giggled, his laugh sounding like he had the hiccups.

Silvan von Arx was the leader of the Opposition, which was the Republicans in the Council. He was well aware his political party was the minority and was not held in high regard by the people; the majority favored monarchy. Silvan was also the justice minister.

Stiff as a board and thin as a reed, Silvan stood in stark contrast to Orell, who was his political adversary. Brown-haired and brown-eyed, Silvan had a Spanish countenance and a matching temper. Yet in the Council Hall, one was hard-pressed to find anyone as dull and uninspiring as Silvan, who managed to lull listeners to a hundred-year sleep with his first sentence alone, which tended to drag on for minutes on end.

Outside of work and underneath that boring facade, though, lived a romantic, pie-in-the-sky dreamer who let loose big-time when night fell. The lavish parties at his mansion were legendary. Last year, Silvan and his husband, Ramos, had dressed up as woodland nymphs, sung operettas for two hours straight, and then showered guests with jelly, enticing them to eat off each other.

Or that was what Max had heard anyway. He'd left before the party devolved into a smutty orgy. As fascinating as it would have been to stay.

"What marvelous food, delicious drink, stunning decor...." Silvan could embellish with the best of them. His high praise certainly stroked one's ego. Suddenly, in the middle of a drink, Silvan asked, "Have you thought about my proposed amendment, Your Highness? It would enrich the lives of everyone in the kingdom."

Max suppressed a sigh. Was Silvan really so tipsy already that he forgot the edicts of court conduct? Everyone seemed so lax today when it came to the rules. Max felt cornered by questions he wasn't prepared to answer.

"How, Silvan, would it improve the lives of the people?" Max asked in return. "While the King and Queen are, by age-old tradition, above the law and cannot be taken to court, they ensure on a daily basis that all their activities are carried out in strict accordance with legal edicts. Unless you have proof to the contrary?"

Silvan pursed his lips, seemingly embarrassed. His cheeks glowed red; he'd had more than one champagne cocktail. "Yes, Your Highness—I mean no, sir. I don't have firsthand knowledge of any transgressions perpetrated by the King and Queen. That is to say, I've heard rumors of falsified royal decrees and stolen signet rings and—"

"Putting stock in rumors is like building a house on quicksand," Max cut in. "Innuendo can drown you."

Deep down, though, Max was shaken to the core. The court had suppressed the story about the stolen signet ring and hidden all evidence in relation to it. As for the document, Karl von Thürer was one of few people who knew about the fake, which had since been destroyed.

Who was spreading these rumors and to what end?

"Yes, sir," Silvan said, slurring his words. "I would never accuse the royal family of any wrongdoing." He tossed back the rest of his drink and added, "Unless they're guilty of something, of course." He stared at Max, though his eyes wandered a bit. "Is a lie illegal?"

Max didn't want anything to do with this conversation. "Silvan, you're a tad drunk. Perhaps you should take a moment to recuperate in the lounge or the bathroom."

Silvan straightened but kept wobbling, which made his intended imperious stance look silly. "Sir, I am a Republican. I demand that Noricia evolve into a republic worthy of its citizens."

Max sighed. The two of them had had this talk many times before. When Silvan was lost in the vapors of alcohol, he tended to forget that fact.

"Silvan, Noricia has a Council composed sixty-three officials duly elected by the citizenry. The only difference between our constitutional monarchy and your idea of a republic is that our head of state is called a sovereign, not a president."

Indignant, Silvan waved his glass about, and Max rejoiced it was empty. "You wound me, sir. A single leader is not worthy to rule over a diverse nation of many."

"But a Republican Council consisting of only wealthy aristocrats is?" Max countered, though he knew he shouldn't goad a drunken fool.

Silvan's eyes rounded into two furious, and unfocused, orbs. "Apparently your family is not only above the law—" *hic* "—but above polite rules of society. How dare you insult a man who only dreams of a better world?"

That was enough, Max thought. He gripped Silvan by the arm, lifted Silvan up so he had to walk on tippytoes, and escorted him to the nearest armchair, where he plopped the man down.

"Sit and calm down." Then, for personal emphasis, Max leaned in and murmured, "And, Silvan, as you well know, the royal family is most certainly not above the law. Or have you forgotten my brother Johann's speeding tickets? Or my aunt Charlotte's hunting accident?"

"Oh. Oh." Silvan blinked and nodded several times.

Charlotte was Colette's younger sister, a fierce and reckless huntress who had an unfortunate habit of shooting rifles without aiming properly. She had been cautioned on the day of the incident, and when that didn't do the trick, Gustav had emptied her manor of arms altogether and relieved her of her weapon permits. Which was a good thing, or she might have shot him.

As a result, she was persona non grata at Riten Castle.

"No one here considers themselves above the law," Max said in a hushed voice.

Silvan stared at his empty glass, forlorn and muttering to himself, "But if a ruler lies to his people… should that be against the law…?"

Max backed away, unwilling to have a reasonable talk with a drunkard. Nothing would come of it. Silvan was a good man. As a sworn pacifist, he would never pursue his ideal republic through violent means. Mostly he made speeches too boring for anyone to listen to and made amendments to reduce royal authority that never passed the Council to become a referendum.

Maybe that was why Silvan drank? Or was his absent husband, Ramos, spending time at yet another wild party in Vindeburg? Max had heard through the grapevine that the von Arx duo had an open marriage with epic fights and scandalous make-up sex.

"I know you're right, my prince, of course I do," Silvan was still whispering under his breath, his eyes dazed, his attention faraway. "But shouldn't ethics be a part of a civilized nation too? What good is the rule of law without conscience or morality?"

His stammering voice, and surprisingly sensible words, faded as Max moved away. It was hard to see Silvan like this, so defeated. Was the monarchy to blame for his misfortunes? Max could no longer give a simple yes or no in response.

His head hurt.

And his heart hurt. Max knew it wasn't illegal to lie to a lover, but it was unethical. Silvan's unintentional jabs had struck home with Max, who was already worried about his relationship with Oliver. There were so many unanswered questions, so many impossible hurdles, so much needless pain.

Damn lies. Damn monarchy. Damn everything.

Well, at least Max hadn't been forced to resort to stormy weather twice today.

A CLOUD of colorful confetti showered over Max, covering his head and shoulders.

"What the—"

Theo danced past Max, waving about merrily, singing a bawdy drinking song and throwing around confetti like a child. Max chuckled, nodding his greeting—and received a garland of flowers on his head for his gesture. Their earthy scent reminded him why summer was so important, with its sunshine, warmth, and glory.

"Dance with me!" Theo exclaimed at the top of his lungs as he grasped Max's hands in his and tried to pull him along into a merry-go-round.

With the experience of numerous prior festivities, Max disengaged himself with a laugh. "I have two left feet while you float effortlessly like a sunbeam. I cannot match your grace."

Theo giggled and moved on. Only then did Max notice everyone else. He had no idea how Theo had managed to entice over three-dozen people into a freaking conga line with him. The music didn't match, but everyone seemed to be having fun, laughing and singing.

A tall black woman pried herself away from the line and stumbled into Max.

"Oh. I'm so sorry, Your Highness. I've not done a conga line in ages. Theo started with a mambo to get me to go along. I couldn't resist."

She was out of breath and excited, her rough panting mixing with her eager giggles, and her permasmile was firmly in place.

Max chuckled. "No apology necessary. Few can resist Theo's childish charms. Besides, it's good to see you let your hair down, Yacine."

She snorted, touching her dark-brown curls with golden stripes. The whole coiffure stood high on her head like an actual Renaissance-era wig. Pins of golden butterflies and white-gold flowers stuck out as decorations, helping to keep the whole rigging in place.

"I try, Your Highness. I do try," she replied and curtseyed, lifting the hem of her white-and-gold Renaissance-style dress, complete with bows and floral patterns and a tight bodice pushing up her breasts. The dark gold in her dress fitted well with her brown skin and eyes.

Yacine Haas was the leader of the Moderate party in the Council, the largest group at the moment over the Royalists by four members. She stood between Orell and Silvan when they argued and brought forth peaceful discourse, compromises, and resolutions. A fitting position for the defense minister, standing between two warring parties.

She was of Caribbean and Dutch descent. Her family had emigrated to Noricia when she'd been a baby. Full of life and a happy disposition, Yacine always had a smile gracing her plump red lips. She was full-figured and had a presence no matter where she went. Her background in the militia showed in her posture and commanding voice.

Had Max been straight, he might have found Yacine irresistible. Alas, they were friends. Well, as much as a royal could be with anyone outside of court.

"I hear you have a friend staying with you here at Riten, sir," Yacine said and took a delicate sip of the champagne cocktail she snatched from a passing waiter's tray, as usual with an expression of innocent curiosity.

"Yes." Max stopped there, smiling kindly and waiting for the other shoe to drop.

Yacine matched his smile and upped the wattage to brilliant. "How splendid for you to spend the summer with a friend, sir."

Max grinned. Yacine was a master in the theater of politics. No wonder it was rumored she led the Council behind the scenes, bringing forth subjects that the two opposing parties would fight over and then solving them with her peacemaking abilities. Max admired her but also refused to give her any ammunition; she tended to bring in the big guns, badass as she was.

"I'm afraid my schedule is not free for the entire length of the summer," Max said ruefully but then perked up. "But you are correct. The right company can improve even the worst moods or the most hectic times. What are your plans, Yacine, during the Council's summer break?"

Yacine inclined her head. "My family and I are headed for a Caribbean cruise. Sunshine, the balmy sea, and a rocking boat. What could be better? Oh, yes, the Mayan ruins will likely be stunning too."

"You have two children, don't you?" Max asked, his memory about the hundreds of people he met every day a little sketchy.

Yacine smiled, seeming pleased at Max taking an interest. "I do, yes. Pepper is eight and Cherry is six."

"They're adopted, aren't they?" Max hoped he wasn't making an ass of himself by asking.

"Yes. Cherry is from China and Pepper from Cambodia." Yacine sighed. "Cherry still has nightmares about her baby brother. He was sick. Cholera outbreak. Can you believe it? A cholera epidemic in this day and age?"

"It shouldn't happen, I agree," Max said with a curt nod. "We have medicines to save sick children."

"Adoption is an important means of ensuring their health," Yacine remarked.

Max felt like testing the ice, so he asked, "Do you think every couple should be allowed to adopt a child?"

Yacine's sharp eyes landed squarely on Max. Though she had a constant sunny disposition, she could be unreadable at times. "There are so many who can and do have children but don't give a fig for them. And there are many who want a child but cannot—me for example. An adoption should be available to everyone, except for those with a criminal record."

"Even gay or lesbian couples?" Max asked, keeping his expression and tone as neutral and casual as he could.

Yacine nodded. "Yes, of course. Children don't care what gender those around them are as long as there is love."

Max felt better about the news than he'd expected. Had he subconsciously been considering wedding a man and then adopting? It was his heart's desire. Normality.

Then his castles in the sky came crashing down.

"Of course, it wouldn't be the same for royalty," Yacine said matter-of-factly. "While there exists no law that prohibits a member of the royal family from adopting a child, there are two reasons why it is not a good idea. First, there is the weight of tradition, culture, religion. The people wouldn't want to see that tradition destroyed."

"No, naturally," Max murmured, nodding as if in agreement.

"Secondly and more importantly is the fact that an adopted child cannot inherit the throne," Yacine said, her voice taking on a somber tone. "According to the Act of Succession, only a blood descendant of the royal lineage can assume the throne."

"Yes, I'm well versed with the law of the land," Max retorted dryly.

Yacine chuckled. "Speaking of which, Norician law extends the same rights to both natural and adopted children. Why should royalty or aristocracy or any hereditary title be held to a different account?"

Max was glad to hear that. Was there a loophole buried in the law that he could exploit for his dream to marry whom he wished and to raise his own children, adopted or not? He would have to do research to determine—

"However, when it comes to royalty, the law of bloodline heredity is paramount, immutable, and vital," Yacine continued, showing her legal expertise. "In your case, Your Highness, for example, the heir must be a Neo-Celtic descendant of Queen Aletta. As adopted children are not part of the line of succession and therefore have no claim to the throne, it is impossible for a First Prince to adopt and make them their heir."

Max nodded. He gulped, unable to trust his voice. He'd read the entirety of the Act of Succession many times and knew the contents. What he'd hoped from Yacine was confirmation that perhaps in modern times public opinion had changed and blood relations were no longer seen as an absolute requirement for inheriting the throne. Alas, apparently not.

Deep down, Max understood. If anyone, regardless of blood or lineage, could be instated onto the Ivy Throne, then the monarchy would truly become obsolete. An elected ruler would then be preferable to an arbitrary choice made by whoever happened to sit on the throne. That opened the door to all sorts of unlawful and unethical abuses of power.

"Still, back to your case, sir," Yacine continued, as if unaware of Max's emotional plight. "Any heir to the throne naturally has the right to pass succession on to the children of siblings, their children, or even first cousins in unusual circumstances. For example, in cases of infertility."

Yacine was smart, Max knew. She'd quickly moved on from adopting children to the other demands of succession, as if she sensed that was where he wanted the discussion to go.

Before Max could change the subject, Yacine chuckled. "I could imagine the Second Prince adopting, since our eminent inventor seems to lose himself in work rather than the ladies. As for the Third Prince, well, I can't see our special party boy adopting anyone to serve as his heir."

Max laughed a little, the polite thing to do. "I don't know. Johann could surprise us all."

Inside, Max doubted his own words. A sense of entitlement, like the one Johann cultivated, lent no credence even to the idea of bringing new blood into the line. Max wished Johann would settle down and stop acting like a petulant brat, but he also prayed that the sensible girl wouldn't be a cousin or too close a relative. Johann needed to widen his gene pool into an ocean, not reduce it to a puddle.

"Do you think we'll see the rules change in our lifetime?" Max asked, mostly to himself.

Yacine smiled. "What are you talking about, sir? Royals change the rules of the game all the time now. No hugs to avoid getting sick or attacked? No selfies to avoid social media getting flooded with fake stories? No autographs to avoid royal signature forgeries? Royals all over the first world break these rules. Think of Meghan Markle, for one…."

Yacine's voice faded as Max became lost in thought. He'd forgotten that last one. He'd been so preoccupied with the false signet-ring emblem on the wax seal that he'd forgotten the culprit had to know Max's signature pretty damn well to make the decree appear legitimate.

To get a grip on the straying topic, Max interjected, "Those are but little things. I meant something more substantive."

Yacine sipped her drink, pensive. "You mean, an adopted child or a gay couple sitting on the throne?" She shrugged, peering past Max and waving when she spotted someone she knew and clearly wanted to speak with. "I don't know, Your Highness. Stranger things have happened."

As Yacine curtseyed and walked off, Max watched her receding back. He was surprised by the positive comment that didn't sound like a complete dismissal. Perhaps there was hope yet.

For now, though, Max had done his duty for the day, spoken with enough people, and entertained the court with his presence. His mind kept drifting to Oliver; his patience was wearing thin. He didn't want to talk to anyone else, even if the topic was as safe and idle as the weather. He was tired of representing the royal family when his heart ached. There were other members of the family in attendance. Let them carry the burden.

In short, Max decided to celebrate the solstice with his beloved instead of the crowds.

I want Oliver, and I want him now.

BACK AT the Snake Tower, Max slouched in and found, to his surprise, Oliver sleeping on an uncomfortable couch intended for guests waiting to see the First Prince. Max's heart skipped a beat, and a hollow pit in his chest filled with warmth and affection.

"Oliver, wake up," Max crooned at his lover, gently shoving his shoulder. "This isn't a good spot to sleep in. Come on."

Oliver blinked, muttered something, and slowly roused enough to recognize Max. "Didn't mean to fall asleep for long. What time is it?"

"Past three, love. Come on. Let me take you to bed." Max lifted Oliver into his arms and carried him to the bedroom.

Oliver wiggled in protest. "I'm not a damsel in distress, man, and I don't need to be carried around like one. Put me down."

"Nope." Max grinned cheekily at his partner until he set Oliver down on the bed.

Oliver promptly stood again. "It's afternoon. What time is that for bed?"

"Siesta." Max chuckled, his intention to seduce his beloved. Oliver's cheeks turned ruddy when he caught on to the plot.

Then their mouths and bodies came crashing together, and all words were forgotten in favor of the lovers' language. Kisses were followed by caresses, then moans, then hot and heavy grinding, and finally two simultaneous sighs of contentment.

After cleaning up, they lounged together in bed, touching each other here and there without hurry, sharing a kiss every now and then.

"Can we order in ice cream and drinks?" Oliver asked, nuzzling Max's neck.

"Yes." Max craned his head to the side to give Oliver better access. A hot, wet tongue licked, sucked, and nipped at his jugular. Max's dick twitched. He wanted more, but he was too tired to make the effort. "How about a movie?"

Oliver's head popped up. An eager light burned in his eyes. "I know the perfect one."

While Oliver busied himself with the TV, Max ordered champagne, caviar, strawberries, canapes, salty snacks, and ice cream. He groaned, anticipating in advance the tummy ache he'd have later on. But Oliver could kiss his boo-boos away.

As they settled in against the headboard and a stack of stuffed pillows, both of them naked, Max was happy. More than happy. This had to be bliss, his ecstatic brain supplied. Good food, sweet drinks, warm bed, and a hot lover. All his for the taking. Max wished he could live forever in this one moment, cuddled next to Oliver.

"What's this comedy about?" Max asked, popping a piece of canape into his mouth.

"It's called *Without a Clue*," Oliver explained, bouncing with excitement. "And it toys with the idea that Doctor Watson is an unappreciated genius and Sherlock Holmes is a bumbling buffoon, drunkard, and skirt-chaser."

"Oh. I thought this would be another *Clue* movie, though I don't see how they could improve on the one we saw from 1985." Max laughed. "Well, this one ought to be good."

Max and Oliver spent the rest of the day watching movies, eating junk food, toasting each other, and making love. Though by evening the bed was sticky and their minibar empty, and the linens had to be changed and the fridge restocked, Max smiled because he couldn't help it. His cheeks almost hurt from smiling so much; his stomach sure did from all the chortling and the junk food. Oliver's taste in comedies was far better than his (former) taste in men.

If this was what life would be like with Oliver, Max wanted it forever.

Chapter 24

MAX AWOKE in agony. His insides were on fire, his stomach burning. He trembled all over, his muscles twitching. His heart thudded a mile a minute, deafening him. He knew the symptoms well enough to realize he wasn't sick; he'd been poisoned.

He stumbled out of bed—noting absentmindedly that it was empty. Oliver had taken to sleeping on the balcony during the hottest summer nights. Max had subcutaneous biochips inside his body, and his poisoning had undoubtedly been detected already. A medical team had been dispatched, he figured, trying to stagger toward the door.

A few seconds later, the door opened with a heavy thud. A white-haired female doctor dressed in a white lab coat rushed in with two guards in tow. These weren't guards in ceremonial uniforms carrying lances but security officers in black armor and carrying assault rifles. This was all business.

"Symptoms?" Doctor Schneider asked, her tone sharp as she checked Max's pulse and other vitals with a high-tech gadget.

"N-nausea… p-pain… in my s-stomach…," Max whispered.

"What's going on?"

Over the doctor's shoulder, Max watched in horror as a sleepy-eyed Oliver slouched in from the balcony in his underwear, the rising sun at his back. He had dozed off there again. This time Max had hoped Oliver had gone out with his family and would not have to see Max in this deplorable state.

When Oliver seemed to understand the seriousness of the situation, he hurried over and knelt beside Max, taking his hand. "What's happening? Max? What's wrong?"

"Pupils dilated. Elevated heart rate. Muscle spasms. Increased salivation." Doctor Schneider studied Max with swift efficiency. "Hemlock poisoning." She waved at the guards. "We must get him to the infirmary now."

Max could do nothing to alleviate Oliver's obvious rising panic. He was too weak and hurting. His muscles gave out, and he couldn't speak. He let the guards lift him and place him onto a gurney. Each room in the castle had a cache of medical supplies and equipment for basically any and all types of emergencies.

He tried to reach out to Oliver but couldn't control his hands. He tried to speak, but nothing came out except wheezing and drool.

He did manage to murmur huskily, "W-water b-bottle…." He'd drunk from a water bottle from the minifridge in his quarters only an hour or so before waking up in torment. Since he'd eaten nothing else in several hours, the poison had to be there.

Oliver was quick, despite his shocked state. He glanced back at the nightstand, observed the half-empty bottle, and nodded to Max. Relief washed over Max. Oliver would preserve the evidence. He'd help. He was truly a godsend.

Max could let go for a while, knowing he was in good hands. Oliver's hands. He allowed darkness to claim him.

GASTRIC SUCTION sounded exactly as awful as it was as an experience. Max hated getting his stomach pumped. But since he'd digested poison hemlock, there was no other choice. That coupled with some one-on-one time with a ventilator, and Max's next day started as badly as it possibly could. And to think yesterday had ended on such a positive note, with him in bed with his lover.

Speaking of which, where was Oliver?

Gustav and Colette were in the room when Max awoke. Their expressions were dire. Max could relate. Why would anyone want to kill him?

His parents hadn't noticed him being awake yet, though.

"This must be connected to the earlier attempt on his life last spring, when he was in France," Colette was saying. "Where he met… that boy."

Max's blood chilled. That was a rather cold thing to say about someone you knew nothing about. Oliver was a great guy. Sometimes Max felt he didn't deserve Oliver. But by the gods, Max wanted him. A special someone just for him. Was that too much to ask?

Collette had never openly disapproved of Max being gay, or bisexual as far as they knew. He hadn't bothered to correct them.

So why was Collette so upset now? Not like this was the first time—

"Do you think this has something to do with that boy?" Collette asked then, breaking Max's train of thought. Where he'd felt cold before, now he was seething, a fiery indignation sparking for his lover who wasn't there to defend himself.

Gustav grunted. "No, dear, I do not. That is a coincidence. Oliver seems like a nice boy. Max cares for him. I doubt he would if Oliver was a bad seed. Max is an excellent judge of character."

Collette harrumphed. "That may be so, but I also don't believe in coincidences. The boy was there the last time an attempt was made on my son's life, and he's here again."

"Both times," Max cut in, rasping like a wounded crow, "Oliver was there because I asked him to be there. He didn't want to enter the hotel vault with me, and he was hesitant about coming here. I insisted on both."

"Hush, darling," Collette crooned as she sat on the medical cot and caressed his forehead and cheek, like she used to do when Max was a child. "Don't try to speak. Rest now."

Max shook his head, though the gesture took all his strength. "And lie here while you throw baseless accusations at Oliver, who has never once lied to me? Unlike me who's lied to him repeatedly about everything." He cast a glance around the soothing, clean-smelling and clean-looking infirmary. "Where is he? I want to see him." When Collette tried to argue, Max demanded louder, his hoarse voice barely above a whisper, "Now."

Collette sighed. "You always had to go your own way, Max. I wish you'd understand that perhaps your way isn't the wisest or the best for you."

Max grimaced. "I do love you, Mom. But you can't live my life for me. I want to make my own decisions—and my own mistakes, should they turn out to be that."

Gustav rested a hand over his wife's shoulder. Collette nodded and stood. Both left the room. Max let out a deep breath, which hurt like a son of a bitch. But he persevered. The assassination attempt had failed. He'd survived. Now it was time for damage control.

The curtain shifted when Lawana ambled to Max's bedside. Max hadn't heard her come in. She must have been a cat in a previous life. Lawana appeared stiff and stony. Max suspected the worst but couldn't tell what that was.

"Your Highness." Even her voice was a mere shadow of its former self. She had her hands clasped rigidly in front of her, clutching a rumpled piece of paper. "Last night I failed egregiously in my sworn duty to keep you safe from harm, sir. I must hand you my resignation, effective immediately. I sincerely apologize and—"

"Denied." Max's throat hurt from all the croaking. Damn pumps down his windpipe. They weren't there now, but he still felt them. This was not something he wanted to grow accustomed to.

Lawana gasped, eyes wide. "But, sir—"

"I refuse your resignation," Max repeated as forcefully as he could. "Tear that damn piece of paper, burn it, eat it—I don't care. Get that damn thing out of my sight. And then, Lawana, I want you to find out who is doing this to us."

Lawana shook her head. "With all due respect, sir, I have failed you once already—"

"Unless you can somehow detect toxic chemicals inside an unopened water bottle with your naked eye, I don't want to hear any more self-recriminations. You're not just my bodyguard; you're my chief of security. I trust you more than anyone else to get to the bottom of things."

At first it looked like Lawana was ready to argue her case again. Then she ripped the letter of resignation to shreds, nodded firmly, and exited the room.

Max sighed in relief. He didn't want to lose Lawana. She was capable but not infallible; she was human. He still had faith in her ability to find out what was going on.

A minute passed. Max could tell because a clock was ticking loudly on the wall. The smell of industrial-strength detergents made him want to gag. Though the infirmary was in the castle, it seemed cold and impersonal, same as a hospital ward. A white curtain separated his custom-made wide cot from the rest of the room, but he knew the layout and the interior. He'd recuperated there more than once. Though the walls were wood-paneled, the room always seemed to lack warmth.

The curtain swung gently, and Oliver peeked in, looking like a lost lamb. His eyes were red and slightly swollen; he'd been crying. Max hated himself for putting tears in those eyes.

"Hey, Oliver," Max said with as much normality as he could muster. Judging from Oliver's deepening frown, Max failed. Nonetheless, he smiled a little, pain making that hard. "I'm fine. Just a… a small bout of…."

This time when Oliver's furrow grew, Max knew he'd said the wrong thing while trying to lift his lover's fears.

Oliver snarled. "Damn you. You promised you'd never lie to me ever again. You think I'm fucking deaf? That I didn't hear that doctor say you were poisoned? You think I'm a fucking idiot?" Max couldn't get a word in edgewise. Oliver was on a rant. "I can't believe I'm here again, with yet another miserable liar."

"Please, Oliver," Max murmured softly, trying to be gentle. "It's okay. I'm a prince. Stuff like this happens all the time—"

Max could have slapped himself silly when he realized what he'd just uttered. Oliver turned white as a sheet, and his jaw quivered.

"No, no, I didn't mean it like that, baby, I swear," Max tried again.

But it was too late. Oliver nodded firmly. "So, let me sum this up, shall I? One, you lied to me again. Two, from what you just said, it's obvious you've been the target of attempted murder before. That signet ring thing was one of them, wasn't it?" Oliver let out a watery laugh and threw up his arms in a sign of defeat. "I give up. I just can't win with you. And I sure as shit can't protect a prince from assassins. That's way above my pay grade."

When Oliver turned to leave, Max pleaded, "Don't leave, Oliver. Please. We can sort this out, I promise."

Oliver didn't face him. His hand hung on the door handle as he whispered, "Fool me once, shame on you. Fool me twice...."

Then he walked out the door. He didn't slam it; he shut it with a soft snick.

Max only realized he was crying when the droplets landed on his neck. Hot streaks covered his cheeks, and his eyes itched. He wanted to stop crying, but he couldn't.

Had Oliver left for good this time?

Max cursed himself. He'd lied again, yes, but with the best of intentions, to prevent Oliver from worrying. Then Max had his word-vomit moment, and now Oliver must have been under the mistaken illusion that Max spent half his time fending off would-be killers. When that wasn't the case at all. The signet ring incident had been the first serious attempt ever made against him. Threats weren't entirely uncommon, but actual attacks, in this day and age? Never.

Gustav entered quietly, his face a portrait of concern. "Are you all right, son?"

Max wiped away his tears. "Fine. Couldn't be better."

Gustav frowned. "No one here deserves your bitterness, Max. We're all trying to help."

Shame washed over Max in hot waves. "Sorry, Dad. I.... Have I asked for too much already from life or the Goddess or the universe? I must have because now I can't seem to have the one thing I really want." He sighed, slumped, and added in a whisper, "What I need."

Gustav sat beside him on the cot. "You mean the boy?"

Max bristled. "He has a name, you know. Oliver is a grown man, Dad. Trust me, I know."

Gustav chuckled. "I believe you."

Max swallowed hard. "D-did he… leave?"

"Just retired to his rooms," Gustav reassured him. "Or that's what he said anyway."

Max buried his face in his hands. "This is all my fault. I shouldn't have lied to him."

"Then why did you?" Gustav asked, scratching his temple in wonderment.

Max growled. "Because that's what you do sometimes to protect someone. You tell a white lie to spare another from hurt."

Gustav pursed his lips in obvious disagreement. "Is that what we've taught you?"

"No. That's what being born into this family has taught me. This castle, the people around us, the politics, the scheming and plotting. Lying is—"

"Wrong," Gustav cut in sharply.

"Necessary sometimes," Max finished his sentence.

Gustav stood and straightened his clothes. His expression was stern and stony. "This does seem to be the age of lies. Fake news here, blatant lies over there. But I thought you were better than that. Besides, look where your well-intentioned lies have gotten you. Perhaps you should consider the alternative and tell the truth for once. Couldn't make things any worse."

After that, while Max was busy grumbling and self-marinating in his justified juices, Gustav left as well. Max was starting to feel rather abandoned. But deep down he was certain he had only himself to blame.

Chapter 25

I STARED at the open suitcase. The bottom was lined with the few clothes I had yet to unpack. With Max, we'd been without a stitch on for so long that the need for attire had lessened.

Now I was faced with a choice. As the song went—should I stay, or should I go?

It seemed I had a type when it came to guys. Liars and cheaters. Somehow either they in their predatory cruelty or I in my stupid desperation seemed to hone in on each other.

But was Max really that? Could I lump him in with the others and wash my hands of him?

In my heart, I knew he wouldn't cheat on me with someone else. Then again, he'd lied about his engagement with Lady Kira.

In my soul, I knew he had lied about the poisoning in order to protect me. But that meant he saw me as a weakling who had to be sheltered from the truth.

"Fuck this!"

I yanked opened two drawers, hurting my fingers in the process, grabbed some clothes I'd stored there, and tossed them haphazardly in the suitcase, which I'd never be able to close if I left it in this state. It was a mess, just like me.

There was a knock on the door.

"Go away," I yelled in response.

Nonetheless, the door opened with a creak. Max peered in, his expression uncertain, his voice timid. "May I come in?"

I snorted. "It's your fucking castle. Do whatever you want."

Max winced. But he came in, closed the door, and leaned against it. His skin glowed with a coat of fresh sweat, and he had dark circles around his eyes. He looked about ready to collapse.

"Jesus. Sit down before you pass out."

Max chuckled a little at my command, shuffled in slow as a sloth, and fell into an armchair, panting like a marathon runner. He wore a lavender-hued hospital gown that I hoped to never ever see on him again for as long as I lived.

I studied him with growing concern. He looked so terrible. Quite literally hot. My protective instincts kicked into high gear. "Man, you shouldn't be out of bed."

Max offered me a wry smile. "You should be in mine with me. I swear, I'm not contagious."

I sighed, drew a stool in front of the armchair, and sat on it, facing him. "I'm not really in a make-out mood."

Max's smile faltered. He nodded with a rueful expression. "I know. I'm sorry. I'm to blame."

I rolled my eyes. Recriminations and self-pity didn't do it for me any more than lies. "Max, you were just poisoned. You need to rest. Go back to the infirmary."

Max grimaced. "I hate that place. The smell, the whiteness, the cool air, the echoing tiles on the floor…. It all reminds me of the previous times I spent there."

I straightened, my heart hardening. "Right. All the other times someone tried to kill you. Which you also neglected to tell me about."

Max slumped. Any more and he'd slide right out of the soft, sunken seat. "I know. I didn't want you to worry. Those other times, you see, they weren't serious." My look must have been utterly incredulous because Max grinned a little. "There were exactly two times before today. The first, a drunken aristocrat tried to challenge me to a duel during a formal banquet. He brandished a butter knife, a sharp one unfortunately. As I tried to stop him, he accidentally cut me on the hand, where a visible vein was. There was blood, and everybody freaked out for no real reason. He was charged with misdemeanor assault, by my insistence, instead of a crime against the crown or lese majesty."

"Would the penalty have been… severe?" I asked, shivering. I'd had my share of drunken incidents in college, but none had involved brawls to the death.

Max nodded. His weary eyes drooped but he clearly made an effort to stay alert and talk to me. "Yes. He was a foolish old man who couldn't hold his liquor. Yes, my injury was dangerous but not life-threatening, despite the acute blood loss. But the only one who sees that as a legitimate assassination attempt is seriously deranged."

"I see," I remarked slowly. And I sort of did understand. That incident didn't seem too grave. "And the other?"

When Max paused, I knew the second wasn't as innocent as the first. Max licked his lips, radiating nervousness in waves. The way he dodged my gaze warned me to expect the worst. "That time, at my birthday party two years ago, I ate a piece of poisoned pie."

I gasped, anger roiling in my stomach. "Another poison attack? And you decided this wasn't relevant? Poison pie, poison ring, poison drink. There's a goddamn pattern. The same person could be behind all those times."

Max shook his head. "The investigation is ongoing. I do not want to jump to conclusions in a matter such as this."

I seethed. "Fine. But what about me? You should have told me about this poison shit."

Max closed his eyes. "I know, Oliver. Believe me, I do."

I let out a bitter laugh. "Believe you? Is that a joke? After all the lies, how could I possibly trust you?"

"They were white lies," Max argued, his voice just a croak now. "To protect you."

"There are no white lies," I replied, angry at him for trying to justify his actions. "Only gray ones, where the truth is blurred or distorted or absent entirely. Keeping me in the dark was the wrong choice."

I held back more furious words that served no purpose. Maybe I was overreacting, but small lies and omissions of truth had a way of piling up until they formed a pattern of behavior, or even became a whole way of life.

For a prince, perhaps stretching the truth was second nature. Due to my past experiences with lies, deception, and cheating, I didn't think I could live like that—or with that.

Max seemed about ready to continue to disagree. Finally, he released a deep breath, as if emptying himself. "You're right. Of course you are. My father said the same. That's why I'm here." He glanced at my half-packed, open suitcase, and his features briefly twisted in pain. "A-are you leaving?"

I fisted my hands. "Is that why you're here? To stop me?"

"No." Max looked out the window, his eyes glossed over. "I came to explain. It's your choice whether to leave or stay." His gaze shifted down to his wringing hands. "You know I've had lovers before. But I've never met anyone with whom I felt… you know, a connection."

I hesitated to burst his soliloquy bubble now that he was opening up to me about, hopefully, everything. But I had to ask. "Why did you fixate on me? You could have anyone, I think."

Max smiled but didn't look at me. "Believe it or not, Oliver, it was love at first sight. There you were, a languid beau in my bed. Your lashes were so long as you slept, like black wavy curtains. Your lips were slightly parted and wet; I wanted to kiss you."

I blushed but countered, "That's physical attraction, not love."

Max chuckled. "I'm not really in the best condition to debate the nature of love with you, my dear. However, I cannot say with absolutely certainty what it was about you that made me fall head over heels for you. All I remember is the feeling, how it bloomed inside my chest and expanded till it filled me with warmth and light and delight and, yes, desire, too."

I stared at Max, conflicted. It was hard to deny or belittle someone's feelings. How could I? Had I myself not fallen for him, too, almost instantly? I recalled the blushes, the boner that wouldn't go away, the sight of his absolute hot gorgeousness when he'd slithered out of bed in nothing but black boxer briefs. Perhaps love was, like beauty, in the eye of the beholder.

I had a sneaking suspicion Elinor wouldn't agree with me. But that was her take on things, her business. Maybe it had something to do with her being a girl.

Then the true meaning of his words finally dawned on me.

"You love me?"

Max chuckled, still avoiding eye contact with me. "Took you long enough." Then he grew serious. "We haven't known each other long. For two seasons, yes, but in reality only a couple of weeks. Is that enough time to know another intimately? I can't speak for everyone."

Finally, he met my gaze, steadfast and strong, even if a bit feverish. I knew what he would say, so I stopped him.

"I appreciate what you're trying to say, Max. I really do." I gulped, forcing the words past the emotions lodged in my throat. "But I can't trust you. In the short time we've known each other, you've kept things from me. Serious, life-or-death stuff. You've given me white lies, saying you did it to protect me. But I don't need you protect me from the truth, no matter how harsh or inconvenient or problematic. You can't rob me of that." I stood and started pacing because my head was a jumble of pent-up grievances and frustrations. "You're a nice guy, Max, when you want to be. But honesty is a skill you lack."

Max bit his lower lip. I could see his jaw trembling and his eyes grow misty. It was tough to hurt him when he was so beaten down. My heart ached. Which told me I was lost already.

Max seemed to struggle to speak. "The poisoned pie incident. Or was it a cake? Anyway, that carrot and ginger dish was a gift. We're generally not allowed to accept them. But this was a private, personal present from… Karl von Thürer."

Though I was mystified by the direction our talk had taken, I snarled. "That bully?"

Max smiled shortly. "Yes, him. Do I believe he's after my head, my crown, my throne? No, I do not. He's a patriot *and* a devout Royalist. To sully the royal family… would be unthinkable for him, an unforgivable offense."

"Really?" I felt only disbelief. "Because he didn't seem like your biggest fan waving that falsified document in front of your face. The dude's a total elitist bigot. What if he, like, thought he'd run the kingdom better than you?"

Max shook his head, appearing wan. "Karl could never hurt the kingdom because that would hurt… my mother."

"Collette?" I blinked in confusion.

"Karl and Collette knew each other when they were teenagers. Karl loved her, but Collette loved Gustav. Though Karl eventually married, he still harbors an unrequited love for my mother."

I blinked some more in astonishment. I couldn't imagine a cold, stony person like Karl loving anyone, let alone pining for them if rejected.

"That is why Karl couldn't hurt me. If I died, Collette would be devastated. And upsetting her is the last thing Karl could ever do. Not even his ambition rivals his passion for Collette."

I cringed. Passion and Karl von Thürer seemed like incompatible opposites that by all laws of nature should cancel each other out. Did there beat a warm heart inside that icy body after all? Who knew?

"Okay, so how'd he explain the poisoned pie or cake or whatever?" I asked.

"That his gift to me had been tampered with." Max nodded to himself. "I believe him."

I could only scratch my head in bafflement. For a man who had such a fluid understanding of truth and lies, Max seemed profoundly naïve to believe such a hateful man. Then again, having a heart full of hate didn't mean a person was up to no good. Some grew embittered but never acted on it. But as global hate reared its ugly head, those inactive ones were few and far between.

"Did Karl have anything to do with your signet ring?" I insisted, not yet ready to give up on such a likely suspect as Karl von Thürer.

Max snickered. "No, of course not. The ring is the sole possession of the royal family. The only time it's ever out of the vault is when it's on my finger. Karl has seen it throughout his life, yes, but only from afar. He has never handled it, not even during official ceremonies."

When Max grew quiet, closing his mouth midbreath, I knew there was more to the story. "What?" I demanded, waiting to see if he would lie to me again.

Max sighed. "I'm sure it has nothing to do with anything but… Karl recommended Janos to my security detail."

I drew in a sharp breath. "The guard who disappeared just before your signet ring was turned into a lethal weapon?"

"Yes." Max locked eyes with me. "Oliver? We've drifted off the subject. Are you going to leave? How can I prove to you I've changed if you're not here?"

I sat on the stool again in front of him. "You've held back the truth and told your white lies for so long that it's become second nature." I straightened up and let him hear me. "Maybe it's weird or old-fashioned, naïve or stupid, to value honesty and integrity in a world where everyone has their own version of things. But my parents raised me right."

"As did mine," Max said quietly, a sad tone to his husky voice. "I grew up to see the value of keeping things close to heart and telling white… uh, gray lies over being direct, frank, and honest to a fault. It wasn't my parents' doing that I became this man. I do believe in those things: honesty, integrity, honor, bravery, and so on. I don't always exercise them, though. And… that probably makes me the wrong man for you, my dear, sweet Oliver."

My chest constricted. My eyes burned. I wanted to cry. But I held back. This was not the time to falter. I could give in, but I doubted that would do either of us any good.

Max stood, his knees buckling and his arms shaking. I steadied him, but he gently pushed me aside. Without another word, he left. The door closed so softly I could barely hear it. The boom in my heart deafened me to the sound anyway.

Had that been goodbye?

Chapter 26

Since Max had left me with barely a semblance of a goodbye, I wondered if that was what I should do. Just leave and go back to my old life when I hadn't known any real-life princes.

I, however, stuck to my guns and stayed. I told myself I was simply curious about Max being poisoned and his signet ring being stolen, and that I remained at Riten Castle to learn the truth so I could leave knowing Max would be safe and sound in the end.

Deep down, though, I was just as stubborn as Max. I'd grown to care for him, maybe even love him. And Max himself had declared his devotion for me, unbidden but not entirely unwelcome. Perhaps if the situation hadn't been so dire and if he hadn't been so secretive….

All I had were maybes and ifs, questions and suspicions. I vowed to get to the bottom of things before returning home, or I'd never sleep well again.

While Max was bound to the infirmary for much needed rest and recuperation, I decided to do a little snooping. And Karl von Thürer was my main target.

Was he a suspect because I despised him? No. He was a person of interest because whenever Max succumbed to an assassin's poison, Karl seemed to be there.

Of course, I could say the same for myself. But I knew *I* didn't do it, so….

Finding von Thürer was easy since he already had a shadow in Elinor. I texted her, and she informed me Karl was presently—in late afternoon of the day Max was poisoned—in the Chapel at the eastern side of the Outer Bailey. So I made my way there.

Outside huge wooden double doors that had carvings of oak trees on them paced a plump man. I recognized him from my meeting with the royal family.

"Mr. Weiss?"

Theo Weiss stopped dead in his tracks and blinked at me. When he recognized me, a smile appeared on his lips. "Oh, Mr. Reed. Didn't see you there."

As I approached, I heard raised voices from inside. Theo grimaced and sighed.

"What's going on?" I asked in confusion.

Then I heard Elinor's clear-as-crystal voice shout, "You're an asshole, man. How do I know? Because everything that comes out of your mouth is shit."

I winced. Elinor could rub everyone the wrong way if and when she tried, but she usually had more common sense than this.

Then Karl bellowed, "You hot-blooded shrew!"

This was followed by Elinor screaming, "You cold-blooded reptile!"

"Should we, uh… interrupt them?" I nervously asked Theo, who stared at the door with a similar expression of frustration mixed with trepidation.

Theo harrumphed. "I was in there when they started. After I tried to intervene and call for peace, they unanimously kicked me out." He grinned shortly at me. "It's good, I suppose, that those two can at least agree on something."

I probably shouldn't have laughed, but I think it was mostly stress relief or perhaps just pure hysteria. Take your pick.

"How has your visit been so far?" Theo asked, his tone rising, probably to mask the noise from inside.

"Okay." I smiled back since Theo seemed to have a resting smile face, and it was impolite not to respond in kind. "Listen. What exactly are the rules about giving gifts to members of the royal family?" I felt like I was onto something with Karl and his poison dessert.

"Unless the giver is a direct relation, by marriage or by blood, to the member in question, it is considered inappropriate. Especially if they are common subjects of the realm. Birthday presents from friends are an exception, of course, but there is a price limit set in advance."

I liked how concise Theo could be. "What kind of gifts are typically given?"

Theo chuckled. "Anything expensive is considered extremely bad form because the desire to impress the royal is otherwise eclipsed by the urge to out-do others and compete for the best-present award. You understand, I'm sure."

I nodded. So, cheap knickknacks? Intriguing. "What about, like, food or drink?"

Theo shrugged. "Drink? Not so much. The temptation to buy expensive wines, you see. But specialty foods are a favorite. The castle kitchen is known far and wide for its high-quality cuisine. But a dish or two as a gift is not unheard of. They do have to be cleared first, of course, or there might be a flood of special dishes for one party. That would be... awkward."

"They have to be cleared in advance?" I asked. "By who?"

"The Council. In case you don't know, the Council is like a parliament. Democracy and all."

I rolled my eyes. Karl von Thürer was a councilman. It would have been easy for him to gain consent for a gift he intended to poison. But... I had no proof.

Then Theo's words sank in. "Wait. Some gifts are only allowed between family members?" I struggled to make sense of the message. "Is Karl von Thürer related to the royal family?"

Theo laughed. "To the Lindau-Arbon family? A distant cousin, thrice removed, I think. The von Thürers belong to the secondary royal lineage of the Mountain Tribe, the Varini-Böhm line."

I had a feeling these ancient lineages crisscrossed to the point it was hard to tell how people were connected to each other without an extensive genealogy map. Could Karl be tied to the royal seat more strongly than anyone knew? Did Karl believe that becoming the next king would win the favor of his unrequited love, Colette?

Seemed insane. Then again, power could make men mad.

I didn't get the chance to ask more because the doors banged open, and Karl stormed out. I don't know if he recognized me, but he shoved past me and Theo, using his palms to push us out of his way. His low curses were only audible when he was close.

Elinor came out in Karl's wake, her expression that of a thunderstorm.

"Ellie—" I started, about to reprimand her yet again for her improper conduct.

Theo, however, beat me to the punch. "Behind you is a Chapel to a peaceful goddess, young lady. I will not have it defiled again by your foul mouth. Is that clear?"

Elinor managed to appear abashed and meek. I had my suspicions, though. Theo seemed like too sweet a guy to come off particularly stern or commanding. But his point was valid.

Elinor stepped aside as Theo passed her, pursing his lips. But I doubt he was as angry as he made it appear. He disappeared inside and closed the doors behind him.

I approached my sister and hissed, "You're in big trouble now, Ellie. I'm going to tell Mom and Dad."

Elinor smirked. "Snitch. Rat. Weasel."

I snorted. "If this is a zoology test, I've got it in the bag." She and I both chuckled. Elinor knew when she'd crossed the line, and I could never stay mad at her. She was my baby sister. "One day, if you keep tailing him, that guy's going to hurt you."

Elinor snickered with derision. "I'd like to see that dueling, pompous git try. I'd rip him a new one."

I gave her that one. She'd probably win. "Listen. We need to talk." I took her aside, to the edge of the outer courtyard where a stone banister overlooked a vista of the valley below. Sunshine and greenery. The sight was stunning. I was really going to miss this. Sighing, I ensured no one was around and then told her what had happened this morning and everything since.

Naturally, Elinor was shocked. But when she spoke, I was taken aback by her words. "You and Max broke up over this? That's the stupidest thing you've ever done. I swear, sometimes guys can be so damn chivalrous that it just defies all reason."

I bristled. "Excuse me? Did you miss the part about Max being poisoned and almost dying?"

"No. Duh." Elinor slapped me on the arm, as she often did, because in her mind, boys only learned through punching. Couldn't say she was entirely wrong. Her corporal punishments sure stuck in my memory. "Why'd you break up?" Elinor whined. "You two are stronger together, as a team of equal partners, than you are apart. How come neither of you morons gets that?"

I couldn't deny her logic, which was sound. But Max had made up his mind. And me? Well, I was still on the fence about trusting Max again. He could lie like the best of them.

As if reading my mind, Elinor scoffed. "He's lying *to himself*, Ollie. Can't you effing see that?" She swung up her arms and stomped her foot. "Boys are so stupid!"

Then she rushed off, stewing, and left me alone to my jumbled thoughts.

So much for getting a woman's opinion on the whole assassination plot.

THE CHAPEL surprised me. There were traditional pews and a pulpit, but beyond that the layout and decor didn't resemble churches. Wood-paneled walls depicted natural motifs, rural scenes, and Celtic gods and goddesses. Rich tapestries, small statues, and a wide array of colorful stained-glass windows showed unicorns wearing crowns.

In the nave, under the sunlight cascading in colored beams, stood a wooden altar on twelve free-standing pillars with lit candles on top. The whole thing was like viewing a miniature wooden Stonehenge inside the Vatican. I didn't know what to make of it. I knew next to nothing about modern Celtic practices.

Theo stood by the altar in his emerald-green robes, shimmying slightly back and forth as if reciting a long prayer. His lips were moving, but even in the echoes of the Chapel I could hear nothing.

"Is that Latin?" I asked softly, as not to startle him.

Theo jumped a little, a hand over his chest in a very theatrical manner. Then he chuckled. "What? Oh, goodness no. Latin is for Catholics. And English is for Protestants. This is the universal language."

"Pig Latin?" I joked.

Theo laughed so hard his big belly jiggled. If I were to picture a summer Santa Claus, he would fit the bill perfectly. "No, child. Song. No words required. Just a melody."

He started to hum a deep tune. I learned he could have been quite the singer had he focused on that instead of religion. Everything was in its proper place, from pitch to tone. As he'd indicated, there were no words, only indistinct sounds. I wasn't sure if I could sit through an entire ceremony of this, but it wasn't wholly unpleasant. Reminded me of hummed mantras from the east.

"Care to try for yourself?" Theo asked once he'd quieted. He waved at me to take his place at the altar.

I chuckled. "Only if you want to bring the whole Chapel down on us. My voice can offend any and all deities."

"Nonsense." Theo dismissed my words with an amused scoff. "I'm sure you have a lovely voice. Youth excels in most things."

I doubted that was true. Natural skills were one thing; a lot had to be learned before excelling in them. Maybe he was trying to be nice.

"What's it like being a druid?" I asked, glancing around, taking it all in.

Theo smiled wide. "Well, I can't speak for everyone who dons the robes, but I love it. I've wanted to be a druid since I was a child." I stared, flabbergasted. Not the sort of dream I'd ever heard of. Theo laughed. "I know. Not a typical career path for most. You see, I cherish nature. I adore every little thing about it. I firmly believe everything in nature has a spirit, a life, an energy. It's like us—intelligent, empathetic, but confined."

I wasn't following. "They don't, like, talk to you, do they?"

Theo threw his head back and laughed so hard he had tears streaming from his eyes. "Oh, you are the absolute funniest young man. Nature would love to have a worshipper in you."

I blushed at the compliment even though I didn't quite get it. "I thought the Celts believed in gods, not spirits."

Theo spread his arms magnanimously. "You say potato, I say potatoh. Besides, ours is not the original faith of the ancient Celts. Ours is a reconstructionist approach. We have room for both gods and spirits. As long as they are a part of nature." He winked at me. "Like you and His Highness, Prince Maximilian."

I flushed with heat, this time not from praise. Theo wasn't being insulting; that much I could tell. But I knew he was referring to Max's and my sexual orientation, and I wasn't sure talking about that ever did anyone any good.

When I didn't speak, Theo nodded to me. "Homosexuality is natural. To call homosexuality a lifestyle choice, or a choice at all, is the most ridiculous—" He caught himself before going too far and cooled off. "It would be like saying all types of sexual orientation are a choice. That would include heterosexuality. And I dare say if I accused straights of that, there'd be hell to pay."

I didn't want to ask him about his sex life, even though I doubted he, as a druid, had the same constraints as some other priesthoods in the chaste religious world. Sexuality, to me at least, was a private matter. No discussion needed.

What I noted, though, was that Theo seemed to know what Max was at heart: a gay man.

"Max is heir to the throne," I remarked. I was curious about his opinion. "If he were gay or bi, wouldn't his orientation be a handicap for the royal lineage, even with the Equal Marriage Act?"

Theo frowned, seemingly weighing every option. I liked his directness and thoughtfulness. Finally he said slowly, "There are two other princes, both of whom are straight as far as I know. So the end of the lineage is not a likely outcome. Besides, history is full of leaders who were gay, but history knew them as impotent or infertile. There are always options."

I stopped to consider Theo's words. There was wisdom there. Max's station as the hereditary prince didn't mean he and I couldn't be together, even if the need for heirs came into play. He could marry and keep me as his lover; he could find a surrogate to carry his child; he could relinquish the burden of offspring to his brothers.

I released a long breath. The children thing had been one of the reasons why I'd initially been hesitant about starting a relationship with a prince. A man like that had obligations to the crown, to his family, to his people, his country.

"Are you two serious?" Theo asked, his tone shyer, his cheeks pinking. Perhaps he rarely asked about people's private lives.

"I don't know," I answered truthfully. Theo seemed like an ally. He didn't condemn Max, me, or homosexuality; he believed it was natural and that gay people were born that way. Therefore, no point in lying.

Theo gave me a sympathetic look. "In that case, this might not be the ideal location for you. I know many who have been seduced by this place and its riches." He let out a mournful sigh, glancing around. "It's hard to see past the glamour, you understand. I don't mean simply because most aren't born to luxury and fame. This place, it can cloud your judgment." Theo chuckled at himself. "In my role, I don't need to come here every day, but I'm drawn here, to this Chapel. Morning, noon, and night, I spend endless hours here, though strictly speaking my presence is only required during official ceremonies and calendrical events. And yet...."

Theo's shrug spoke volumes. He couldn't explain the allure of this place any more than I could. But ever since we'd arrived, I'd loved the rolling hills, the snowy peaks, the dense forests, the idly flowing rivers, the meadows dotted with wildflowers, even the sheep and the cows…. I had loved this land before I'd let myself start falling for Max.

"I mean no offense, young man," Theo said with a hushed, reverent tone. "I only wish to help if I can. This castle isn't always conducive to that outcome."

I smiled ruefully. "I'm aware. Thanks for the advice."

Theo bowed, the hems of his robes sweeping the floor. "Any time, Mr. Reed. Any time. I'll be here if you ever need to talk."

Absentmindedly, I wandered out, conflicted about what to do, what course to take.

I WAS so preoccupied with my thoughts that I nearly ran into Lady Kira.

Her laugh bubbled liked fine champagne. "The sun was in my eyes. The fault is mine. I beg your pardon."

I snorted. "The sun shining is your fault now? Becoming a queen is not enough; you aspire to be a goddess?"

Kira laughed harder, with her whole body. Something told me she didn't often get to do that. When she looked at me, her eyes glistened. "You are a good man, Mr. Reed."

"Please, call me Oliver."

"I'd be happy to. If you call me Kira."

"Will do." I saluted her, and she tittered some more. A question popped into my head. "I didn't see you at the Solstice Festival. I mean, sure, everyone was in costume, with many wearing a mask or face paint, but I'm pretty sure I would've remembered seeing you."

Kira shrugged. "I was there. One of those hiding behind a mask. I didn't feel like talking to anyone, so I spent all my time on the dance floor. Kept me from having to exchange awkward words about, um… Max and… things."

For the first time, I looked at the situation from her point of view. It must have been hard for her to be the subject of so much public conjecture. And it must have been equally troublesome for her to be constantly accosted about her relationship with Max by strangers with a vested interest and no concept of privacy. No wonder she chose to celebrate in anonymity.

I felt bad for her. "I'm sorry," I murmured.

Kira touched my arm gently. "Don't worry. With Theo leading a conga line, who in their right mind could possibly stay sad? I had a wonderful time, I assure you." She smiled and I smiled back. Then she glanced over my shoulder at the closed Chapel doors. "A moment of prayer?"

I shook my head. "Nah. I'm not religious or spiritual."

She pointed at my left arm, bare since I wore a white T-shirt, where one of my tattoos was. "Is that not a religious symbol? The Lady of Guadalupe, if memory serves."

I looked down at the familiar, slightly faded artwork. "It's there for cultural reasons. Plus, one can never have too much luck."

"Ah." Kira nodded, her curious gaze flicking between my arm and the Chapel. "Was Theo in there? I was hoping to speak with him, but he wasn't in the Conservatory or the gardens."

I waved behind me. "Yeah, he's in there." I studied her with curiosity. "Is he interested in gardening?" I knew Theo was a lover of nature, so it made sense.

Kira giggled. "Theo Weiss is one of this country's leading biologists, I'll have you know. Before he donned the robes, he was a brilliant scientist, specializing in flora."

I swallowed hard, trying not to show my sudden chill in spite of the sunshine and warmth. I said as casually as I could, "Theo knows a lot about plants, huh?"

"More than anyone here, I dare say, including Queen Colette." Kira rounded me and headed to the door. "I'll see you later… Oliver."

With an amiable wink, she entered into the shadows and was gone.

I steadied my racing heart. So I had a new suspect and a new lead. But what did it all mean?

I slowly made my way through the castle grounds toward my quarters in the Swan Tower. As I did, I went over what I knew, or thought I knew. The culprit had to have means, motive, and opportunity.

My number one suspect, Karl von Thürer, had all three. He was ambitious about his career, patriotic about leading the country right, and envious of Gustav and Colette. As a councilman, he could come and go as he pleased in the castle. He had given Max the poisoned pie, or whatever it was, and he'd arranged for Jonas to work for him as a bodyguard. Also, as a personal note, I didn't like him.

Who else was on my list?

Lady Kira was a possibility. She could have had a motive: Hell hath no fury like a woman scorned. But was that a strong enough reason to kill someone? Maybe an average Joe, but a prince? Perhaps not. Opportunity presented a problem because she hadn't been in France when the signet ring had been tampered with. As for means, well, sitting in the Conservatory didn't mean she liked or knew anything about lethal plants like hemlock.

In short, Kira was a poor suspect.

Now there was a new addition to the list: Theo Weiss. As a biologist, he had the means. As a virtual resident of the castle, he had the opportunity. But what the heck would be his motive for attacking Max? None that I could see. Theo seemed content to be the Grand Druid and harbored no aspirations for the throne. He didn't hate gays. And he didn't seem greedy for either the luxury or the wealth of the royal family.

As far as I could tell, Theo was a better suspect than Kira but worse than Karl.

Who else?

I grimaced when I considered Prince Johann.

He sure hated me, being an elitist dickhead. But did he hate his big brother? Could he kill his own brother or arrange for his death? If hate wasn't the motive, perhaps ambition was. Johann wasn't next in line for succession but that wouldn't stop a determined man who had already murdered someone.

While Johann had motives up the wazoo and also had opportunities aplenty, since he lived in the castle, did he have the means? Somehow, I doubted a man like Johann, so focused on frivolous pursuits and a life of leisure, would bother learning something complicated, like poison, to get what he wanted. Could laziness suggest a person's innocence?

As a suspect, Johann stood on par with Theo: possible but unlikely.

Karl still held the number one position.

Of course, none of this was evidence. Especially since anyone could google hemlock, come in on a visitor's pass, and give the guards the slip. Everyone hated something with a vengeance, so why not a prince? In addition, all my suspects had the resources to contract a specialist to do the deed if they themselves felt squeamish or wanted to establish credible alibis.

So, my list of who had motive, means, and/or opportunity was a lead, nothing more. Certainly not proof positive. I lacked evidence to make accusations.

Trouble was, I had no idea where to get it.

I sighed. "I should've become a cop or a journalist or a private dick."

Too late now, I thought.

Chapter 27

THE FIRST thing I noticed upon entering my quarters was that the curtains were drawn, casting the room into shadow. Had the maids been in here? I grumbled since the room wasn't even facing south or west, so there was no need to ward off afternoon heat or glare.

"Shut the door."

I started, blind in the shade. Someone inside the room had spoken in a hushed voice, nothing but hisses pronounced.

"If you run, I'll shoot you where you stand." The sound of a gun being cocked confirmed as much.

I gulped. No escape, then. I entered fully, closed the door, and leaned against it. I waited for my eyes to adjust to the dimness.

After a few breaths, I saw a dark shape sitting in the corner armchair. Every movie cliché flashed before my eyes as I took in the invader—who held me at gunpoint.

"Who are you?" I asked cautiously. No sense in antagonizing a lone gunman.

The man sneered. "We met in France in passing, though we didn't speak."

I drew in a sharp breath. "*Janos?*"

"Oh, you know my name." The bodyguard who had vanished under mysterious, suspicious circumstances didn't move. His gun-hand didn't falter once. "Did the prince tell you about me?"

"Vaguely," I replied, not really sure what to do or say. "How did you get in here? There are guards and locked doors and surveillance—"

Janos snorted. "I can get into a lot of places."

I frowned at the mysterious statement. "Everyone's looking for you," I said. Janos barked out a laugh. The fact that he was in my quarters aiming a gun at me didn't necessarily mean he had ill will at heart. "Did you switch the real signet ring in the hotel vault with the fake, poisoned one?"

Janos shrugged. "Yeah, I did."

One down, another to go, I thought to myself. "Did you poison the water bottle last night?"

Janos grunted. "Yes, I did that too."

My hands clenched at my sides as anger replaced my dread. I stepped closer to him. Most of the space remained between us, though. "Why do you want to kill Max?"

"Not kill, incapacitate." Janos stood and approached me. I barely recalled him from before in France. Now I saw the buzz cut, broad shoulders, and the brooding expression, accentuated by a once-broken nose. He glowered at me. "I didn't want the prince dead. He was just supposed to get real sick, so he couldn't be judged healthy enough to inherit the throne."

"But the hotel manager died," I countered in confusion.

Janos dismissed the death with a swish of his wrist. "Turned out the poor bastard had a preexisting heart condition. How could I have anticipated that, or that he'd try to put the stupid thing on his own finger? Fucking dumbass prince-wannabe."

I hadn't known that. Details about the investigation hadn't reached me; why would they? The court was keeping the whole incident under wraps.

"Why did you poison the ring at all?" I asked. "Do you hate Max?"

Janos grunted. "I don't hate the prince. It was a job."

I gasped in shock. Finally, we were getting somewhere. "You were hired to tamper with the ring? Who contracted you? Tell me, please."

Janos never got the chance.

The front door burst open with a deafening bang. Shouts about getting down were lost in the noise, and the red lights on the automatic weapons' scopes blinded me.

Janos grabbed me and threw me aside, cursing and snarling. I fell onto the floor on my face, barely in time to avoid the bullets flying. I covered my head while trying to crawl away.

When a hand landed on my back, I screamed. It wasn't my proudest moment.

A black-clad guard with a Venetian-red fox symbol on his chest helped me up. "You're all right now, sir. The threat has been eliminated." A strong Australian accent told me this hireling was a foreign powerhouse, probably ex-military.

That impression was strengthened when I spotted Janos's dead, bullet-ridden body bleeding on an expensive carpet. A death grimace bared his teeth and his sharklike gray eyes were wide-open, the left one bleeding a little.

I cringed, nauseated as my stomach roiled.

"Shouldn't we try to help him? Get paramedics in here or something?" I asked faintly.

The guard shook his head. "We've called it, sir. You need to vacate the premises until the all-clear." He waved briskly over my shoulder. "This officer will take you to a more secure location."

From the sound of the order, there was no refusing. I stared at Janos's fresh corpse. A wave of sympathy rolled over me, followed again by nausea. Only then, as I walked out with a guard beside me, did justified anger replace other feelings.

With Janos dead, the investigation was back to square one.

"THAT'S IT. We're leaving. Kids, pack your bags." My mother's judgment call rang harsh in my ears. To her, a chance that I could have been killed half an hour ago was reason enough to vacate.

For once, Elinor didn't argue. She sat on the edge of my parents' bed and stared at nothing.

My father stood by the open balcony doors, arms crossed over his chest, his head lowered, and his brow furrowed. As usual, he kept his thoughts to himself.

In the meantime, Valerie did all the talking, in a shrill voice growing sharper and louder with each sentence as she hurried us along.

I stepped in front of her to stop her. "We can't leave, Mom. Who knows if we'll be any safer back home? No, we have to stay and help Max solve this. That's the only way to make sure."

Valerie's eyes flashed, and her chin jutted out stubbornly. "No, Ollie. I will not sit idly by as my eldest child is in mortal danger. I'm calling this one. Mother's prerogative."

I chuckled. "What? There's no such thing."

Laughing proved to be a bad idea. Valerie was so mad she practically had steam coming out of her ears. I'd never seen her so upset. But I knew she wasn't really angry; she was worried.

Regardless, she wasn't stupid. She could see which path served us best.

"Paul? What do you think?" she asked, her tone placating but her face remaining twisted in hard, edgy lines.

Paulito looked up at each of us in turn. "We stay and see this thing through."

The decision silenced us all. I think we realized the very real danger we were in as long as we stayed here at Riten Castle. But the alternative, that we tucked our tails and ran, would be worse, especially if someone got hurt. Such as a member of the royal family.

"Thanks, guys." I blinked back tears. I was touched they sided with me. "Those men in black will keep us safe. That's their job."

"The Black Steed Brigade or the Fox Tails?" Elinor asked. Judging from my expression, I must have made a pretty, if baffled, picture, because she giggled. "Those men in black. They have a name. The Black Steed Brigade is an elite unit of Noricia's militia, showing a horse badge on their chest armor. They cover the perimeter of the grounds. The Fox Tails are the royal guard, with two flanks: the ceremonial sentries standing around in colored uniforms, holding lances, and the men in black full-body armor who patrol the castle with semiautomatic weapons, displaying a red fox logo." She rolled her eyes. "Dude, it was in the brochure."

I blushed. I admit, I'd been far more preoccupied with getting laid than learning about the rich history and culture of Noricia. "Uh-huh," I murmured. To turn attention away from my ignorance, I decided to bring my family into my confidence. "I've been doing my own snooping," I confessed.

Elinor yelped. "I freaking knew it!" She jumped to me, punched me in the arm, and resumed her former position on the bed. "What do you have so far? And don't tell me nothing."

I related to them the facts about Jonas's involvement, the signet ring and how it had been used, and my four suspects: Karl, Kira, Theo, and Johann. In short, I didn't have as much as I'd hoped and certainly not enough to publicly accuse anyone. This wasn't a game of Clue; this was real life, and I couldn't go around pointing at people willy-nilly. Especially high-standing people like Johann or Karl who had enough clout to shut me down for good.

"Wish we could recruit the Cat's Paws to help us," Elinor murmured to herself, a pensive expression on her face as she leaned forward with her elbows on her knees.

"The who?" I asked, understanding that yet again I should have studied more.

"The Black Steeds guard all royal holdings, and the Fox Tails guard the royals in public, but the Cat's Paws do so in… more clandestine ways."

"You learned that from the brochure?"

Elinor laughed. "No, silly. I googled Norician conspiracy theories, of course. According to internet rumors, the Cat's Paw is Noricia's intelligence agency. You know, spies. It's said they lurk and sneak inside hidden chambers at the Cat Tower, right here in Riten Castle."

"Well, if it's on the internet, it must be true." I let my tone drip sarcasm. Elinor chuckled. I went on, "Unless those spies are here to help us in the next five minutes, I'm ruling them out as an option." I narrowed my eyes, surveying my sister. "Unless you know something I don't…."

Elinor stage-whispered, "Well, I heard a rumor that Max might be the spymaster."

I barked out an incredulous laugh. "That's the stupidest thing ever. He's way smart, but come on, that he'd be some kind of James Bond? That's ridiculous."

Elinor shrugged. "Just repeating the talk of the town."

I waved dismissively at her. "Max is not a spy or a master of spies. No chance." I glared at her since she'd tried to mess with my head, which was already a jumble of nerves. "Do you have anything concrete to add?"

We were interrupted by the door opening so fast it hit the wall with a bang. We jumped, all four of us on edge.

Max stumbled in, as haggard as before. Pure horror shone in his widened, wild eyes. When he saw me, a strangled sound escaped his throat. He came to me and grabbed me into a hard embrace. I more felt than heard him sob against my neck.

"Max, what's wrong?" I asked in alarm, patting his back to try to calm him down.

"Are you all right, Oliver?" he whispered. "I'd die if anything happened to you."

I cringed. So Max had only just learned about my encounter with Janos in my quarters. "It's okay. I'm fine. See? Not a hair out of place."

Max shook. I had to hug him tighter to stop his violent trembling. He sniffled and nodded. "Oh, Oliver, I never wanted you to get hurt coming here. The worst I thought would happen was a sex-related injury."

I chuckled into his hair, ruffling it. "There's still time. It's good to have plans."

Max's watery laugh lasted only a moment. When he pulled away, he'd regrouped. A kind, if a bit stiffly polite, smile and a straightened back showed no signs of the distress from a second ago.

"I will speak with my parents and arrange for a private plane to take you back home." When Elinor drew in a breath to reject the offer, as I knew she would, Max brought up his hands. "I apologize, but with the threat of mortal danger hanging over my head *and* yours, I cannot in good conscience endanger any of you."

"I appreciate your concern, Max," I cut in, determined in a way I doubted I'd ever been. "But we're staying." When Max tried to speak, I stopped him with a glare. "If you think for one second that I'm going to leave now when the shit's hitting the fan, you're out of your mind."

Max glowered right back at me. "I will not have this insubordination—"

"It'd only be that if I were working for you as an underling," I interjected like a smartass.

"Fine." Max raised his chin with equal resolution. "Then I will throw you and your family out of the castle."

"Your call," I countered, refusing to budge an inch. "Then we'll come back as tourists."

"Then I will banish you from Noricia altogether."

"I'll smuggle myself in here."

Max sighed and slumped. "You're being an obstinate child."

I growled, defiant. "And you're a pigheaded fool. Listen carefully, Max: We. Are. Staying."

Max didn't seem to have the energy to argue further. He regarded everyone and saw a sea of determined faces. I know because I followed his gaze. My mother had doubts, but I wasn't going anywhere, so neither was she. My father was harder to read; he always had been. Elinor's feistiness complemented my own.

"Anyone else have anything to say?" Max asked, using a commanding princely tone that failed to make a sufficient impact on account of him looking like a poor zombie dragged behind a truck for a week.

Elinor drew in a breath.

I had a hunch what she would say, so I clapped a hand over her mouth, smiled sweetly, and said, "Nothing."

Naturally, Elinor kicked me in the shin, broke free, and asked, "Are you the Black Cat?"

Max's blue eyes widened to near-saucers. Then he burst out laughing. "Let me guess. You've been listening to castle gossip."

I harrumphed. "Forgive her. Ellie's a total conspiracy nut."

"I am not," Elinor sputtered. "It's not like I believe the government faked the Apollo moon landing or that secret agents dose medicines and vaccines with mind-altering drugs or that aliens are slicing up cows on a nightly basis all over America's pastures."

I rolled my eyes. "True. But you do believe silly stuff like there's a nuclear reactor under the Pentagon."

Elinor whined theatrically. "Oh, come on. It's a government facility. Not like it'd be a stretch of the imagination for there to be a missile silo."

Max chuckled. "She's got you there, Oliver."

"Oh, Max, don't you start," I complained. I gave him my most piercing gaze. "Or is there a nuclear weapon under this castle?"

Max snorted. "Riten Castle is an historic site with innumerable people about each day. It would hardly have gone unnoticed if we had built an underground base, especially with radiation involved."

"You're stalling," Elinor accused. "That makes me think you are the Black Cat."

Max smiled. "The leader of the infamous Cat's Paws, the supposed intelligence service of the kingdom? I hate to break it to you, my dear, but there is no such organization in Noricia."

"Ha!" Elinor pointed a finger at him. "Plausible deniability, eh?"

Max shook his head. "Like all male royals before me, I'm a member of the Fox Tails, which is the royal guard. And no, I'm not the Black Fox either."

"That's from a Danny Kaye movie," I noted offside, speaking to no one in particular.

Max smiled wide at me. "Yes, it is. *The Court Jester*. Thank you for introducing it to me."

"Switching topics now? Sus-pi-cious…," Elinor singsonged, doing a little twirl on her tippytoes.

"Knock it off," I told her. She flicked her tongue at me, the impudent little brat. "See what I have to deal with?" I waved toward her while watching Max.

Max giggled. "I don't know. I kind of love your sister."

"See?" Elinor blew me a kiss. Then she said, "I'd be more inclined to believe you, Max—if that is your real name—if you let me search the Cat Tower."

Max laughed so bad he was wheezing. "Why stop at one? Why not search all thirteen towers for spies and assassins?"

Elinor snapped her fingers as though she'd had a brilliant insight. "Hey, that's not a bad idea. Let's do that."

"Search for what?" I countered as the voice of reason. "Janos, the would-be killer, is dead."

"For the real signet ring, of course." Elinor clapped her hands, somehow managing to appear like a Bond villain. "There's a plot afoot, and we should explore this castle, top to bottom."

I was about to argue, but Max beat me to it. "If it will set your mind at ease and prompt you to return to the States and be safe, I'm all for that plan."

I gasped. "What? You're both nutty as a fruitcake!"

Chapter 28

"WHY DO all the towers look so different?" Oliver asked as he, Max, and Elinor stood outside the Cat Tower in the outer courtyard, peering up at the intact stonework. This tower was round, while the Stag and Swan Towers were square. Some towers were shorter, others taller. A few were sturdy, a couple were delicate. There was no rhyme or reason.

Max liked Oliver's inquisitiveness, which was quite different from his sister's. Elinor was more perceptive and direct; Oliver had an overall childlike curiosity that Max appreciated, as if Oliver saw the world anew every day.

Max shrugged. "They were built in different times by different masons, designed by different architects, and funded by different rulers. To each his own, I suppose."

Oliver nodded and shaded his eyes as he studied the Cat Tower. "You mentioned earlier that the Snake Tower is yours, and the Stag Tower belongs to your parents."

"Yes." Max glanced over his shoulder at the largest spire, its blocky construct imposing and majestic. Long green banners depicting a unicorn hung from the ramparts, undulating in the wind. "The Throne Room is on the ground floor, and the King and Queen's quarters are above it, as you well know."

"Do you have your own princely throne room?" Elinor inquired.

Max chuckled. "No. But I have my own private reception hall. All towers have one on the ground floor. It's just called something different at the Stag Tower."

"Let me guess," Elinor remarked, appearing pensive. "The Fox Tower is where the Fox Tails hold fort?"

Max nodded. "Yes. Their barracks and watchtower are at the Fox Tower. The Steed Tower houses a small garrison of our military forces, called the Black Steed Brigade."

Oliver waved toward a thin, delicate, pinkish-white tower next to the Chapel. Vines and roses grew along its cylindrical shape. "I thought I saw a bell in that one."

"Ah, yes. The Wren Tower is the castle belfry. It was built to resemble a minaret during a time when exotic cultures were seen as inspiration for design, art, and architecture."

"It's really pretty," Elinor said with an infatuated sigh. "A real princess's tower. It should belong to a lady."

Oliver barked out a laugh. "Go ahead then, milady, and let down your luscious locks."

Max laughed while Elinor shot daggers at them with her eyes. The relationship between brother and sister seemed carefree, humorous, and close, Max estimated as he observed the two siblings being snarky at each other. He suppressed a sigh, wishing he were closer to his brothers. Alas, one was always too preoccupied with scientific experiments and the other with frivolous parties. If it wasn't for official functions and family gatherings, Max doubted he'd ever see them. A twinge of envy twisted his insides. He shoved the feeling away, for it did no good to dwell. He had as much responsibility for the brotherly distance as the others; Max had stopped trying to reach them.

To set gloomy thoughts aside, Max continued, "The Bull Tower houses the castle kitchen, pantry, and staff quarters. The Seahorse Tower has a number of bathing facilities, namely saunas and hot tubs, as this country is known for spas, like Iceland. In the hills, we have several bathhouses with natural hot springs."

"Oh, I didn't know that. I want to try them!" Elinor exclaimed, abuzz with excitement.

"What? Didn't you read about that in the brochure?" Oliver quipped.

Elinor huffed. "Just for that, I'll be sure to bring a bucket of hot water to your room so I can pour it over your thick head at night when you're fast asleep."

Oliver feigned shock. "Scolding and burning your own brother? Shame on you."

Then brother and sister burst out laughing. Max chimed in. He liked their company. Too bad they wouldn't stay.

"My brother Ben, or Prince Berengar, lives in the Salmon Tower, while John resides in the Butterfly Tower," Max explained.

Elinor scoffed, crossing her arms over her chest. "Right 'cause that guy's the perfect social butterfly. Yeah, maybe in a fascist party or a lynch mob."

"Ellie!" Oliver scolded softly, looking embarrassed. He cast a shy glance at Max, as if to ensure there was no perceived offense. Max wasn't too upset.

"Believe it or not," he said slowly. "John wasn't always like that. He's been spending time with the wrong crowd ever since he came of age."

"Company is as company does," Elinor retorted, looking away. Clearly, she had formed an opinion of Johann, and nothing would deter her from that negativity.

Max decided it was best to change the subject. "The Swan Tower is the guest quarters, where you're staying; the Hawk Tower is the guardhouse and control room; and last but not least, the Wolf Tower has a small gaol on the basement level, a bigger donjon on top, and storage space in between."

Elinor scrunched her nose, forming a frown. "*Gaol* sounds like *jail*, but in the brochure it's spelled g-a-o-l. Is it the same thing? And why's the dungeon at the top of the tower?"

"They are the same. G-a-o-l is the original spelling and is still used here and in the UK, for example," Max explained. "And donjon used to mean a fortified tower or main keep, the most secure spires, but now dungeons are seen as underground structures."

"Cool," Elinor commented dryly. Then she waved at the building before them. "What's the Cat Tower used for? You know, other than being the secret headquarters of a clandestine intelligence service?"

Max laughed. "You have a wonderfully wild imagination, my dear."

Elinor winked at him. "My code name could be Little Sister." While Max was busy laughing his ass off, Elinor went on. "Also, don't think I didn't notice how you avoided answering me."

"I simply didn't get the chance," Max defended himself with a courteous smile and a slight bow. Elinor curtsied back theatrically.

The double doors to the Cat Tower opened suddenly, startling them all.

Out limped a young man in old-fashioned pants, dress shirt, and vest. His ash-blond hair was a mess of curls, his fair skin and short-trimmed beard as sooty and dirty as his leather gloves, and he kept coughing. He looked like a figure escaped out of a steampunk movie. Behind him a billow of smoke expanded out through the crack in the door.

Max gasped. "*Ben?*"

The young man blinked. Then a smile broke out. "Max?" He closed the gap between them and hugged his brother. The warm solidity of his body embracing Max was welcome. "I thought you were in the States, or was it Canada?"

Max drew back, holding on to Ben's shoulders. "No, I came home a while back." He peeked past Berengar but couldn't see anything through the darkness and the smoke. "What are you doing in there?"

Ben chuckled. "Conducting experiments, brother. No one was using the Cat Tower, so I claimed it for myself and rebuilt my laboratory."

Max frowned in confusion. "I thought you had a lab in the Salmon Tower."

Ben shrugged. "I did. It's a bit, um, busted up at the moment."

Max closed his eyes and prayed for patience. "You blew up another lab? Mom and Dad will kill you. This is an historic site, dammit. You're not supposed to set off explosions. The historical society and the Council will be so mad at you."

Ben smiled bright. "I've been in trouble with them before. All three parties. If I have to remind them yet again that I am a prince, I will." Only then did he seem to notice Oliver and Elinor. "Oh, hello." He took a hold of Elinor's hand and bussed a kiss on the back, bowing. "I am Prince Berengar. How may I be of assistance?"

Elinor blushed. Oliver stared at her, eyes wide. Max bit his own lip to stop himself from laughing. The siblings were so adorable. And Ben was laying it on pretty thick. Ben had always been a damnable smooth talker, able to convince anyone of anything.

"H-hi, Your Highness. I'm Ellie Reed." Elinor curtsied ever so quickly.

"Greetings, Ellie. Please call me Ben." The shameless smile Ben flashed could have made a lady of the night blush. Elinor's cheeks reddened as well.

Oliver extended a hand. "Hi. I'm Oliver Reed, Ellie's brother."

Ben took Oliver's hand, if a bit hesitantly. "Oliver?" He glanced at Max with a knowing twinkle. "That Oliver?"

It was Max's turn to flush with heat. "Yes, that one."

Ben chuckled. "Max talked about you all spring long. Never thought I'd meet you, though." He frowned a little and only briefly. "Have you, uh, met our parents?"

Both Oliver and Elinor nodded.

Max snorted. "Brother, they've been here for weeks already."

Out of the blue, Ben switched to German and said, "I hate to be the bearer of bad news, big brother, but Kira is here. I think Johann invited her. If I didn't know better, I'd say he was either stirring up trouble or trying to seduce your fiancée."

Max slumped. "I already know. And you don't have to speak in German. Oliver knows about Kira. They've met and talked—with and without me."

Ben's eyebrows rose to his hairline. "Really? How, uh, progressive? Are you thinking of an open marriage or a threesome perhaps?"

Max groaned. "Stop. Kira is my problem."

Before the discussion escalated, Elinor cut in, "You have a lab in the Cat Tower, do you? Have you noticed anything odd going on in there?"

Both Max and Oliver sighed deeply.

Ben gave them each an odd look. "Uh, why do you ask?"

Elinor smiled wickedly. "Well, the Cat's Paws are rumored to hide in there."

Ben's surprised expression grew. Then he started to laugh. "A conspiracy theorist, eh? I've heard that Americans believe in silly things. It seems there may be some truth to it." Then he shrugged and coughed a little. "You're welcome to search the place, provided you touch none of my ongoing experiments. Just wait until the smoke clears. My assistants are busy opening windows and putting the ventilation on full. Soon it'll be safe to go in."

Ben seemed amused by the idea of a secret intelligence agency hiding in the Cat Tower. Max agreed. This whole thing was ridiculous. Spies in the shadows? Weren't assassins enough?

"We're searching all the towers," Elinor offered, raising her chin defiantly as she studied Ben. "For anything suspicious."

Ben winked. "Something like a mad scientist who nearly blew up the castle?"

Elinor quirked an eyebrow. "Scientific research would be a perfect cover for a secret agent conducting his own, eh, stuff."

Ben laughed harder. "I wish I had time for two jobs. Alas, as the Royal Inventor of Noricia and the CEO of Lindau-Arbon Industries, I do not have the time to play cloak-and-dagger games. If you want someone with an abundance of free time on his hands, I suggest you track down my brother Johann."

"*Pfft!*" Elinor waved a dismissive hand. "That elitist jerk isn't smart enough to be a secret agent."

Ben blinked. He exchanged glances with Max, who understood. They were both aware of Johann's bad habits, prejudices, and sense of entitlement. But to hear such a harsh judgment from an outsider, well, it was a jolt. Took the wind out of their sails.

Elinor seemed to realize her faux pas. "I'm sorry. I'm sure he's a… a nice guy underneath all that, eh—"

"Hostility and bluster?" Ben finished. He sounded sad. "Johann is young. Maybe when he's older and wiser, he'll see the error of his ways." Then Ben clapped his hands and straightened. "Anyway, I'm pretty sure it's safe to go into the tower by now. Most of the smoke seems to have dissipated. But watch out for soot and ash." He walked away across the yard and declared as he went, "I'm off to find new equipment and a clean room. Again."

"Don't blow anything else up!" Max called out after him.

Ben's laughter was carried along with the wind.

"We still doing this?" Oliver asked, pointing at the Cat Tower. He rolled his eyes. "Though I think this is a dumb idea. Nothing but a smoky lab in there, and I prefer clean lungs."

"Don't worry," Max remarked next to him. "If need be, I'll give you mouth-to-mouth."

He loved seeing red slashes appear on Oliver's cheeks and his hazel eyes darken. Those signs suggested their relationship might still be salvaged. Even if Max was determined to send Oliver away for his own safety.

This search had to be the final hours of their time together—for now at least.

Chapter 29

"WHAT'S WRONG with Ben's leg?" Elinor asked as the three of us walked into the Cat Tower. Ben's lab appeared to take up the bulk of the bottom floor—what might have been the reception hall in another tower.

I coughed to clear my throat. The stench of fresh smoke lingered thickly despite the doors and windows being open. Three assistants, all wearing outfits similar to Ben's, hurried about, one waving a fan, another cleaning lab equipment, and a third swiping smudged desks with a rag and foul-smelling cleaning agent.

"What kind of scientist is your brother?" I asked, covering my mouth, though I doubted it did any good.

I had my own reasons to ask—since I'd recognized Ben upon seeing him. He was the man I'd seen at the Solstice Festival speaking with journalist Tulip de Lange in a shadowy alcove. A girlfriend? Or something more sinister?

"Ben is… well, some might call him a Renaissance man, dabbling in all sorts of scientific endeavors, while others would dub him an aimless dilettante." Max shrugged. "In general, I try to stay out of his way when he's working. Less chance of death by incineration."

I chuckled at Max's dry wit. I could tell the brothers cared for each other. But were they as close as Ellie and me? That remained a mystery. "It's been a while since you two talked, I could tell. Ben didn't seem to know about you being here at Riten Castle, and he seemed oblivious, even awfully cavalier, about your recent near-death experience. Mine too for that matter."

Max cast a bashful glance at me. "Ben probably does know. But he's a man whose focus rarely veers away from his science. It might have simply slipped his mind."

I frowned, not feeling the warm and fuzzies. "He's your brother."

Max worried his lower lip. I saw he sought to clam up. "He is. But he has other priorities too. We're both princes. I understand his predicament."

Elinor punched me in the arm and scowled at me. "Dude, I was talking." She faced Max. "What's up with Ben's leg?"

"I fell off a horse when I was thirteen, so now I have a metal pin and occasional pains in my knee," a spooky voice spoke behind us.

We all jumped. Ben sure had a soft step, like a feline. He grinned at our reaction. Ben held a steaming cup of coffee, judging by the scent, and sipped it slowly, regarding us with amusement.

"Found anything?" he asked slyly, in an exaggerated conspiratorial manner.

Elinor scoffed. "We just got here. But now that you ask...."

She proceeded to ransack the lab. She pulled open each cabinet and drawer, surveyed every bottle and dish, perused the contents of every notebook and file she got her hands on, and left no stone unturned.

Ben watched her progress with awe. "She's quite enthusiastic, isn't she?"

I grimaced. "Ellie's driven, yeah. Sorry about her taking over your lab."

Ben leaned into me. "What would she do if I offered to help her?"

I scanned his face for a sign of what he was after. I found mischief and suspended laughter. He would prove quite the adversary for Elinor. "Go for it," I dared him.

With a short bow, Ben walked off and joined Elinor, who seemed none too pleased about the company. But from her reddened cheeks I guessed she wasn't holding back anger as much as some more positive emotion. I smiled. It might do her good to have a dalliance, too, as Max called it.

Speaking of Max....

The heir to the throne looked pale and fragile. His golden curls hung lifeless, his eyes were dull, and he seemed two steps away from collapsing.

"You should be resting," I accused him gently.

Max smiled but didn't look at me. "I find I can't sleep without you next to me."

I narrowed my eyes. That sure didn't sound like a send-off. Max seemed to want me both in his life and out of it. Because of the unknown threat, he was conflicted.

I wasn't.

"Come on, my hero. Time for bed."

"I'LL BE fine after a good night's sleep," Max declared in a thin voice as I put him to bed. His eyes fluttered closed, but he reached for me as if he couldn't bear to let me go, his grip surprisingly strong.

I settled beside him on the bed and spooned him. The scent of his hair had grown fainter, as if he were a mere shadow of the powerful, beautiful man I'd met back in France.

"Max? You're a good man. Never doubt that, okay?" I whispered against his neck.

Max's breathing evened out. He was asleep. But he held my arms around him and kept me plastered against him like a man-blanket. His body felt good against mine, yet his skin was a little too hot. He was still sick. He needed someone to take care of him.

Could that someone be me?

The realization that I would want to be with him even if he weren't a prince struck me like a lightning bolt, sparking the truth, undeniably bright, within me.

"I love you, Max," I murmured to the back of his neck and planted a kiss at his hairline. Max didn't stir; his breathing remained slow and shallow.

Careful not to disturb him, I untangled myself from his grip, climbed out of bed, and left the room, closing the door with a soft snick. Two of Lawana's guards in black stood outside, their watchful eyes on my surreptitious exit.

"Didn't want to wake him," I said quietly.

If the guards seemed less ill at ease thanks to my explanation, they didn't show it. In fact, their expressions registered no emotion of any kind.

I hurried down to the ground floor of the Snake Tower, my intention to rejoin Elinor's search party. This had to stop. Max and I could never see what we could have together with assassins and schemers hiding in every damn shadow.

The Snake Tower was situated in the northwestern corner of the castle grounds, while the Cat Tower stood to the west, at the back of a large park. The quickest way was the covered colonnade that connected almost all of the buildings on the grounds. One could walk from one end of the castle to the other in fresh air but without actually being out in the open.

I walked at a normal pace, not wanting to attract attention. I suspected all the guards would question or detain me if I ran amok or dawdled about.

Since I'd chosen a route with a vantage point slightly above the inner courtyard, I was in a perfect place to observe the well-maintained green lawns, vibrant flowerbeds bursting with colorful plants, and stone and wooden benches dotted about.

Outside the Banquet Hall, by a set of open french doors, I noticed two shapes standing close together. As I got nearer, I could make out Theo Weiss and Karl von Thürer—the younger one, that is. They seemed engrossed in discussion, so I didn't want to interrupt them.

From my higher angle, though, I could piece together parts of the conversation.

"Your recklessness is causing your father great grief," Theo was saying, his tone stern like that of a teacher. "You must use better judgment, especially in your dealings with Johann."

Karl Jr. scoffed. "Johann despises these filthy commoners and foreigners same as me. These immigrants and colored folk are taking our jobs, stealing our women, taking over our country. It has to stop."

Theo huffed in obvious fury. "That is your father talking. You're going too far. You're both stepping out of line. This hatred has no basis in reality."

Karl Jr. chuckled with derision. "Spoken like a true commoner. You're the one who doesn't know his place, Theo. Our family line helped build this kingdom. Remember who we are."

That said, the young aristocrat walked off, chin raised, whistling as he went. Apparently, he was under the impression he'd won the argument.

Theo stood there, watching him go, his expression dark. "And you should remember who I am, child," he muttered, though Karl Jr. was too far away to hear him.

Then Theo stormed into the Banquet Hall and vanished from sight.

I went over the dialogue. The young man had shown the same hate both he, his twin brother, and Prince Johann had displayed when we'd met. So, they were born and raised racists. That didn't surprise me. The elite tended to grow hard at heart the more wealth and power they accumulated. Perhaps someone should research that connection.

Theo, on the other hand, seemed to have taken license, speaking to his colleague's son in such a scolding manner. Perhaps Theo felt the need to offer moral guidance to a young man who had none. Maybe he had assumed that role since Karl Sr. sure didn't offer his twin sons ethical guidelines about charity, compassion, or equality. I was impressed that

Theo dared to be so forthcoming. The von Thürer lineage didn't seem one inclined to tolerance or forgiveness.

I continued onward, my head a mess with unresolved questions. The stonework beneath my feet was solid and unblemished, and the wooden beams above me smelled of pine and tree sap, sweet and tart. Made me think of desserts. And that made my stomach rumble.

Before proceeding to the Cat Tower, I considered dropping by the Bull Tower and the kitchens in the northeastern corner of the inner courtyard. I was hungry. That adrenaline surge with Janos and the shooting had drained me of energy.

So I decided to skip the Cat Tower, stuff my belly with good food, and only then seek my rebellious sister and the mischievous middle prince.

Then I had a thought. The Banquet Hall probably might have snacks—leftovers from the Solstice Festival yesterday, or at least a bowl of fruit somewhere. Would save me a trip to the Bull Tower.

I entered the Banquet Hall, spotted indeed a porcelain bowl filled with fresh apples, snatched one, and headed through the room toward the covered colonnade on the other side. This one was even higher than the previous colonnade since the Outer Bailey was actually on a lower elevation than the Inner Ward.

As I reached the colonnade, I observed another, different pair standing by the Conservatory, conversing rather heatedly, if their wild gestures were any indication. It was Lady Kira and Prince Johann.

I made a casual beeline to hide behind one of the columns to eavesdrop.

"What you're doing is unconscionable," Kira was saying acrimoniously, pointing her index finger at Johann's chest. "He is your brother."

Johann swatter her hand aside. "I'd grown accustomed to the reality of having a gay future king as a brother, but does he have to cavort with that—"

"If you say the word, I swear I will smack you in the face, prince or not," Kira threatened, her eyes alight with righteous indignation.

Johann did seem to consider his words, and his cheeks pinked. Finally, he said, "That man. I mean, I know we white men are a dying breed, but couldn't he find a single one?"

"That is preposterous," Kira countered, every inch of her on fire with rage. "He is a human being. Underneath our skin, whatever the color may be, we are all the same. How dare you judge him over something so trivial? You're being so closedminded."

Yup, Johann was a total snob and a bigot, I thought. But Kira was more diplomatic about it. I really liked her. And she seemed like a person who believed in true human equality.

Johann snorted. "Doesn't it bother you? You're supposed to marry that moron, only he sleeps around with men, and colored men to boot. Don't you think he's being—"

"Honest with himself," Kira cut in. She shook her head in desperation, and a sad sheen of moisture appeared to glisten in her eyes. "Why are you doing this, John? All this hate for someone you know nothing about? And for your brother? Do you want the crown that badly? That you're willing to hurt him and his beloved for the throne?"

I slapped a hand over my mouth to silence the shocked gasp. So, Johann did want the throne? And he was willing to surrender to hate and even destroy his brother to get it?

I paused for thought. Hadn't I already considered this theory?

Johann didn't seem the type to resort to poison. He would do something daring and foolhardy and utterly devoid of reason, like challenge Max to a duel to the death. He wouldn't sit back behind the curtain and wait for a chemical agent to do its job. Johann would declare his dissatisfaction to the world and expect everyone to agree with him because, as a prince, he would always be right.

Then what was Kira referring to? Was Johann up to something else to become the next king?

Then Johann surprised me a bit by saying, "Whoever sits on the throne should be a native Norician, not a Mexican-American foreigner."

So the youngest prince didn't care who was in charge, as long as it was a white guy and a native to the kingdom. That confirmed yet again that Johann was a jackass racist, which I already knew, but it didn't help me with my investigation.

Johann grabbed Kira by the shoulders and shook her. "Don't tell me you wouldn't feel better if Max was with a pureblooded Norician woman, someone like you, because I know you better than that."

Kira frowned… and hesitated. I chewed on the inside of my cheek till I tasted blood. Did she really think that? Man, I'd assumed I had an ally in her, perhaps even a friend. Maybe I was mistaken?

Kira stepped back, twisting out of Johann's hold. "You're wrong. And you don't know how wrong. There is no such thing as a pureblood. That is a fantasy that exists only in the minds of people who wish eugenics were real. Do I wish that Max would be with a woman instead of a man? Only because I know it would make being a king easier for him in the eyes of his people. But do I wish for Max to betray his own heart and pretend to care for a woman for the sake of the royal lineage, the kingdom, or his subjects? No. Not even if that someone is me. I want Max to stay true to himself. And that truth you will never understand."

She quickly wiped away tears, turned on her heels, and walked away, disappearing into the Conservatory. Johann stood in place, a stupefied expression on his face.

I suppressed a growl. So, Johann was not just a bigot, he was also an idiot. Johann couldn't even see in his hate-filled state that Kira was in love with him? *Dumbass*. I guess that explained to an extent why Kira wasn't interested in Max.

She might have aspired to becoming queen, but not with Max as king. Would she have aided Johann to become a king with a little hemlock? Poison was often seen as a woman's weapon. But after listening to Kira just now, I ruled her out. Kira had a strong moral center, and not even ambition shook that rock.

I left Johann in his own pickle and decided to go back to the Snake Tower to check on Max. I wanted to talk to him about all that I had heard. So I walked through the Banquet Hall and saw, to my surprise, Max walking shakily toward the building connecting the Stag and Bull Towers.

The damn guy should've been in bed. Huffing with frustration, I hurried after him and found myself in the Great Hall—as an unintentional spy.

Chapter 30

MAX HADN'T slept long. He'd had a short, fitful nap. When he awoke, he'd been alone. He remembered going to bed with Oliver, but the young man was nowhere to be found.

When Max's cell phone pinged to indicate a text, he grabbed the device and read a message from his mother, asking him to meet her at the Great Hall. So that was where Max went.

He felt light-headed and nauseous, but he persevered. After everything that had happened lately, he couldn't ignore his mother. Perhaps she had news about the investigation into the attack on both his person and on Oliver?

As he crossed the inner courtyard, the sun blazed hotly over him, blinding him. He hated he couldn't wear common, loose attire like everyone else, even when it was extremely hot or cold. He was forced to show his face at his best at all times. Strictly speaking, he wouldn't have needed to even go outside, since his tower was connected to every other tower and building via corridors and covered walkways. But he needed fresh air. He paused for a few seconds, breathed in deep, and felt better. His mind cleared, and his stomach stopped acting up.

With swift, if unsteady, steps, Max made his way to the Great Hall that connected the Stag and Bull Towers.

A Great Hall was a staple of castles everywhere. It was the main room and often the biggest, warmest, and most comfortable. It could function as a dining hall, meeting area, or even throne room. Sometimes it was all the above, and more. Riten Castle had separate spaces for all of them.

Therefore, the Great Hall was used mostly as a dining hall during official functions, public holidays, calendrical feasts, and on occasion familial assemblies.

This purpose was reflected in the decor, with its two long wooden tables covering most of the available space, running from one end to the other, white linen tablecloths on them immaculate. On the eastern end was the screen passage where guests came in. On the western end, where Max entered, was a dais raised by three steps, like a stage in a theater. That was where the royal family sat at their own high table. To the right, facing south, were tall windows, the middle one a bay window, that let the sunshine in. On the left wall, a huge fireplace, unlit for now and flanked by rich tapestries and ceremonial armors holding halberds, would have added warmth and brightness into the cavernous space. The thrice-domed high ceiling had elaborate wooden beams and struts in place, as well as pillars, but they were all decorative. Green royal banners depicting the unicorn hung from the rafters, waving about ever so slightly.

It was clear it had been a while since the last use of the Great Hall, for no delicious odors wafted about and dust particles danced in the light beams through the windows. Still, there wasn't a speck on the tables or floor; the place was ever ready to host a large gathering.

Max looked around. Oliver wasn't there. But Colette and Valerie Reed were. This did not bode well.

Max gritted his teeth but approached with a smile and a bow. "Mother. Mrs. Reed."

Colette nodded stiffly. She looked concerned. "Valerie and I have been talking, and we feel it would be best if the Reeds returned to the States posthaste."

Max prayed for patience. "I would normally agree with you, Mother. But there are issues left to be resolved. You must know your son well, Mrs. Reed. Oliver refuses to go."

"Then make him," Valerie snapped but quickly collected herself. "Oliver is a sweet boy, but he doesn't always make the best decisions for himself."

"Neither does my son," Colette cut in, her gaze flicking over Max, who felt all of five years old again, being reprimanded by his mother for some childish act.

Max clenched his fists, trying to rein in his temper. "With all due respect, you're not giving your son enough credit, Mrs. Reed. Oliver is a resourceful young man, smart and capable." Max glanced at his mother. "And so am I."

"There was a killer in his room," Valerie cried out, her desperation showing.

"Janos wasn't there to kill him." Max calmed the panicking woman. "He was there to deliver a message. That is my theory at least. Don't you see? It makes sense. The whole kingdom was looking for him. Whatever he knew, he had to ensure it would reach the right people. Oliver is an outsider, so to Janos he must have served a purpose."

"But Oliver didn't get anything from that man," Valerie argued, her voice lower now, her demeanor more in control, but baffled.

Max sighed. "Perhaps Janos didn't get the chance to say what he came to say or give the proof needed. As for his profession, Janos was a trained soldier, yes, but as far as I know, his track record was zero kills."

Despite saying that aloud, Max suspected Janos had been the one to poison the fake signet ring. Thus, Janos had caused the hotel manager's death. That had been unintentional; Max was the more likely target. The attempt had failed, however, and since Max couldn't prove Janos had poisoned the ring, he decided not to mention it at all.

"Even if that bodyguard hadn't intended to harm Oliver," Colette said, "that still leaves your assassination attempt, Max. Both of them. Two poisonings tell me the threat is real. You must see the wisdom of sending the Reeds back home to safety."

"Oliver won't go," Max repeated.

"Then tell him you no longer care for him," Valerie suggested. Her tone was cold, but her jaw trembled. She didn't like the idea, but she wanted to keep her son safe—no matter what. Even at the risk of a broken heart. That would mend; a bullet-ridden heart would not.

Max swallowed hard. His own heart hurt. "I-I don't think Oliver would believe me."

Valerie frowned. "Why ever not?"

Max closed his eyes and drew in a breath before confessing, "I've already told him I love him."

Colette gasped. "D-do you?"

Max raised his chin, knowing the resolute effect it would reflect. "Yes, Mother, I do."

Colette gulped and visibly paled. But she remained silent, possibly because she and her son weren't alone.

Valerie had no such qualms. "Love is all well and good, but who could either of you two love if the other were dead? You're in danger, Max, and by association, so is Oliver. Love will not protect you from a bullet."

Max had to stop the shaking before it began. Had he not thought the exact same thing just a moment ago? He was going to argue that they were in one of the safest places in the kingdom, but he couldn't. The claim didn't hold water—not after recent events.

"What is it you want from me, Mrs. Reed?" Max asked, starting to lose his calm. "Haven't I lied to him enough?"

Valerie's jaw worked; she must have been clenching her teeth. "You have lied, so what is one more—if it saves Oliver's life?"

Max slumped. "I promised him I would never lie to him again."

"That's a noble sentiment, but you'd be doing it for all the right reasons." Valerie laid a hand Max's arm, her touch shaky but sturdy. "You must have known this day would come eventually. I mean, you two can't be together."

Max stepped back, and her grip on him loosened and released. "Why not?"

Valerie harrumphed, clearly vexed. "Come on, Max. You couldn't marry him. Princes marry princesses." Before Max could tell her that was the most ludicrous, antiquated thing to say, Valerie went on. "But even if a prince could marry a man, let's not forget, for example, the reception someone like Meghan Markle got. An outsider, a foreigner, a woman of color. First there were doubts, then love and worship, and now a shitstorm of epic proportions." Valerie paused and glanced at Colette apologetically. "So sorry, Your Majesty."

Max had had enough. He raised a hand in a universal stop sign. "No more, Mrs. Reed. Now you will listen to me. As the crown prince and heir to the throne, I am accountable to my subjects; that much I freely admit. However, there is a difference between my public and my private persona. People, and I mean not only my subjects but the media and the world at large, may dictate aspects of the former but not the latter. That I reserve for myself as a human being with inalienable rights. As for the haters, a ruler must represent his people, yes. But I say a ruler should always represent the best, and only the best, of his people. We must rise above the mire, for we do not exist in a damn swamp. And lastly, as for Oliver, I will not lie to him anymore. I refuse. If he is stubborn enough to stay in spite of my argument to the contrary, he can stay. It is his right as an informed adult. And yes, if Oliver were at some later date so inclined, I would propose marriage to him. Oliver is no Meghan Markle."

After what he himself dubbed a great speech, Max twirled around and walked off. He didn't get far.

Johann's mocking laughter interrupted him as the man approached them from the other side of the Great Hall. "All commoners make poor spouses. They don't understand how we live and work."

"You never work," Max accused, getting angrier by the second. Perhaps he needed more rest after all.

Johann scoffed, stopping in front of his big brother. "At least I work in favor of the Norician kingdom instead of planning to marry someone completely unsuitable, like your Latin lover."

That was it. Max saw red. He punched Johann straight in the mouth. Colette screamed. But Max was far from done.

Johann lay on the stone floor on his back, holding his busted, bleeding nose and whimpering.

Max hissed at him, "I've had enough of you. For the first time since I was poisoned, I wish I had died so I wouldn't have to take any more of your bullshit. I used to think you were just stupid, John, too dumb to realize your mistakes. But now I know better. You're a vicious, mean-spirited bully. I'm done with you. I will never call you brother again. And just so we're clear, even if I were gone, you would never be king. You know why? It's because you never understood that power is not a fucking privilege for yourself but a challenge to do your best for other people. But you failed at that, like you fail at everything else."

Max stormed off. His head throbbed. He could feel the fever rising. He wasn't well at all. Pretending to be made things worse.

If Colette protested, Max didn't hear it. Maybe he'd gone too far, but he'd be damned if he'd apologize. Johann had deserved it, the prick. Deep down, though, Max hated having done that to his own baby brother. First, he'd been the gentleman prince, making a grand speech—and then he had brawled like a common thug.

"I guess stupidity runs in the family," he muttered to himself as he crossed the large anteroom of the Stag Tower and entered the Mural Room that connected the Stag and Snake Towers.

To call it a room was misleading.

The Mural Room was really a long corridor that stretched the length of the building. Murals, tapestries, paintings, and reliefs hung on the walls, depicting the history of the kingdom, its people, and its past kings and queens. Each work of art had its own mellow spotlight, a thick rug masked any footsteps, and from the door the passageway appeared to extend into infinity.

As Max walked, he let his exhaustion show. His hand hurt from the punch.

At about the middle of the corridor, which in Max's mind could have been called an art room or a history hall, stood Gustav and Paulito, conversing. Max was pleased that the two had discovered a common interest in history.

Max tried to walk past them without getting dragged into a lecture on art history. But both men noticed him.

"Ah, Maximilian." Gustav smiled. Max knew he wouldn't be smiling anymore once he found out about him punching his brother smack on the nose. "Mr. Reed is very knowledgeable about the past."

Max's eyebrows rose to his hairline. That was pretty high praise coming from his father, who had assumed the role of history master back in Max's school days. It was rare for him to acknowledge the range of another's knowledge.

Paulito nodded, his smile smaller than Gustav's, but Max had a feeling Paulito was never boisterous. "Your history is fascinating."

He pointed at the painting on the wall. It was a famous scene from the past, the culmination of the War of the Three Rings. Three war-weary chieftains stood on a bloody battlefield littered with fresh corpses and declared a cessation of hostilities. Less than a month later, the Peace of the Three Crowns was signed in a formal treaty, and the unified kingdom of Noricia was born.

"To think that three tribes could form such a kingdom in such a relatively small area as Noricia. It boggles the mind." Paulito was shaking his head in awe. "Of course, people have fought over far less."

Gustav nodded firmly. "The day the three native tribes—mountain, forest, and river—set the foundation of our kingdom was the proudest in our history. To create peace after so much bloodshed. For a time it seemed impossible. But the human spirit perseveres."

Max was exhausted but also felt obliged to participate in the dialog. He stared at the painting. The artist had captured the distinctive likeness of all three chiefs well. Sigismund, the chief of the Mountain Tribe, was portrayed as a large hulk of a man with an impressive beard, wearing the fur coat of a wolf over his broad shoulders and carrying a huge battle-axe; Alette, the female chief of the River Tribe, was short and svelte, with flaming red hair and wearing tight chainmail that covered her chest and her sword arm; and Gunthard, the chief of the Forest Tribe, was clean-shaven, average height, and fit like a race hound, and he carried a spear and wore hardened leather armor.

"In a land where three spheres—the Alps, the woods, and the Rhine River—exist in such close proximity to each other, it is imperative we work together," Max said diplomatically. "All three chiefs needed something from the others. And there'd been enough death. If peace hadn't been forged, the tribes would have vanished from the face of the earth. Dead and unburied, for there would have been no one left to perform the funeral rites."

Paulito smiled approvingly. "And your family are direct descendants of Chief Alette of the River Tribe."

Gustav raised his hand and almost touched the painting. "Yes. We are proud to name her as our chief ancestor. House Lindau-Arbon is the primary royal lineage, descended from Alette's eldest child."

"The way the original kingship was handled." Paulito whistled low. "I've never heard of such an arrangement before."

Gustav chuckled. Max listened, blinking in surprise; his father rarely opened himself up so with a virtual stranger. Then again, Paulito had a low-key likeability factor, much like his son. Their appeal was undeniable. He suspected Paulito made for an excellent friend. Oliver sure made for a perfect companion.

"Rotating kingships aren't unheard of," Gustav said, waving at the painting. "The kingdom of Zaria, for example, had rotating kingship, as did the Yoruba, if memory serves. Of modern nations, Malaysia has a practice of rotational kingship for five-year periods."

Max joined in the conversation. "In Noricia, each chieftain ruled as king for a year. Then the title rotated to another chief. In three-year intervals, each ruler had a chance to sit on the throne and wear the Triskelion Crown."

"Only direct descendants of the original chieftains were eligible for succession," Gustav said with pride in his voice. "And that hasn't changed to this day."

"But there has been no rotation for a long time," Paulito noted, growing serious and clearly intrigued.

"Unfortunately, the last descendants of the Forest Tribe's primary royal lineage were killed in World War II," Max said, sadness creeping into his tone. That had been a loss to the world. "The Mountain Tribe's primary royal line had already died off in the late nineteenth century, though they have secondary line members alive and well. The River Tribe's primary royal lineage was unbroken and plentiful, so the status quo fell into place naturally. There were no objections at the time, and so the practice of rotational kingship was discontinued in favor of rebuilding the kingdom after the war."

"I understand you and Lady Kira are part of the same tribe?" Paulito asked.

Max nodded. "Yes. My family are direct descendants of Queen Alette's firstborn. Lady Kira belongs to the tertiary royal line. But basically, we are all River Tribe."

Paulito's eyes narrowed a little, but beyond that it was hard for Max to tell what the man was feeling or thinking. "Karl von Thürer belongs to the Mountain Tribe, doesn't he?"

"Yes, to the secondary royal lineage." Gustav raised his chin. He was immensely proud of the continued cooperation of the tribes; that much Max knew well. "There are members of all three tribes on the Council, as it should be. We are now a constitutional monarchy, after all. I am no despot and have no desire to create a dictatorship. This kingdom was founded on the unity of the three tribes, and I will not be the king to end it and bring ruin to our great nation."

Max decided to placate his father, who could summon forth too much vitriol sometimes. "The von Thürer line belongs to a secondary royal lineage of the Mountain Tribe. We Lindau-Arbons are primaries. Our claim to the throne and the crown are greater. The Council accepts this as fact."

Paulito shrugged. "Perhaps being prime minister is enough. I know some people who would never be content with anything less than what they in their selfishness and lust for power think they're owed. Maybe your people are different, sir."

Max wasn't sure how to take Paulito's words. He didn't seem to intend to offend on purpose. The political climate in the States wasn't the greatest at present, so the reference could have been about that.

Max didn't get the chance to contemplate the matter further or comment at all because that was when someone put a hand over his shoulder. Max nearly jumped out of his skin.

"You were wonderful."

Max released a long breath and turned when he recognized Oliver's voice.

"Was I?" he asked. Oliver's words penetrated his dull brain slowly. "Wait. You were there at the Great Hall?" He escorted Oliver away from their fathers, out of earshot.

"Yes." Oliver looked bashful but he was smiling. "Behind the dais curtain. You stormed out so fast you nearly bumped into me. Man, that would have ruined the exit and the drama." Oliver faked a heavy hit with a fist. "Kapow! You just socked that guy in the chin like a champ."

Max grimaced. "I lost my temper. I shouldn't have."

Oliver snorted. "You're human. We all lose our cool sometimes."

Max shook his head. "John shouldn't have called you... that."

Oliver chuckled. "What, Latin lover? I've been called way worse. One guy I dated, and who also cheated on me, called me a brownie in bed. I think he meant a cookie, like a sweet endearment, you know, because I love baking. But it was offensive nonetheless. Told him to stuff 'em brownies where the sun don't shine."

Max laughed. Some of the tension plaguing him eased. The knot in his belly unwound. His knuckles seemed less bruised and aching. This was one of the reasons why he loved Oliver. The man could make him laugh and feel that the world was beautiful and full of light and laughter and love. Pain and fear and doubt seemed to disappear.

Oliver stepped closer, placed his hands over Max's hips, and rubbed the tip of his nose over Max's. "Did you mean it?"

Max didn't need to ask. "Yes. All of it. The whole wise speech wasted on account of—"

"Forget John," Oliver purred. "Let me take you back to bed. You'll rest, I'll rest with you, and when we wake up, we can...." He whispered the rest in Max's ear.

Max flushed with heat. His heart leaped. Oh yes, he smiled to himself. Things were looking up.

Chapter 31

MAX AWOKE to the song of birds. He cracked open an eyelid and saw that the balcony doors were open. A soft, warm breeze ruffled his hair.

And a hot, eager mouth engulfed his cock.

Max groaned in delight, waves of fiery pleasure washing over him, and he arched his back, letting the tingling sensation move along his spine. His hand wandered underneath the covers and found a head of hair bobbing up and down.

A clever tongue licked his shaft and probed his slit. A vacuum formed with a ring of lips, sucking the animalistic responses right out of him. Max wanted to cry, the feeling was so good. He'd missed this, even though it hadn't been that long.

"Ollie...," Max whispered. He let love blossom in his chest and expand outward till he felt aglow with it, his body thrumming with ecstasy. He longed to reciprocate. "Come here, babe, and let me—"

A head popped out from under the covers. An impish smile greeted Max. "No can do. This is my breakfast in bed." He winked at Max, vanished under the blanket, and retook Max's dick into his mouth.

At first, in his haze, Max decided to go with the flow and let Oliver do what he pleased. Then Max had another thought, a sweet epiphany.

"Ride me, Oliver," he murmured. "You can do all the work, and I won't exert—"

Before Max could even finish his sentence, Oliver had already tossed aside the covers and climbed on top of Max. Oliver gripped Max's shaft and aimed the tip at his hole.

Max gasped. "What are you doing? Stop. I don't want to hurt—"

Oliver giggled breathlessly, his skin flushed and ruddy. "You won't. Before you were so kind as to wake up, I was playing with myself. Feel it for yourself if you don't believe me."

Max reached under Oliver, who rose to his haunches to accommodate Max's efforts. Oliver's hole was stretched and wet with lube. Max grinned. "You really did prep yourself. All right then. Hop on."

Grinning, Oliver nodded. He kept Max's cock straight as he slowly lowered himself, taking Max into a hot, wet, tight channel. Max's pulse surged with desire. He felt light-headed but didn't care about anything except keeping his lover close. He touched Oliver's thighs, feeling the muscles twitch, bunch, and relax.

Then Oliver slammed down, Max's cock buried deep in one sudden lust-fueled move. Max's breath hitched, and his heart skipped a beat.

"By the gods, Oliver. What was that?"

Oliver flushed, his cheeks, neck, and upper body now sporting a shade of rouge. "I-I couldn't wait any longer. Had to feel you inside me."

Max gulped. The darkness of desire burning in Oliver's eyes undid something in him. He was speechless. Oliver could be so bashful at times and so forward at other times. Max savored the conundrum that was Oliver Reed.

Oliver rested his hands over Max's chest, his hot palms spreading fire through Max's skin. Then he tweaked Max's nipples, and a jolt of lightning struck straight to Max's cock. His hips jumped at the feeling on pure instinct.

"Ah, yes...." Oliver licked his lips so salaciously Max had a hard time holding back his need.

Oliver's eyelids fluttered closed, and he threw his head back. Then he rose up and slammed right back down, as if he were riding a trotting horse. Max grunted as pleasure washed over him at the shocking sensation. Every nerve ending in his body seemed to ignite at once.

How he could feel Oliver all over, inside and out, baffled him to no end. No other lover had ever made him feel like this.

Oliver leaned back, his palms on Max's thighs, and he panted, a thin sheen of sweat soon covering his skin, giving him a golden glow in the slivers of sunshine peeking through the curtains. Max's need grew into an almost animalistic urge to fuck Oliver through the mattress. But Oliver was in control, rising and dropping onto Max's prick, again and again, swallowing Max into his body as if Oliver never wanted him to leave.

Max rose halfway, wrapped his arms around Oliver to pull him close, and sucked on Oliver's nipples. Oliver moaned and jerked, his arms threading through, even pulling at, Max's hair. Oliver's scent, now slightly musky from sex, filled Max's senses. The tender nub hardened, and Max bit gently into it, then smoothed the sting with his lapping tongue.

"Shit, Max, you're going to make me come," Oliver whimpered.

"That's the idea," Max muttered, knowing he was too close himself, as he always was right after waking up.

He watched enthralled as Oliver's thick dick jutted upward and bounced back and forth with his ride, slapping against first one belly, then the other. Max fisted Oliver's erection, wet with precome and a touch of lubricant, and stroked up and down. From the sensitive slit, he squeezed translucent droplets that glistened like crystalized rain and wished he had his mouth where his hand was.

"Not fair," Oliver whispered, glaring down at Max, who loved the look of the rapt dark angel above him.

"All's fair in love," Max replied with a smirk.

Oliver quirked an eyebrow. "Oh, is it?" Then he squeezed his ass and as a result Max's cock too.

Pleasure mixed with a flash of discomfort, almost pushing Max over the edge. "You play hardball, I see," he breathed out—and clasped Oliver's cock harder on the upstroke, his slick palm moving around the thick shaft with ease.

"Oh!" Oliver exclaimed. Then he cupped Max's face and dove in for a kiss.

Max couldn't resist the sweet temptation of Oliver's mouth, so he slid his tongue in to play as well. Oliver's voracious craving was apparent when he plunged his tongue deep into Max's mouth in turn and sucked on Max's tongue, licked his lips, and inhaled his breath. Max had never felt so coveted or desired in his whole life.

Oliver kept moving, impaling himself on Max's cock. Every time his body jerked and he let out a guttural groan, Max knew he'd hit the sweet spot. Heck, everything about Oliver was sweet. He couldn't get enough.

For now, though, his balls hiked up and his cock was about to burst at the seams. Max knew he had to come, so he doubled his efforts to jerk off Oliver. Max also started to thrust up his hips to meet Oliver when he came down. The first time Max did that, Oliver's whole body lurched. His moan, cracking and wanton, was music to Max's ears.

Too many sensations caused Max to orgasm without warning, spilling his creamy seed into Oliver's willing body. Oliver released Max's kiss-stinging lips and cried out, hot and sticky spunk exploding from his dick over Max's hand and between their thrashing bodies.

For a while they panted roughly against each other, the potent smells of sex and semen and man floating around them. Max felt like he was floating too, gliding over undulating waters of pure satisfaction and love.

When Oliver kissed him again, it was slow and sloppy and breathy. But Max didn't want it any other way, kissing back as best he could.

Then Oliver squirmed a little, but not enough to dislodge Max from inside him.

"Stop it," Max moaned. "I'm too sensitive."

Oliver giggled—and tensed his muscles. Max's cock was in trouble, caught in a hot, slippery vise. Then Oliver wiggled, and the tension was too much, bordering on excruciating delight.

"I said enough," Max reprimanded and shoved Oliver off him.

Unfortunately, Oliver had been in the middle of shifting his weight, so he couldn't catch himself in time. Instead, he fell on the floor in a heap of flailing limbs, shouting in shock.

"Oliver!" Max cried out and reached for Oliver, though it was too late. He peered over the edge of the bed. "I'm so, so sorry—"

His apology was cut short when he saw Oliver on the floor on his back, laughing till he wheezed with tears streaming down his cheeks.

"You jerk, I really thought you were hurt." Max pouted and scowled.

Oliver just giggled some more. "Oh my God, you should have seen your face."

Max scoffed in indignation and moved away to lie back on the bed. "I hate you."

Oliver peered over the edge, a smile in his eyes. "No, you don't."

Max grumbled, but he wasn't angry at all. He was drifting on blissful clouds, sailing on an ocean of euphoria. He'd never been this happy. Was it really so selfish of him to want this to continue? Why was it wrong for a prince to seek happiness?

"Whoa. What's this? It's awesome. Can I have it?"

Oliver came up again, this time holding a wooden ring in his hand. An emerald glittered in the setting, the wooden band brown and gleaming.

Max frowned. "Where'd you get that?"

Oliver shrugged. "It was lodged under your bed, between the mattress and the frame." He winked at Max shamelessly, like an imp. "If this isn't yours, to what dashing young knight does it belong?"

Max pursed his lips and snatched the ring off Oliver's hand. "Yoink!"

Oliver chuckled as he climbed back into bed next to Max. "You're such a kid, I swear."

Max ignored him in favor of inspecting the object. The fine finish, the style of the setting, the artistry of the woodwork, they all pointed to a highly skilled jeweler. But Max had never worn a wooden ring, and he'd never bedded anyone in his quarters who wore one.

"How odd," he murmured. "It looks familiar. And yet I've no idea how it got here."

Oliver harrumphed playfully. "Geesh, man. You said Riten Castle was the most secure place in the kingdom, and here we have yet another piece of evidence to suggest people are coming and going at all hours, as if you guys had an open-door policy."

Max could hardly disagree. "I'm sorry, Oliver, for—"

"Don't you dare," Oliver cut in with a growl Max found surprisingly sexy. "You didn't put a gun to my head. Janos—and whoever hired him—did. They're responsible. No one else. Certainly not you."

Max kissed Oliver, cherishing the taste, the warmth, the solid softness. He longed to spend every day with his lips against Oliver's at least three times a day.

"Hey, lost you there for a second," Oliver admonished with a sweet, teasing smile. He kissed Max, who kissed back. Though Max had just come like a shooting star, he felt rejuvenated.

Oliver, however, drew back, his eyes wide and his mouth forming a little O. "Janos!"

Max grimaced. "Way to think about another man while kissing—"

"He did this," Oliver interjected, excited for a whole other reason than Max. Oliver took the wooden ring and turned it around in his fingers. "Janos left this here." Oliver chuckled to himself. "That's why he said that 'I can get into a lot of places' when I asked him how he got into my room."

Max blinked in confusion. "I don't get it. Why would he do that?"

Oliver grinned. "Him being in *my* room was a diversion. His real target was you. I mean, your room. My room was searched by the guards. But he left the evidence in *your* room instead."

Max frowned. "How is this generic ring proof of anything?"

"It must belong to the man, or woman, who hired Janos," Oliver suggested. Then he frowned in bafflement. "Wait. I was sneaking up behind you in the Mural Room. My dad and Gustav and you were talking about something. The War of the Three Rings?"

Max went back to his lessons on Noricia's history. "Yes, the war was fought because all three of the chieftains wanted to rule the land. The three tribes were about the same strength. Where they lacked one thing, another balanced them out. The River Tribe had the greatest number of warriors and the finest weapons, plus access to a fast river trading route, the Forest Tribe had plenty of timber, clever tactics and booby-traps, and the Mountain Tribe had the high ground and deceptive terrain, not to mention both raw and refined metals."

"Yes, yes," Oliver cut in impatiently. "What's with the rings?"

"Oh," Max uttered sheepishly. "All three chiefs had a ring as a sign of their station and as a symbol of their tribe. The River Tribe's chief had a silver ring, which in later centuries was made of glass, and it had a diamond on it. The Mountain Tribe had a ring made of stone, gneiss I believe, with a sapphire embedded in it. And the Forest Tribe…" His voice faded into obscurity when isolated things started adding up. "The Forest Tribe had a ring made of wood with an emerald in it."

Oliver gasped. "C-could it be this ring?"

"No, no." Max waved his hand to dismiss the notion. "The original rings are in the Treasury Vault, like the other crown jewels. The one in the Throne Room display case is another replica." He studied the ring more carefully. Its presence mocked him. Why bring the Forest Tribe into this when their primary royal lineage was gone? There was no one left to contest Gustav's kingship. In short, the ring made no sense. "I wonder, could this be that copy from the Throne Room display case…?"

Oliver shook his head, seemingly frustrated. "Why make these ring replicas at all? I mean, I figured that your fake ring was meant to incapacitate or kill you while the real ring was used to verify that false document." Suddenly Oliver's eyes went wide. "Holy shit. If that's true, it means—" Oliver cut himself off, leaving Max in the dark. Finally, Oliver said, "We must go to the Throne Room and get everyone there."

Max had read, seen, and listened to his share of whodunit-mysteries to realize this was the moment when the hero figured out the bad guy's plot and revealed the culprit to every member of the quaint little drama.

"You know who's doing this to us?" Max asked, though he suspected the answer already.

Oliver nodded. "I do." But to Max's surprise, the buzzing excitement seemed to have left Oliver, who now appeared dark and gloomy.

That did not bode well, Max thought and mentally prepared for the worst.

Chapter 32

AN HOUR later, once Max and I had showered, gotten dressed, and called for a meeting, we met up in the Throne Room.

I admitted to myself I was scared. So much could go wrong if I was right. And shit would hit the fan if I was plain wrong. But I didn't think I was. I'd done more research while waiting for Max to finish primping, which apparently was something princes did. My findings had solidified my conclusions. I was reasonably certain that my theories were correct.

But not 100 percent sure. And that was where the doubts came in to harass and bully me till my knees buckled and I feared I really would run.

Max gripped my hand. The warmth of his touch grounded me. My fears ran away screaming in the face of all that love.

"If I fail spectacularly—" I started.

Max's kiss on my lips silenced me quite effectively. "You'll do great. I know because you're with me. And I never fail."

The ridiculous statement made me laugh. What remained of my hesitation evaporated.

We entered the Throne Room and found everyone present.

King Gustav and Queen Colette stood by the Ivy Throne. They didn't speak, but their similar expressions told me they were in perfect mutual understanding. Whatever happened, they would sport a unified front.

Elinor hung back with our parents beside her. Valerie seemed subdued; I think Max's speech had broken her resolve. Paulito… well, he'd always been a hard man to read. He did appear curious, though. He nodded to me as greeting and boost of confidence.

Elinor gave me a thumbs-up, which elicited a chuckle from Prince Berengar who stood close by, in front of the crown jewels. He winked at Elinor, who blushed and glared. That seemed to amuse Ben more. I liked him.

Prince Johann, back ramrod straight, had taken up a position by the arches into the anteroom. Theo Weiss, the Grand Druid, was beside him.

They didn't talk. In addition to sporting two black eyes and a bandaged nose, Johann looked like he'd sucked on a lemon for an hour, and Theo seemed fidgety and positively ill.

Lady Kira studied one of the many reliefs in the room, this one of the Maiden Goddess. Though she must have seen the artwork before, one couldn't tell from her apparent interest. If she was faking, she would have made a world-class actress.

Karl von Thürer and his twin sons, Karl Jr. and what's-his-name, dominated the space by the door, as if they wanted to exit as soon as humanly possible. Karl's stern face could have been carved out of rock, Karl Jr. seemed bored and the other one baffled like a village idiot.

All eyes turned to me and Max when we walked in with Lawana in tow.

"Max," Gustav greeted his son with a curt nod. He didn't say my name.

I felt a distinct chill in the air. Then I glanced at Max, who smiled at me with encouragement. My heart thawed, and I braved on.

"Ladies and gentlemen," I began, my voice breaking at first. "I'm sorry if this meeting has inconvenienced—"

"I have government business to attend to," Karl von Thürer cut in, like a knife to my self-esteem. "I have no time for political niceties. Get to it."

Before others could comment on his rudeness, I stepped in. "You should be glad you're here because I'm here to vindicate you."

Karl blinked. I think this was the first time he really and truly looked at me. His astonishment was plain as day, his eyebrows raised, his eyes wide, and his mouth gaping. "Wh-what?" Then he seemed to remember who he was because he coughed to clear his throat and straightened up. "Well, of course. I've nothing to do with the attempts on Prince Maximilian's life. To think differently would be utterly preposterous."

"That may be so," I said. "But you did give Max a poisoned dish as a gift."

"Th-that is completely misleading, and I-I object to this line of accusations," Karl sputtered. When no one spoke, not even me, but with all eyes on him, Karl gulped. "I swear, Your Majesties, I had nothing to do with that. I would never harm any of the princes."

In the following silence, one could have heard a pin drop.

Then, surprising even myself, I said, "I believe you." Karl blinked and finally nodded a little. Perhaps that was the best he could do. "Do you know why?" I asked. "That's because you didn't bake a pie, as Max remembered at first; you baked a carrot *cake*." After a pause, I went on. "I had to look at three separate incidents. One, the first poisoning attempt on Max at his birthday party two years ago. Two, the stolen ring and second poisoning attempt in France. And three, the latest poisoning attempt here at Riten Castle. The whole butter knife incident was an accident and is irrelevant. Anyway, I had other suspects in addition to Karl von Thürer."

"Such as?" Max prompted with a kind tone.

I glanced at Kira. "Ladies first." She inclined her head minutely, a tiny polite smile present. True class, I thought, and hated having to take on this role as accuser. "Your ladyship had means and motive. You spend a lot of time in the Conservatory, surrounded by plants, some of them poisonous. And while you don't love Max the way a would-be wife should, maybe you felt scorned when Max turned out to prefer men. Also, you could harbor secret aspirations for the throne. Goodness knows, the world could use more competent women leaders."

Kira chuckled courteously. "Thank you kindly for your high praise, Mr. Reed. Even under these peculiar circumstances."

I nodded. "You had motive and means—but not opportunity. According to Max, you weren't there for his birthday bash, and you weren't in France this spring. You were here for the third attempt, but that's beside the point."

"I'm delighted that you're in the clear, my dear," Max remarked with a quirky smile shared between friends. Kira giggled behind her hand.

I moved on. "Another suspect was Theo Weiss."

The Grand Druid's eyes widened, and his plump mouth formed a perfect surprised O. "I... I...," he stammered helplessly.

"Your Holiness had means and opportunity," I said. "You're a renowned biologist, and you frequent woods, meadows, herbalist shops, apothecaries, and the Conservatory here. Using hemlock would be natural for you. And you are a daily visitor to the castle in your priestly role and thus have access to most areas."

Poor Theo gulped, looking ever so pale and sweaty at the same time. He wrenched his hands and shifted weight from one foot to the other, anxious as a cat in a room full of rocking chairs.

"What you don't have, Mr. Weiss, is motive." Theo released a visible breath. I smiled. "You have no apparent desire or access to the throne, and wealth, power, or luxury don't seem to motivate you. Plus, you like Max and express no animosity toward different sexual orientations."

Theo managed a shaky smile. "Th-thank you, young man."

I glanced around. I had a captive audience. Everyone was listening intently.

I locked gazes with Johann, who seemed unusually subdued. His eyes did flash when they met mine, and his mouth turned into a thin, tight line.

"Prince Johann is next," I murmured. Colette gasped but didn't intervene. Out of the corner of my eye, I saw Gustav hold her hand.

Johann sneered in protest. "This is preposterous. You are not an official investigator but a mere amateur sleuth from another country. None of us need stand these baseless accusations."

"Yes, you must," Gustav cut in, his voice razor-sharp. I watched Johann blink and pale with trepidation, and finally offer an assenting nod. While I wasn't sure why exactly Gustav was on my side, I was happy to receive his support.

I licked my lips to fight off nervousness. "Johann had motive and opportunity. He resents his brother for myriad reasons. His motives include envy, jealousy, hate, and so on. Many possibilities to choose from. Johann believes in his own entitlement and that he would undoubtedly make a better future king than Max."

Johann harrumphed and crossed his arms over his chest. "Anyone would."

When I observed Gustav turning red with anger, I quickly moved on. "You also had ample opportunity to poison your brother. You both live right here in Riten Castle."

"As do hundreds of others," Johann pointed out like a brat.

"True," I agreed slowly. "What you didn't seem to have was means. I'm sorry to say this, Your Majesties, but a man with your son's, eh, free-time activities wouldn't bother learning about complex poisons or have the patience to wait for his revenge to take hold. His weapon wouldn't be hemlock but a gun or a blade."

Johann's mouth gaped in confusion. "What?"

"He said you're too dumb to be a murderer," Elinor clarified and earned herself a deadly glare, which she bypassed with a sweet smile and a shrug.

I hurried onward. "None of you three had the full trifecta of the prerequisites to commit this crime. Only one suspect had motive, means, and opportunity." I turned to him, as did everyone else. "Karl von Thürer."

"Oh, so we can finally get back to the prime minister's cake," Elinor commented amusedly.

I nodded and faced Karl. "You baked a carrot cake." Everyone seemed confused, including Karl. "You didn't buy the cake, did you? You actually made it yourself from scratch."

Karl hesitated, appearing uncertain. "Yes. Yes, I did." His cheeks pinked a hint. "I-I'd never tried my hand at baking, but I wanted to do something special for Maximilian on his birthday."

I smiled. "That was sweet of you. Being a baker myself, I know how hard that can be on the first try, or the second, or the millionth. And as a baker, I have to be able to tell the difference between edible and poisonous plants. Some can be very hard to distinguish. Just out of curiosity, where'd you get the ingredients?"

"From the greenhouse at my family's estate," Karl replied. The more flummoxed his face grew, the more convinced I was that I was on the right track. "My late wife grew a number of herbs and medicinal plants there."

"And you maintain it still?"

"Yes, and I get help—"

"Yes," I quickly cut him off. "When Max was poisoned with hemlock in the water bottle, I started my own investigation. I'm not an expert, of course, but I didn't think it could do any harm. I had several suspects but only one had means, motive, and opportunity." I stared at Karl, who opened his mouth to protest, his expression like that of a blustering gale. I beat him to the punch. "By your own admission, you have a greenhouse and you grow herbs. Why not hemlock? You both honor the royal family and detest Max for—"

"That's not true!" Karl called out, taking a step forward. As did Lawana. Karl glanced at her and backed up again.

"It's okay to have mixed feelings about leaders," I said. "I come from a country split in half because of a wannabe despot and his cabinet of horrors. Not that Gustav is one, let alone Max. But I think some of us know why you have conflicting feelings."

I didn't want to declare out loud that Karl harbored an unrequited love, or maybe obsession, for Colette. I wasn't sure if Gustav knew, and

I had no idea how many other people in the room were in the know. So I held back.

Karl seemed to realize this because his face darkened, but he said nothing.

"So you have means and motive," I continued. "And you have opportunity. In your role as prime minister, you have full access in here and could easily make the arrangements to hurt Max."

"But I didn't," Karl growled, glaring at me.

I nodded. "I know. You're the perfect suspect. But despite your love and hate for the royal family, I don't believe you'd actually harm them, let alone murder any of them."

"So who is responsible, then?" Max asked me, gently steering me away from Karl and back to the matter at hand.

"I mentioned I had two reasons for not believing Karl von Thürer to be the guilty party." I sighed. "First was the carrot cake you baked yourself, which I already talked about. The second reason has to do with your volatile nature."

"I beg your pardon?" Karl huffed, indignant. Then he seemed to realize his behavior matched the accusation to a tee, and he flushed red.

I glanced at Max, who gave me an encouraging smile. "When you burst into Max's quarters with the falsified document, you proved your innocence."

Karl appeared flummoxed, his gaze wandering from me to everyone else and then right back to me. For the first time, he seemed speechless.

"If you had been responsible for the theft and assassination attempt against Max in France," I pointed out, "why would you draw attention to yourself by waving the fake decree in front of Max's face? After all, the swapping of the signet ring was done to facilitate forging official royal decrees."

Karl wasn't the only one who paused for thought at that. I watched them all, their expressions belying the wheels hard at work in their heads. All but one.

"You're right, Oliver," Max said with a steadfast tone. "He wouldn't. Or to be precise, the guilty party wouldn't."

"Right. Because the real signet ring was exchanged with the fake one to do political damage," Elinor murmured to herself. "Otherwise, there would have been no need for another ring because the bad guy could have just poisoned the real one."

"Yes," I agreed. "The real signet ring was needed elsewhere."

"And I led you on the right track when I, um, showed up at the First Prince's quarters with the falsified decree," Karl said, quite needlessly.

I nodded. "Yup. You revealed yourself to be a hot-tempered nincompoop—"

"Excuse me?" Karl roared.

"—but not the villain," I concluded.

"What's that got to do with the carrot cake?" Valerie asked, surprising me because until now she'd been silent. "I mean, if according to you, Mr. von Thürer had the means."

And there it was. The part where I'd cut things off last time. Now the moment had come.

"Why not simply cut to the chase, Mr. Reed?" Prince Berengar asked from the sidelines, his amiable expression unbecoming for what was happening. I couldn't read him at all. "Who are we looking for?" He winked at me, though I doubt anyone else saw since general attention had returned back to me.

"Fine." So much for my sleuth stardom scene. I felt bad already and doubted I'd feel any better later on. "The culprit is Karl von Thürer—" The communal gasp could have sucked out all the air in the room had I not continued. "—Junior."

Chapter 33

MAX GULPED. His eyes turned to the older twin, who had gone pale and stiff like a stone statue.

"Is this true?" Max asked, startling everyone in the silence that reigned in the room.

Karl Jr. blinked. Then, like a sleepwalker, he nodded his affirmation.

Oliver took charge again, for which Max was grateful. Max doubted he could have provided much in the way of intelligent conversation; he was too livid.

"Your father," Oliver addressed the young man. "He decided to ingratiate himself at Max's birthday party by baking a carrot cake with his own hands. Thanks to the tutelage you received in plant life, you knew wild carrots look an awful lot like hemlock. At your estate's herb garden, you ensured your father collected the wrong plants."

"Wh-what?" Karl Sr. cried out, his voice shrill and shaky, his stony facade crumbling at last. "Th-that's impossible."

"Why, Dad?" Karl Jr. retorted, his tone dripping disdain. "Because I'm not smart enough? Well, let me tell you, I almost singlehandedly brought down the future king of this nation."

"Almost," Oliver cut in, not letting anyone else go on a rant about this. Max appreciated his swift resolve. "But you didn't do it alone, did you?" Oliver asked.

Max was watching Oliver while others waited for Karl Jr. to respond. Because of that, Max saw where Oliver's gaze flitted briefly— and his heart broke. Now Max understood what the wooden ring Janos had hidden under his bed signified.

"You taught him everything he knew," Max said, his cold tone aimed at his old friend. People started catching on, and a restless shifting made way for low murmurs. Max trembled with rage. "You were supposed to teach him about love and life and the divine beauty of existence, just like you taught me. But instead, you fed him hate and power-lust and death? Why, Theo?"

The Grand Druid frowned a little, as if bewildered. Had he believed he would get away with it? He looked about as mesmerized as Karl Jr. had a moment ago. Finally his head moved minutely to the side. His eyes held an odd dark light.

"Why? I…." He seemed at a loss for words. It was strange for Max to watch the man he had known his whole life as an exuberant, amiable man who loved all living things change into an enemy. "I-I was forced," Theo muttered, his gaze aimed at everything else but other people's eyes. "Yes, he blackmailed me." He pointed at Karl Jr.

Karl Jr. drew in a sharp breath, his eyes wide and wild. "He's lying! I never had to make him do anything. He came to me about his plan to—"

"To reinstate the rotational kingship," Oliver interjected.

Max reeled slowly from the shock. Others seemed to share his flummoxed state of mind. No one knew what to say.

"You wanted to be king," Theo exclaimed, still pointing at his coconspirator. "And I helped you because you promised a smooth, stable transition of power."

The two ended up in a shouting match, each trying to one-up the other and convince listeners of their viewpoint and honesty. Max couldn't hear himself think, which probably was the whole point of the ensuing noise.

"Have we not been good kings and queens?" Max asked Theo. "What have we done wrong to earn your contempt and treason?"

Theo shook his head. "No, no, you misunderstand. It's the Great Goddess, you see. She's angry at humanity. We've done wrong by her. Nature is dying all around us, from the deepest ocean to the highest sky and everything in between. We're destroying the earth."

"Noricians alone aren't at fault there, and certainly not this royal family," Max said. "The whole world is culpable, to an extent."

"We had balance before," Theo growled. "When the Three Crowns reigned as one. Noricia had respect for nature then. We had to reset the balance. I had to. And he promised to help me by declaring environmental initiatives across the board. We could have salvaged this land."

"I doubt that was what he had in mind," Elinor cut in dryly, nodding at Karl Jr. "Not that little pissant. No way he's that progressive or altruistic." She scowled at the von Thürer father. "Not with him in the driver's seat."

For the first time since the Reed-Ruíz family had met Karl von Thürer, the prime minister did not rise to the bait. He looked… defeated. Max had never seen the man so utterly devastated.

"You tried to murder your future king?" Karl Sr. asked, his voice hoarse and trembling. "You must have known you could never be king."

"Why not?" Karl Jr. shouted. "Our blood is just as good and pure as the Lindau-Arbon line. We, the Varini-Böhm, are royal lineage too."

"No, we're not," Karl Sr. denied adamantly. "We're secondary—"

"We'd be first once they were removed from the throne," his son declared, chin raised in childlike defiance, eyes ablaze. "Theo wanted to reinstate the rotational kingship. The Forest Tribe is dead and buried, and the River Tribe has no secondary royal line left like us mountain folk do, just a tertiary line. So once the Lindau-Arbons are gone, we'd be left, Dad. Don't you see? I'd agree to rotate my kingship but in the end I wouldn't. I'd rule supreme alone."

"Actually, you're wrong about that," Max said, taking center stage from Oliver and recalling the meaning of the wooden ring. "No one outside the royal family knows about this but… Theo Weiss is a direct descendant of the Forest Tribe's secondary royal lineage. Close enough to the throne. Just like you, Junior, if my primary line was removed from the equation."

Oliver chuckled at Karl Jr.'s pure shocked expression. "He didn't mention that, did he?"

"Y-you mean, I would've had to… to share the throne… with him?" Karl Jr. screamed like a banshee and dashed in a mad spurt toward Theo, pulling his arm back for a blow. "I'd never share power with you, you stupid hippie!"

Before he even got close, armed military men and women, clad in black, swarmed the room, swift on their feet, effective in their movements. The Fox Tails tripped Karl Jr. with ease, pushed him hard down onto the floor on his stomach, yanked his hands back, and restrained him with plastic handcuffs—all in less than five seconds.

"That's not all," Oliver whispered to Max, who hoped that the commotion would prevent anyone from overhearing. "There was a third person tied to the conspiracy." He met Max's gaze. Max swallowed. Oliver looked so sad. Whatever he knew, he didn't want to say it.

Max found the last remaining ounces of strength within himself and quietly asked, "Kira or Johann?" He suspected it was one or the other.

Oliver lowered his head. "Your brother. He stole your signet ring while it was still here in Riten Castle and swapped it for the fake one Karl Jr. had had made. I don't think he knew his friend would try to kill you. Perhaps he thought it was a prank, you know, to declare ridiculous, outlandish laws to discredit you or embarrass you in front of your parents and the Council."

Max stood still. He loved Oliver right then, the young man who had been wronged but still defended the offender because he knew the truth made Max sad beyond belief. Max wasn't as close to his brothers as he would have wanted. Clearly, with his youngest sibling out to get him, it was too late to mend fences.

The guards arrested Theo as well and escorted both him and Karl Jr. out of the room. Where the young man was still ranting and foaming at the mouth like a mad dog, the older man seemed confused about why he was being treated like this. Perhaps Theo had lost some sense of sanity along the way as he plotted murder and treason. Max shivered; he didn't want to go into it.

"Lust for power versus the wish to do good, and yet both went astray," Paulito Ruíz said, his wise words and serene tone releasing some of the tension in the air. Max noted how many appeared to relax and draw breath for the first time in what seemed like ages.

"What an ordeal," Johann said out of the blue, standing straight and dignified, like a man who had done nothing wrong in his whole life. "I sure could use a drink."

Max saw red. He would have lunged at Johann had Oliver not taken his hand and squeezed hard. The touch grounded Max, and he settled down.

"Are you sure you want to do this?" Oliver asked with a low voice. "In front of everyone? Your parents? Wouldn't it better to confront him in private? He might be more inclined to be honest if there are no witnesses."

Max considered Oliver's advice. He seriously weighed both sides. Finally, he shook his head. "Johann has never learned to take responsibility for his actions. He's never had to face the music and the true consequences of his choices. But no more."

"Max…." Oliver sounded concerned, and Max knew then who he wanted by his side forever.

"I'll be fine," Max reassured his anxious lover.

"I'm not a fan of public spectacles, even to humiliate a bad guy. You really need to hold a private family meeting." Oliver's cool tone told Max a great deal about Oliver's character. Oliver brought fingers to his mouth and whistled. People jumped, lost in conversation or their own thoughts. Oliver waved. "Okay, everybody. Hustle! Reed family, out. Von Thürer family, exit as well, please."

Surprisingly, Karl Sr. didn't argue. He seemed beaten. Had he truly not seen his son growing up hating the way his father did? How could a parent be so oblivious? Children learned from their elders. And the von Thürers harbored a lot of resentment, bitterness, and envy. Now the pater familias was reaping what he had sown so long ago.

Otto von Thürer, the younger twin, followed in his father's wake, eyes wide in stupor and mouth hanging open. Clearly, he wasn't in on the conspiracy and treason. Entitlement had come to mean for him utter lack of knowledge of the world outside his own sphere.

Max didn't feel sorry for them. Perhaps he should have, but he couldn't muster forgiveness in his heart. Not yet.

Paulito escorted Valerie and Elinor out with a hand on their backs, not pushing but simply holding. Max suspected it was a case of protective instinct. After what Karl Jr. had tried to do, caution was the better part of valor.

As Oliver passed Max, he bussed a quick kiss on Max's cheek—and whispered in his ear.

MAX KEPT his face impassive until the room was cleared of everyone but for the royal family and the royal guards. The only outsider remaining was Lady Kira, who stood to the side. She was a distant cousin but part of the family and definitely a member of the tribe.

Once the doors closed, Max spoke. "John, give me back my signet ring. Right now."

Johann's eyes widened in shock. He hadn't expected that. For a second his gaze flicked between the exits and Max. In the end, he apparently decided not to flee. His face fell as he dug into the inside jacket pocket and produced Max's signet ring.

"*You* had it?" Gustav asked, his tone rising. That was alarming in itself. The King almost never raised his voice.

"I, uh… Karl Jr. gave it to me after—" Johann scrambled to say.

"You're lying," Max cut in, swathing through his brother's falsehoods like a blade. Johann cringed. "You're the third conspirator."

"No!" Johann denied, his voice high-pitched. "It was just a prank."

"So you didn't know your best friend intended to kill your brother?" Ben asked, composed as ever, a flicker of a smile gracing one corner of his lips.

"No, I didn't. Max, I swear." Johann pleaded with his eyes, his voice, his whole body.

Max was inclined to believe him, but he wasn't about to let Johann off the hook this time. "You've been given every opportunity to show what you're made of, John. If I haven't been enough of a brother to you, for that I am sorry. But the hate you let fester in your heart…. Your actions were directly responsible for the death of an innocent hotel manager and for both Oliver and me almost getting killed. No, John. I can't forgive you."

Johann's jaw quivered, and his eyes grew misty. "I never meant to hurt you."

Max shook his head. "I don't believe you. Not anymore." He stared at the signet ring he'd put back on his finger. The familiar unicorn seemed somehow tarnished. "You stole my ring, maybe for a prank with the falsified document, maybe to humiliate me in public. That thoughtlessness lead to a man's death. Two deaths, if you count Janos."

Johann gasped. He looked pale and wan, his knees shaky, as if he was about to collapse at any moment. "B-but I didn't mean for that to happen. I didn't know Karl Jr. had poisoned the fake ring."

"Once the hotel manager died, you should have come to me then, or our parents. You should have told someone. Come clean about what you had done," Max growled, so angry with his baby brother that the emotion damn near broke his spirit. "No. You've had enough privileges, enough excuses, enough forgiveness. No more."

Max faced his father, who was watching Johann with a mix of emotions. Max could relate. But that was all. "Father," he said in a tight voice, "I will make a formal request in writing later today that Prince Johann be stripped of his allowance, his duties, and his station."

Johann hurried to his father, grabbed his lapels, and made a melodramatic spectacle, playing the victim. "Dad, you can't. Please don't let him do that to me. I was stupid, I admit that. But I'm not a murderer. I was used. My friend tricked me."

Max snarled. "Well, at least you didn't claim you were blackmailed like Theo or seduced into a game of thrones like Karl Jr. But all in all, you three sound the same. Three conspiring, lying peas in a pod."

Johann ignored him. "Dad, I'll change. I'll be good. I'll follow the rules and behave like the perfect prince. I promise."

Gustav sighed. "You will *not* be stripped of your position as the Third Prince." Max waited patiently, and Gustav nodded to him, acknowledging Max's acquiescence to any decision being made. "But your allowance will be cut to zero. No more parties, no more lavish lifestyle, no more wrong crowds. You will be sent to Hohenstamm Hall—"

"But it's in the middle of nowhere," Johann cried out his protest, referring to a family castle secluded on a mountaintop. It had once belonged to the Mountain Tribe, as the name suggested. The place was where family members went to be alone—or where they were sent as a punitive measure. There was nothing to do there, as even hiking was dangerous on those steep slopes. The only diversion the castle had was an extensive library.

Gustav's face hardened, and his eyes glinted like steel. "What was that?"

Johann stepped back, exuding nervousness. "N-nothing, Father. I will obey."

"Yes, you will." Gustav's tone ended the debate. "Go to your quarters and stay there until I come for you. You are hereby under house arrest. You will speak to no one and do nothing, is that clear?"

Johann nodded, his head bowed. The fight had left him. He was just a boy being scolded by a parent, a boy who had lost the battle and the war. Max felt a twinge of sympathy he wasn't prepared for. Guess that confirmed that in spite of everything, he still loved his baby brother.

Under his brow, Johann stole a glance at Lady Kira, whose presence had slipped Max's mind. Had the man finally realized how she felt about him?

Stiffly, like a puppet moving on its own for the first time, Johann walked over to Kira. He cleared his throat and murmured, "M-milady, I-I know I'm not welcome here at home right now. And I know I've treated you badly. For that I sincerely apologize." He bowed like a jack-in-the-box, back and forth in an instant. "I-I hope that when this is settled, I might have your permission to, uh, court you?"

Max quirked an eyebrow in surprise. Johann was a prince into whom had been drilled the same codes of gentlemanly conduct as into Max, but Johann never behaved according to those rules. Max had assumed Johann didn't even know them.

Kira stared at Johann, who stared in turn at a spot below her jaw. A whole host of emotions flitted across her face. Max saw hope there, a dream come true. Then the castle in the sky crumbled.

Kira shook her head. "You've no idea how long I've waited to hear you say that, Johann." He met her gaze, a light of hope shining in his eyes. But Kira frowned. "I used to believe love conquered all. That nothing was more powerful than love." Then she raised her chin and her brow cleared. "Now I know that I love myself more than you. You filled yourself with hate, and I with wishful thinking. We both need to move on. You may be a prince, Johann, but I can do better. Much better. I deserve better."

Then she turned around and headed for the doors. They parted as if by magic, let her leave, and promptly closed again. A whiff of her expensive perfume, the scent of summer strawberries, was all that remained.

Johann blinked in confusion. Then he gulped, and his face fell. Max estimated that the full depth of what he'd lost hit Johann right then. With a deep sigh, Johann left the room, flanked by his bodyguard and castle security.

Max was conflicted. One part of him was glad that Johann had finally experienced the loss of something he couldn't have in spite of trying to get it by all the wrong means. On the other hand, Johann was Max's brother, and the instinct to offer comfort was strong.

Yet Max stayed in place. They all needed time.

"CAN WE keep this contained?" Colette asked then, seemingly addressing no one in particular. Just when Max thought her quite heartless, she added, "Is there something we can do for that poor man's family? The hotel manager, I mean. I think we should."

Gustav stood with a hand under his jaw, pensive. "According to the information released to the public, the man died of an undiagnosed medical condition. But since it is known he was in the First Prince's company at the time, a gesture of good will seems appropriate."

"Theo and Karl's son will both have to be tried for treason," Colette remarked, and she didn't sound happy about that. The way she chewed on the inside of her cheek and kept blinking to ward off tears told Max she was quite upset. "I can't believe Theo would do this. Stand against us over some silly superstition?"

"He was morally misguided and spiritually lost," Max offered in reconciliation. "Perhaps we could do something about those environmental initiatives caught in Council limbo?"

Colette perked up. "Yes. We shall do that. Find something positive in all this misery." She studied Max with a discerning eye and a small smile. "Speaking of which... Max, what about you and Oliver? Should we expect an autumn wedding?"

Max laughed. It felt good to show positivity after so much anger. "Let's not set any dates yet. He and I still have a lot to work out."

"As do I," Colette said like a mysterious soothsayer foretelling the tale of an impending royal marriage.

Max wisely ignored her. Gustav and Colette left the room, leaving Max alone with his second brother. He closed the gap between them. Ben grinned as usual. He seemed unaffected by all that had transpired.

"So," Max started, observing his brother's features. "You're in charge of the Cat's Paws?"

Ben quirked an eyebrow. Then he chuckled. "All right, fine. Yes, I'm the current Black Cat. How did you figure it out?"

Max snorted. "I didn't. Oliver did. And Elinor's suspected all along, I think."

Ben laughed. "I quite like that girl. I might have to recruit her."

"I hear she's an excellent engineer," Max stated, knowing that would interest Ben even more.

And sure enough, Ben's eyes flashed, and he rubbed his trendy beard, a musing expression on his face. "Is she now? Intriguing."

"The Cat Tower?" Max asked, though he had a feeling he knew the answer.

"My laboratory is, of course, a front, as you might have guessed," Ben confessed sheepishly. "Explosions in scientific research tend to keep the curious at bay. Yes, the Cat Tower is the secret lair of the Cat's Paws, Noricia's finest intelligence service."

"And only one, I sincerely hope," Max interjected with a chuckle. Ben replied with a smirk and a shrug. He'd never reveal all his secrets, Max surmised, and found he didn't mind. The world was better with a hint of mystery.

"If Theo hadn't confessed or Karl Jr. hadn't shown his treacherous ways, would you have interceded?" Max asked. "I'm assuming you had the proverbial goods on them?"

Ben sighed. "We've been following Theo Weiss, the von Thürer family, and many others of late, since hate groups and terrorist attacks have become the norm in the political field. Like Oliver, we couldn't deduce Theo's motives. Remind me to thank him for that insight."

"I will," Max vowed. He was pleased his brother complimented his beloved. It warmed his heart.

"With the von Thürers, the case got trickier." Ben frowned, lost in thought. "We suspected Karl Sr. of attempted murder when he poisoned your pie—"

"Cake," Max corrected him.

"Yes, that. Dang, but that alliteration sounded so nice: poison pie. Like in a fairy tale." Ben rolled his eyes. "But Karl's love for our mother seemed to exclude him, as he didn't and still doesn't want to do anything that would hurt Colette. We should be grateful our mother is so irresistible."

Max grimaced. "I'll, uh, be sure to send my thanks to the Goddess."

Ben grinned, but it quickly faded. "We missed Karl Jr.'s seriously disturbed tendencies. He's not part of any hate group per se, but his social media accounts reveal him to be a troubled young man, full of anger and not knowing where to direct it."

Max sighed. "At least some of it is probably aimed at his father. I wonder what will become of either of them now."

Ben shrugged. "Otto seems the only one out of the circle of hate. That is most likely due to his being totally clueless. He snickers at the poor as an elitist, but beyond that? He might not be so bad. A few civics lessons and a little sensitivity training might help him."

Though Max knew better than to pry too much information out of his brother, the leader of a clandestine spy organization, he still had many questions. "How did Janos get into the castle?"

For the first time, Ben appeared abashed. His cheeks pinked. He even rubbed the back of his neck and cleared his throat. "Well, actually, um, we let him in. We were hoping he would lead us to the real signet ring and the person or persons who hired him."

Max grimaced. "Your men shot Janos before he could actually reveal anything."

Ben blushed and coughed. "Yes, well… not our finest hour."

"No, it wasn't." Max clenched his hands. "He could have killed Oliver."

Ben ducked his head. "I doubt he would have, being a professional and all, with nothing to gain by Oliver's death, but… yes, there might have been a faint, very faint chance of Oliver possibly getting hurt. And for that, I'm sorry. I promise I will never endanger your boyfriend's life again."

In his heart, Max had a feeling Ben meant what he said. He'd better, or else…. Max studied his brother, wondering what more he had planned. "Will the Cat's Paws arrange a cover-up?"

Ben waved about indistinctly. "What is gained by exposure? I doubt either Theo or Karl Jr. will mention Johann's involvement. Theo does seem to believe in the premise of royalty, even if it's a little screwed up. As for Karl Jr., when he starts to rant about what he's owed, how everyone's out to get him, and the way he views his imaginary subjects, I don't think anyone will take him seriously." Ben paused for thought. "Perhaps to coincide with the trials, we'll arrange for Johann to do a public display of charity. Leave a good impression in people's minds."

"How calculating of you, brother. Taken right out Freddie's playbook," Max remarked dryly. He didn't view their subjects as sheep who needed to be herded toward manufactured truths, or fake news as a certain tyrant named it. Max believed people were smart and capable of figuring things out for themselves. If they cared enough about more than themselves, that is.

Ben chuckled. "Ah, brother. You're so naïve sometimes. A single person is smart and able to discern the truth from lies; people as a group believe whatever they're told. Herd mentality."

Max grimaced. Ben had an uncanny ability to read minds. How come Max hadn't made the rather obvious connection between the elusive scientist and the covert intelligence agency?

"Besides, dear brother," Ben added, back to his jovial self, "we're not lying to the people. We're just omitting the involvement of their favorite party prince in a plot to seize the throne. Unless you actually believe he meant to kill you?"

Max shook his head. "No, I don't. John can be a vicious and petty bully, but a murderer in a scheme for fratricide and regicide? No."

"Well, then, there you have it." Ben yawned and stretched as if he'd just awoken from a nap. "You should probably find you special guy and figure out a way to keep him in your life. I have, uh, another function to attend."

"Don't blow up our only intelligence service!" Max yelled at Ben's receding back as he left the room, laughing his ass off.

Max smiled at Ben, though the man couldn't see it. The door had closed. Max stood in place and pondered what he wanted out of life. The crown? Sure, it was his heritage. His family together, alive and well? Absolutely, if a little difficult to arrange for now. Oliver? Yes, yes, and yes. That was the one thing Max no reservations about.

Max had some planning to do.

Chapter 34

THE FOLLOWING day came the fallout. All I could do, standing on the sidelines, was read the newspapers and try to anticipate what would happen next.

"Plot to kill the future king uncovered. Two treacherous suspects unmasked," screamed the headlines, courtesy of Tulip de Lange. "Sources inside Riten Castle speak of poisonings, shots fired, deaths of assassins, and a rattled royal family."

I cringed. Sources inside the castle? Tulip really could be shameless. Yet not a word was false or an outright lie. What she wrote about, as a representative of the free media, was accurate and true.

That didn't make the news any less inconvenient.

I was glad I wasn't the Royal Press Officer. Poor Freddie. She had to stretch in a million different directions and skate around the truth without going into detail. Precarious were the icy fields of politics.

The Inner Ward was devoid of people but not quiet. Wind rustled softly in the bushes, and birds sang whole arias. I swore I caught sight of a bunny hopping across the lawn from one bush to another. Summer days seemed so long, yet they went by so fast.

Reading the news from my iPhone didn't help matters. Sure, my relationship with Max had become less of a mystery in favor of the threat against the royal family and therefore against all of Noricia. I couldn't help but wonder what could be salvaged from this mess.

"Oliver."

I started. Ben sat down next to me, a minor grunt escaping his lips as he kept his injured leg straight and rubbed the knee.

"Your Highness."

Ben chuckled. "Not my name."

I smiled a little. "Ben." When he nodded to acknowledge my change of words, I studied him closely. "So Tulip is one of your agents?"

Ben didn't so much as flinch. He faced me with an amused shine in his eyes. "Oliver, you are too sharp for your own good."

Since he kept his tone light, I didn't take offense or worry. "Correct me if I'm wrong."

Ben grinned at me. "Why do you assume Tulip is one of my operatives?"

I shrugged. "It's true I don't know for a fact. I saw you two together at the Solstice Festival, being all secretive and shit, but perhaps you're having an affair with her? Yet somehow I just can't see it."

Ben stared ahead at the Swan Tower, which cast a shadow over parts of the Inner Ward. Then again, the same could be said about all the towers despite the courtyards both being quite vast.

"I'm thinking about hiring your sister, Elinor. What would she say?"

I laughed at Ben's proposal. "She'd scream *yes*. Then she'd play it cool. Then she'd probably punch you where it hurt. But in the long run, you couldn't find anyone better, smarter, more creative, resourceful, or inquisitive."

Ben nodded, seeming pleased at my assessment, as if it coincided with his own evaluation of Elinor's character.

"You prefer to hire women?" I asked, curious.

"No one can be as duplicitous as a woman." Ben winked at me, showing he wasn't serious. "So. You and my brother?"

I shrugged. "There's no future in it."

Ben leaned back, serious for the first time since I'd met him. "Why not?"

I snorted. "That's a weird question coming from a prince who knows full well the numerous reasons why."

Ben sighed, rubbing his knee again. "You and Max together might create a constitutional crisis. That much is true. There are no easy answers." He glanced at me. "Do you love him?"

"Yes." There was no hesitation in my voice, but neither was there any emotion. I kept that to myself. The truth was my heart belonged to Max, but the other truth was we couldn't be together. I locked gazes with Ben. "Why fight the inevitable? Your mother said that once summer was over, so were Max and me. I love him, and he is worth fighting for, but against everyone and everything? I don't know if I have it in me."

Ben chuckled, his usual mirthful disposition making a comeback. "That's funny. Yesterday my mother said something quite the opposite. An autumn wedding was mentioned."

I gasped in shock. "The hell she did!"

Ben laughed out loud. "My father may be King, but what my mother wants, she gets."

I swallowed hard. "Why would she want me? She wants Max to marry Kira." I stared at Ben with suspicion. "Kira's not one of your agents, is she?"

Ben wiped tears of joy from his eyes as he chortled. "Contrary to what you might think, not every woman in the land, or even in court, is." Slowly, his mirth subsided, and he grew serious. "The speech Max gave in the Great Hall earlier got to Colette. Add to that Kira having feelings for Johann, though now quashed, and I think Colette finally sees that all her matchmaking efforts have come to nothing."

"Maybe. But that still doesn't mean she'd want her firstborn son and heir to the throne to marry a dude, least of all me," I commented dryly. Then his words hit me. "Wait. You weren't there in the Great Hall when…. Right. The Black Cat. Do you have eyes and ears everywhere?"

With an arduous effort, Ben stood, appearing composed. "Consider what I said. If my family expresses no objections about you and Max being together, then who else's opinion really matters?"

As Ben walked off with a slight limp, I noted he hadn't answered my questions, especially about Tulip. I figured my theory about her was correct, but I also surmised I'd never get a straight answer from either of them.

Instead, I focused on the idea that Max and I could forge a relationship beyond the summer. We still had a month left. Back on Whidbey Island, Max had indicated he wouldn't have minded if our arrangement continued. But what kind of relationship would that be? A clandestine affair kept by secret agents and security details? More lies, deceit, and secrets. Could I be that for him, something hidden in daylight, only taken out at night?

To consider anything else was folly. Max, a prince, and me, a poor Mexican-American boy, getting married? I didn't care what anyone said. It was impossible. Times hadn't changed that much. Even if I had won Colette and Gustav over, I was an unknown to their subjects. And there was no way in the world a whole country would sign off on their future king having a gay husband and royal consort, especially a foreign one. Keeping the primary royal lineage and the line of succession intact was one thing; the entire gay thing would be another.

The sad truth was, love didn't conquer all.

Glum and depressed, I refreshed the front page of the *Vindeburg Tribune* to see if there had been any updates.

When I saw the additional headlines, my heart very nearly stopped.

AFTER ASKING a passing staff member, I found Max in the Chapel. He stood before the altar, a faraway look in his eyes. I think he grieved over the loss of his friend, ally, and confidant, Theo. The druid wasn't dead, but he might as well have been.

I touched his shoulder gently.

Max blinked at me. For a second, I don't think he recognized me. Then he smiled and sagged in relief. "Oliver."

"I'm here." I took his hand and squeezed.

Max stared at our joined hands. "I rely too much on you," he said quietly. "What will I do without you?"

I bit my lower lip to keep the sob at bay. "Summer's not over yet." Then I remembered why I'd come here and sighed. "Although… for both our sakes, maybe it should be."

Frowning, Max looked at me. "What do you mean?"

I handed him my iPhone for him to read the latest news from the *Tribune*.

"First Prince's secret gay lover's identity discovered."

And there, for the whole world to see, was my face, my name, my ethnicity, the whole effing enchilada. The photo was my college graduation picture. I was smiling goofily. The sun was in my eyes, so I was squinting. It wasn't terrible, but it could have been better.

Max's face darkened, and he held the phone with a white-knuckled grip. "Tulip."

"Who else? She seems to keep her fingertips on the pulse of the kingdom." I rested a hand over Max's arm and felt him tense and then relax. "If I were you, I wouldn't jump to conclusions. For one, she and I met at the Solstice Festival, but she made no mention of that encounter or show pictures of me at the party."

Max frowned in obvious confusion. "So? Perhaps she didn't have a cameraman with her."

I chuckled. "Come on, man. Someone like Tulip always has means of recording something. Besides, everyone's got a cell phone these days, especially reporters. Even if they are banned at the castle, I bet it's like inside prison: stuff gets through."

Max chewed on the inside of his cheek; I saw his face move. "To reiterate, so?"

"Second," I said, "Tulip made only a passing remark about me being a guest here at Riten Castle. But nothing beyond that. Also, apart from the headline, she makes no direct allusions to our relationship. If anything, she's downright vague."

Max nodded slowly as understanding seemed to dawn on him. "I admit that is unusual for a journalist of her caliber."

I hesitated to tell him my theory about Tulip being an agent of the Cat's Paws. That should have been a topic of conversation between Max and his brother Ben.

Then Max glanced over my shoulder, and he gritted his teeth. "Looks like we'll get to ask her ourselves."

I swiveled on my heels and saw Frederica, the Royal Press Officer, approach us side by side with Tulip de Lange. Tulip was smiling, as was Frederica, but she had dark circles around her eyes. Too much demanding her attention lately, I surmised, and felt for her.

Tulip curtseyed. "Your Highness. Mr. Reed."

Max kept a straight face, but his bow was so diminutive that it came off as rude. I smiled at Tulip as best I could to relieve the tension crackling in the air.

"Your Highness," Frederica said. "Ms. de Lange is here to conduct an interview with you and Mr. Reed. This has been approved by the King and Queen."

Max squared his shoulders as if readying for a fight.

I stepped in fast. "Thanks, Freddie. I'm sure Tulip and we will manage."

Hesitating only for a second, Frederica nodded, turned around, and left.

Tulip faced me with a wicked grin. "Such familiarity in address already, Mr. Reed. Almost like you're settling in."

I waved at her to sit down on the bench. Church pews were uncomfortable in any religion, I concluded. "Would it do any good if Max and I categorically deny a close personal relationship?"

Tulip smirked. "Not really."

"You don't write the headlines, do you?" I asked, seeking confirmation.

"No, that would be the editor-in-chief. Us poor grunts only write the articles." Tulip seemed pleased that I made the distinction. "Flashy, provocative headlines sell. The actual article could be dull as mud, but as long as readers click on the link…." She shrugged, leaving the sentence hanging.

"Clickbait," I clarified. "And here I thought you wrote for a reputable publication, not for a cheap tabloid."

Tulip sighed. "Unfortunately, I have no say in some matters. But I take pride in publishing only what's—"

"Vague?" I interjected with a smirk.

Tulip chuckled. "—true. The *Tribune* might have a populist for a current editor-in-chief, but that doesn't mean *I* have to cater to the whims of the populace."

"Then why write such a scandalous piece?" Max asked, his tone as cold as ice. I exchanged glances with Tulip. Max seemed to sense she and I were on the same wavelength. His mouth thinned into a white line of disapproval. "Explain," he commanded.

"Sometimes even awkward truths must be said out loud," Tulip spelled out in her cautious diplomatic fashion. "And someone must always be the first."

Max studied her for a time in silence. Then his attention turned to me, his eyes narrowed. "I see." I could tell there was more he wanted to say to me, but he refrained. Instead, he faced Tulip again. "And you want a soundbite for your puff piece from the court?"

Tulip smiled softly and shook her head. "No. A small comment from both of you to dispel any… nasty rumors."

"They do spread like wildfire," I cut in dryly. Before Max could make a snarky retort of his own to Tulip, I asked, "How long have you known about Max's, um, situation?"

"You mean, how long have I held back the story? Years."

I watched as Max's sullen expression changed into a portrait of utter surprise. He'd been so preoccupied with keeping his orientation in the closet that it probably hadn't occurred to him that an expert reader of human character could sniff out his secret.

"I figured," I said, trying to prompt Max into joining our talk.

And Max did. "Why would you keep such a scoop from the public?"

"I'm a patriot and a Royalist," Tulip replied coolly. "Though if that last part is ever repeated outside this little gathering of ours, I will deny it and sue for slander."

"Are you sure you're not American?" I asked, grinning at her. Tulip laughed.

Max locked gazes with me. "How long have you known about her?"

"Tulip? We met at the Solstice Festival and got to talking." I bit my lip, as I almost spilled the beans about Tulip and Ben.

Max spotted the hedging and grew suspicious. "What aren't you telling me?"

Glowering, I almost reproached Max about his own tendency to withhold things. But that was a private matter. Max seemed to guess where my thoughts had taken me, and he bowed his head minutely.

It was Tulip who came to our rescue. "The Second Prince told me about your fanciful theory about me, Mr. Reed."

"Oliver, please," I said, sighing in relief. "Ben works fast, apparently."

Tulip winked at me. "There you go again with the familiarities. If you intend to claim there's nothing going on between you and the First Prince, you should take care how you talk. Mind your p's and q's."

"Wait." Max raised his hands to stop Tulip and me. "You're one of Ben's agents?"

Tulip smiled sweetly and batted her eyelashes. "Perhaps I'm dating your brother."

Max snorted. "I'll believe it when I see it."

"Unfortunately for you two, the world believes it when it hears a rumor," Tulip said. "You must get ahead of this. I'm here to interview you first. Others will follow."

I slumped a little, defeated. This was the time when Max and I had to come to terms with the temporary nature of our relationship. I still had one card left to play, though.

"Would everyone believe us if we made an official statement, backed by the court, that Max and I are just good friends? Or is it necessary for Max to say I was a last foreign affair before he settles down, gets married, and rules the kingdom?"

Max stiffened next to me, but I couldn't worry about that now.

"These are hard times for the kingdom," Tulip said carefully. "But also advantageous. You see, there's talk of a motion fueled by the Republicans—"

"A vote of no-confidence," Max said, a bitter smile gracing his lips. "They certainly wasted no time. As if assassins weren't enough...."

"Exactly. Their timing couldn't be poorer," Tulip offered. "There's been an attempt on your life, Max, and part of the reason is your sexual orientation. Excuse me, rumored orientation. Whatever opinion the people have about homosexuality or bisexuality or whatever, the majority back up the royalty with fierce loyalty. Especially now."

"You're saying this is the time to come out?" Max asked, his bitterness growing stronger with each word he spat out. I worried about him.

"Yes." Tulip nodded. "Two traitors tried to kill you. The people will rally to your defense if the Republicans make a move against you."

"Um...." I coughed to get their attention. "Could someone explain to me what's going on?"

"You know of the Council, right?" Tulip asked and carried on before I could say anything. "The King and the people have their own independent roles in society. Legislation, for example, must be approved by both parties. The people's consent comes either via their representatives, as in the Council, or by a kingdom-wide referendum, which is direct democracy where every citizen can vote on the matter. I told you all this at the festival, didn't I, Oliver? A motion of no-confidence requires at least fifteen hundred registered voters, which is not a problem for the Republicans."

I swallowed hard. My forehead grew hot and sweaty. "So, a vote of no-confidence means... what? That Noricians don't want Max to be a prince anymore?"

Max sighed. "No, it means they could block me from becoming the next king. A motion of no-confidence accepted by the people would mean that succession would bypass me and fall on the next eligible person in the royal line."

"Ben," I whispered.

Max nodded, a wry smile on his face. "Yes. Ben is the Second Prince." He glanced at Tulip. "Is that what the infamous Black Cat wants? The Ivy Throne?"

Tulip snorted. "Not bloody likely." A pink hue rose to her cheeks. "Sorry." She straightened and said, "No, Max. Your brother does not want the throne. Certainly not if you are removed from the line of succession in shame and disgrace."

"This suggestion for me to come out…." Max stared at Tulip, a steely light in his eyes. "Does it come from you or Ben?"

Tulip grunted in frustration. "Don't you see? There's been no motion to vote you out of the line of succession. Yet. Public support is on your side. But that window of opportunity closes fast."

"Clearly you and Ben have an idea," Max stated, asking a question without raising his tone.

Tulip nodded. "Yes. Admit the truth about your orientation. Throw yourself at the mercy of the people. There's no better time."

"But…?" Max asked, waving his hand about to encourage Tulip to elaborate. Like me, he clearly knew there was more to the notion.

"Having a gay king is one thing, and your press corps and my media can spin it. Press packets could go out right away," Tulip said. "The knowledge there will be no heirs is another matter. The main concern here. The continuity of the royal lineage."

Max chuckled. "Let me guess. Since I won't beget any offspring, I should name Ben's future children as heirs to the throne to succeed me."

"Actually," Tulip corrected him slyly. "Ben suggests adopting an heir from the tertiary royal line of the River Tribe."

I had no idea what was going on.

Max, however, gasped in evident shock. "Kira?"

It was my turn to draw in a sharp breath. "Kira?"

Tulip grinned in triumph. "She'd make an excellent regentess and mother of a future king, don't you think?"

Max nodded immediately, though I could tell from his glassy stare that he wasn't all there. Then he looked at me. "What about Oliver?"

Tulip shrugged. "A brief affair or permanent consort, it won't matter. Not if you come out now and settle the heir predicament at the same time. That is what everyone will focus on."

This was my chance. I saw the opening a mile away. I'd vowed to stay and help Max find out who was trying to kill him and stop them. I'd done that. As for my relationship with Max, there were problems, as evidenced by this whole debacle in the news right now. But more importantly, the issues of trust, honesty, and truth-telling still hung unresolved between us.

In short, I had to take a stand for myself. No one else would.

"A brief affair it is," I declared to Tulip. Max opened his mouth, but I spoke over him. "Can you ensure the piece about me will be positive enough so that I can get back to my old life and be forgotten once summer is over?"

Tulip licked her lips, perhaps to buy time. She switched between me and Max, who was fuming next to me. Finally, Tulip said, "I can do that, yes. If that's what you want."

"Great." I nodded, forced a smile, and waved about. "Let's do the interview, then. Best to get it over with." I faced Max, who had gotten a grip on his emotions and sat there, rigid and cold. "A lot of people already suspect the truth about your orientation, so… coming out should be like ripping off a Band-Aid. Easy-peasy."

Both Tulip and I waited for Max to say something. Anything at this point. Then Max stood, bowed to us, and walked away without another word or a backward glance.

I clenched my fists to hold back the tears I felt forming, hot and itchy in my eyes. Tulip touched my arm gently, the contact fleeting. But I understood. This couldn't be easy for anyone, and my dismissal had made things worse. Especially since I'd just denied my true relationship with Max in front of a journalist. Even if said reporter knew the truth.

Honestly, though, what else could I do? Wanting to be with Max, the man, was one thing; Max, the prince, who was already in trouble with his people and government was quite another.

It was best for everyone if our affair was downplayed and I took off. Since leaving now would send a weird signal, I couldn't go yet. But Max could say that he and I weren't exclusive and had no permanent plans.

Hell, it was the truth. Wasn't it?

Chapter 35

MAX FOUND his parents in the Western Drawing Room. Unlike the Eastern, the look of this room was modern and minimalist. The room color scheme was white and light gray, except for bright yellow chairs and pillows, cherry-red lamps and curtains, and paintings depicting orange flowers and flames.

"Is this a bad time?" Max asked as he sat down in an armchair across from the coffee table, facing his parents who were sitting on a large white velvet settee.

"No," Gustav said, shaking his head. "We have a quarter of an hour. Schedule's tight today, but according to Freddie, there might be quick changes."

Max noted his tone, strained just enough for his son to catch on. "Ms. de Lange is to conduct an interview, then? About me?"

Gustav and Colette exchanged glances.

"It seems best," Colette remarked slowly.

Max bristled. "Don't you think there are serious legal issues at stake here? A gay man on the throne could throw the kingdom into a constitutional crisis."

"The Republicans will have a field day," Colette cut in, her brow scrunched. Officially the royal family and its members took no sides among the political parties. But Colette held no love for those who sought to destroy her family's legacy.

"Without an heir, possibly," Gustav agreed. "I understood Ben had an idea about that?"

Max nodded. "I become king, Oliver or another man my royal consort, and Ben's children or Kira my heirs."

Again, Max's parents glanced at each other. Whatever passed between them, no words were necessary. They'd had that bond as long as Max could remember.

"Does that seem unreasonable to you?" Gustav asked carefully, his tone level, his demeanor unemotional.

Max hedged. "It would solve a few problems, but it would create a whole lot of new ones." He leaned forward, knowing what he was about to say would hurt his family. But it was an option he had to explore. "What if… if I abdicate?" Colette gasped and Gustav frowned. "We could put it to a vote with the people," Max added.

"A referendum on abdication?" Gustav asked, his usually serene tone now a mere growl.

"Don't you think that would be preferable to the constitutional crisis that would wreak havoc on our land?" Max tried to reason with his parents. "I mean, who knows? If I don't abdicate, this might be exactly what the Republicans need to call for a referendum on the abolition of the monarchy, not just our family's right to the throne."

Colette stood in a rush, withdrew to the windows, and hugged herself. But she said nothing. Max suspected this idea had hit her hard.

Gustav leaned forward as well. "Son, I know you mean well."

"I don't want my orientation to end our family," Max said, emphatic and a bit desperate too. "This way, Ben can be named heir, and since he's straight, the promise of offspring is high. Please, Father, think about it."

"We have stood for centuries," Colette said, staring out the window, rigid as a marble statue. "Our family, House Lindau-Arbon, has withstood countless calamities and lived to tell the tale. We have ruled over this land for generations. And you would throw it all away… for Oliver?"

Max reined in his temper, though it was tough. "Actually, Oliver is speaking with Tulip right now about how he's just a passing fancy for me. A brief affair before taking the throne. Nothing more. Oliver… will not be sticking around."

Colette turned to Max, her puzzlement clear. "He doesn't love you?"

Max gritted his teeth, having seen through Oliver's intentions from the beginning. "He leaves because he loves me and because he doesn't want to add more problems for me."

"And you wish you could leave with him and be ordinary?" Gustav asked quietly.

Max straightened. "I wouldn't be the first royal to abdicate over love. Think Edward VIII of England or the Grand Duchess of Luxembourg. But my love isn't the main reason, and you two know it. The *Tribune* is riddled with photos of Oliver. He might be able to convince the world he's nothing more than a part-time lover. But that won't end the trouble for *me*. I'm gay. And my very existence is a threat to the continuation of this monarchy. One way or another, I must go."

Silence fell into the room, thick with tension. There really didn't seem to anything more to say. Max had said his piece and settled in to wait for what would come. In the meantime, he prayed for the Great Goddess to grant her mercy to two lonely lovers.

"PLEASE, YOUR Highness. Reconsider this foolish plan. I'm aware this is my last day as prime minister and that my duties are at an end, but I urge you in the strongest terms possible to reconsider."

Max stared out the window of his room. He didn't need to look at Karl von Thürer.

The radio was on. Max caught the tail end of what was already dubbed a landmark speech.

> *Ours is a progressive nation. Where other nations stall*
> *or go back, we push forward and set the gold standard.*
> *Noricia stands as a flagship for the future. It is time for us*
> *to decide, as a people and as individuals, if we stand for*
> *love or hate.*

Max sighed without turning. "It's too late to back out now, Karl. I've delivered the speech and brought the referendum before the people."

Two weeks had passed since the news broke about Oliver. Tulip had splashed an entire month's worth of articles about Oliver on the front page, each positive in its own way. Oliver, the aspiring pastry chef, wasn't painted as a queer gold digger but as a young man who had helped the First Prince accept the truth about himself. While that turned Oliver into something of a media darling, not all Royalists were happy about him even drawing breath.

Max had done as advised. Well, to an extent. He'd come out of the closet as a gay man. He'd given Tulip an exclusive interview, and three days later new interviews to everyone who came to him. A gay future king was front-page news all over the world.

What Max hadn't done right away was confirm to the press that he was still the heir apparent or announced what he would do about the continuity of the royal lineage. Instead, he'd bypassed the Council and ordered a referendum about a vote of no-confidence.

Now if the people voted on Max's behalf, he'd continue as First Prince and heir to the Ivy Throne. If they voted against him, Max would be stripped of his station as heir and would no longer be eligible to rule; Ben would assume that role as next in the line of succession.

"No." Max finally faced Karl, head held high. "Whatever the people want, they shall have. If they believe a gay man cannot rule, I will accept that. If they decide a ruler must be able to conceive children, which drops me from consideration, I'll accept their judgment." He looked out the window. The familiar vista outside the Snake Tower gave him no comfort today. "I may be the First Prince and they my subjects, but I will adhere to their will."

Karl joined his side. "The Republicans have fanned the flames of revolution. There has been civil unrest in Vindeburg, small-scale rioting, a few brawls...."

Max clenched his fists. He recalled today's press conference where the prime minister had asked the people of Noricia to stand united against the unfounded hate that threatened to divide them. The speech had been in response to the agitation on the streets before they flamed into the wildfire of a civil war. No one wanted that.

Karl spoke right behind him. "The monarchy could fall."

"If our way of life falls over one gay man, then it should fall."

Max knew he was being naïve to expect a perfect fantasy from his subjects. When fear and hate governed a person, compassion and reason left the building.

A bitter laugh escaped his lips. "This status quo we're supposed to be defending, Karl... is it really something worth preserving? Is the system good enough for us to become the best versions of ourselves—or do we cling to it out of fear fueled by self-serving politicians and the greedy richest one percent?"

Karl sighed. "Ours is not a perfect system, but it is hardly the worst."

In fresh memory, Max replayed his own desperate appeal to the public.

As history teaches us, someone always has to be the first. Neither my coming out nor my notable referendum are a stand on public policy but a personal entreaty to you. People have come to expect exaggerations from their politicians, but outright lies or deception from their rulers? Unacceptable. No more. I must be true to myself and, as a result, to you. I stand before you as a Norician and wait for your judgment.

Max waved a hand at Karl. "Leave me. I grow weary of this pointless discussion."

Karl seemed like he wasn't finished. But he merely bowed and walked away.

Before Karl left the room, though, Max said, "I wish you had talked to us before handing in your resignation to the Council. For you have not lost our confidence." The royal *we* wasn't a term Max often used, but it seemed appropriate for this juncture.

Karl sighed, hands clasped behind his back. In a week, he'd aged years. Not that he'd been particularly youthful to begin with.

"My son betrayed you, the monarchy, our traditions, the whole nation, and me. It would have been highly improper of me to continue as head of the Council."

Max smiled shortly. "And what of my crime, Karl? I betrayed the country too, just by being myself. A treasonous act. What your son did as a thoughtless prank, I've done on purpose."

"It's not the same, sir." Karl sighed. "My son endangered the security of the monarchy and the nation. You… all you've ever done is serve this kingdom to the best of your abilities."

Max was touched by Karl's words. "Th-thank you, Karl."

A dry smile flitted across Karl's lips. "All of my ambitions have come to naught. I would give it all away for a chance to relive the past and be with my sons more. The hatred they harbored, their sense of entitlement, it came from me. It is high time I learned the lesson of humility. Goddess knows, if this hadn't happened, I might never have understood it." He bowed. "With your permission, Your Highness, I take my leave of you."

"Granted." Max bowed as well, though he wasn't expected to. But Karl had served them and the kingdom with distinction his whole life.

Once the door closed, Max slumped, releasing a long breath. All these changes were taking their toll. He'd had a headache for three days straight. Would it ever go away?

Another knock sounded, and a perky young woman with a short, twenties-style pitch-black hairdo, small round glasses, and a pointy nose peeked in. "Ministers Schaffhausen, von Arx, and Haas are here to see you, sir. Shall I show them in?"

Max suppressed a new sigh. "Yes, Hannah. Thank you."

Hannah Falk was his personal secretary. She controlled whom he would see in the course of a day in a formal capacity. Her role was like that of a key to a locked door. No one entered without her permission. Three Council members qualified for entry, though.

Max plastered a blank, patient, and polite expression on his face.

Orell Schaffhausen entered with the force of a blustering gale. His round face was red and angry. "Your Highness, you leave me no choice. I fear that in my role as interior minister I must lodge a formal protest. Your actions of late have proven unsuitable for a crown prince. Why, you have shaken the very foundations of the monarchy and—"

"Don't be silly, Orell. Can't you see that what the First Prince is trying to do is save your precious monarchy?" Yacine Haas sidestepped Orell, curtsied to Max, and smiled apologetically.

"I agree with the honorable defense minister," concurred Silvan von Arx. "I may be a full-blooded Republican, but I am in awe of the crown prince's responsible and mature conduct in this difficult matter. Your Highness, I am proud of you."

Red streaks appeared on Silvan's cheeks when the justice minister realized his words might be interpreted as overly familiar. Max smiled. Silvan was a good man, ethical and just. To have his respect meant a lot to Max. This surprised him since he and Silvan weren't on the same side politically.

Orell, however, harrumphed. He held his hands in front of him like a penguin. Max struggled not to laugh at the mental image.

"While my colleagues shower you with praise, sir," Orell chastised. "I myself cannot, not in good conscience. As a prince of the realm, sir, your first and only duty should always be to the kingdom, not yourself."

"You should be glad he chose selfishness this time," Silvan retaliated, albeit good-naturedly. "If he hadn't gone through with the referendum, no one would know about his proclivities. He would become king—and never sire heirs. What would that do for your glorious monarchy, hmm?"

If at all possible, Orell's face turned even ruddier, like a red balloon being filled with hot air. "The primary royal lineage should remain unbroken if the traditions of our nation are to stand the test of time and—"

"Enough." Max cut the others off as they seemed inclined to chime in, but he addressed Orell directly. "After so many centuries, only a genius geneticist could determine the actual percentage of Alette's blood flowing through my family's veins. Who could honestly say I am more worthy than either of my brothers or, say, Lady Kira or even you, Orell? The primary lineage is a word, an idea, an abstraction. It may be the basis of our kingdom, yes—but it doesn't have to be the foundation to end all royal foundations."

"Well said, Your Highness," Yacine cut in softly, an admiring smile curving her lips. "In my opinion, and I trust no one present considers this treasonous, all lineages hailing from the chief of the River Tribe could be eligible to take the Ivy Throne. Why only the firstborn's family line? It's old-fashioned, redundant, and—"

"You're the defense minister, Haas, for Goddess's sake," Orell raged. "Defend our customs and traditions, for they are what made our kingdom great."

"If we all thought as you, nothing would ever change or progress," Silvan countered. "Our kingdom would stagnate like a swamp. And aren't there enough of those in the world already? Not to mention the fact that valuing our monarchy doesn't have to mean that every opposing concept or practice be abolished."

Orell scoffed, crossing his arms, his demeanor belligerent. "You don't value monarchy at all, Silvan. You wish to see it destroyed."

Much to Max's surprise, Silvan shrugged. "I don't know. I did... before. But today, after hearing Max's speech, I find myself less inclined to overthrow the crown. Why would I when there is a man worthy of leading us right here?"

Max blushed. Had he turned Silvan into a Royalist? If not, he at least seemed to have made a friend. "Th-thank you kindly, Silvan."

Out of the corner of his eye, Max spotted Orell's jaw dropping in utter shock.

Silvan smiled shyly. "As the justice minister, all I've ever wanted is to be certain that those who rule over this kingdom aren't tyrants. As a firm believer in democracy, I've always thought that the best way to ensure that is through a leader chosen by the people, not one who inherits the status by mere birthright. Today, sir, I heard the words of a true prince and saw the actions of a man who would make an excellent king."

Max found it ironic beyond belief that Silvan, the Republican, had suddenly become his strongest supporter—while Orell, the Royalist, seemed hell bent on rebuking Max for everything he'd said and done lately. Funny how life turned out sometimes.

"Well?" Yacine quirked an eyebrow. "What say you to that, Minister Schaffhausen?"

For once, Orell appeared speechless. He stared at Silvan in bafflement, then blinked hard and regrouped, clearing his throat. "Well, yes, of course I…." He faced Max, studied him in silence for a while, and then sighed. "As a prince, it is your right to ask for a vote of no-confidence. While I am not pleased you did so, as the future monarch perhaps this was your… duty." Frowning, Orell glared at Max. "I just hope the kingdom doesn't fall over this silliness."

Then he swiveled on his heels and sailed out the room like a royal barge. He didn't even wait for Max to excuse him. Max rolled his eyes; Orell would never change.

Silvan bowed deeply before Max. "You Highness, whichever way the vote goes, you have an ally and a friend in me and my husband." With a coy half smile, he, too, left the room, though without turning his back on the prince.

Yacine touched Max's shoulder. Strictly speaking this was a no-no, but Max didn't care.

"What Silvan said echoes me as well, sir." She winked then. "Just so you know, I voted for you. If my children were older, I know they would have voted for you as well. And speaking of kids, I'm sure you and I will revisit that topic in the future. Good night."

Max bowed as she curtsied. Once the doors closed behind her, Max was still smiling. He was disappointed by Orell's reaction, but not surprised. What Silvan and Yacine had done, though, declaring their faith in him, did throw Max for a loop.

Perhaps things might work out after all?

By midnight the count should be in. This might be his last day as First Prince.

He wandered about the room, touching things, memorizing them. He sought a semblance of solace but found none. Cabinets, bedposts, doors—they were his home but not his home. Not now.

Max missed Oliver more than he could say.

Between the time when Oliver was revealed to the public as Max's lover and when Max ordered the referendum about his own future status as heir apparent, the King and Queen had decided there was no need to give the Republicans, the public, the media, or the paparazzi further fodder. As a result, the Reed-Ruíz family was sent back home to the States.

Once more, Max had said au revoir to Oliver and given him the continental cheek kiss. His heart broke as he recalled the pain of that separation.

Had that been the final goodbye this time?

A KNOCK from the door was what he needed to compose himself. If he was to go down for being gay, he would do so with pride. He would not hang his head in shame; he would not wail in self-pity. He was born First Prince; he would leave his royal office like a goddamn prince.

He was so consumed by his inner turmoil that he forgot the knock until it repeated, louder this time. "Enter."

Ben hobbled in with his usual irreverent grin. "Brother."

Max sat heavily on the foot of the bed. "I'm tired, Ben. Can't this wait?"

Ben came to sit beside him. "This might be your final night here at Riten. When else would work for you?"

"I'll find a place somewhere," Max replied vaguely.

"You are family, dummy," Ben reminded him. "Even if the people accept your inane exit strategy, you're still a member of the royal family. You can stay here. Well, maybe not in this tower." Ben studied Max, his face unreadable. "Or are you planning on going to Oliver? Is he worth it?"

Max smiled, his heart light for the first time in days. "Yes, Ben. He is."

"He left," Ben reminded him.

"Oliver thought he was doing the right thing," Max explained wearily. "That by leaving he could clean up my mess. He's sweet like that."

Ben stretched his arms and rubbed his knee. "If you and Oliver end up together, it won't matter where you are. Your days will be hectic and chaotic, and you will attract attention wherever you go. It won't be easy."

"Easy-peasy." Max chuckled at the memory. Back then it had hurt, like a knife cutting into his heart. But he'd understood Oliver's motives. As he recalled those hazel eyes, veiled in tears, Max knew Oliver loved him. Oliver had sacrificed his future with the man he loved for what he saw as the greater good.

Max was done with the greater good. He'd held his tongue long enough. He'd had so much growing up, but freedom to be his true self hadn't been available to him. Wealth and luxury weren't adequate compensation for a life without love.

Not now, when Max had finally had a taste of Oliver's sweet flavor and knew what love was.

"If Oliver wants to get back together with you, you two should come back here. You'll be safe at Riten. Yes, despite the recent unpleasantness. As the Black Cat, I promise no one will get at you again."

Ben pledged with a hand over his heart. His sincere look was dampened by the mischievous smile ever-present on his lips.

Max chuckled. "I'll take your word for it." He flopped backward onto the comforter that welcomed him, soft and billowy, as he sank into it. "It's a long wait until midnight. Want to wait with me?"

Ben snorted. "And do what, exactly? Lie in bed and commiserate? Pass."

"No. We can watch a movie." Max jumped up, found the remote, and pushed a button. The TV rose from a hidden compartment inside a credenza set up against the wall opposite the foot of the bed. The 98-inch TV filled out a large section of the wall. Max found Netflix on the menu screen and then the film he wanted to laugh with.

"*The Court Jester*?" Ben squinted at the screen. "Never heard of it."

Max grinned. "We watched this, me and Oliver, before he left. It's really funny. Trust me."

"Okay," Ben agreed grudgingly and settled with his back against the foot of the bed. Max slid down next to him, placing a cushion under his behind. "What's this about again?"

Max smiled. "Well, there's an heir to the throne who is just a baby. He has a birthmark on his buttcheek: the purple pimpernel."

"You're joking," Ben cut in, his jaw dropping, his eyes widening.

Max giggled. "Nope. A ruthless king who rules under false pretenses is searching high and low for the child. His chief advisor is an evil swordsman, and there's a beautiful love-sick princess, and then there's the Black Fox, the leader of a rebel force. And... well, you'll see."

Ben shrugged. "Wish we had popcorn."

"I'll call room service. One last serving before sentencing, eh?" Max got up, pulled on the cord next to the bed—the old, still-functional way to call for a servant—and reclaimed his position beside his brother. "Danny Kaye is amazing in this role. You'll love him."

Ben nudged Max with his shoulder. "I already love Oliver and miss him too. Whatever the count of the referendum vote, brother... go get your man."

Max grinned from ear to ear. He was happy. The vote would change things no matter which way it went. But he still had his family. He could have Oliver back, too, couldn't he?

Chapter 36

BACK HOME *again*. My room seemed so empty and small when I walked in with my bags. The last red rays of the sun bathed everything in a maroon glow. I didn't need to turn on the lights. I set my suitcase down and sat on the bed.

As soon as I drew a breath, a hollow sadness overtook me. I shuddered, and tears brimmed in my eyes.

"You'll see him again," Elinor said, leaning on the doorjamb, a kind look on her face. "Trust me, I know these things."

I smiled. "Yeah."

I didn't believe my own words. Max had let his parents send me away. While I understood the reasoning, I didn't accept it. Or was that my foolish and stubborn heart? Max had embraced me goodbye, but he'd only given me the formal cheek kiss that meant... nothing. I missed the feel of his lips on me.

Summer was nearly over. The reporters who'd flocked our house when we'd left for Noricia were gone. I was yesterday's news. I'd been reduced to a fling, and not only by the yellow press. I told myself the same, mostly to preserve what was left of my heart.

Why? Because he had made no promises, nary a mention of seeing me again. Our separation felt like goodbye, not like see you soon. Like before. Like France. Did I dare hope?

I straightened on the bed and changed the subject. "I need a job."

Elinor sighed but nodded. "I'll help you find an awesome one. I know all the best restaurants. Who knows? We could use your recent—"

"No." I stood, adamant. "We'll not breathe a word about Max or any of them. None of us. As far as they're concerned, we're mute."

Elinor saluted me in proper military fashion. "Sir. Yes, sir."

I loved her so much. Maybe I should say it to her more often.

I LEANED against the wooden railing of our balcony, overlooking the strait. Pines rustled in the wind, and in the distance, waves created whitewash out at sea. Scents of evergreen and sea salt filled my senses, their familiar mix comforting.

In my head, I heard Lana Del Rey singing about how nothing lasted forever, not love, not the sun, nor sweet summer days. "Music to Watch the Boys To" was a song I'd listened to many times, the original version and the numerous dance mixes. I could never have imagined the lyrics matching my situation.

I needed solace. Pining for Max grew stronger when I was idle.

"I'm sorry things didn't work out for you and Max."

Valerie came to stand next to me, her hand on my shoulder, warm and kind. But my bitterness hadn't yet turned sweet.

"Are you, Mom?" I asked with venom in my tone.

She flinched. I was being needlessly cruel. It wasn't her fault Max and I had fallen apart. She'd tried to separate us, but she'd seen the error of her ways, and there were other, more powerful, forces at play too.

"I'm sorry, Mom." I bumped her with my shoulder, not knowing what else to say or do.

She sighed and rested her head against mine. "I love you, my sweet baby boy. And just when I'd started to accept the idea of you two together."

I snorted, facing her. She seemed as worn as I felt. She had dark circles around her eyes and wrinkles where there'd been none before. She smiled in response, though, which took off years.

"Really?" I asked, half-incredulous, half-hopeful.

Valerie nodded firmly. "Yes. I mean, what was the point of all those press photos and official interviews and positive articles about you if they weren't planning on announcing publicly that you and Max were an item?"

I shook my head. "I think at that point they were on the fence about me. But then later they decided I was suitable as more of, uh, a mentor than a future husband for a king. I imagine they'll scour the country for eligible bachelors, aristocratic and picture-perfect male candidates. Born and bred Norician men. Not like me."

"You stop that this instant," Valerie commanded with a hard edge to her voice. "You might not have been what they were looking for, but you were, and are, what Max wants."

I smiled ruefully, my heart aching. "I think in this Max will defer to them, for the sake of the kingdom. He might care about me—"

"Might? He does," my mother interjected.

"—but he cares about his homeland, his people, and his family more. As he should." I bussed Valerie on the cheek. "Love is mighty, but it doesn't always conquer all."

"Well, it should." My mother's jaw trembled and her eyes watered.

I hugged her, and she embraced me back. I heard her sniffle.

"A-are we good?" she asked, her voice small and timid.

I hugged her tighter. "Of course. I love you, Mom, more than anything."

"I love you too," Valerie declared, hoarse and emotional.

Then a gleeful shout came from the backdoor: "Group hug!"

Elinor launched herself at us. We were lucky to not get thrown over the railing and down the steep incline into the sea. Valerie screamed good-naturedly while I grunted, my side bruised by my sister's ridiculous antics.

By the time we managed to disengage from one another, we were all a bit ruffled.

Valerie scowled at Elinor, who feigned innocence, hands behind her back, eyes wide with wonder like a child. Then my mother sighed, defeated, and turned to me.

"I want you to know that if there's a chance you and Max will get back together—"

"Unlikely," I cut in bitterly. I didn't know for sure, but in my bouts of self-pity, I wouldn't have placed any bets on me to win the race. Beating a dead horse; that was me.

"—your father and I will support you," Valerie finished, pretending not to have heard me. "It's clear you two love each other. Your father and I had little else when we started our life together. So you see, Oliver, sometimes love does win."

She kissed my forehead, the way she did when I was a kid. Her words warmed my heart and eased my soul. Some of the emotional weight on my shoulders lifted. I didn't believe in my chances with Max, but my mother's words instilled hope.

In the end, hope was all we had.

I ACQUIRED an apprenticeship at one of the top restaurants in Seattle. Not quite five Michelin stars, but a top-notch menu, state-of-the-art kitchen, and a great chef, if the rumors were to be believed.

Instead of glamour, though, that meant dull drudgery, torturous hours, and a chef whose sole form of communication was shouting and throwing pans around. I hated him, but he knew his cuisine. I learned a lot about food I wanted to make and a lot about the kind of chef I didn't want to be.

So everything balanced itself out. Days flew by, turning into weeks without my barely noticing.

One boring Saturday in early autumn, when three weeks had passed since we'd come home from Noricia, I was playing the part of busboy-slash-waiter, trying my best at both. It was supposed to be my night off, but my favorite coworker had called in sick and asked me to fill in for her. I'd grudgingly agreed because I knew she'd have my back in the future.

It was game night, so the bar area was packed with big burly men screaming at the TV. I had no idea who was playing; I was too busy to steal so much as a glimpse. Dishes didn't clear themselves, and drinks didn't deliver themselves.

A commercial break came on. I could finally, for five minutes anyway, hear myself think. The noise level went down fast. Low murmurs took its place. Someone who had the remote started flipping stations.

A pretty girl in a pink cocktail dress who sat at the bar called out, "Oh! Leave that on. Raise the volume, please? Oh, isn't he handsome? I wish he'd make me his princess."

Hearing a halfway familiar word, I glanced over my shoulder as I was clearing a table of dirty dishes into a beige plastic bucket. My breath hitched.

Max was on TV!

In answer to the adoring fangirl's request, someone had indeed raised the volume of the news show. I could hear my prince making an official statement, his familiar baritone like a shot of pure pleasure.

"Ladies and gentlemen," Max said politely. "From the bottom of my heart I thank you for your continued support in these trying times. I assure you, Noricia has faced calamities before and risen from the ashes. No two traitors will bring down our kingdom."

A polite cacophony of impromptu clapping followed, lasting only a moment. Reporters kept throwing questions at Max, one of them about the vote of no-confidence referendum and its results, but I couldn't hear the response.

A group of men at the bar were tipsy enough to start a scuffle about the game, and I couldn't hear Max anymore. The bouncers broke up the almost-fight and threw two guys out.

On TV, Max said, "…am honored to be so warmly welcomed into your beautiful country."

I frowned in bafflement. Max wasn't at home? Perhaps he was on a diplomatic mission? Too bad the background consisted of a group of men and women in business attire and indistinct gray pillars and steps. He could have been anywhere.

I shivered, remembering how things had changed after the exposure of Theo and Karl Jr.

Our lovemaking had become a quiet affair. An air of reverence descended and silenced our words. Instead, we communicated through touch and glance and kiss. Max pulled me on top of him and cradled me in his arms as if I were made of spun glass. I'd let him because I felt the same about him, even though he had recuperated since the poisoning incident.

It was as if we hung in a strange in-between, a state of uncertainty somewhere between what we'd been and what we could be. Undecided, we didn't speak about what troubled us, even though I sensed we thought and felt the same.

Yet a bond between souls didn't necessarily translate into an understanding without words. So we stayed close, the sex as hot and passionate as ever, but we drifted apart, too, because of all the things we left unsaid.

But that was a month ago. Time flies, except when your heart is broken. Then every hour is an eon of agony. I'd tried to forget Max but… he'd settled in there pretty firmly.

I was still unprepared to see his face, even if it was on TV.

Suddenly Max smiled. His gesture wasn't polite as much as it was a full-blown wicked grin.

"And now, if you please, I come to the real reason for this press conference. I am searching for someone." Questions by the reporters silenced him briefly, but he persevered. "This person is a young man who is close to my heart. Unfortunately, he is not answering his phone, so I'm forced to resort to unusual methods. Please, if anyone knows the current whereabouts of Oliver Reed, kindly call the number you see on the bottom of the screen. Oh and by the way, for all you reporters and royalty fans out there, this is a special number for this occasion only and not my personal line."

I gasped. *My phone's in my locker, on silent.* Utter shock flooded me.

The platter fell from my numb fingers, thankfully only onto the table. The clatter of dishes caught a few patrons' attention. I stared at the TV, undoubtedly resembling a fish on dry land, mouth gaping, trying and failing to breathe. I started to feel light-headed.

A guy in a ball cap who sat at the bar called out to me, "Are you the guy he's looking for?"

I couldn't speak. The man's words had aroused the attention of everyone at the bar by then.

On the screen, Max declared, "My intentions are time-honored and true. Please, help me find this man."

Then the phone on the makeshift podium in front of him buzzed. The microphones picked up the noise loud and clear. Max answered. Then the bearded, ball-capped man shoved a phone in my face.

"H-hello…?" I whispered.

On the TV, Max's grin widened, and his eyes burned. "Oliver."

The word purred in my ear, and my stomach flipped. "Wh-what are you doing?"

Max chuckled. "No. Ask me *where* I am." But I didn't get the chance. "No. Where are *you*?" Someone at the bar yelled out the restaurant's name and address. Max nodded in reply and winked at the camera. "Don't move."

The line disconnected. The cameras shook as Max walked off-screen even though reporters from all over the world hollered more questions. A newscaster appeared and started speaking in a formal tone, but no one was listening.

"Oh my God, you're that prince's sweetheart!" someone shouted.

Lights flashed in my eyes as people started taking pictures. Me in my stained work clothes—two sizes too big—sweaty skin, red eyes, and one cringe following another. *Wonderful. Quite the cover model I'll make.*

Panic turned me into a statue. Why did Max ask where I was? If he was half a world away, what did it matter where I was?

Holly, one of the four waitresses, dashed over to me and started pulling off my filthy apron, talking a mile a minute, though I couldn't make out a single word. Tara, another waitress, yanked on my mussed-up hair, trying to get it to go where she pleased.

I had no concept of time. People were shoving and prodding me. Patrons took photos with their camera phones, sometimes bringing their smiling faces next to my stunned one. People talked incessantly. My brain couldn't compute. I felt I might pass out.

Then a room-wide gasp heralded total and utter silence. For once, no one was looking at me. Everyone's gazes were glued to the door.

My heart skipped a beat. When I turned—*God, how long does a head-turn take?*—I swear I could hear my joints creak and pop.

There he was. My dream prince…. Well, with Lawana in tow, looking badass as usual.

Max stood on the threshold, smart in his impeccable charcoal-gray business suit and sky-blue tie, grinning like a loon. "Oliver…," he whispered in a sensual hiss.

I heard him faintly, like I was underwater. I couldn't move my feet.

Max seemed to realize this because he came to me, as smoothly as if he were sailing through the air on winged feet. He smiled at me, and a cute pink blush graced his high cheekbones.

"Oliver," he said again.

Then he cupped my face, brought me close, and kissed me on the lips.

He took my breath away.

In the background, I heard clapping, whooping, and wolf whistles. I blushed midkiss, feeling the heat beneath my skin.

When he pulled back, he said, "I'm sorry to spring this on you, my dear Oliver. I know how much you hate public displays."

I smiled, a fever burning me inside and out. "Only negative ones." Breathless with want and love, I asked, "Why are you here? How?"

"So many questions," Max said with a laugh, pulled me into an embrace, and pressed his cheek against mine. "I missed you. Did you miss me?"

I buried my face in the crook of his neck. Tears burned my eyes. "A little."

"Only a little?" he teased.

"Okay, a lot," I confessed, fisting the back of his jacket in a fit of emotion. Then, lowering my voice so no one else could possibly hear, I admitted, "I thought I'd never see you again."

"Funny. I knew with absolute, crystal-clear certainty I would see you again." Max bussed my temple and rocked me back and forth, as if soothing away pains I hadn't been aware I had. "To be honest, I couldn't stand it anymore. Mother was pestering me constantly about the autumn wedding your departure had denied her. I surrendered to her whining."

I pushed him off and glared, though I wasn't serious. "Oh really?"

Max laughed. "I came all the way to the States, halfway across the world, to tell you, Oliver Reed, that I am in love with you and that I wish to spend the rest of my life with you."

There was no holding back the tears any longer. "M-me too. I love you, Max."

Max gathered me into his arms and kissed me breathless. When we parted, I panted, my head swimming in a daze of happiness. He caressed my cheek and made me feel like I was the only person in the world he adored.

"Remember how you once asked me if I wanted a concubine?" Max asked, smiling at me in that wicked way he did. I was confused but nodded hesitantly. Max chuckled. "Well, I still don't need one—but I would love a consort. Would you be amenable to that sort of arrangement?"

I gasped in shock that reverberated through me like wildfire. Was he really asking me what I thought he was asking me? "A-are you, uh, p-proposing to me…?"

Then Max knelt on the floor of the restaurant, pulled a small velvet-covered box out of his pocket, and raised it toward me. "My dearest Oliver, will you—"

"Yes!" I exclaimed loudly. Then I flushed with embarrassment. I'd interrupted my prince's proposal. A very public proposal that would go down in history books and internet archives. "Sorry."

Max chuckled. "Don't be. Not when the outcome is favorable to us both. Here." With steady, strong hands, Max slipped a golden engagement ring onto my finger. Like a vine or snake, it wrapped around my digit. "It's a Celtic knot. Plant or animal, whichever one you wish to see there. Nature, in the end."

I stared at my hand, dumbfounded. "I-I love it." I looked up at him. "I love you."

Max smiled. "I love you, my sweetest Oliver, more than I could ever say."

When he hugged and kissed me again, I didn't care that strangers took my picture. My dream man was here, he had declared his feelings, and he would carry me away to a beautiful castle in a faraway land. I was fortunate.

And this time I'd sleep with my prince totally on purpose. Double entendre intended.

Chapter 37

WEARY TO the bone, I drudged out of the Bull Tower. My eyes refused to stay open, but I tried to maintain a decent facade when out and about at Riten Castle.

"You look like something the cat dragged in."

I smiled, buoyant again, and turned to Max, who leaned against the wall, gorgeous and put-together as usual, dashing in his dress pants, white dress shirt, and vest that matched the color of his eyes. Max disengaged from the wall and approached me with a wicked grin.

"You look amazing," I drawled, letting him wrap his arms around me and kiss me. "Good thing you're mine. You make me hungry." My stomach rumbled on cue. "Well, I'm overall famished."

Max nuzzled my neck. "I have dinner waiting for you in our room."

I buzzed with warm excitement. Our room. The Snake Tower was truly ours now, mine and Max's. He, the First Prince, and me, the royal consort-to-be. The royal wedding was scheduled for next spring. For now, Max and I were engaged. I wore a golden engagement ring that twined around my finger, reminding me every day what a lucky man I was.

Side by side with our arms around each other, we slouched across the immaculate lawn toward the entrance to the Snake Tower.

"What have you been up to today?" I asked, stifling a yawn that brought tears to my eyes. "Representing the nation to the best of your abilities?"

Max laughed. "Yes, my dear. Business as usual."

I shook my head. "Not anymore. Noricia will be the first nation in the world governed by a married gay royal. It's insane. I still can't believe the people's vote went your way."

The vote hadn't been unanimous, but voter turnout had been unprecedented. Ninety-seven percent of the people had voted. Fifty-six percent had voted for Max to remain as the First Prince and Heir no matter whom he wed; thirty-five percent had voted for Max *if* he named

Ben's future children as heirs (which Max did right after the vote); and nine percent had voted flat out against.

Max pressed his head against mine for a moment, perhaps for support. "I guess my subjects had enough confidence in me to accept me for who I am. Love won. No constitutional crisis. No end for the monarchy."

"Having Ben's and John's future kids named as heirs probably helped," I noted.

"True," Max agreed, inclining his head minutely. "An unbroken royal lineage is important in unprecedented situations like this. Plus, in a crunch, the tertiary lineage could provide a future king or queen as well. Personally, I would love to see Kira on the Ivy Throne."

I laughed at the thought, agreeing with it wholeheartedly.

As historical a vote as it had been, the end result for Max and me meant that if he and I ever planned to have children of our own, whether via surrogacy or adoption, they would never be called princes or princesses, nor would they be in the line of succession. They would be seen as lesser royals. I was fine with that. Kids didn't need to grow up inside castles or be burdened by a litany of titles to be loved by their parents.

Clearly Max didn't want to talk about that anymore because he changed the topic. "You seem tired. Did Ariana give you a hard time?"

This time I didn't bother to hide the yawn. My jaw nearly dislodged. "She always does. Quite the ballbuster. But she knows so much, and she runs a tight ship in the kitchens. I could only ever hope to be her equal."

"How do you find the Confectionary?" Max asked, licking his lips.

I chuckled. "Keep that tongue away from me, you horndog."

"I can't." Max licked his finger and swiped it across my cheek, hot and wet. I suppressed an *ick* sound when he smacked his lips in delight. "Mmm, chocolate. I love how I associate you with sweets."

I giggled, blushing. "Today we made mousse with fourteen different kinds of chocolate. I never knew there were so many ways to make mousse or that one could get it so smooth." I stole a glance at Max. He looked happy, a constant secret little smile on his lips; I gave him that. "Ariana suggested I design a dessert for the wedding reception. Not the main event wedding cake but one of the desserts."

Max's eyebrows rose. "Wow. That is a huge undertaking. Your signature dish?"

"No. I don't want my signature dish to be popular just because it was in a royal wedding."

"Even if it's the royal wedding of the century?"

"No." I remained adamant. "Ariana wants me to let my imagination fly with the dish, since hundreds of people will get to taste my recipe on the first try and people all over the world will want to try it out later." I shuddered. "Scary."

"You'll do fine," Max assured me, his soft voice soothing my fears. Then his tone changed. "Johann has written our father and asked to return for the Winter Solstice Gala."

"Oh." I was aware Johann was still secluded in the hillside castle, Hohenstamm Hall, because of his actions. Almost four months and counting. The King and Queen had visited him but hadn't allowed him to come home. "Will Gustav agree, do you think?"

Max's expression was pensive. "I don't know. Father's pretty angry still. Johann's betrayal hit him hard. Colette… she's tougher to interpret. I think she might allow it, but only for the celebration and then send him packing again. Neither of them are in a forgiving mood."

"John is a bit lost right now, but he didn't mean permanent harm," I said in his defense. "He was playing a prank."

"A stupid prank that could have ended the monarchy," Max exclaimed, shaking his head in vexation. "No, I'm not ready to forgive him either." Then, with a quieter voice, he added, "I do miss him, though."

"Maybe we could ask your parents to let him have visitors besides them?" I suggested. "Lady Kira, for example?"

Max glanced at me. "You think she'd want to?"

I shrugged. "I think she was teaching Johann a lesson. That with all that hatred inside him, he stood to lose all the love that could have been there. But… I'm not sure. Have you spoken to her?"

"I called her last week," Max replied. "She seems hesitant to visit Riten Castle again. I think the wounds might be too raw still."

I nodded. "Broken hearts take forever and a day to mend."

Max smiled at me. "What's that? Rather poetic."

I blushed. "Shut up." Then I said, "Ask your parents first. Depending on what they say, then we can plan how to best ask Kira about it."

Max frowned. "You think she's still in love with Johann? He turned out to be such a… a…."

"Douchebag?" I helped him with a smirk.

"A thoughtless, reckless young man," Max corrected me with a sidelong mock glare. "His crime was stupidity. Karl Jünger's was ambition and insensibility. And Theo's…."

I took Max's hand in mine to offer comfort. "What will become of Karl Jr.?"

Max frowned. "Karl Jr. is in prison, awaiting the trial of the century for treason and crimes against the crown; he was denied bail. His lawyers aren't optimistic about his chances of avoiding a life sentence, but he might not be executed. That option's still in the air. My parents haven't made a decision yet, and neither has the Council."

"And Theo?" I asked as gently as I could. I wanted Max to talk about his old friend, but so far, my prince had remained quiet about the whole betrayal. I think Max had decided to wait for a sentence before delving into the trauma of it all.

Max grimaced. "Theo's lawyers asked for a psychological evaluation. Theo's mental state has deteriorated since his incarceration. I can't help but be amazed at how long Theo was able to convince people he was sane. The question is, to what extent is he culpable for his treasonous acts in the eyes of the law. If he's deemed mentally unfit to stand trial, he'll spend the rest of his life in a padded room instead of a prison cell."

I nodded, keeping my thoughts to myself. For my beloved's sake, I prayed Theo wouldn't be executed. I feared that outcome would break Max's spirit. But I also couldn't be sure if Theo really was as unhinged as he seemed of late, or if he was a great actor. His facade had certainly never broken before he was caught.

Max and I entered the relieving shade of the Snake Tower. Summer was over, but autumn remained sunny and warm. No trees in the Inner Ward meant that the only shadows were cast by the towers and surrounding buildings. It was late in the afternoon, the start of the evening, but the bright, hot weather hadn't yet leveled off into cool, dusky night.

Though this wasn't like the oceanside home my family and I had left behind, it was my new home with Max. At times, the sloping hills, green meadows, snow-topped peaks, and gushing streams still felt strange to me, but this place was growing on me.

I missed the sound of waves every now and then, but Max got me a ten-hour recording of ocean sounds I could fall asleep to. He complained the noise made him go to the toilet ten times a night now, but all in all, he took it in stride.

A narrow staircase rose on the left side, but on the right was an elevator, added for modern convenience. A guard stood in front of the stairs with his eyes on the lift as well. He followed us with his gaze like a hawk. As we ascended, the ride slow and silent, I hugged Max. In his embrace, I felt safe and cherished.

The elevator halted before we'd gotten up to the private suite.

"Why'd we stop here?" I asked with a slight whine when Max released me and opened the door to his study. He rarely brought a guest up here. It was where he handled the affairs of his station, namely tons and tons of official paperwork.

"I wish to check the mail," Max explained absentmindedly.

I understood. "Still waiting for a letter from Karl? You know he doesn't want to be the prime minister again. He's too, I don't know, defeated?"

Max nodded as he went over the stack of letters and other papers left on his desk by his secretary, a young lady by the name of Hannah Falk, one of the few with an entry pass onto this floor. Hannah might have been on-call twenty-four seven, but since the hour was late, she had no doubt left for the day, and we had the study to ourselves.

"It is the prerogative of the royal family to nominate a prime minister for the Council. If Karl stubbornly refuses to reconsider his retirement, I will make damn sure he nominates someone exactly as capable as he was."

I chuckled. "Good luck with that. From what I've heard, Karl was exemplary in the office. His successor will have a hell of a long learning curve."

Max sighed. "Despite the occasional animosity and sense of entitlement, Karl was one of the best prime ministers in the history of the Council. I regret to see him go before his time." A wily expression appeared in his eyes. "Maybe I could ask him to be a Royal Advisor.... Would he accept, do you think?"

I rolled my eyes. "I think you can make anyone do whatever you want if you put your mind to it. Look at me. I'm living proof. I wasn't sure if I could trust you after all the white lies and willful deceptions. But

I learned the reasons behind them. You promised never to lie to me again, and you've kept your word, so… here I am."

Max chuckled. "Yes. You and me, two regular Joes."

As Max went back to the stacks of papers, letters, and proposals on his desk, I checked the news on my cell phone. I whistled at the latest. "Tulip's been promoted to vice editor-in-chief. Wow, that's a terrible title; what a mouthful."

Max harrumphed, not glancing up from the papers he was studying. "I still don't understand how that is supposed to work. A journalist by day, a spy by night. I see a glaring conflict of interest."

"Don't be so hard on her," I admonished gently. "After all, without her, you and I wouldn't be together. Or did that fact slip your mind?"

Max pursed his lips and glared at me over the letter in his hands. "Tulip doesn't need more advocates on her behalf."

I snorted. "I'm not her advocate, whatever that means. Tulip's my friend."

Max quirked an eyebrow but wisely kept his mouth shut when I scowled at him. Shrugging, Max finally sighed. "I can't say I wholeheartedly approve of you and Tulip. But… I'm glad you found a friend in her."

I approached the desk. "Don't worry, scaredy-cat. I'll keep a tight lid on court stuff."

Max nodded but his attention had veered to the letter. I watched a frown form between his eyebrows. "Johann's written to me too, it seems." I was itching to ask what was in the letter, but Max got there first. "He's *not* asking me to persuade our parents to let him come back."

"He's not?" I asked, more than a little incredulous.

"No." Max's face melted into a smile. "He's begging me to arrange a meeting between him and Kira."

I burst out laughing. "Holy shit. Looks like your baby brother's on a learning curve." I came to stand next to Max. The only other person allowed on this side of the desk was his secretary, Hannah. I felt privileged. "What are you going to do?"

Max took a deep breath and tossed the letter back on the desk. "I don't know. On the one hand, it might do some good for the two of them to talk things through. On the other… Johann still has a lot to learn. Like patience. And humility."

I touched Max's hand. "Who better to teach him than Kira, who's been both those things for ages? Ask Kira if she'd be willing. If she's not, then let Johann down easy. But if Kira considers it... there might a chance for both of them to find happiness." Then I rolled my eyes at my own thoughts. "Not that I'm implying a woman can't be happy without a man. Elinor would kill me."

Max laughed. "Goodness no." He regarded me with an amused look. "I heard Ben hired her for the Cat's Paws. I bet that didn't go over well with your mother."

I snorted. "Nope. They screamed so loud it was a miracle the roof didn't cave in on them."

"Valerie must have gone over to Elinor's side since your whole family is now here."

Buzzing within, I nodded. "Yeah. Sort of. Elinor and Ben both promised that Elinor would be restricted to the agency's garage area for now. She is an engineer, after all." I giggled. "Mom really should have thought that through better. Elinor can cause worse trouble near engines and machines than out there."

Max chuckled, his gaze wandering the room, laugh lines around his eyes. "I spied Ellie and my mother in the Great Hall the other day. Elinor suggested that Colette needed more lederhosen in her wardrobe— and called her Inga." He gave me a mischievous look. "Ellie does know leather pants didn't originate in this country, doesn't she?"

I flicked my tongue at him. "Yeah. It's a joke from *Trading Places*. Remember that movie? Everyone in their silly costumes on the party train on New Year's Eve, trying to steal a briefcase from a killer?"

"Oh." The frown on Max's forehead smoothed and he snapped his fingers. "Inga. Jamie Lee Curtis. Mixing Austrian and Swedish. Oh, how could I have forgotten that comedy gem?"

"Dude, that was pretty embarrassing." Max swatted a hand at me, missing on purpose, and growled, murmuring how naughty I was. I smiled but then grew serious again. "My parents are still trying to find their place in a new country."

Max smiled softly at me. "We're all in the dark here, my love. This is novel territory. I hope they understand that the parents of the first gay royal consort in history should stay here where we can keep everyone safe and sound."

I nodded, suppressing a sigh. "I know. We're lucky to be given this chance. They just don't want to be a burden, you know."

We *were* all kind of in the dark, I thought. It was an odd thing to know I soon would be joining House Lindau-Arbon through the bonds of holy matrimony. That would connect me with a lot of foreign royal families all over Europe. Max's lineage was tied to other royals outside of Noricia throughout generations in a complex web of blood and marital relations, cousins and more distant cousins, aunts and uncles, and so forth. It was scary. No wonder we were all seeking a niche where we fit. My parents were still searching. But I knew with Gustav and Colette's help, Paulito and Valerie would be all right.

Shaking off the weirdness of it all, I took Johann's letter from the desk and stared at it. "What are you going to do about this?"

After a moment Max nodded firmly, his decision made. "I'll contact Kira, propose the idea, and see what happens." I bussed his cheek, and he smiled at me. My heart bloomed with love. Max studied the stacks in front of him and made a frustrated grunt. "This is never-ending. Invitations to charity fundraisers, cocktail parties, formal dinners, special events…. So tiring."

I chuckled. "Don't be like that. You could get an invitation to, oh I don't know, Ambassador Fowler's daughter's wedding reception, eh? A flighty debutante getting hitched with your ex-lover? Can't imagine anything more embarrassing and awkward."

Max grimaced. "Don't even go there. Alois made his bed. Now he has to lie in it."

"For the rest of his life." I mused at the whole debacle with the Fowlers and Alois. "Do you think Alois—"

"Stop right there." Max clapped a hand over my mouth. "Don't even think it."

I chortled behind his hand but nodded obediently. Stating out loud that my prince's ex-lover might have slept with a foreign ambassador *and* his daughter would be surreal as fuck. Of course, that was merely a rumor circulating in court.

I put down Johann's letter and maneuvered myself between Max and the desk, hopping onto the table. "No more flipping through papers. Your hands have other priorities, as do mine." I wound my arms around his neck and pulled him into a kiss.

Max murmured against my lips, but I ignored him. I slid my hands down to grab his buttocks and yank him close, between my splayed legs, which I wrapped around him tight. Our groins pressed together, and Max groaned. His tongue entered my mouth, and mine entangled with his. I wanted to kiss him for hours. He tasted so good, like cinnamon coffee and some kind of pastry.

Cue my stomach rumbling again.

Max laughed into the kiss, pulling back. "Stop. You're not helping."

I noticed him readjusting himself in his pants with glee. My own cock was swollen and hot and ready to be manhandled. "I'm not trying to help you work. I'm trying to help you play."

Max sighed, groped my butt, and lifted me off his desk. "Did you know, darling, that official correspondence of every member of the royal family will be stored in the Royal Archives?" He gave a pointed look at the desk, now stacked with rumpled pieces of paper.

I snorted. "So? It's not like my buttocks are imprinted on them now." I gripped Max's arm and dragged him toward the stairs. "Come on, babe. Do this later. It's my first fucking free weekend in over a month, and I have plans."

Max followed me, chuckling good-naturedly. "Oh, what did you have in mind?"

I smirked when we entered the bedroom and closed the door behind us. "Movie marathon."

Max snorted. "A what?"

Then I smelled the food. Delectable savory and sweet aromas floated in the room. My stomach rumbled again, reminding me I'd skipped lunch. My gaze found the three metal trolleys with covered trays on them, and I knew to expect only the best. I dashed over and started lifting lids.

"Mmm, roast pork belly with chargrilled peach salsa." I inhaled deeply. "Ariana's favorite sinful comfort food. Oh, and maple and pecan pudding. Look at that creamy sauce—it's just dribbling like…."

I salivated. Max snickered beside me.

I almost sobbed at the sights and scents. "Ah, soy-poached chicken with lemongrass brown rice. Skirt steak with salsa verde. Caramel pumpkin frozen yogurt. Chicken roulade with pineapple jam and pistachio nuts."

Max laughed so hard he had tears in his eyes. "You spend every day at the kitchens, and you are still in awe of what Ariana can whip up for you on the spot? Especially since she knew full well it was your first time off since taking the job at the Confectionary?"

I gasped in shock. "Y-you told her?"

"She knew. And she wanted to do something nice for you." Max waved me toward the bed. "You can do something nice for her next week. In the meantime, I'll fill up your plate if you get the movies ready. What are we watching again?"

I grinned, buzzing as I placed enough cushions on the floor at the foot of the bed to satisfy a horde. Eating off the floor in a castle seemed so naughty and decadent. But in truth, I didn't want to get crumbs in the bed, since I knew we'd be using it after we'd dined and watched a few flicks.

"A couple of classics, such as *Some Like It Hot*," I started and received an approving wink from my handsome prince. "And a number of my personal favorites, like *What's Up, Doc?* and *The Pink Panther*—the original with Peter Sellers—and *Galaxy Quest* and *A Fish Called Wanda* and—"

"That last one, is it the one where the leading lady has a, uh, kink for foreign languages?"

"Yup." I giggled, blushing. "I can totally relate. That first time we met, you and your looks and that sexy French accent, I was hooked."

"Is that so? *Est-ce vrai, mon chér?*" Max drawled.

I chuckled. "You know, you never told me what your favorite comedy is."

Max glanced over his shoulder. "Didn't I?" Then he shrugged. "I like all the movies you and I have watched together. But I'd have to say my favorite is… *All of Me*. Steve Martin at his best."

I smiled, remembering the movie well though I hadn't seen it in ages. "Why that particular movie?"

"A man with two distinctly different personalities inside him? Sure, in the movie it's a man and a ghost woman sharing one body. But I guess I felt there were several similarities with my own life and situation. I have dualities within as well. My public and private personas. My fake straight and true gay sides. Sometimes it's hard to tell who's running the show."

I nodded. "You felt a connection with the main character. I get it."

"Yes. That plus Steve Martin being absolutely amazing in the role. I love comedies."

Max ambled over with a sexy swagger, carrying a plate in each hand filled to the brim with food. He'd popped open the top three buttons of his bright white dress shirt, and I could see honey-golden skin, a hint of strong muscles, and the lines of his clavicles. There were sculpted abs underneath, and my mouth watered. His charcoal-gray slacks showcased his powerful thighs and long legs. The absolutely delicious bulge at his groin didn't hurt either.

I was hungry for him, not dinner.

"Can I eat off you?" I asked, rising to my knees in anticipation, ready to either take the plates or play. I longed to lick something sweet or savory off every inch of his skin, to taste the musk and smell the salt of his aroused body.

Max groaned with a laugh. "Oh, not again, sweetheart. Last time we did that, I was sticky in awkward places even after two showers." I gave him the puppy-dog eyes and made my jaw tremble in the most convincing of manners. Max released a long-suffering sigh. "You're incorrigible."

When I took the plates off his hands and started unbuttoning his shirt the rest of the way, Max stopped me gently. I grumbled. Max shook his head like a patient master to his pupil and chuckled.

"Eat first, my love. You've not eaten all day. I don't want you passing out when your blood rushes south of the border."

"Hey, man, I'm part Mexican. Did you really make a south-of-the-border joke with m… mmm…."

Max kissed me silent. I let him. In fact, I let him do a lot to me—after dinner and a movie.

Cast of Characters

* Oliver Reed: college senior studying culinary arts.
* Maximilian IX Lukas, or Max: First Prince of Noricia.
* Elinor Reed: Oliver's younger sister.
* Paulito Ruíz: Oliver and Elinor's father, Mexican-American.
* Valerie Reed: Oliver and Elinor's mother, Canadian-American.
* Gustav IV Caspar: King of Noricia and Head of House Lindau-Arbon.
* Colette II Sophia: Queen of Noricia.
* Berengar I Clovis, or Ben: Second Prince of Noricia.
* Johann VII Lothair, or John: Third Prince of Noricia.
* Kira von Montfort-Bregenz: Norician noblewoman and Max's bride-to-be.
* Karl von Thürer: Prime Minister of Noricia and father of Karl Jr. and Otto.
* Theo Weiss: Grand Druid.
* Lawana: the First Prince's personal bodyguard and chief of security.
* Orell Schaffhausen: leader of the Royalists and interior minister.
* Silvan von Arx: leader of the Republicans and justice minister.
* Yacine Haas: leader of the Moderates and defense minister.
* Frederica Hoffman: Royal Press Secretary.
* Gudrun Kühl: Marshal of Ceremonies.
* Wilhelmina van Apeldoorn: Lady Usher.
* Ariana Delacroix: Royal Chef.
* Hannah Falk: Max's private secretary.
* Tulip de Lange: journalist from the *Vindeburg Tribune*.
* Robert Fowler: US ambassador to Noricia and father of Madeleine.
* Alois Zest: radio host from Norician Public Radio and Max's ex-lover.

SUSAN LAINE, an award-winning, multipublished author of LGBTQ erotic romance and a Finnish native, was raised by the best mother in the world, who told her daughter time and again that she could be whatever she wanted to be. The spark for serious writing and publishing kindled when Susan discovered the gay erotic romance genre. Her book, *Monsters Under the Bed*, won the 2014 Rainbow Award for Best Gay Paranormal Romance.

Anthropology is Susan's formal education, and she could have been happy as an eternal student. But she's written stories since she was a kid, and her long-term goal is still to become a full-time writer. Susan enjoys hanging out with her family and friends in movie theaters, libraries, bookstores, and parks. Her favorite pastimes include singing along (badly) to the latest pop songs, watching action flicks, doing the dishes, and sleeping till noon, while a few of her dislikes are sweating, hot and too-bright summer days, tobacco smoke, purposeful prejudice and hate speech.

Website: www.susan-laine-author.fi
Email: susan.laine@hotmail.com
Blog: www.goodreads.com/author/show/5221828.Susan_Laine/blog
Facebook: www.facebook.com/Susan-Laine-128697277229180
Twitter: @Laine_Susan

www.ingramcontent.com/pod-product-compliance
Lightning Source LLC
Chambersburg PA
CBHW070052030726
47506CB00002B/442